VINTAGE **CLASSICS**

ITALO CALVINO

Italo Calvino was born in Cuba in 1923 and grew up in Italy. He was an essayist and journalist and a member of the editorial staff of Einaudi in Turin. His other books include *If on a winter's night a traveller*, *Invisible Cities* and *Our Ancestors*. In 1981 he won the prestigious Premio Feltrinelli. He died in 1985.

ITALO CALVINO

Difficult Loves

TRANSLATED FROM THE ITALIAN BY
William Weaver and Ann Goldstein

Smog

TRANSLATED FROM THE ITALIAN BY
William Weaver

A Plunge into Real Estate

TRANSLATED FROM THE ITALIAN BY
D.S. Carne-Ross

VINTAGE

2 4 6 8 10 9 7 5 3 1

Vintage
20 Vauxhall Bridge Road,
London SW1V 2SA

Vintage Classics is part of the Penguin Random House group
of companies whose addresses can be found at
global.penguinrandomhouse.com.

 Penguin
Random House
UK

First published in Great Britain in two volumes in 1983
by Martin Secker and Warburg Ltd
This edition, with the addition of 'The Adventure of a Skier' and
'The Adventure of a Motorist' first published in 2018 by Vintage

www.vintage-books.co.uk

A CIP catalogue record for this book is available
from the British Library

ISBN9781784874841

Typeset in 11/14 pt Sabon
by Integra Software Services Pvt. Ltd, Pondicherry

Printed and bound in Great Britain by Clays Ltd, Elcograf S.p.A.

Penguin Random House is committed to a sustainable future
for our business, our readers and our planet. This book is
made from Forest Stewardship Council® certified paper.

CONTENTS

The Adventure of a Soldier

In the compartment, a lady came and sat down, tall and
buxom, next to Private Tomagra. She must have been a
widow from the provinces, to judge by her dress and her
veil: the dress was black silk, appropriate for prolonged
mourning, but with useless frills and furbelows, and the
veil went all around her face, falling from the brim of a
massive, old-fashioned hat. Other places were free, Private Tomagra noticed, there in the compartment; and he
had assumed the widow would surely choose one of them.
But, on the contrary, despite the vicinity of a coarse soldier like himself, she came and sat right there, no doubt
for some reason connected with comfortable traveling,
the soldier quickly decided, a draft, or the direction of the
train.

Her body was in full bloom, solid, indeed a bit square. If its high curves had not been tempered by a matronly softness, you would have said she was no more than thirty; but when you looked at her face, at the complexion both marmoreal and relaxed, the unattainable gaze beneath the heavy eyelids and the thick black brows, at the sternly sealed lips, hastily colored with a jarring red, she seemed, instead, past forty.

Tomagra, a young infantry private on his first leave (it was Easter), huddled down in his seat for fear that the lady, so ample and shapely, might not fit; and immediately he found himself in the aura of her perfume, a popular and perhaps cheap scent, but now, out of long wear, blended with natural human odors.

The lady sat down with a composed demeanor, revealing,there beside him, less majestic proportions than he had imagined when he had seen her standing. Her hands were plump, with tight, dark rings; she kept them folded in her lap, over a shiny purse and a jacket she had taken off, exposing round, white arms. At her first movement, Tomagra had shifted, to make space for a broad maneuvering of her arms; but she had remained almost motionless, slipping out of the sleeves with a few brief twitches of her shoulders and torso.

The railroad seat was therefore fairly comfortable for two, and Tomagra could feel the lady's extreme closeness, though without any fear of offending her by his contact. All the same, Tomagra reasoned, lady though she was, she had surely not shown any sign of repugnance towards him, towards his rough uniform; otherwise she would have sat farther away. And, at these thoughts, his muscles, till now contracted and tensed, relaxed freely, serenely; indeed, without his moving, they tried to expand to their greatest extension, and his leg, its tendons taut, at first detached even from the cloth of his trousers, settled more broadly, not tightening the material that covered it, and the wool grazed the widow's black silk. And now, through this wool and that silk, the soldier's leg was adhering to her leg with a soft, fleeting movement, like two sharks grazing each other, and sending waves through its veins to those other veins.

It was still a very light contact, which every jolt of the train could break off and recreate; the lady had strong, fat knees, and Tomagra's bones could sense at every jerk the lazy bump of the kneecap. The calf had raised a silken cheek that, with an imperceptible thrust, had to be made to coincide with his own. This meeting of calves was precious, but it came at a price, a loss: in fact, the body's weight was shifted and the reciprocal support of the hips no longer occurred with the same docile abandon. In order to achieve a natural and satisfied position, it was necessary to move slightly on the seat, with the aid of a curve in the track, and also of the comprehensible need to shift position every so often.

The lady was impassive, beneath her matronly hat, her gaze fixed, lidded, and her hands steady on the purse in her lap. And yet her body, for a very long while, rested against that stretch of man: hadn't she realized this yet? Or was she preparing to flee? To rebel?

Tomagra decided to transmit, somehow, a message to her: he contracted the muscle of his calf into a kind of hard, square fist, and then with this calf-fist, as if a hand inside it wanted to open, he quickly knocked at the calf of the widow. To be sure, this was a very rapid movement, barely time for some flicker of the tendons; but in any case, she didn't draw back, at least not so far as he could tell. Because immediately, needing to justify that covert movement, Tomagra extended his leg as if to get a kink out of it.

Now he had to begin all over again; that patient and prudently established contact had been lost. Tomagra decided to be more courageous; as if looking for something, he stuck his hand in his pocket, the pocket towards the woman, and then, as if absently, he left it there. It had been a rapid action, Tomagra didn't know whether he had touched her or not, an inconsequential gesture; and yet he realized what an important step forward he had made, and in what a risky game he was now involved. Against the back of his hand, the hip of the lady in black was pressing; he felt it weighing on every finger, every knuckle; now any movement of his hand would have been an act of incredible intimacy towards the widow. Holding his breath, Tomagra turned his hand inside his pocket; in other words, he set the palm towards the lady, open against her, though still in the pocket. It was an impossible position, the wrist twisted. And yet, at this point, he might just as well attempt a decisive action: and so he ventured to move the fingers of that contorted hand. There could no longer be any possible doubt: the widow couldn't have helped but notice his maneuvering, and if she didn't draw back, but pretended to be impassive and absent, it meant that she wasn't rejecting his advances. When he thought about it, however, her paying no attention to Tomagra's mobile hand might mean that she really believed he was hunting for something in that pocket: a railway ticket, a match ... There: and if now the soldier's fingertips, the pads, seemingly endowed with a sudden clairvoyance, could sense through those different stuffs the hems of subterranean garments and even very minute roughnesses of skin, pores and moles, if, as I said, his fingertips arrived at this, perhaps her flesh, marmoreal and lazy, was hardly aware that these were, in fact, fingertips and not, for example, nails or knuckles.

Then, with furtive steps, the hand emerged from the pocket, paused there, undecided, and, with sudden haste to adjust the trouser along the side seam, proceeded down all the way to the knee. It would have been more accurate to say it cleared a path: because to go forward, it had to dig in between himself and the woman: a route, even in its speed, rich in anxieties and sweet emotions.

It must be said that Tomagra had thrown his head back against the seat, so one might also have thought he was sleeping: this was not so much an alibi for himself as it was a way of offering the lady, in the event that his insistence didn't irritate her, a reason to feel at ease, knowing that his actions were divorced from his consciousness, surfacing barely from the depths of sleep. And there, from this alert semblance of sleep, Tomagra's hand, clutching his knee, detached one finger, the little finger, and sent it out to reconnoiter. The finger slid along her knee, which remained still and docile; Tomagra could perform diligent figures with the little finger on the silk of the stocking which, through his half-closed eyes, he could barely glimpse, light and curving. But he realized that the risk of this game was without reward, because the little finger, scant of surface and awkward in movement, transmitted only partial hints of sensations and was incapable of conceiving the form and substance of what it was touching.

Then he reattached the little finger to the rest of the hand, not withdrawing it, but adding to it the ring-finger, the middle-finger, the fore-finger: now his whole hand rested, inert, on that female knee, and the train cradled it in a rocking caress.

It was then that Tomagra thought of the others: if the lady, whether out of compliance or out of a mysterious intangibility, didn't react at his boldness, facing them, there were still seated other persons who could be scandalized by that non-soldierly behavior of his, and by that possible silent complicity on the woman's part. Chiefly to spare the lady such suspicion, Tomagra withdrew his hand, or rather he hid it, as if it were the only guilty party. But this hiding it, he later thought, was only a hypocritical pretext: in fact, abandoning it there, on the seat, he intended simply to move it closer to the lady, who occupied, in fact, such a large part of the space.

Indeed, the hand groped around. There: like a butterfly's lighting, the fingers already sensed her presence; and there; it was enough merely to thrust the whole palm forward gently, and the widow's gaze beneath the veil was impenetrable, the bosom only faintly stirred by her respiration. But no! Tomagra had already withdrawn his hand, like a mouse scurrying off.

She didn't move – he thought – maybe she wants this. But he also thought: another moment and it would be too late. Maybe she's sitting there, studying me, preparing to make a scene.

Then, for no reason except prudent verification, Tomagra slid his hand along the back of the seat and waited until the train's jolts, imperceptibly, made the lady slide over his fingers. To say he waited is not correct: actually, with the tips of his fingers, wedge-like between the seat and her, he pushed with an invisible movement, which could also have been the effect of the train's speeding. If he stopped at a certain point, it wasn't because the lady had given any indication of disapproval, but because, as Tomagra thought, if she did accept, on the contrary, it would be easy for her, with a half-rotation of the muscles, to meet him halfway, to fall, as it were, on that expectant hand. To suggest to her the friendly nature of his attention, Tomagra, in that position beneath the lady, attempted a discreet wiggle of the fingers; the lady was looking out of the window, and her hand was idly toying with the purse-clasp, opening and closing it. Were these signals to him, to stop? Was it a final concession she was granting him, a warning that her patience could be tried no longer? Was it this? – Tomagra asked himself – Was it this?

He noticed that this hand, like a stubby octopus, was clasping her flesh. Now all was decided: he could no longer draw back, not Tomagra. But what about her? She was a sphinx.

With a crab's oblique scuttle, the soldier's hand now descended her thigh: was it out in the open, before the eyes of the others? No, now the lady was adjusting the jacket she held folded on her lap, allowing it to spill to one side. To offer him cover, or to block his path? There: now the hand moved freely and unseen, it clasped her, it opened in fleeting caresses like brief puffs of wind. But the widow's face was still turned away, distant; Tomagra stared at a part of her, a zone of naked skin, between the ear and the curve of her full chignon. And in that dimple beneath the ear a vein throbbed: this was the answer she was giving him, clear, heart-rending, and fleeting. She turned her face all of a sudden, proud and marmoreal; the veil hanging below the hat moved like a curtain; the gaze was lost beneath the heavy lids. But that gaze had gone past him, Tomagra, perhaps had not even grazed him; she was looking beyond him, at something, or

nothing, the pretext of some thought, but anyway something more important than he. This he decided later; because
earlier, when he had barely seen that movement of hers, he
had immediately thrown himself back and shut his eyes
tight, as if he were asleep, trying to quell the flush spreading
over his face, and thus perhaps losing the opportunity to
catch in the first glint of her eyes an answer to his own
extreme doubts.

His hand, hidden under the black jacket, had remained as
if detached from him, numb, the fingers drawn back towards
the wrist: no longer a real hand, now without sensitivity
beyond that arboreal sensitivity of the bones. But as the
truce the widow had granted to her own impassivity with
that vague glance around soon ended, blood and courage
flowed into the hand again. And it was then that, resuming
contact with that soft saddle of leg, he realized he had
reached a limit: the fingers were running along the hem of
the skirt, beyond there was the leap to the knee, and the
void.

It was the end, Private Tomagra thought, of this secret
spree: and now, thinking back, he found it a truly poor thing
in his memory, though he had greedily blown it up while
experiencing it: a clumsy feel on a silk dress, something that
could in no way have been denied him, simply because of his
miserable position as a soldier, and something that the lady
had discreetly condescended, without any show, to
concede.

In the intention, however, of withdrawing his hand, deso-
late, he was interrupted, as he noticed the way she held her
jacket on her knees: no longer folded (though it had seemed
so to him before), but flung carelessly, so that one edge fell
in front of her legs. His hand was thus in a sealed den:

perhaps a final proof of trust that the lady was giving him, confident that the disparity between her station and the soldier's was so great that he surely wouldn't take advantage of the opportunity. And the soldier recalled, with effort, what had happened so far between the widow and himself, as he tried to discover something in her behavior that hinted at further condescension, and he now considered his own actions insignificant and trivial, casual grazings and strokings, or, on the other hand, of a decisive intimacy, committing him not to withdraw again.

His hand surely agreed with this second consideration, because, before he could reflect on the irreparable nature of the act, he was already passing the frontier. And the lady? She was asleep. She had rested her head, with the pompous hat, against a corner of the seat, and she was keeping her eyes closed. Should he, Tomagra, respect this sleep, genuine or false as it might be, and retire? Or was it a consenting woman's device, which he should already know, for which he should somehow indicate gratitude? The point he had now reached admitted no hesitation: he could only advance.

Private Tomagra's hand was small and plump, and its hard parts and calluses had become so blended with the muscle that it was uniform, flexible; the bones could not be felt, and its movement was made more with nerves, though gently, than with joints. And this little hand had constant and general and minuscule movements, to maintain the completeness of the contact alive and burning. But when, finally, a first stirring ran through the widow's softness, like the motion of distant marine currents through secret underwater channels, the soldier was so surprised by it that, as if he really supposed the widow had noticed nothing till then, had really been asleep, he drew his hand away in fright.

Now he sat there with his hands on his own knees, huddled in his seat as he had been when she came in. He was behaving absurdly: he realized that. Then, with a scraping of heels, a stretching of hips, he seemed eager to reestablish the contacts, but this prudence of his was absurd too, as if he wanted to start his extremely patient operation again from the beginning, as if he were not sure now of the deep goals already gained. But had he really gained them? Or had it been only a dream?

A tunnel fell upon them. The darkness became deeper and deeper, and Tomagra then, first with timid gestures, occasionally drawing back as if he were really at the first advances and were amazed at his own temerity, then trying more and more to convince himself of the profound intimacy he had already reached with that woman, extended one hand, shy as a pullet, towards the bosom, large and somewhat abandoned to its own heaviness, and with an eager groping he tried to explain to her the misery and the unbearable happiness of his condition, and his need of nothing else but for her to emerge from her reserve.

The widow did react, but with a sudden gesture of shielding herself and rejecting him. It was enough to send Tomagra crouching in his corner, wringing his hands. But it was, probably, a false alarm caused by a passing light in the corridor which had made the widow fear the tunnel was suddenly going to end. Perhaps: or else, had he gone too far, had he committed some horrible rudeness towards her, who was already so generous towards him? No, by now there could be nothing forbidden between them; and her action, on the contrary, was a sign that this was all real, that she accepted, participated. Tomagra approached again. To be sure, in these reflections a great deal of time had been wasted, the tunnel wouldn't last much longer, it wasn't wise to allow oneself to be caught by the sudden light. Tomagra was already expecting the first grayness on the wall, there: the more he expected it, the more risky it was to attempt anything. To be sure, however, this was a long tunnel; he remembered it from other journeys as very, very long. Certainly, if he took advantage immediately, he would have a lot of time ahead of him. Now it was best to wait for the end, but it never ended, and so this had perhaps been his last chance. There, now the darkness was being dispelled, it was ending.

They were at the last station of a provincial line. The train was emptying; some passengers in the compartment had already got out, now the rest were taking down their bags, moving off. In the end they were alone in the compartment, the soldier and the widow, very close and detached, their arms folded, silent, eyes staring into space. Tomagra still had to think: Now that all the seats are free, if she wanted to be nice and comfortable, if she were fed up with me, she would move...

Something restrained him and frightened him still, perhaps the presence of a group of smokers in the passage, or a light that had come on because it was evening. Then he thought of drawing the curtains on the passage, like somebody wanting to get some sleep. He stood up with elephantine steps; with slow, meticulous care be began to unfasten the curtains, draw them, fasten them again. When he turned, he found her stretched out. As if she wanted to sleep: but apart from the fact that she had her eyes open and staring, she had slipped down, maintaining her matronly composure intact, with the majestic hat still on her head, which was resting on the seat arm.

Tomagra was standing over her. Still, to protect this image of sleep, he chose also to darken the outside window; and he stretched over her, to undo the curtain. But it was only a way of shifting his clumsy actions above the impassive widow. Then he stopped tormenting that curtain's snap and understood he had to do something else, show her all his own, compelling condition of desire, if only to explain to her the misunderstanding into which she had certainly fallen, as if to say to her: You see, you were kind to me because you believe we have a remote need for affection, we poor lonely soldiers, but here is what I really am, this is how I received your courtesy, this is the degree of impossible ambition I have reached, you see, here.

And since it was now evident that nothing could manage to surprise the lady, and indeed everything seemed somehow to have been foreseen by her, then Private Tomagra could only make sure that no further doubts were possible, and finally the urgency of his madness managed also to grasp its mute object: her.

When Tomagra stood up and, beneath him, the widow remained with her clear, ste gaze (she had blue eyes), with her hat and veil still squarely on her head, and the train never stopped its shrill whistling through the fields, and outside those endless rows of grapevines went on, and the rain that throughout the journey had tirelessly streaked the panes now resumed with new violence, he had again a brief spurt of fear, thinking how he, Private Tomagra, had been so daring.

(1949)

The Adventure of a Crook

The important thing was not to get himself arrested immediately. Gim flattened himself in the recess of a doorway, the police seemed to run straight past, but then, all at once, he heard their steps come back, turn into the alley. He darted off, in agile leaps.

"Stop or we'll shoot, Gim!"

Sure, sure, go ahead and shoot! he thought, and he was already out of their range, his feet thrusting him from the edge of the pebbled steps, down the slanting streets of the old city. Above the fountain, he jumped over the railing of the stairs, then he was under the archway, which amplified the pounding of his steps.

The whole circuit that came into his mind had to be rejected: Lola no, Nilde no, Renée no. Those guys would soon be all over the place, knocking at doors. It was a mild night, the clouds so pale they wouldn't have looked out of place in the daytime, above the arches set high over the alleyways.

On reaching the broad streets of the new city, Mario Albanesi alias Gim Bolero slowed his pace a little, tucked behind his ears the strings of hair that fell from his temples. Not a step was heard. Determined and discreet, he crossed over, reached Armanda's doorway, and climbed to her apartment. At this time of night she surely didn't have anybody with her; she would be sleeping. Gim knocked hard.

"Who's there?" a man's voice asked, irritated, after a moment. "At this time of night people get their sleep ..." It was Lilin.

"Open up a minute, Armanda. It's me, it's Gim," he said, not loud, but firmly.

Armanda rolled over in bed, "Oh, Gim boy, just a minute, I'll open the door ... uh, it's Gim." She grabbed the wire at the head of the bed that opened the front door and pulled.

The door clicked, obedient; Gim went along the corridor, hands in his pockets; he entered the bedroom. In Armanda's huge bed, her body, in great mounds under the sheets, seemed to take up all the space. On the pillow, her face without make-up, under the black bangs, hung slack, baggy and wrinkled. Beyond, as if in a fold of the blanket, on the far side of the bed, her husband Lilin was lying; and he seemed to want to bury his little bluish face in the pillow, to recover his interrupted sleep.

Lilin has to wait till the last customer has gone before he can get into bed and sleep off the weariness that accumulates during his lazy days. There is nothing in the world that Lilin knows how to do or wants to do; if he has his smokes, he's content. Armanda can't say Lilin costs her much, except for the packets of tobacco he consumes in the course of a day. He goes out with his packet in the morning, sits for a while at the cobbler's, at the junk dealer's, at the plumber's, rolls one paper after another and smokes, seated on those shop stools, his long, smooth, thief's hands on his knees, his gaze dull, listening like a spy to everyone, hardly ever contributing a word to the talk except for brief remarks and unexpected smiles, crooked and yellow. At evening, when the last shop has closed, he goes to the wine counter and drains a liter, burns up the cigarettes he has left, until they also pull down the shutters. He comes out, his wife is still on her beat along the Corso in her short dress, her swollen feet in her tight shoes. Lilin appears around a corner, gives her a low whistle, mutters a few words, to tell her it's late now, she should come to bed. Without looking at him, on the step of the sidewalk as if on a stage, her bosom compressed in the armature of wire and elastic, her old woman's body in her young girl's dress, nervously twitching her purse in her hands, drawing circles on the pavement with her heels, suddenly humming, she tells him no, people are still around, he must go off and wait. They woo each other like this, every night.

"Well then, Gim?" Armanda says, widening her eyes.

He has already found some cigarettes on the night-table and lights one.

"I have to spend the night here. Tonight."

And he is already taking off his jacket, undoing his tie.

"Sure, Gim, get into bed. You go onto the sofa, Lilin, go on, Lilin honey, clear out now, let Gim get to bed."

Lilin lies there a bit, like a stone, then he pulls himself up, emitting a complaint without distinct words; he gets down from the bed, takes his pillow, a blanket, the tobacco from the table, the cigarette-papers, matches, ashtray. "Go on, Lilin honey, go on." Tiny and hunched, he goes off, under his load, towards the sofa in the corridor.

Gim smokes as he undresses, folds his trousers neatly and hangs them up, arranges his jacket around a chair by the head of the bed, brings the cigarettes from the dresser to the night-table, matches, an ashtray, and climbs into bed. Armanda turns off the lamp and sighs. Gim smokes. Lilin sleeps in the corridor. Armanda rolls over. Gim stubs out his cigarette. There is a knocking at the door.

With one hand Gim is already touching the revolver in the pocket of his jacket, with the other he has taken Armanda by the elbow, warning her to be careful. Armanda's arm is fat and soft; they stay like that for a while.

"Ask who it is, Lilin," Armanda says in a low voice.

Lilin, in the hall, huffs impatiently. "Who is it?" he asks rudely.

"Hey, Armanda, it's me. Angelo."

"Angelo who?" she says.

"Angelo the sergeant, Armanda. I happened to be going by, and I thought I'd come up ... Can you open the door a minute?"

Gim has got out of the bed and is signalling her to be quiet. He opens a door, looks into the toilet, takes the chair with his clothes and carries it inside.

"Nobody's seen me. Get rid of him fast," he says softly and locks himself in the toilet.

"Come on, Lilin honey, get back into bed, come on, Lilin," from the bed Armanda directs the rearrangement.

"Armanda, you're keeping me waiting," the other man says, beyond the door.

Calmly, Lilin collects blanket, pillow, tobacco, matches, papers, ashtray, and comes back to bed, gets in, and pulls the sheet to his eyes. Armanda grabs the wire and clicks open the door.

Sergeant Soddu comes in, with the rumpled look of an old policeman in civilian clothes, his mustache gray against his fat face.

"You're out late, sergeant," Armanda says.

"Oh, I was just taking a walk," Soddu says, "and I thought I'd pay you a call."

"What was it you wanted?"

Soddu was at the head of the bed, wiping his sweaty face with his handkerchief.

"Nothing, just a little visit. What's new?"

"New how?"

"Have you seen Albanesi by any chance?"

"Gim? What's he done now?"

"Nothing. Kid stuff... We wanted to ask him something. Have you seen him?"

"Three days ago."

"I mean now."

"I've been asleep for two hours, Sarge. Why are you asking me? Go ask his girls: Rosy, Nilde, Lola ..."

"No use. When he's in trouble, he stays away from them."

"He hasn't shown up here. Next time, Sarge."

"Well, Armanda, I was just asking. Anyway I'm glad to pay you a visit."

"Good night, Sarge."

"Good night, eh."

Soddu turned, but didn't leave.

"I was thinking ... it's practically morning, and I don't have any other rounds to make. I don't feel like going back to that cot. So long as I'm here, I've half a mind to stay. What about it, Armanda?"

"Sergeant, you're always great, but to tell you the truth, at this time of night, I'm not receiving. That's how it is, Sarge. We all have our schedule."

"Armanda ... an old friend like me," Soddu was already removing his jacket, his undershirt.

"You're a nice man, Sergeant. Why don't we get together tomorrow night?"

Soddu went on undressing. "It's to pass the night, you understand, Armanda? Well, make some room for me."

"Lilin will go on the sofa then. Go on, Lilin honey, go on out now."

Lilin groped with his long hands, found the tobacco on the table, pulled himself up, grumbling, climbed from the bed almost without opening his eyes, collected pillow, blanket, papers, matches. "Go on, Lilin honey." He went off, dragging the blanket along the hall. Soddu turned over between the sheets.

Next door, Gim looked through the panes of the little window at the sky, turning green. He had forgotten his cigarettes on the table, that was the trouble. And now the other man was getting into bed and Gim had to stay shut up until daylight between that bidet and those boxes of talcum powder, unable to smoke. He had dressed again in silence, had combed his hair neatly, looking at himself in the washstand mirror, above the fence of perfumes and eye-drops and syringes and medicines and insecticides that adorned the shelf. He read some labels in the light from the window, stole a box of tablets, then continued his tour of the toilet.

There weren't many discoveries to be made: some clothes in a tub, others on a line. He tested the taps of the bidet; the water spurted noisily. What if Soddu heard? To hell with Soddu and with jail. Gim was bored, he went back to the basin, sprinkled some cologne on his jacket, spread Brilliantine on his hair. The fact was, if they didn't arrest him today, they would tomorrow, but they hadn't caught him red-handed, and if all went well, they'd turn him loose right away. To wait there another two or three hours, without cigarettes, in that cubbyhole ... why did he bother? Of course, they'd let him out right away. He opened a closet: it creaked. To hell with the closet and everything else. Inside it, Armanda's clothes were hanging. Gim stuck his revolver into the pocket of a fur coat. I'll come back and get it, he thought, she won't be wearing this till winter anyhow. He drew out his hand, white with naphthalene. All the better: the gun won't get moth-eaten. He laughed. He went to wash his hands again, but Armanda's towels turned his stomach and he wiped himself on a topcoat in the closet.

Lying in bed, Soddu had heard noises next door. He put one hand on Armanda. "Who's there?"

She turned, pressed to him, and put her big, soft arm around his neck. "It's nothing ... Who could it be? ..."

Soddu didn't want to free himself, but still he heard movements in there and he asked, as if playing: "What is it, eh? What's that?"

Gim opened the door. "Come on, Sarge, don't play dumb. Arrest me."

Soddu reached out one hand to the revolver in his jacket, hung on a peg; but he didn't let go of Armanda. "Who's that?"

"Gim Bolero."

"Hands up."

"I'm not armed, Sarge, don't be silly. I'm turning myself in."

He was standing at the head of the bed, his jacket around his shoulders, his hands half-raised.

"Oh, Gim," Armanda said.

"I'll come back to see you in a few days, 'Anda," Gim said.

Soddu got up, mumbling, and slipped on his trousers. "What a lousy job ... Never a moment's peace ..."

Gim took the cigarettes from the table, lighted one, slipped the pack into his pocket.

"Give me a smoke, Gim,' Armanda said, and she leaned out, lifting her flabby bosom.

Gim put a cigarette in her mouth, lighted it for her, helped Soddu on with his jacket. "Let's go, Sarge."

"Another time, Armanda," Soddu said.

"So long, Angelo," she said.

"So long, eh? Armanda," Soddu said again.

"Bye, Gim."

They went out. In the corridor Lilin was sleeping, perched on the edge of the broken-down sofa; he didn't even move.

Armanda was smoking, seated on the big bed; she turned off the lamp because a gray light was already coming into the room.

"Lilin," she called. "Come on, Lilin, come to bed, come on, Lilin honey, come."

Lilin was already gathering up the pillow, the ashtray.

(1949)

The Adventure of a Bather

While enjoying a swim at the beach at ***, Signora Isotta Barbarino had an unfortunate mishap. She was swimming far out in the water, and when it seemed time to go back in and she turned towards the shore, she realized that an irreparable event had occurred. She had lost her bathing-suit.

She couldn't tell if it had slipped off just then, or if she had been swimming without it already for some time; of the new two-piece suit she had been wearing, only the halter was left. At some twist of her hip, some buttons must have popped, and the bottom part, reduced to a shapeless rag, had slipped down her leg. Perhaps it was still sinking a few feet below her; she tried dropping down underwater to look for it, but she immediately lost her breath and only vague green shadows flashed before her eyes.

She stifled the anxiety rising inside her, and tried to think in a calm, orderly fashion. It was noon; there were people around, in the sea, in kayaks and in rowboats, or swimming. She didn't know anyone; she had arrived the day before, with her husband, who had had to go back to the city at once. Now there was no other course, the Signora thought (and she was the first to be surprised at her clear, serene reasoning), but to find among these people a beach-attendant's boat, which there had to be, or the boat of some other person who inspired trust, hail it, or rather approach it, and manage to ask for both help and tact.

This is what Signora Isotta was thinking, as she kept afloat, huddled almost into a ball, pawing the water, not daring to look around. Only her head emerged and, unconsciously, she lowered her face towards the surface, not to delve into its secrecy, now held inviolable, but like someone rubbing eyelids and temples against the sheet or the pillow to stem tears provoked by some night-thought. And it was a genuine pressure of tears that she felt at the corners of her eyes, and perhaps that instinctive movement of her head was really meant to dry those tears in the sea: this is how distraught she was, this is what a gap there was in her between reason and feeling. She wasn't calm then: she was desperate. Inside that motionless sea, wrinkled only at long intervals by the barely indicated hump of a wave, she also kept herself motionless, no longer with slow strokes, but only with a pleading movement of the hands, half in the water; and the most alarming sign of her condition, though perhaps not even she realized it, was this usury of strength she observed, as if she had a very long and exhausting time ahead of her.

She had put on her two-piece suit that morning for the first time; and at the beach, in the midst of all those strangers, she realized it made her feel a bit ill-at-ease. But the moment she was in the water, on the contrary, she felt content, freer in her movements, with a greater desire to swim. She liked to take long swims, well away from the shore, but her pleasure was not an athlete's, for she was actually rather plump and lazy; what meant most to her was the intimacy with the water, feeling herself a part of that peaceful sea. Her new suit gave her that very impression; indeed, the first thing she had thought, as she swam, was: It's like being naked. The only irksome thing was the recollection of that crowded beach. It was not unreasonable: her future beach acquaintances would perhaps form an idea of her that they would have to some extent to modify later: not so much an opinion about her behavior, since at the seaside all the women dressed like this, but a belief, for example, that she was athletic, or fashionable, whereas she was really a very simple, domestic person. It was perhaps because she was already feeling this sensation of herself as different from usual that she had noticed nothing when this mishap took place. Now that uneasiness she had felt on the beach, and that novelty of the water on her bare skin, and her vague concern at having to return among the other bathers: all had been enlarged and engulfed by her new and far more serious dismay.

What she would have preferred never to look at was the beach. And she looked at it. Bells were ringing noon, and on the sand the great umbrellas with black and yellow concentric circles were casting black shadows in which the bodies became flat, and the teeming of the bathers spilled into the sea, and none of the boats was on the shore now, and as soon as one returned it was seized even before it could touch bottom, and the black rim of the blue expanse was disturbed by constant explosions of white splashing, especially behind the ropes, where the horde of children was roiling; and at every bland wave a shouting arose, its notes immediately swallowed up by the blast. Just off that beach, she was naked.

Nobody would have suspected it, seeing only her head rising from the water, and occasionally her arms and her bosom, as she swam cautiously, never lifting her body to the surface. She could then carry out her search for help without exposing herself too much. And to check how much of her could be glimpsed by alien eyes, Signora Isotta now and then stopped and tried to look at herself, floating almost vertically. And with anxiety she saw in the water the sun's beams sway in limpid, underwater glints, and illuminate drifting seaweed and rapid schools of little striped fish, and on the bottom the corrugated sand, and on top, her body. In vain, twisting it with clenched legs, she tried to hide it from her own gaze: the skin of the pale revealing belly gleamed, between the tan of the bosom and the thighs, and neither the motion of a wave nor the half-sunken drift of seaweed could merge the darkness and the pallor of her abdomen. The Signora resumed swimming in that mongrel way of hers, keeping her body as low as she could, but, never stopping, she would turn to look out of the corner of her eye over her shoulder: at every stroke, all the white breadth of her person appeared in the light of day, in its most identifiable and secret forms. And she did everything to change the style and direction of her swimming, she turned in the water, she observed herself at every angle and in every light, she writhed upon herself; and always this offensive, naked body pursued

her. It was a flight from her own body that she was attempting, as if from another person whom she, Signora Isotta,
was unable to save in a difficult juncture, and could only
abandon to her fate. And yet this body, so rich and so impossible to conceal, had indeed been a glory of hers, a source of
self-satisfaction; only a contradictory chain of circumstances, apparently sensible, could make it now a cause for
shame.

Or perhaps not, perhaps her life always consisted only of
the clothed lady she had been all of her days, and her nakedness hardly belonged to her, was a rash state of nature
revealed only every now and then, arousing wonder in
human beings and foremost in her. Now Signora Isotta
recalled that even when she was alone or in private with her
husband she had always surrounded her being naked with
an air of complicity, of irony, part embarrassed and part
feline, as if she were temporarily putting on joyous but out-
rageous disguises, for a kind of secret carnival between
husband and wife. She had become accustomed with some
reluctance to owning a body, after the first disappointed,
romantic years, and she had taken it on like someone who
learns he can command a long-yearned-for property. Now,
the awareness of this right of hers disappeared again among
the old fears, as that yelling beach loomed ahead.

When noon had passed, among the bathers scattered
through the sea a reflux towards the shore began; it was the
hour of lunch at the pensioni, of picnics in front of the cab-
ins, and also the hour in which the sand was to be enjoyed
at its most searing, under the vertical sun. And the keels of
boats, and the pontoons of the catamarans passed close to
the Signora, and she studied the faces of the men on those
boats, and sometimes she almost decided to move towards

them; but each time a flash, a glance beneath their lashes, or the hint of an abrupt jerk of shoulder or elbow, put her to flight, with false-casual strokes, whose calm masked an already burdensome weariness. The men in the boats, alone or in groups, boys all excited by the physical exercise, or gentlemen with wily claims or insistent gaze, encountering her, lost in the sea, her prim face unable to conceal a shy, pleading anxiety, with her cap that gave her a slightly peevish, doll-like expression, and with her soft shoulders heaving around, uncertain, immediately emerged from their self-centred or brawling nirvana. Those who were not alone pointed her out to their companions with a snap of the chin or a wink; and those who were alone, braking with one oar, swerved their prow deliberately, to cross her path. Her need for trust was met by these rising barriers of slyness and double-entendre, a hedge of piercing pupils, of incisors bared in ambiguous laughter, of oars pausing, suddenly interrogatory, on the surface of the water; and the only thing she could do was flee. An occasional swimmer passed by, ducking his head blindly, and puffing out spurts of water without raising his eyes; but the Signora distrusted these men and evaded them. In fact, even though they passed at some distance from her, the swimmers, overcome by sudden fatigue, let themselves float and stretched their legs in a senseless splashing, until, by moving away, she displayed her disdain. And thus this net of compulsory hints was already spread around her, as if lying in ambush for her, as if each of those men for years had been daydreaming of a woman to whom what had happened to her would happen, and these men spent the summers at the sea hoping to be present at the right moment. There was no way out: the front of preordained male insinuations extended to all men, with no

possible breach, and that savior she had stubbornly dreamed
of as the most anonymous possible creature, almost angelic,
a beach-boy, a sailor, could not exist: she was now sure of
that. The beach guard she did see pass by, certainly the only
one who would be out in a boat to prevent possible acci-
dents with this calm sea, had such fleshy lips and such tense
muscles that she would never have had the courage to
entrust herself to his hands, even if – she actually thought in
the emotion of the moment – it were to have him unlock a
cabin or set up an umbrella.

In her disappointed fantasies, the people to whom she had
hoped to turn had always been men. She hadn't thought of
women, and yet with them everything should have been
more simple; a kind of female solidarity would certainly
have gone into action, in this serious crisis, in this anxiety
that only a fellow-woman could completely understand. But
possibilities of communication with members of her own
sex were rarer and more uncertain, unlike the perilous ease
of encounters with men; and a distrust – reciprocal this
time – blocked such communication. Most of the women
went by in catamarans accompanied by a man, and they
were jealous, inaccessible, seeking the open sea, where the
body, whose shame she suffered passively, was for them the
weapon of an aggressive and calculable strategy. Now and
then a boat came out packed with chirping, over-heated
young girls, and the Signora thought of the distance between
the profound vulgarity of her suffering and their volatile
heedlessness; she thought of how she would have to repeat
her appeal to them because they surely wouldn't understand
her the first time; she thought of how their expression would
change at the news, and she couldn't bring herself to call out
to them. A blonde also went by, alone, tanned, in a

catamaran, full of smugness and egoism; surely she was going far out to take the sun completely naked, and it would never remotely occur to her that nakedness could be a misfortune or a torment. Signora Isotta realized then how alone a woman is, and how rare, among her own kind, is solidarity, spontaneous and good (destroyed perhaps by the pact made with man), which would have foreseen her appeals and come to her side at the merest hint in the moment of a secret misfortune no man would understand. Women would never save her: and her own man was away. She felt her strength abandoning her.

A little, rust-colored buoy, till then fought over by a cluster of diving kids, suddenly, at a general plunge, remained deserted. A seagull lighted on it, flapped its wings, then flew off as Signora Isotta grasped its rim. She would have drowned, if she hadn't grabbed it in time. But not even death was possible, not even that indefensible, excessive remedy was left her: when she was about to faint and couldn't manage to keep her chin up, drawn down towards the water, she saw a rapid, tensed alertness among the men on the boats around, all ready to dive in and come to her rescue. They were there only to save her, to carry her naked and unconscious among the questions and stares of a curious public; and her risk of death would have achieved only the ridiculous and vulgar result that she was trying in vain to avoid.

From the buoy, looking at the swimmers and rowers, who seemed to be gradually reabsorbed by the shore, she remembered the marvelous weariness of those returns, and the cries from one boat to another – "We'll meet on shore!", or "Let's see who gets there first!" – filled her with a boundless envy. But then, when she noticed a thin man, in long trunks, the only person left in the middle of the sea, standing erect in a motionless motorboat, looking at something or other in the water, immediately her longing to go ashore burrowed down, hid within her fear of being seen, her anxious effort to conceal herself behind the buoy.

She no longer remembered how long she had been there: already the beach crowd was thinning out, and boats were already in line again on the sand, and the umbrellas, furled one after the other, were now only a cemetery of short poles, and the gulls skimmed the water, and on the motionless motorboat the thin man had disappeared and in his place a dumbfounded boy's curly head peered from the side; and over the sun a cloud passed driven by a just-wakened wind against a cumulus collected above the hills. The Signora thought of that hour as seen from the land, the polite afternoons, the destiny of unassuming correctness and respectful joys she had thought was guaranteed her and of the contemptible incongruity that occurred to contradict it, like the chastisement for a sin not committed. Not committed? But that abandonment of hers in bathing, that desire to swim all alone, that joy in her own body in the two-piece suit recklessly chosen: weren't these perhaps signs of a flight begun some time past, the defiance of an inclination to sin, the progressive stages of a mad race towards this state of nakedness that now appeared to her in all its wretched pallor? And the society of men, among whom she thought to pass intact like a big butterfly, pretending a compliant, doll-like nonchalance, now revealed its basic cruelties, its doubly diabolical essence, the presence of an evil against which she had not sufficiently armed herself and, at once, the agent, the instrument of her sentence.

Clinging to the studs of the buoy with bloodless fingertips now with accentuated wrinkles from the prolonged stay in the water, the Signora felt herself cast out by the whole world, and she couldn't understand why this nakedness that all people carry with themselves forever should banish her alone, as if she were the only one who was naked, the only being who could remain naked under heaven. And as she raised her eyes, she saw now the man and boy together on the motorboat, both standing, making signs to her as if to say she should remain there, that she shouldn't distress herself pointlessly. They were serious, composed, the two of them, unlike anyone else earlier, as if they were announcing a verdict to her: she was to resign herself, she alone had been chosen to pay for all; and if, as they gesticulated, they tried to muster a kind of smile, it was without any hint of maliciousness: perhaps an invitation to accept her sentence good-naturedly, willingly.

Immediately the boat sped off, faster than one would have thought possible, and the two paid attention to the motor and the course and didn't turn again towards the Signora, who tried to smile back at them, as if to show that if she were accused only of being made in this way so dear and prized by all, if she had only to expiate our somewhat clumsy tenderness of forms, well, she would take the whole burden on herself, content.

The boat, with its mysterious movements, and her own tangled reasoning had kept her in a state of such timorous bewilderment that it was a while before she became aware of the cold. A sweet plumpness allowed Signora Isotta to take long and icy swims that amazed her husband and family, all thin people. But now she had been in the water too long, and the sun was covered, and her smooth skin rose in grainy bumps, and ice was slowly taking possession of her blood. There, in this shivering that ran through her, Isotta realized she was alive, and in danger of death, and innocent. Because the nakedness that had suddenly seemed to grow on her body was something she had always accepted not as a guilt but as her anxious innocence, as the secret fraternity with others, as flesh and root of her being in the world. And they, on the contrary, the smart men in the boats and the fearless women under the umbrellas, who did not accept it, who insinuated it was a crime, an accusation: only they were guilty. She didn't want to pay for them; and she wriggled, clinging to the buoy, her teeth chattering, tears on her cheeks ... And over there, from the port, the motorboat was returning, even faster than before, and at the prow the boy was holding up a narrow green sail: a skirt!

When the boat stopped near her, and the thin man stretched out one hand to help her on board, and covered his eyes with the other, smiling, the Signora was already so far from any hope of someone saving her, and the train of her thoughts had traveled so far afield, that for a moment she couldn't connect her senses with her reasoning and action, and she raised her hand towards the man's out-stretched hand even before realizing that it wasn't her imagination, that the boat was really there, and had really come to her rescue. She understood and, all of a sudden, everything became perfect and ordained, and her thoughts, the cold, fear were forgotten. From pale, she turned red as fire, and standing on the boat, she slipped on that garment, while the man and the boy, facing the horizon, looked at the gulls.

They started the motor, and seated at the prow in a green skirt with orange flowers, she saw on the bottom of the boat a mask for underwater fishing and she knew how the pair had learned her secret. The boy, swimming below the surface with mask and harpoon, had seen her and had alerted the man, who had also dived in to see. Then they had motioned her to wait for them, without being understood, and had sped to the port to procure a dress from some fisherman's wife.

The two were sitting at the poop, hands on their knees, and were smiling: the boy, an urchin of about eight, was all eyes, with a dazed, coltish smile; the man, a gray, shaggy head, a brick-red body with long muscles, had a slightly sad smile, a dead cigarette stuck to his lip. It occurred to Signora Isotta that perhaps the two of them, looking at her dressed, were trying to remember her as they had seen her underwater; but this didn't make her feel ill-at-ease. After all, since someone had perforce to see her, she was glad it had been these two, and also that they had felt curiosity and pleasure. To arrive at the beach, the man took the boat past the docks and the port and the vegetable gardens along the sea; and anyone who saw them from the shore no doubt believed that the three were a little family coming home in their boat as they did every evening during the fishing season. The gray fishermen's houses overlooked the dock; red nets were stretched across short stakes; and from the boats, already tied up, some youths lifted lead-colored fish and passed them to girls standing with square baskets, the low rim propped against their hip; and men with tiny gold earrings, seated on the ground with spread legs, were sewing endless nets; and in some tubs they were boiling tannin to dye the nets again; and little stone walls divided off tiny vegetable gardens on the sea, where the boats lay beside the canes of the seed-beds; and women with their mouth full of nails helped their husbands, lying under the keel, to patch holes; and every pink house had a low roof covered with tomatoes split in two and set out to dry with salt on a grille; and under the asparagus plants the kids were hunting for worms; and some old men with bellows were spraying insecticide on their loquats; and the yellow melons were growing under creeping leaves; and in flat pans the old women were frying squid and polyps or else pumpkin-flowers dredged in flour; and the prows of fishing-boats rose in the yards redolent of wood just planed, and a brawl among the boys caulking the hulls had broken out with threats of brushes black with the little sand castles and volcanoes adandoned by the children

Signora lsotta, seated in the boat with that pair, in that excessive green and orange dress, would ever have like the trip to continue. But the boat was aiming its prow at the beach, attendants were carrying away the deck-chairs, and the man had bent over the motor, turning his back: that brick-red back divied by the knobs of the spin, on which the hard, salty skin rippled as if moved by a sigh.

(1951)

The Adventure of a Clerk

It so happened that Enrico Gnei, a clerk, spent a night with a beautiful lady. Coming out of her house, early, he felt the air and the colors of the spring morning open before him, cool and bracing and new, and it was as if he were walking to the sound of music.

It must be said that only a lucky conjunction of circumstances had rewarded Enrico Gnei with this adventure: a party at some friends' house, a special, fleeting mood of the lady's – a woman otherwise controlled and hardly prone to obeying whims – a slight alcoholic stimulation, whether real or feigned, and in addition a rather favorable logistic combination at the moment of goodbyes: all this and not any personal charm of Gnei's – or, rather, only his discreet and somewhat anonymous looks which would mark him as an

34

undemanding, unobtrusive companion – had produced the unexpected result of that night. He was well aware of all this and, modest by nature, he considered his good luck all the more precious. He knew also that the event would have no sequel; nor did he complain of that, because a steady relationship would have created problems too awkward for his usual way of living. The perfection of the adventure lay in its having begun and ended in the space of a night. Therefore Enrico Gnei that morning was a man who has received what he could most desire in the world.

The lady's house was in the hill district. Gnei came down a green and fragrant boulevard. It was not yet the hour when he was accustomed to leave home for the office. The lady had made him slip out now, so the servants wouldn't see. The fact that he hadn't slept didn't bother him, in fact it gave him a kind of unnatural lucidity, an arousal no longer of the senses but of the intellect. A gust of wind, a buzzing, an odor of trees seemed to him things he should somehow grasp and enjoy; he couldn't become accustomed again to humbler ways of savoring beauty.

As he was a methodical sort of man, getting up in a strange house, dressing in haste, without shaving, left in him an impression of disturbed habits; for a moment he thought of dashing home to shave and tidy himself up before going to the office. He would have had the time, but Gnei immediately dismissed the idea; he preferred to convince himself it was late, because he was seized by the fear that his house, the repetition of daily acts, would dispel the rich and extraordinary atmosphere in which he now moved.

He decided that his day would follow a calm and generous curve, to retain as far as possible the inheritance of that night. His memory, if he could patiently reconstruct the hours he had passed, second by second, promised him boundless Edens. And letting his thoughts stray thus, without haste Enrico Gnei went to the tram terminus.

The tram, almost empty, was waiting for the hour when its schedule began. Some drivers were there, smoking. Gnei whistled as he climbed aboard, his overcoat open, flapping; he sat down, sprawling slightly, then immediately assumed a more citified position, pleased that he had thought to correct himself promptly but not displeased by the carefree attitude that had come to him naturally.

The neighborhood was sparsely inhabited, and the inhabitants were not early risers. On the tram there was an elderly housewife, two workmen having an argument, and himself, the contented man. Sound, morning people. He found them likeable; he, Enrico Gnei, was for them a mysterious gentleman, mysterious and content, never seen before on this tram at this hour. Where could he come from? they were perhaps asking themselves now. And he gave them no clue: he was looking at the wistaria. He was a man who looks at the wistaria like a man who knows how wistaria should be looked at: he was aware of this, Enrico Gnei was. He was a passenger who hands the money for his ticket to the conductor, and between him and the conductor there is a perfect passenger-conductor relationship; it couldn't be better. The tram moved down towards the river; it was a great life.

Enrico Gnei got off downtown and went to a café. Not the usual one. A café with mosaic walls. It had just opened; the cashier hadn't arrived yet; the barman was starting up the coffee-machine. Gnei strode like a master to the center of the place, went to the counter, ordered a coffee, chose a sweet biscuit in the glass pastry case, and bit into it, first with hunger, then with the expression of a man with a bad taste in his mouth after a wild night.

A newspaper lay open on the counter, Gnei glanced at it. He hadn't bought a paper this morning, and to think that, on leaving his house, that was always the first thing he did. He was a habitual reader, meticulous; he kept up with even the slightest events and there wasn't a page he skipped without reading. But that day his gaze ran over the headlines and his thoughts remained unconnected. Gnei couldn't manage to read: perhaps, who knows?, stirred by the food, by the hot coffee or by the dulling of the morning air's effect, a wave of sensations from the night came over him. He shut his eyes, raised his chin, and smiled.

Attributing this pleased expression to the sports news in the paper, the barman said to him: "Ah, you're glad Boccadasse will be playing again on Sunday?", and he pointed to the headline that announced the return of a center-half. Gnei read, recovered himself, and instead of exclaiming, as he would have liked, Ah, I've got something a lot better than Boccadasse to think about, my friend!, he confined himself to saying: "Hm ... right ..." And, unwilling to let a conversation about the forthcoming match disrupt the flow of his feelings, he turned towards the cashier's desk where, in the meanwhile, a young girl with a disenchanted look had installed herself.

"So," Gnei said, in a tone of intimacy, "I owe you for a coffee and a cake." The cashier yawned. "Sleepy? Too early for you?" Gnei asked. Without smiling, the cashier nodded. Gnei assumed an air of complicity: "Aha! didn't get enough sleep last night, eh?" He thought for a moment, then, persuading himself he was with a person who would understand, he added: "I still haven't gone to bed." Then he was silent, enigmatic, discreet. He paid, said good morning to everyone, and left. He went to the barber's.

"Good morning, sir. Have a seat, sir," the barber said in a professional falsetto that to Enrico Gnei was like a wink of the eye.

"Um hum, give me a shave!" he replied with sceptical condescension, looking at himself in the mirror. His face, with the towel knotted around his neck, appeared like an independent object, and some trace of weariness, no longer corrected by the general bearing of his person, was beginning to show; but it was still quite a normal face, like that of a traveler who has got off the train at dawn, or a gambler who has spent the night over his cards; except there was a certain look that marked the special nature of his weariness – Gnei observed smugly – a certain relaxed, indulgent expression, that of a man who has had his share of things, and is prepared to take the good with the bad.

Far different caresses – Gnei's cheeks seemed to say to the brush that encased them in warm foam – far different caresses from yours are what we're used to!

Scrape, razor – his skin seemed to say – you won't scrape off what I have felt and know!

It was, for Gnei, as if a conversation filled with allusions were taking place between him and the barber, who, on the contrary, was also silent, devoting himself to handling his implements. He was a young barber, somewhat taciturn, more from lack of imagination than from a reserved character; and in fact, attempting to start a conversation, he said: "Some year, eh? The good weather's already here. Spring …"

The remark reached Gnei right in the middle of his imaginary conversation, and the word "Spring" became charged with meanings and hidden references. "Aaah! Spring ..." he said, a knowing smile on his foaming lips. And here the conversation died.

But Gnei felt the need to talk, to express, to communicate. And the barber didn't say anything further. Two or three times Gnei started to open his mouth when the young man lifted the razor, but he couldn't find any words, and the razor came down again over his lip and chin.

"What did you say?" the barber asked, having seen Gnei's lips move, without any sound coming from them.

And Gnei, with all his warmth, said: "Sunday, Boccadasse'll be back with the team!"

He had almost shouted; the other customers turned their half-lathered faces towards him; the barber had remained with his razor suspended in air.

"Ah, you're a *** fan?" he said, a bit mortified. "I'm a follower of ***", and he named the city's other football team.

"Oh, *** has an easy game Sunday; they can't lose ...' but his warmth was already extinguished.

Shaven, he came outside. The city was loud and bustling, there were glints of gold on the windows, water flew over the fountains, the trams' poles struck sparks from the overhead wires. Enrico Gnei proceeded as if on the crest of a wave, bursts of vigor alternating in his heart with fits of lassitude.

"Why, it's Gnei!"

"Why, it's Bardetta!"

He ran into an old schoolmate he hadn't seen for ten years. They traded the usual remarks, how time had gone by, how they hadn't changed. Actually Bardetta had rather faded, and the vulpine, slightly crafty expression of his face had become accentuated. Gnei knew that Bardetta was in business, but had a rather murky record and had been living abroad for some time.

"Still in Paris?"

"Venezuela. I'm about to go back. What about you?"

"Still here," and, in spite of himself, he smiled in embarrassment, as if he were ashamed of his sedentary life, and at the same time irked because he couldn't make it clear, at first sight, that his existence in reality was more full and satisfied than might be imagined.

"Are you married?" Bardetta asked.

To Gnei this seemed an opportunity to rectify the first impression. "Bachelor!" he said. "Still a bachelor, ha, ha! We're a vanishing race!" Yes, Bardetta, a man without scruples, about to leave again for America, with no ties now to the city and its gossip, was the ideal person; with him Gnei could give free rein to his euphoria, to him alone Gnei could confide his secret. Indeed, he could even exaggerate a little, talk of last night's adventure as if it were, for him, something habitual. "That's right," he insisted. "The old guard of bachelors, us two, eh?", meaning to refer to Bardetta's one-time reputation as a successful chaser of chorus girls.

And he was already studying the remark he would make to arrive at the subject, something in the order of "why, only last night, for example ..."

"To tell the truth," Bardetta said, with a somewhat shy smile, "I'm married and have four children ..."

Gnei heard the remark as he was recreating around himself the atmosphere of a completely heedless, epicurean world; and he was thrown a bit off-balance by it. He stared at Bardetta; only then did he notice the man's shabby, down-trodden look, his worried, tired manner. "Ah, four children ..." he said, in a dull voice. "Congratulations! And how are things going over there?"

"Hmph ... not much doing ... It's the same all over ... Scraping by ... feeding the family ..." and he stretched out his arms with a defeated attitude.

Gnei, with his instinctive humility, felt compassion and remorse: how could he have thought of trumpeting his own good luck to impress a wreck of a man like this? "Oh, here too, I can tell you," he said quickly, changing his tone again, "we barely manage, living from day to day ..."

"Well, let's hope things will get better ..."

"Yes, we have to keep hoping ..."

They exchanged all best wishes, said goodbye, and each went off in a different direction. Immediately, Gnei felt overwhelmed with regret: the possibility of confiding in Bardetta, that Bardetta he had first imagined, seemed to him an immense boon, now lost forever. Between the two of them – Gnei thought – a man-to-man conversation could have taken place, good-natured, a shade ironic, without any showing off, without boasting, his friend would have left for America, bearing a memory that would remain unchangeable; and Gnei vaguely saw himself preserved in the thoughts of that imaginary Bardetta, there, in his Venezuela, remembering old Europe – poor, but always faithful to the cult of beauty and pleasure – and thinking instinctively of his friend, the schoolmate seen again after so many years, always with that prudent appearance and yet completely sure of himself: the man who hadn't abandoned Europe and virtually symbolized its ancient wisdom of life, its wary passions ... Gnei grew excited: thus the adventure of the previous night would have been able to leave a mark, take on a definitive mean-ing, instead of vanishing like sand in a sea of empty days, all alike.

Perhaps he should have talked about it to Bardetta any-way, even if Bardetta was a poor wretch with other things on his mind, even at the cost of humiliating him. And besides, how could he be sure that Bardetta really was a failure? Perhaps he just said that and he was still the old fox he had been in the past ... I'll overtake him – Gnei thought – I'll start a conversation, and I'll tell him.

He ran ahead along the sidewalk, turned into the square, proceeded under the arcade. Bardetta had disappeared. Gnei looked at the time; he was late; he hurried towards his job. To calm himself, he decided that this telling others of his affairs, like a schoolboy, was too alien to his character, his ways; and this was why he had refrained from doing it. Thus, reconciled with himself, his pride restored, he punched the time-clock at the office.

For his job, Gnei harbored that amorous passion that, though unconfessed, makes clerks' hearts warm, once they come to know the secret sweetness and the furious fanati-cism that can charge the most habitual bureaucratic routine, the answering of indifferent correspondence, the precise keeping of a ledger. Perhaps this morning his unconscious hope was that amorous stimulation and clerkish passion would become a single thing, merge one with the other, to go on burning and never be extinguished. But the sight of his desk, the familiar look of a pale green folder with "pend-ing" written on it, was enough to make him feel the sharp contrast between the dizzying beauty from which he had just parted and his usual days.

He walked around the desk several times, without sitting down. He had been overwhelmed by a sudden, urgent love for the beautiful lady. And he could find no rest. He entered the next office where the accountants, careful and dissatisfied, were tapping on their adding-machines.

He began walking past each of them, saying hello, nervously cheery, sly, basking in the memory, without hopes for the present, mad with love among the accountants. As I move now in your midst, in your office – he was thinking – so I was turning in her blankets, not long ago. "Yes, that's right, Marinotti!" he said, banging his fist on a fellow-clerk's papers.

Marinotti raised his eyeglasses and asked slowly: "Say, did they take an extra four thousand lire out of your salary this month, too, Gnei?"

"No, my friend, in February," Gnei began, and at the same time he recalled a movement the lady had made, late, in the morning hours, that to him had seemed a new revelation and had opened immense, unknown possibilities of love – "no, they already deducted mine then, " he went on, in a mild voice, and he moved his hand gently before him, in mid-air, pursing his lips, "they took the whole amount from my February pay, Marinotti."

He would have liked to add further details and explanations, just to keep talking, but he wasn't able to.

This is the secret – he decided, going back to his office – at every moment, in everything I do or say, everything I have experienced must be implicit. But he was consumed by an anxiety, that he could never live up to what he had been, could never succeed in expressing, with hints or, still less, with explicit words, and perhaps not even with his thoughts, the fullness he knew he had reached.

The telephone rang. It was the general manager. He was asking for the background on the Giuseppieri complaint.

"It's like this, sir," Gnei explained over the telephone, "Giuseppieri and Company on the sixth of March ..." and he wanted to say: You see, when she slowly said: are you going? ... I realized I shouldn't let go of her hand ...

"Yes, sir, the complaint referred to goods previously billed ..." and he thought to say: Until the door closed behind us, I still wasn't sure ...

"No," he explained, "the claim wasn't made through the local office ..." and he meant: But I realized only then that she was entirely different from the way I had imagined her, so cold and haughty ...

He hung up. His brow was beaded with sweat. He felt tired now, burdened with sleep. It had been a mistake not to stop by at the house and freshen up, change: even the clothes he was wearing irked him.

He went to the window. There was a large courtyard surrounded by high walls, full of balconies, but it was like being in a desert. The sky could be seen above the roofs, no longer limpid, but bleached, covered by an opaque patina, as in Gnei's memory an opaque whiteness was wiping out every memory of sensations, and the presence of the sun was marked by a vague, still patch of light, like a secret pang of grief.

(1953)

The Adventure of a Photographer

When spring comes, the city's inhabitants, by the hundreds of thousands, go out on Sundays with a leather case over their shoulder. And they photograph one another. They come back as happy as hunters with bulging game-bags; they spend days waiting, with sweet anxiety, to see the developed pictures (anxiety to which some add the subtle pleasure of alchemistic manipulations in the dark-room, forbidding any intrusion by members of the family, relishing the harsh acid smell), and it is only when they have the photos before their eyes that they seem to take tangible possession of the day they spent, only then the mountain stream, the movement of the child with his pail, the glint of the sun on the wife's legs take on the irrevocability of what has been and can no longer be doubted. The rest can drown in the unreliable shadow of memory.

Seeing a good deal of his friends and colleagues, Antonino Paraggi, a non-photographer, sensed a growing isolation. Every week he discovered that the conversations of those who praise the sensitivity of a filter or discourse on the number of DINs were swelled by the voice of another to whom he had confided until yesterday, convinced that they were shared, his sarcastic remarks about an activity that to him seemed so unexciting, so lacking in surprises.

Professionally, Antonino Paraggi occupied an executive position in the distribution department of a production firm, but his real passion was commenting to his friends on current events large and small, unraveling the thread of general reasons from the tangle of details; in short, by mental attitude, he was a philosopher, and he devoted all his thoroughness to grasping the significance of even the events most remote from his own experience. Now he felt that something in the essence of photographic man was eluding him, the secret appeal which made new adepts continue to join the ranks of the amateurs of the lens, some boasting of the progress of their technical and artistic skills, others, on the contrary, giving all the credit to the efficiency of the camera they had purchased, which was capable (according to them) of producing masterpieces even when operated by inept hands (as they declared their own to be, because wherever pride aimed at magnifying the virtues of mechanical devices, subjective talent accepted a proportionate humiliation). Antonino Paraggi understood that neither the one nor the other motive of satisfaction was decisive: the secret lay elsewhere.

It must be said that his examination of photography to discover the reasons of a private dissatisfaction – as of someone who feels excluded from something – was to a certain extent a trick Antonino played on himself, to avoid having to consider another, more evident process that was separating him from his friends. What was happening was this: his acquaintances, of his age, were all getting married, one after the other, starting families, while Antonino remained a bachelor. And yet between the two phenomena there was undoubtedly a connection, inasmuch as the passion for the lens often develops in a natural, virtually physiological way as a secondary effect of fatherhood. One of the first instincts of parents, after they have brought a child into the world, is to photograph it; and given the speed of growth, it becomes necessary to photograph the child often, because nothing is more fleeting and unmemorable than a six-month-old infant, soon deleted and replaced by one of eight months, and then one of a year; and all the perfection that, to the eyes of parents, a child of three may have reached cannot prevent its being destroyed by that of the four-year-old, the photograph album remaining the only place where all these fleeting perfections are saved and juxtaposed, each aspiring to an incomparable absoluteness of its own. In the passion of new parents for framing their offspring in the sights to reduce them to the immobility of black-and-white or a full-color slide, the non-photographer and non-procreator Antonino saw chiefly a phase in the race towards madness lurking in that black instrument. But his reflections on the iconography-family-madness nexus were summary and reticent: otherwise he would have realized that actually the person running the greatest risk was himself, the bachelor.

In the circle of Antonino's friends, it was customary to spend the weekend out of town, in a group, following a tradition that for many of them dated back to their student days and that had been extended to include their girl-friends, then their wives and their children, as well as wet-nurses and governesses, and in some cases in-laws and new acquaintances of both sexes. But since the continuity of their habits, their getting together, had never lapsed, Antonino could pretend that nothing had changed with the passage of the years and that they were still the band of young men and girls of the old days, rather than a conglomerate of families in which he remained the only surviving bachelor.

More and more often, on those excursions to the sea or the mountains, when it came time for the family group or the multi-family picture, an outsider was asked to lend a hand, a passer-by perhaps, willing to press the button of the camera already focused and aimed in the desired direction. In these cases, Antonino couldn't refuse his services: he would take the camera from the hands of a father or a mother, who would then run to assume his or her place in the second row, sticking his head forward between two heads or crouching among the little ones; and Antonino, concentrating all his strength in the finger destined for this use, would press. The first times, an awkward stiffening of his arm would make the lens veer to capture the masts of ships or the spires of steeples, or to decapitate grandparents, uncles and aunts. He was accused of doing this on purpose, reproached for a joke in poor taste. It wasn't true: his intention was to lend the use of his finger as docile instrument of the collective wish, but also to exploit his temporary position of privilege to admonish both photographers and their subjects as to the significance of their actions. As soon as the pad of his finger reached the desired condition of detachment from the rest of his person and personality, he was free to communicate his theories in well-reasoned discourse, framing at the same time well-composed little groups. (A few accidental successes had sufficed to give him nonchalance and assurance with finders and light-meters.)

"... Because, once you've begun," he would preach, "there is no reason why you should stop. The line between the reality that is photographed because it seems beautiful to us and the reality that seems beautiful because it has been photographed is very narrow. If you take a picture of Pierluca because he's building a sand-castle, there is no reason not to take his picture while he's crying because the castle has collapsed, and then while the nurse consoles him by helping him find a sea-shell in the sand. You only have to start saying of something: 'Ah, how beautiful! We must photograph it!' and you are already close to the view of the person who thinks that everything that is not photographed is lost, as if it had never existed, and that therefore in order really to live you must photograph as much as you can, and to photograph as much as you can you must either live in the most photographable way possible, or else consider photographable every moment of your life. The first course leads to stupidity; the second, to madness."

"You're the one who's mad and stupid," his friends would say to him, "and a pain in the ass, into the bargain."

"For the person who wants to capture everything that passes before his eyes," Antonino would explain, even if nobody was listening to him any more, "the only coherent way he can act is to snap at least one picture a minute, from the moment he opens his eyes in the morning to when he goes to sleep. This is the only way the rolls of exposed film will represent a faithful diary of our days, with nothing left out. If I were to start taking pictures, I'd see this thing through, even if it meant losing my mind. The rest of you, on the contrary, still insist on making a choice. What sort of choice? A choice in the idyllic sense, apologetic, consolatory, at peace with nature, the fatherland, the family. Your choice isn't only photographic; it is a choice of life, which leads you to exclude dramatic conflicts, the knots of contradiction, the great tensions of will, passion, aversion. So you think you are saving yourselves from madness, but you are falling into mediocrity, into hebetude."

A girl named Bice, someone's ex-sister-in-law, and another named Lydia, someone else's ex-secretary, asked him please to take a snapshot of them while they were playing ball among the waves. He consented, but since in the meanwhile he had worked out a theory against snapshots, he dutifully expressed it to the two friends:

"What drives you two girls to cut from the mobile continuum of your day these temporal slices, the thickness of a second? Tossing the ball back and forth, you are living in the present, but the moment the scansion of the frames is insinuated between your acts it is no longer the pleasure of the game that motivates you but rather that of seeing yourselves again in the future, of rediscovering yourselves in twenty years' time, on a piece of yellowed paper (yellowed emotionally, even if modem printing procedures will preserve it unchanged). The taste for the spontaneous, natural, lifelike snapshot kills spontaneity, drives away the present. Photographed reality immediately takes on a nostalgic character, of joy fled on the wings of time, a commemorative character, even if the picture was taken day before yesterday. And the life that you live in order to photograph it is already, at the outset, a commemoration of itself. To believe that the snapshot is more *true* than the posed portrait is a prejudice ..."

So saying, Antonino darted around the two girls in the water, to focus the movements of their game and cut out of the picture the dazzling glints of the sun on the water. In a scuffle for the ball, Bice, flinging herself on the other girl, already submerged, was snapped with her behind in close-up, flying over the waves. Antonino, so as not to lose this angle, had flung himself back in the water, holding up the camera and nearly drowning.

"They all came out well; and this one's stupendous," they commented a few days later, snatching the proofs from each other. They had arranged to meet at the photographer's shop. "You're good; you must take some more of us."

Antonino had reached the conclusion that it was necessary to return to posed subjects, in attitudes denoting their social position and their character, as in the nineteenth century. His anti-photographic polemic could be fought only from within the black box, setting one kind of photography against another.

"I'd like to have one of those old box cameras," he said to his girl-friends, "the kind you put on a tripod. Do you think one could still be found?"

"Hm, maybe at some junk-shop ..."

"Let's go see."

The girls found it amusing to hunt for this curious object; together they ransacked flea-markets, interrogated old street-photographers, followed them to their lairs. In those cemeteries of objects no longer serviceable, lay wooden columns, screens, backdrops with faded landscapes; everything that suggested an old-fashioned photographer's studio, Antonino bought. In the end he managed to get hold of a box camera, with a bulb to squeeze. It seemed in perfect working order. Antonino also bought an assortment of plates. With the girls helping him, in a room of his apartment, he set up the studio, all fitted out with old-fashioned equipment, except for two modem spotlights.

Now he was content. "This is where to start," he explained to the girls. "In the way our grandparents assumed a pose, in the convention that decided how groups were to be arranged, there was a social meaning, a custom, a taste, a culture. An official photograph or one of a marriage or a family or a school group conveyed to what extent each role or institution was serious and important but also how far they were false or forced, authoritarian, hierarchical. This is the point: to make explicit the relationship with the world that each of us bears within himself, and which today we tend to hide, to make unconscious, believing that in this way it disappears, whereas ..."

"Who do you want to have pose for you?"

"You two come tomorrow and I'll begin by taking some pictures of you in the way I mean."

"Say, what's in the back of your mind?" Lydia asked, suddenly suspicious. Now, as the studio was all set up, she saw that everything about it had a sinister, threatening air. "If you think we're going to come and be your models, you're dreaming!"

Bice giggled with her, but the next day she came back to Antonino's apartment, alone.

She was wearing a white linen dress with colored embroidery on the hems of the sleeves and pockets. Her hair was parted and gathered over her temples. She laughed, somewhat slyly, bending her head to one side. As he let her in, Antonino studied her ways, a bit coy, a bit ironic, to discover what were the traits that defined her true character.

He made her sit in a big armchair, and stuck his head under the black cloth that complemented his camera. It was one of those boxes whose rear wall was of glass, where the image is reflected as if already on the plate, ghostly, a bit milky, deprived of every link with space and time. To Antonino it was as if he had never seen Bice before. She had a docility, in her somewhat heavy way of lowering her eyelids, of stretching her neck forward, that promised something hidden, as her smile seemed to hide behind the very act of smiling.

"There. Like that. No, head a bit further; raise your eyes. No, lower them." Antonino was pursuing, within that box, something of Bice that all at once seemed most precious to him, absolute.

"Now you're casting a shadow, move into the light. No, it was better before."

There were many possible photographs of Bice and many Bices impossible to photograph, but what he was seeking was the unique photograph that would contain the former and the latter.

"I can't get you," his voice emerged, stifled and complaining from beneath the black hood, "I can't get you any more; I can't manage to get you."

He freed himself from the cloth and straightened up again. He was doing it all wrong, from the beginning. That expression, that accent, that secret he seemed on the very point of capturing in her face was something that drew him into the quicksands of moods, humors, psychology: he too was one of those who pursue life as it flees, a hunter of the unattainable, like the takers of snapshots.

He had to follow the opposite path: aim at a portrait completely on the surface, evident, unequivocal, that did not elude conventional appearance, the stereotype, the mask. The mask, being first of all a social, historical product, contains more truth than any image claiming to be "true"; it bears a quantity of meanings that will gradually be revealed. Wasn't this precisely Antonino's intention in setting up this fair-stall of a studio?

He observed Bice. He should start with the exterior elements of her appearance. In Bice's way of dressing and fixing herself up – he thought – you could recognize the somewhat nostalgic, somewhat ironic intention, widespread in the mode of those years, to hark back to the fashions of thirty years earlier. The photograph should underline this intention: why hadn't he thought of that?

Antonino went to find a tennis racket; Bice should stand up, in a three-quarters turn, the racket under her arm, her face in the pose of a sentimental postcard. To Antonino, from under the black drape, Bice's image – in the slimness and suitability to the pose and in the unsuitable and almost incongruous aspects that the pose accentuated – seemed very interesting. He made her change position several times, studying the geometry of legs and arms in relation to the racket and to an element in the background. (In the ideal postcard in his mind there should have been the net of the tennis court, but you couldn't demand too much and Antonino made do with a ping-pong table.)

But he still didn't feel on safe ground: wasn't he perhaps trying to photograph memories, or rather, vague echoes of recollection surfacing in the memory? Wasn't his refusal to live the present as a future memory, as the Sunday photographers did, leading him to attempt an equally unreal operation, namely to give a body to recollection, to substitute it for the present before his very eyes?

"Move! Don't stand there like a stick! Raise the racket, damn it! Pretend you're playing tennis!" All of a sudden he was furious. He had realized that it was only by exaggerating the poses that he could achieve an objective alien-ness; only by feigning a movement arrested halfway could he give the impression of the unmoving, the non-living.

Bice obediently followed his orders even when they became vague and contradictory, with a passivity that was also a way of declaring herself out of the game, and yet somehow insinuating, in this game that was not hers, the unpredictable moves of a mysterious match of her own. What Antonino now was expecting of Bice, telling her to put her legs and arms this way and that way, was not so much the simple execution of a plan, as her response to the violence he was doing her with his demands, an unforeseeable aggressive reply to this violence that he was being driven more and more to wreak on her.

It was like a dream, Antonino thought, contemplating, buried in the darkness, that improbable tennis-player filtered in the glass rectangle: like a dream, when a presence coming from the depth of memory advances, is recognized, and then suddenly is transformed into something unexpected, something that even before the transformation is already frightening, because there's no telling what it might be transformed into.

Did he want to photograph dreams? This suspicion struck him dumb, hidden in that ostrich refuge of his like an idiot, the bulb in his hand; and meanwhile Bice, left to herself, continued a kind of grotesque dance, freezing in exaggerated tennis poses, backhand, drive, raising the racket high or lowering it to the ground as if the gaze coming from that glass eye were the ball she continued to slam back.

"Stop, what's this nonsense? This isn't what I had in mind," and Antonino covered the camera with the cloth and began pacing up and down the room.

It was all the fault of that dress, with its tennis, pre-war connotations ... It had to be admitted that in a street-dress the kind of photograph he described couldn't be taken. A certain solemnity was needed, a certain pomp, like the official photos of queens. Only in evening dress would Bice become a photographic subject, with the décolleté that marks a distinct line between the white of the skin and the darkness of the fabric underlined by the glitter of jewels, a boundary between an essence of woman, almost atemporal and almost impersonal in her nakedness, and the other abstraction, social this time, the dress, symbol of an equally impersonal role, like the drapery of an allegorical statue.

He approached Bice, began to unbutton the dress at the neck, over the bosom, and slip it down on her shoulders. He had thought of certain nineteenth-century photographs of women in which from the white of the cardboard the face emerges, the neck, the line of the bared shoulders, and all the rest disappears into the whiteness.

This was the portrait outside of time and of space that he now wanted: he wasn't quite sure how it was achieved, but he was determined to succeed. He set the spotlight on Bice, moved the camera closer, fiddled around under the cloth adjusting the aperture of the lens. He looked into it. Bice was naked.

She had made the dress slip down to her feet; she wasn't wearing anything underneath it; she had taken a step forward; no, a step backward, which was like her whole body's advancing in the picture; she stood erect, tall, before the camera, calm, looking straight ahead, as if she were alone.

Antonino felt the sight of her enter his eyes and occupy the whole visual field, removing it from the flux of casual and fragmentary images, concentrating time and space in a finite form. And as if this visual surprise and the impression of the plate were two reflexes connected among themselves, he immediately pressed the bulb, loaded the camera again, snapped, put in another plate, snapped, and went on changing plates and snapping, mumbling, stifled by the cloth: "There, that's right now, yes, again, I'm getting you fine now, another.'

He had run out of plates. He emerged from the cloth. He was pleased. Bice was before him, naked, as if waiting.

"Now you can dress," he said, euphoric, but already in a hurry. "Let's go out."

She looked at him, bewildered.

"I've got you now," he said.

Bice burst into tears.

Antonino realized that he had fallen in love with her that same day. They started living together, and he bought the most modern cameras, telescopic lens, the most advanced equipment; he installed a dark-room. He even had a set-up for photographing her at night when she was asleep. Bice would wake at the flash, annoyed; Antonino went on taking snapshots of her as she disentangled herself from sleep, of her becoming furious with him, of her trying in vain to find sleep again plunging her face into the pillow, of her making up with him, of her recognizing as acts of love these photographic rapes.

In Antonino's dark-room, strung with films and proofs, Bice peered from every frame, as thousands of bees peer out of the honeycomb of a hive, always the same bee: Bice in every attitude, at every angle, in every guise; Bice posed or caught unawares, an identity fragmented into a powder of images.

"But what's this obsession with Bice? Can't you photograph anything else?" was the question he heard constantly from his friends, and also from her.

"It isn't just a matter of Bice," he answered. "It's a question of method. Whatever person you decide to photograph, or whatever thing, you must go on photographing it always, exclusively, at every hour of the day and night. Photography has a meaning only if it exhausts all possible images."

But he didn't say what meant most to him: to catch Bice in the street when she didn't know he was watching her, to keep her within the range of hidden lenses, to photograph her not only without letting himself be seen but without seeing her, to surprise her as she was in the absence of his gaze, of any gaze. Not that he wanted to discover any particular thing; he wasn't a jealous man in the usual sense of the word. It was an invisible Bice that he wanted to possess, a Bice absolutely alone, a Bice whose presence presupposed the absence of him and everyone else.

Whether or not it could be defined as jealousy, it was, in any case, a passion difficult to put up with. And soon Bice left him.

Antonino sank into deep depression. He began to keep a diary: a photographic diary, of course. With the camera slung around his neck, shut up in the house, slumped in an armchair, he compulsively snapped pictures as he stared into the void. He was photographing the absence of Bice.

He collected the photographs in an album: you could see ashtrays brimming with cigarette butts, an unmade bed, a damp stain on the wall. He got the idea of composing a catalogue of everything in the world that resists photography, what is systematically omitted from the visual field not only by cameras but also by human beings. On every subject he spent days, using up whole rolls, at intervals of hours, so as to follow the changes of lights and shadows. One day he became obsessed with a completely empty corner of the room, containing a radiator pipe and nothing else: he was tempted to go on photographing that spot and only that till the end of his days.

The apartment was completely neglected, old newspapers, letters, lay crumpled on the floor, and he photographed them. The photographs in the papers were photographed as well, and an indirect bond was established between his lens and that of distant news-photographers. To produce those black spots the lenses of other cameras had been aimed on police assaults, charred automobiles, running athletes, ministers, defendants.

Antonino now felt a special pleasure in portraying domestic objects framed by a mosaic of telephotos, violent patches of ink on white sheets. From his immobility he was surprised to find he envied the life of the news-photographer, who moves following the movements of crowds, bloodshed, tears, feasts, crime, the conventions of fashion, the falsity of official ceremonies; the news-photographer, who documents the extremes of society, the most rich and the most poor, the exceptional moments that are yet produced at every moment and in every place.

Does this mean that only the exceptional condition has a meaning? Antonino asked himself. Is the news-photographer the true antagonist of the Sunday photographer? Are their worlds mutually exclusive? Or does one give a meaning to the other?

And reflecting like this, he began to tear up the photographs with Bice or without Bice that had accumulated during the months of his passion, ripping to pieces the strips of proofs hung on the walls, snipping up the celluloid of the negatives, jabbing the slides, and piling the remains of this methodical destruction on newspapers spread out on the floor.

Perhaps true, total photography, he thought, is a pile of fragments of private images, against the creased background of massacres and coronations.

He folded the corners of the newspapers into a huge bundle to be thrown into the trash, but first he wanted to photograph it. He arranged the edges so that you could clearly see two halves of photographs of different newspapers that in the bundle happened, by chance, to fit together. In fact he reopened the package a little so that a bit of shiny pasteboard would stick out, the fragment of a torn enlargement. He turned on a spotlight; he wanted it to be possible to recognize in his photograph the half-crumpled and torn images and at the same time to feel their unreality as casual inky shadows, and also at the same time their concreteness as objects charged with meaning, the strength with which they clung to the attention that tried to drive them away.

To get all this into one photograph he had to acquire an extraordinary technical skill, but only then would Antonino quit taking pictures. Having exhausted every possibility, at the moment when he was coming full circle, Antonino realized that photographing photographs was the only course that he had left, or rather, the true course he had obscurely sought all this time.

(1955)

The Adventure of a Traveler

Federico V., who lived in a Northern Italian city, was in love with Cinzia U., a resident of Rome. Whenever his work permitted, he would take the train to the capital. Accustomed to budgeting his time strictly, at work and in his pleasures, he always traveled at night: there was one train, the last, which was not crowded – except in the holiday season – and Federico could stretch out and sleep.

Federico's days in his own city went by nervously, like the hours of someone between trains who, as he goes about his business, cannot stop thinking of the schedule. But when the evening of his departure finally came and his tasks were done and he was walking with his suitcase towards the station, then, even in his haste to avoid missing his train, he began to feel a sense of inner calm pervade him. It was as if all the bustle around the station – now at its last gasp, given the late hour – were part of a natural movement, and he also belonged to it. Everything seemed to be there to encourage him, to give a spring to his steps like the rubberized pavement of the station, and even the obstacles, the wait, his minutes numbered, at the last ticket-window still open, the difficulty of breaking a large bill, the lack of small change at the newsstand, seemed to exist for his pleasure in confronting and overcoming them.

Not that he betrayed any sign of this mood: a staid man, he liked being indistinguishable from the many travelers arriving and leaving, all in overcoats like him, case in hand; and yet he felt as if he were borne on the crest of a wave, because he was rushing towards Cinzia.

The hand in his overcoat pocket toyed with a telephone token. Tomorrow morning, as soon as he landed at the Rome Termini Station, he would run, token in hand, to the nearest public telephone, dial the number, and say: "Hello, darling, I'm here …" And he clutched the token as if it were a most precious object, the only one in the world, the sole tangible proof of what awaited him on his arrival.

The trip was expensive and Federico wasn't rich. If he saw a second-class coach with padded seats and empty compartments, Federico would buy a second-class ticket. Or rather, he always bought a second-class ticket, with the idea that, if he found too many people there, he would move into first, paying the difference to the conductor. In this operation, he enjoyed the pleasure of economy (also the cost of first class, being paid in two instalments, and through necessity, upset him less), the satisfaction of profiting by his own experience, and a sense of freedom and expansiveness in his actions and in his thoughts.

As sometimes happens with men whose life is most conditioned by others, extrovert Federico tended constantly to defend his own condition of inner concentration, and actually it took very little, a hotel room, a train compartment all to himself, and he could adjust the world in harmony with his life, the world seemed created specially for him, as if the railroads that swathed the peninsula had been built deliberately to bear him triumphantly towards Cinzia. That evening, again, second-class was almost empty. Every sign was favorable.

Federico V. chose an empty compartment, not over the wheels, but not too far into the coach either, because he knew that as a rule people who board a train in haste tend to reject the first few compartments. The defense of the necessary space to stretch out and travel lying down is made up of tiny psychological devices; Federico knew them and employed them all.

For example, he drew the curtains over the door, an act which, performed at this point, might even seem excessive; but it aimed, in fact, at a psychological effect. Seeing those drawn curtains, the traveler who arrives later is almost always overcome by an instinctive scruple, and prefers, if he can find it, a compartment, perhaps with two or three people already in it, but with the curtains open. Federico strewed his bag, overcoat, newspapers on the seats opposite and beside him. Another elementary move, abused and apparently futile but actually of use. Not that he wanted to make people believe those places were occupied: such a subterfuge would have been contrary to his civic conscience and to his sincere nature. He wanted only to create a rapid impression of a cluttered, not very inviting compartment, a simple, rapid impression.

He sat down and heaved a sigh of relief. He had learned that being in a setting where everything can only be in its place, the same as always, anonymous, without possible surprises, filled him with calm, with self-awareness, freedom of thought. His whole life rushed along in disorder, but now he found the perfect balance between interior stimulus and the impassive neutrality of material things.

It lasted an instant (if he was in second; a minute, if he was in first) then he was immediately seized by a pang: the squalor of the compartment, the plush threadbare in places, the suspicion of dust all about, the faded texture of the curtains in the old-style coaches, gave him a sensation of sadness, the uneasy thought of sleeping in his clothes, on a bunk not his, with no possible intimacy between him and what he touched. But he immediately recalled the reason why he was traveling, and he felt caught up again in that natural rhythm, as of the sea or the wind, that festive, light impulse; he had only to seek it within himself, closing his eyes, or clasping the telephone token in his hand, and that sense of squalor was defeated, only he existed, alone, facing the adventure of his journey.

But something was still missing: what? Ah: he heard the bass voice approaching under the canopy: "Pillows!" He had already stood up, was lowering the window, extending his hand with the two 100-lire pieces, shouting: "I'll have one!" It was the pillow-man who, every time, gave the journey its starting signal. He passed by the window a minute before departure, pushing in front of him the wheeled rack with pillows hanging from it. He was a tall old man, thin, with a white moustache and large hands, long, thick fingers: hands that inspire trust. He was dressed all in black: military cap, uniform, overcoat, a scarf wound tight around his neck. A character from the times of King Umberto I; something like an old colonel, or only a faithful quartermaster sergeant. Or a postman, an old rural messenger: with those big hands, when he extended the thin pillow to Federico, holding it with his fingertips, he seemed to be delivering a letter, or perhaps to be posting it through the window. The pillow now was in Federico's arms, square, flat, just like an envelope, and, what's more, covered with postmarks: it was the daily letter to Cinzia, also departing this evening, and instead of the page of eager scrawl there was Federico in person to take the invisible path of the night post, through the hand of the old winter messenger, the last incarnation of the rational, disciplined North before the incursion among the unruly passions of the Center-South.

But still, and above all, it was a pillow; namely, a soft object (though pressed and compact) and white (though covered with rubber-stamp marks) from the steam laundry. It contained in itself, as a concept is enclosed within an ideographic sign, the idea of bed, the twisting and turning, the privacy; and Federico was already anticipating with pleasure the island of freshness it would be for him, that night, amid that rough and treacherous plush. And further: that slender rectangle of comfort prefigured later comforts, later intimacy, later sweetness, whose enjoyment was the reason he was setting out on this journey; indeed, the fact itself of departing, the hiring of the cushion was a form of enjoying them, a way of entering the dimension where Cinzia reigned, the circle enclosed by her soft arms.

And it was with an amorous, caressing motion that the train began to glide among the columns of the canopies, snaking through the iron-clad fields of the points, hurling itself into the darkness, and becoming one with the impulse that till then Federico had felt within himself. And, as if the release of his tension in the speeding of the train had made him lighter, he began to accompany its race, humming the tune of a song that this same speed brought to his mind: "*J'ai deux amours. Mon pays et Paris ... Paris toujours ...*"

A man entered; Federico fell silent. "Is this place free?" He sat down. Federico had already made a quick, mental calculation: strictly speaking, if you want to make your journey lying down, it's best to have someone else in the compartment, one person stretched out on one side, and the other opposite, and then nobody dares disturb you; but if on the other hand, half the compartment remains free, when you least expect it a family of six boards the train, complete with children, all bound for Siracusa, and you're forced to sit up. Federico was quite aware then that the wisest thing to do, on entering an uncrowded train, was to take a seat not in an empty compartment but in a compartment where there was already one traveler. But he never did this: he preferred to aim at total solitude, and when, through no choice of his, he acquired a traveling companion, he could always console himself with the advantages of the new situation.

And so he did now. "Are you going to Rome?" he asked the newcomer, so that he could then add: Fine, let's draw the curtains, turn off the light, and nobody else will come in. But instead the man answered: "No. Genoa." It would be fine for him to get off at Genoa and leave Federico alone again, but, for a few hours' journey, he wouldn't want to stretch out, probably would remain awake, wouldn't allow the light to be turned off, and other people could come in at the stations along the way. Thus Federico had the disadvantages of travelling in company with none of the corresponding advantages.

But he didn't dwell on this. His forte had always been an ability to dismiss from the area of his thoughts any aspect of reality that upset him or was of no use to him. He erased the man seated in the corner opposite his, reduced him to a shadow, a gray patch. The newspapers that both held open before their faces assisted the reciprocal impermeability. Federico could go on feeling himself soar in his amorous flight. "*Paris toujours ...*" No one could imagine that in that sordid setting of people coming and going, driven by need and by patience, he was flying to the arms of a woman the like of Cinzia U. And to feed this sense of pride, Federico felt impelled to consider his traveling companion (at whom he had not even glanced so far) to compare – with the cruelty of the nouveau riche – his own fortunate state with the grayness of other existences.

The stranger, however, didn't look the least downcast. He was a still-young man, sturdy, hefty; his manner was satisfied, active; he was reading a sports magazine, and had a large suitcase at his side. He looked, in other words, like the agent for some firm, a commercial traveler. For a moment, Federico V. was gripped by the feeling of envy always inspired in him by people who seemed more practical and vital than he; but it was the impression of a moment, which he immediately dismissed, thinking: He's a man who travels in corrugated iron, or paints, whereas I... And he was seized again by that desire to sing, in a release of euphoria, clearing his mind. "Je *voyage en amour!*" he warbled in his mind, to the earlier rhythm that he felt harmonized with the race of the train, adapting words specially invented to enrage the salesman, if he could have heard them. "*Je voyage en volupté!*" underlining as far as he could the lilt and the languor of the tune, "Je *voyage toujours ... l'hiver et l'été. . .*"

He was thus becoming more and more worked up, "*l'hiver et... l'été!*" to such a degree that a smile of complete mental beatitude must have appeared on his lips. At that moment he realized the salesman was staring at him.

He promptly resumed his staid mien, concentrated on the reading of his paper, denying even to himself that he had been caught a moment before in such a childish mood. Childish? Why? Nothing childish about it: his journey put him in a propitious condition of spirit, a condition characteristic, in fact, of the man who knows the good and the evil of life, and now is preparing himself to enjoy, deservedly, the good. Serene, his conscience perfectly at peace, he leafed through the illustrated weeklies, shattered images of a fast, frantic life, in which he sought something of what also moved him. Soon he discovered that the magazines didn't interest him in the least, mere scribbles of immediacy, of the life that flows on the surface. His impatience was voyaging through loftier heavens. "*L'hiver et... l'été!*" Now it was time to settle down to sleep.

He received an unexpected satisfaction: the salesman had fallen asleep sitting up, without changing position, the newspaper on his lap. Federico considered people capable of sleeping in a seated position with a sense of estrangement that didn't even manage to be envy: for him, sleeping on the train involved an elaborate procedure, a detailed ritual, but this, too, was precisely the arduous pleasure of his journeys.

First, he had to take off his good trousers and put on an old pair, so he wouldn't arrive all rumpled. The operation would take place in the W.C.; but before – to have greater freedom of movement – it was best to change his shoes for slippers. From his bag Federico took out his old trousers, the slippers' bag, took off his shoes, put on the slippers, hid the shoes under the seat, went to the W.C. to change his trousers. "*Je voyage toujours!*" He came back, arranged his good trousers on the rack so they would keep their crease. "*Trallalà-la-la!*" He placed the pillow at the end of the seat, towards the passage, because it was better to hear the sudden opening of the door above your head than to be struck by it visibly as you suddenly opened your eyes. "*Du voyage je sais tout!*" At the other end of the seat he put a newspaper, because he didn't lie down barefoot; he kept his slippers on. He hung his jacket from a hook over the pillow, and in one pocket he put his change-purse and his bill-clip, which would have pressed against his leg if left in his trouser-pocket. But he kept his ticket, in the little pocket below his belt: "*Je sais bien voyager ...*" He replaced his good sweater, so as not to wrinkle it, with an old one; he would change his shirt in the morning. The salesman, waking when Federico came back into the compartment, had followed his maneuvering as if not completely understanding what was going on. "*Jusqu'à mon amour ...*" He took off his tie and hung it up, took the celluloid stiffeners from his shirt collar and put them in a pocket of his jacket, along with his money. "*. . .j'arrive avec le train!*" He took off his suspenders (like all men devoted to an elegance not merely external, he wore suspenders) and his garters; he undid the top button of his trousers so they wouldn't be too tight over the belly. " *Trallalà-la-la!* " He didn't put the jacket on again over his old pullover, but his overcoat instead, after having taken his house-keys from the pocket; he left the precious token, though, with the heart-rending fetishism of children who put their favorite toy under the pillow. He buttoned up the overcoat completely, turned up the collar; if he was careful, he was able to sleep in it without leaving a wrinkle. "*Maintenant voilà!*" Sleeping on the train meant waking with your hair all disheveled and maybe finding yourself in the station without even the time to comb it; so he pulled a beret all the way down on his head. "*Je suis prêt, alors!*" He swayed across the compartment in the overcoat which, worn without a jacket, hung on him like a priestly vestment; he drew the curtains over the door, pulling them until the metallic buttons reached the leather button-holes. With a gesture towards his companion, he asked permission to turn off the light; the salesman was sleeping. He turned the light off: in the bluish penumbra of the little safety light, he moved just enough to close the curtains at the window, or rather to draw them almost closed; here he always left a crack open: in the morning he liked to have a ray of sunshine in his bedroom. One more operation: wind his watch. There, now he could go to bed. With one bound, he had flung himself horizontally on the seat, on his side, the overcoat smooth, his legs bent, hands in his pockets, token in his hand, his feet – still in his slippers – on the newspaper, nose against the pillow, beret over his eyes. Now, with a deliberate relaxation of all his feverish inner activity, a vague anticipation of tomorrow, he would fall asleep.

The conductor's curt intrusion (he opened the door with a yank, with confident hand unbuttoned both curtains in a single movement as he raised his other hand to turn on the light) was foreseen. Federico, however, preferred not to wait for it: if the man arrived before he had fallen asleep, fine; if his first sleep had already begun, a habitual and anonymous appearance like the conductor's interrupted it only for a few seconds, just as a sleeper in the country wakes at the cry of a nocturnal bird but then rolls over as if he hadn't waked at all. Federico kept the ticket ready in his pocket and held it out, not getting up, almost not opening his eyes, his hand remaining open until he felt the ticket again between his fingers; he pocketed it and would immediately have fallen back to sleep, if he hadn't been obliged to perform an operation that nullified all his earlier effort at immobility: namely, get up and fasten the curtains again. This trip, he was still awake, and the ticket-check lasted a bit longer than usual, because the salesman, caught in his sleep, took a while to get his bearings, to find his ticket. He doesn't have prompt reflexes like mine, Federico thought, and took advantage to overwhelm him with new variations on his imaginary song. "*Je voyage l'amour ...*" he crooned. The idea of using the verb *voyager* transitively gave him the sense of fullness that poetic inspiration, even the slightest, gives, and the satisfaction of having finally found an expression adequate to his spiritual state. "*Je voyage amour! Je voyage liberté! Jour et nuit je cours ... par les chemins-de-fer ...*"

The compartment was again in darkness. The train devoured its invisible road. Could Federico ask more of life? From such bliss to sleep, the transition is brief. Federico dozed off as if sinking into a pit of feathers. Five or six minutes only: then he woke. He was hot, all in a sweat. The coaches were already heated, since it was well into autumn, but he, recalling the cold he had felt on his previous trip, had thought to lie down in his overcoat. He rose, took it off, flung it over himself like a blanket, leaving his shoulders and chest free, but still trying to spread it out so as not to make ugly wrinkles. He turned on his other side. The sweat had spread over his body a network of itching. He unbuttoned his shirt, scratched his chest, scratched one leg. The constricted condition of his body that he now felt evoked

thoughts of physical freedom, the sea, nakedness, swimming, running, and all this culminated in the embracing of
Cinzia, the sum of the good of existence. And there, half-
sleeping, he could no longer distinguish present discomforts
from the yearned-for good; he had everything at once; he
writhed in an uneasiness that presupposed and virtually
contained every possible well-being. He fell asleep again.

The loudspeakers of the stations that waked him every so
often are not as disagreeable as many people suppose. Waking and knowing at once where you are offers two different
possibilities of satisfaction: you can think, if the station is
farther along than you imagined: How much I've slept!
How far I've gone without realizing it!, or, if the station is
way behind: Good, I have plenty of time to fall asleep again
and continue sleeping without any concern.

Now he was in the second of these situations. The salesman
was there, also stretched out, asleep, softly snoring. Federico
was still warm. He rose, half-sleeping, groped for the regulator of the electric heating system, found it on the wall opposite
his, just above the head of his traveling companion, extended
his hands, balancing on one foot, because one of his slippers
had come off, and angrily turned the dial to "minimum". The
salesman had to open his eyes at that moment and see that
clawing hand over his head: he gulped, swallowed saliva,
then sank back into his haze. Federico flung himself down.
The electric regulator let out a hum, a red light came on, as if
it were trying to explain, to start a dialogue. Federico impatiently waited for the heat to be dispelled; he rose to lower the
window a crack, but as the train was now moving very fast,
he felt cold and closed it again. He shifted the regulator
towards "automatic". His face on the amorous pillow, he lay
for a while listening to the buzzes of the regulator like

mysterious messages from ultra-terrestrial worlds. The train was traveling over the earth, surmounted by endless spaces, and in all the universe he and he alone was the man who was speeding towards Cinzia U.

The next awakening was at the cry of a coffee-vendor in the Principe Station, Genoa. The salesman had vanished. Carefully, Federico stopped up the gaps in the wall of curtains, and listened with apprehension to every footstep approaching along the passage, to every opening of a door. No, nobody came in. But at Genoa-Brignole a hand opened a breach, groped, tried to part the curtains, failed; a human form appeared, crouching, and cried in dialect towards the passage: "Come on! It's empty here!" A heavy shuffling replied, of boots, scattered voices, and four Alpine soldiers entered the darkness of the compartment and almost sat down on top of Federico. As they bent over him, as if over an unknown animal – "Oh! Who's this here?" – he pulled himself up abruptly on his arms and confronted them: "Aren't there any other compartments?" "No. All full," they answered, "but never mind. We'll all sit over on this side. Stay comfortable." They seemed intimidated, but actually they were simply accustomed to curt manners, and paid no attention to anything; brawling, they flung themselves on the other seat. "Are you going far?" Federico asked, meeker now, from his pillow. No, they were getting off at one of the first stations. "And where are you going?" "To Rome." "Madonna! All the way to Rome!" Their tone of amazed compassion was transformed, in Federico's heart, into a heroic, melting pride.

And so the journey continued. "Could you turn off the light?" They turned it off, and remained faceless in the dark, noisy, cumbersome, shoulder to shoulder. One raised a curtain at the window and peered out: it was a moonlit night. Lying down, Federico saw only the sky and now and then the row of lights of a little station that dazzled his eyes and cast a rake of shadows on the ceiling. The Alpini were rough country-boys, going home on leave; they never stopped talking loud and hailing one another, and at times in the darkness they punched and slapped one another, except for one of them who was sleeping and another who coughed. They spoke a murky dialect. Federico could grasp words now and then, talk about the barracks, the brothel. For some reason, he felt he didn't hate them. Now he was with them, almost one of them, and he identified with them for the pleasure of then imagining himself tomorrow at the side of Cinzia U., feeling the dizzying, sudden shift of fate. But this was not to belittle them, as with the stranger earlier; now he remained obscurely on their side; their unaware blessing accompanied him towards Cinzia; in everything that was most remote from her lay the value of having her, the sense of him being the one who had her.

Now Federico's arm was numb. He lifted it, shook it; the numbness wouldn't go away, turned into pain, the pain turned into slow well-being, as he flapped his bent arm in the air. The Alpini, all four of them, sat there staring at him, their mouths agape. "What's come over him ... He's dreaming ... Hey, what are you doing? ..." Then with youthful fickleness they went back to teasing one another. Federico now tried to revive the circulation in one leg, putting his foot on the floor and stamping hard.

Between dozing and clowning an hour went by. And he didn't feel he was their enemy; perhaps he was no one's enemy; perhaps he had become a good man. He didn't hate them even when, a little before their station, they went out, leaving the door and the curtains wide. He got up, barricaded himself again, savored once more the pleasure of solitude, but with no bitterness towards anyone.

Now his legs were cold. He pushed the cuffs of his trousers inside his socks, but he was still cold. He wrapped the folds of his overcoat around his legs. Now his stomach and shoulders were cold. He turned the regulator up almost to "maximum," tucked himself in again, pretended not to notice that the overcoat was making ugly creases, though he felt them under him. Now he was ready to renounce everything for his immediate comfort, the awareness of being good to his neighbor drove him to be good to himself and, in this general indulgence, to find once more the road to sleep.

From now on the awakenings were intermittent and mechanical. The entrances of the conductor, with his practiced movement in opening the curtains, were easily distinguishable from the uncertain attempts of the night travelers who had got on at an intermediary station and were bewildered at finding a series of compartments with the curtains drawn. Equally professional, but more brusque and grim, was the appearance of the policeman, who abruptly turned on the light in the sleeper's face, examined him, turned it off, and went out in silence, leaving behind him a prison chill.

Then a man came in, at some station buried in the night. Federico became aware of him when he was already huddled in one corner, and from the damp odor of his coat realized that outside it was raining. When he woke again the man had vanished, at God knows what other invisible station, and for Federico he had been only a shadow smelling of rain, with a heavy respiration.

He was cold; he turned the regulator all the way to "maximum", then stuck his hand under the seat to feel the heat rise. He felt nothing; he groped there; everything seemed cut off. He put his overcoat on again, then removed it, he hunted for his good sweater, took off the old one, put on the good one, put the old one on over it, put the overcoat on again, huddled down, and tried to achieve once more the sensation of fullness that earlier had led him to sleep, but he couldn't manage to recall anything, and when he remembered the song he was already sleeping and that rhythm continued cradling him triumphantly in his sleep.

The first morning light came through the cracks like the cry "hot coffee!" and "newspapers!" of a station perhaps still in Tuscany or at the very beginning of Latium. It wasn't raining; beyond the damp windows the sky displayed an already southern indifference to autumn. The desire for something hot and also the automatic reaction of the city man who begins all his mornings by glancing at the newspapers acted on Federico's reflexes; and he felt that he should rush to the window and buy coffee or the paper or both. But he succeeded so well in convincing himself that he was still asleep and hadn't heard anything that this persuasion still held when the compartment was invaded by the usual people from Civitavecchia who take the early morning trains into Rome. And the best part of his sleep, that of the first hours of daylight, had almost no breaks.

When he really did wake up, he was dazzled by the light that came in through the panes, now without curtains. On the seat opposite him a row of people were lined up, and actually there was also a little boy on a fat woman's lap, and a man was seated on Federico's own seat, in the space left free by his bent legs. The men had different faces, but all had something vaguely bureaucratic about them, with the one possible variant of an air force officer in a uniform bright with ribbons; and also the women, it was obvious, were going to call on relatives who worked in some government office: in any case these were people going to Rome to deal with red-tape for themselves or for others. And all of them, some looking up from the conservative newspaper *Il Tempo*, observed Federico stretched out there at the level of their knees, shapeless, bundled into that overcoat, without feet like a seal, as he was detaching himself from the saliva-stained pillow, disheveled, the beret on the back of his head, one cheek marked by the wrinkles of the pillowcase, as he got up, stretched with awkward, seal-like movements, gradually rediscovering the use of his legs, slipping the slippers on the wrong foot, and now unbuttoning and scratching himself between the double sweaters and the rumpled shirt, while running his still sticky eyes over them, and smiling.

At the window, the broad Roman *campagna* spread out. Federico sat there for a moment, his hands on his knees, still smiling; then, with a gesture, he asked permission to take the newspaper from the knees of the man facing him. He glanced at the headlines, felt as always the sense of finding himself in a remote country, looked olympically at the arches of the acqueducts that sped past outside the window, returned the newspaper, and got up to look for his toilet-kit in his suitcase.

At the Stazione Termini the first to jump down from the car, fresh as a daisy, was Federico. He was clasping the token in his hand. In the niches between the columns and the news-stalls, the gray telephones were waiting only for him. He put the token in the slot, dialed the number, listened with

beating heart to the distant ring, heard Cinzia's "Hello ..."
still suffused with sleep and soft warmth, and he was already
in the tension of their days together, in the desperate battle
against the hours; and he realized he would never manage
to tell her anything of the significance of that night, which
he now sensed was fading, like every perfect night of love,
at the cruel explosion of day.

(1958)

The Adventure of a Reader

The coast road ran high above the cape; the sea was below, a sheer drop, and on all sides, as far as the hazy mountainous horizon. The sun was on all sides, too, as if the sky and the sea were two glasses magnifying it. Down below, against the jagged, irregular rocks of the cape, the calm water slapped without making foam. Amedeo Oliva climbed down a steep flight of steps, shouldering his bicycle; which he left in a shady place after closing the padlock. He continued down the steps amid spills of dry, yellow earth and agaves jutting into the void, and he was already looking around for the most comfortable stretch of rock where he could lie down. Under his arm he had a rolled-up towel and, inside the towel, his bathing trunks and a book.

The cape was a solitary place: a few groups of bathers dived into the water or took the sun, hidden from one another by the irregular conformation of the place. Between two boulders that shielded him from view, Amedeo undressed, put on his trunks, and began jumping from the top of one rock to the next. Leaping in this way, on his skinny legs, he crossed half the rocky shore, sometimes almost grazing the faces of half-hidden pairs of bathers stretched out on beach-towels. Having gone past an outcrop of sandy rock, its surface porous and irregular, he came upon smooth stones, with rounded corners; Amedeo took off his sandals, held them in his hand, and continued running barefoot, with the confidence of someone who can judge distances between rocks, and whose soles nothing can hurt. He reached a spot directly above the sea; there was a kind of shelf running around the cliff at the halfway point. There Amedeo stopped. On a flat ledge he arranged his clothes, carefully folded, and set the sandals on them, soles up, so no gust of wind would carry everything off (in reality the faintest breath of air was stirring from the sea; but this precaution was obviously a habit with him). A little bag he was carrying turned into a rubber cushion; he blew into it until it had filled out, then set it down, and below it, at a point slightly sloping from that rocky ledge, he spread out his towel. He flung himself onto it, supine, and already his hands were opening his book at the marked page. So he lay stretched out on the ledge, in that sun glaring on all sides, his skin dry (his tan was opaque, irregular, as of one who takes the sun without any method, but doesn't burn), on the rubber cushion he set his head sheathed in a white canvas cap, moistened (yes, he had also climbed down to a low rock, to dip his cap in the water), immobile except for his eyes (invisible behind his dark glasses) which followed, along the black and white lines, the horse of Fabrizio del Dongo. Below him opened a little inlet of greenish-blue water, transparent almost to the bottom. The rocks, according to their exposure, were bleached white or covered with algae. A little pebbled beach was at their foot. Every now and then Amedeo raised his eyes to that broad view, lingered on a glinting of the surface, on the oblique dash of a crab; then he went back, gripped, to the page where Raskolnikov counted the steps that separated him from the old woman's door or where Lucien de Rubempré, before sticking his head into the noose, gazed at the towers and roofs of the Conciergerie.

For some time Amedeo had tended to reduce his participation in active life to the minimum. Not that he didn't like action: on the contrary, love of action nourished his whole character, all his tastes; and yet, from one year to the next, the yearning to be someone who did things declined, declined, until he wondered if he had ever really harbored that yearning. His interest in action survived, however, in his pleasure in reading; his passion was always the narration of events, stories, the tangle of human situations. Nineteenth-century novels, especially, but also memoirs and biographies; and so on, down to thrillers and science fiction, which he didn't disdain but which gave him less satisfaction because they were short. Amedeo loved thick tomes, and in tackling them he felt the physical pleasure of undertaking a great task. Weighing them in his hand, solid, closely printed, squat, he would consider with some apprehension the number of pages, the length of the chapters, then venture into them, a bit reluctant at the beginning, without any desire to overcome the initial chore of remembering the names, catching the drift of the story; then, entrusting himself to it, running along the lines, crossing the grid of the uniform page, and beyond the leaden print the flame and fire of battle appeared, the cannonball that, whistling through the sky, fell at the feet of Prince Andrei, and the shop filled with engravings and statues where Frédéric Moreau, his heart in his mouth, was to meet the Arnoux family. Beyond the surface of the page you entered a world where life was more alive than here, on this side: like the surface of the water that separates us from that blue and green world, rifts as far as the eye can see, expanses of fine, ribbed sand, creatures half-animal and half-vegetable.

The sun beat down hard, the rock was burning, and after a while Amedeo felt he was one with the rock. He reached the end of the chapter, closed the book, inserting an advertising coupon to mark his place, took off his canvas cap and his glasses, stood up, half-dazed, and with broad leaps went down to the far end of the rock, where a group of kids, at all hours, were constantly diving in and climbing out. Amedeo stood erect on a shelf over the sea, not too high, a couple of meters above the water; his eyes, still dazzled, contemplated the luminous transparence below him, and all of a sudden he plunged. His dive was always the same, headlong, fairly correct, but with a certain stiffness. The passage from the sunny air to the tepid water would have been almost unnoticeable, if it hadn't been abrupt. He didn't surface immediately, he liked to swim underwater, down, down, his belly almost scraping bottom, as long as his breath held out. He very much enjoyed physical effort, setting himself difficult assignments (for this, he came to read his book at the cape, making the climb on his bicycle, pedaling up furiously under the noonday sun). Every time, swimming underwater, he tried to reach a wall of rocks that rose at a certain point from the sandy bed, covered by a thick patch of sea grasses. He surfaced among those rocks and swam around a bit; he began to do "the Australian crawl" methodically, but expending more energy than necessary; soon, tired of swimming with his face in the water, as if blind, he took to a freer side-stroke; seeing gave him more satisfaction than movement, and in a little while he gave up the side-stroke to drift on his back, moving less and less regularly and steadily, until he stopped altogether, in a dead-man's float. And so he turned and twisted in that sea as if in a bed without sides, and he would set himself the goal of a sandbar to be reached, or he would limit the number of strokes, and he couldn't rest until he had carried out that task; for a while he would dawdle lazily, then he would head out to sea, taken by the desire to have nothing around him but sky and water; for a while he would move close to the rocks scattered along the cape, not to overlook any of the possible itineraries of that little archipelago. But, as he swam, he realized that the curiosity occupying more and more of his mind was that of knowing the outcome – for example – of the story of Albertine. Would Marcel find her again, or not? He swam furiously or floated idly, but his heart was between the pages of the book left behind on shore. And so, with rapid strokes, he would regain his rock, seek the place for climbing up, and almost without realizing it, he would be up there, rubbing the Turkish towel over his back. Sticking the canvas cap on his head once more, he would lie again in the sun, to begin the next chapter.

He was not, however, a hasty, voracious reader. He had reached the age when re-reading a book for the second, third, or fourth time affords more pleasure than a first reading. And yet he still had many continents to discover. Every summer, the most laborious packing before the departure for the sea involved the heavy suitcase to be filled with books. Following the whims and dictates of the months of city life, each year Amedeo would choose certain famous books to re-read and certain authors to essay for the first time. And there, on the rock, he went through them, lingering over sentences, often raising his eyes from the page to ponder, to collect his thoughts. At a certain point, raising his eyes in this way, he saw that on the little pebble beach below, in the inlet, a woman had appeared and was lying there.

She was deeply tanned, thin, not very young, nor of great beauty, but nakedness became her (she wore a very tiny "two-piece", rolled up at the edges to get as much sun as she could), and Amedeo's eye was drawn to her. He realized that, as he read, he raised his eyes more and more often from the book to gaze into the air; and this air was the air that lay between that woman and himself. She was stretched out on the sloping shore, on a rubber mattress, and at every flicker of his pupils Amedeo saw her legs, not shapely but harmonious, the excellently smooth belly, the bosom slim in a perhaps not unpleasant way but probably sagging a bit, the shoulders a bit too bony and then the neck and the arms, and the face masked by the black eyeglasses and by the brim of the straw hat. Her face was slightly lined, lively, aware, and ironic. Amedeo classified the type: the independent woman, on holiday by herself, who dislikes crowded beaches and prefers the more deserted rocks, and likes to lie there and become black as coal; he evaluated the amount of lazy sensuality and of chronic frustration there was in her; he thought fleetingly of the likelihood of a rapidly consummated fling, measured them against the prospect of a trite conversation, a program for the evening, probable logistic difficulties, the effort of concentration always required to become acquainted, even superficially, with a person; and he went on reading, convinced that this woman couldn't interest him at all.

But he had been lying on that stretch of rock for too long, or else those fleeting thoughts had left a wake of restlessness in him; anyway, he felt an ache, the harshness of the rock under the towel that was his only pallet began to chafe him. He got up to look for another spot where he could stretch out. For a moment, he hesitated between two places that seemed equally comfortable to him: one more distant from the little beach where the tanned lady was lying (actually behind an outcrop of the rock which blocked the sight of her), the other closer. The thought of approaching and of then perhaps being led by some unforeseeable circumstance to start a conversation and thus perforce to interrupt his reading, made him immediately prefer the farther spot; but when he thought it over, it actually would look as if, the moment that lady had arrived, he wanted to run off, and this might seem a bit rude; thus he picked the closer spot, since his reading so absorbed him anyway that the view of the lady – not specially beautiful, for that matter – could hardly distract him. He lay on one side, holding the book so that it blocked the sight of her, but it was awkward to keep his arm at that height and, in the end, he lowered it. Now the same gaze that ran along the lines encountered, every time he had to start a new line, just beyond the edge of the page, the legs of the solitary vacationer. She, too, had shifted slightly, looking for a more comfortable position, and the fact that she had raised her knees and crossed her legs precisely in Amedeo's direction, allowed him to observe better her proportions, not at all unattractive. In short, Amedeo (though a shaft of rock was sawing at his hip) couldn't have found a finer position: the pleasure he could derive from the sight of the tanned lady – a marginal pleasure, something extra, but not for that reason to be discarded, since it could be enjoyed with no effort – did not mar the pleasure of reading, but was inserted into its normal process; now he was sure he could go on reading without being tempted to look away.

Everything was calm; only the course of his reading flowed on, for which the motionless landscape served as frame, and the tanned lady had become a necessary part of this landscape. Amedeo naturally was relying on his own ability to remain for a long time absolutely still, but he hadn't taken into account the woman's restlessness: she now rose, was standing, proceeding among the stones towards the water. She had moved – Amedeo understood immediately – to see, closer, a great medusa, that a group of boys was bringing ashore, poking at it with some reeds. The tanned lady bent towards the overturned body of the medusa and was questioning the boys; her legs rose from wooden clogs with very high heels, unsuited to those rocks; her body, seen from behind as Amedeo now saw it, was that of a woman more attractive, younger than she had first seemed to him. He thought that, for a man seeking a romance, that dialogue between her and the fisher-boys would have been a "classic" opening: approach, also remark on the capture of the medusa, and, in that way, engage her in conversation. The very thing he wouldn't have done for all the gold in the world! he added to himself, plunging again into his reading. To be sure, this rule of conduct of his also prevented him from satisfying a natural curiosity concerning the medusa, which seemed, as he saw it there, of unusual dimensions, and also of a strange hue between pink and violet. This curiosity about marine animals, too, was in no way a side-track; it was coherent with the nature of his passion for reading; at that moment, in any case, his concentration on the page he was reading – a long descriptive passage – had been relaxing; in short, it was absurd that to protect himself against the danger of starting a conversation with that woman he should also deny himself spontaneous and quite legitimate impulses such as that of amusing himself for a few minutes by taking a close look at a medusa. He shut his book at the marked page and stood up: his decision couldn't have been more timely: at that same moment the lady moved away from the little group of boys, preparing to return to her mattress. Amedeo realized this as he was approaching and felt the need of immediately saying something in a loud voice. He shouted to the kids: "Watch out! It could be dangerous!"

The boys, crouched around the animal, didn't even look up: they continued, with the lengths of reed they held in their hands, to try to raise it and turn it over; but the lady turned abruptly and went back to the shore, with a half-questioning, half-fearful air. "Oh, how frightening! Does it bite?"

"If you touch it, it stings," he explained and realized he was heading not towards the medusa but towards the lady, who, for some reason, covered her bosom with her arms in a useless shudder and cast almost furtive glances first at the supine animal then at Amedeo. He reassured her and so, predictably, they started conversing; but it didn't matter, because Amedeo would soon be going back to the book awaiting him: he only wanted to take a glance at the medusa, and so he led the tanned lady over, to lean into the center of the circle of boys. The lady was now observing with repulsion, her knuckles against her teeth, and at a certain moment, as she and he were side by side, their arms came into contact and they delayed a moment before separating them. Amedeo then started talking about medusas: his direct experience wasn't great, but he had read some books by famous fishermen and underwater explorers, so – skipping the smaller fauna – he promptly began talking about the famous *manta*. The lady listened to him, displaying great interest and interjecting from time to time, always irrelevantly, the way women will. "You see this red place on my arm? That wasn't a medusa, was it?" Amedeo touched the spot, just above the elbow, and said no. It was a bit red because she had been leaning on it, while lying down.

With that, it was all over. They said goodbye, she went back to her place, he to his and resumed reading. It had been an interval lasting the right amount of time, neither more nor less, a human encounter, not unpleasant (the lady was polite, discreet, unassuming) precisely because it was barely adumbrated. Now in the book he found a far fuller and more concrete attachment to reality, where everything had a meaning, an importance, a rhythm. Amedeo felt himself in a perfect condition: the printed page opened true life to him, profound and exciting and, raising his eyes, he found a pleasant but casual juxtaposition of colors and sensations, an accessory and decorative world, which couldn't commit him to anything. The tanned lady, from her mattress, gave him a smile and a wave, he replied also with a smile and a vague gesture, and immediately lowered his eyes. But the lady had said something.

"Eh?"

"You're reading. Do you read all the time?"

"Mm ..."

"Interesting?"

"Yes."

"Enjoy yourself!"

"Thank you."

He mustn't raise his eyes again. At least not until the end of the chapter. He read it in a flash. The lady now had a cigarette in her mouth and motioned to him, as she pointed to it. Amedeo had the impression that for some time she had been trying to attract his attention. "I beg your pardon?"

"... match. Forgive me ..."

"Oh, I'm very sorry. I don't smoke ..."

The chapter was finished. Amedeo rapidly read the first lines of the next one, which he found surprisingly attractive, but to begin the next chapter without concern he had to resolve as quickly as possible the matter of the match. "Wait!" He stood up, began leaping among the rocks, half-dazed by the sun, until he found a little group of people smoking. He borrowed a box of matches, ran to the lady, lighted her cigarette, ran back to return the matches, and they said to him, "Keep them, you can keep them." He ran again to the lady to leave the matches with her, she thanked him, he waited a moment before leaving her, but realized that after this delay he had to say something and so he said: "You aren't swimming?"

"In a little while," the lady said. "What about you?"

"I've already had my swim."

"And you're not going to take another dip?"

"Yes, I'll read one more chapter, then have a swim again."

"Me, too, when I finish my cigarette, I'll dive in."

"See you later then."

"Later ..."

This kind of appointment restored to Amedeo a calm such as he – now he realized – had not known since the moment he became aware of the solitary lady: now his conscience was no longer oppressed by the thought of having to have any sort of relationship with that lady; everything was postponed to the moment of their swim – a swim he would have taken anyway, even if the lady hadn't been there – and now he was able to abandon himself without remorse to the pleasure of reading. So thoroughly that he didn't notice when, at a certain point – before he had reached the end of the chapter – the lady finished her cigarette, stood up, and approached him to invite him to go swimming. He saw the clogs and the straight legs just beyond the book, his eyes moved up, he lowered them again to the page – the sun was dazzling – and read a few lines in haste, looked up again, and heard her say: "Isn't your head about to explode? I'm going to have a dip!" It was nice to stay there, to go on reading and to look up every now and then. But, since he could no longer put it off, Amedeo did something he never did: he skipped almost half a page, to the conclusion of the chapter, which he read, on the other hand, with great attention, then he stood up. "Let's go. Shall we dive from the point there?"

After all the talk of diving, the lady cautiously slipped into the water from a ledge on a level with it. Amedeo plunged headlong from a higher rock than usual. It was the hour of the still-slow inclining of the sun. The sea was golden. They swam in that gold, somewhat separated: Amedeo at times sank for a few strokes under water and amused himself by frightening the lady, swimming below her. Amused himself, after a fashion: it was kid stuff, of course, but for that matter, what else was there to do? Swimming with another person was slightly more tiresome than swimming alone; but the difference, in any case, was minimal. Beyond the gold glints, the water's blue deepened, as if from down below an inky darkness rose. It was useless: nothing equalled the savor of life found in books. Skimming over some bearded rocks in midwater and leading her, frightened (to help her onto a sandbar, he also clasped her hips and bosom, but his hands, from the immersion, had become almost insensitive, with white, wrinkled pads), Amedeo turned his gaze more and more towards land, where the colored jacket of his book stood out. There was no other story, no other possible expectation beyond what he had left suspended, between the pages where his book-mark was; all the rest was an empty interval.

However, the return to shore, giving her a hand, drying himself, then each rubbing the other's back, finally created a kind of intimacy, so that Amedeo felt it would have been impolite now to go off on his own once more. "Well," he said, "I'll stretch out and read here; I'll go get my book and pillow." And *read:* he had taken care to warn her. And she said: "Yes, fine. I'll smoke a cigarette and read *Annabella* a bit myself." She had one of those women's magazines with her, and so both of them could lie and read, each on his own. Her voice struck him like a drop of cold water on the nape of the neck, but she was only saying: "Why do you want to lie there on that hard rock? Come onto the mattress: I'll make room for you." The invitation was polite, the mattress was comfortable, and Amedeo gladly accepted. They lay there, he in one direction and she in the other. She didn't say another word, she leafed through those illustrated pages, and Amedeo managed to sink completely into his reading. The sun was that of a lingering sunset, when the heat and light hardly decline but remain only barely, sweetly attenuated. The novel Amedeo was reading had reached the point where the darkest secrets of characters and plot are revealed, and you move in a familiar world, and you achieve a kind of parity, an ease between author and reader: you proceed together, and you would like to go on forever.

On the rubber mattress it was possible also to make those slight movements necessary to keep the limbs from going to sleep, and one of his legs, in one direction, came to graze a leg of hers, in the other. He didn't mind this, and kept his leg there; and obviously she didn't mind either, because she also refrained from moving. The sweetness of the contact mingled with the reading, and as far as Amedeo was concerned, made it the more complete; but for the lady it must have been different, because she rose, sat up, and said: "Really ..."

Amedeo was forced to raise his head from the book. The woman was looking at him, and her eyes were bitter.

"Something wrong?" he asked.

"Don't you ever get tired of reading?" she asked. "You could hardly be called good company! Don't you know that, with women, you're supposed to make conversation?" she added, with a half-smile perhaps meant only to be ironic though to Amedeo, who at that moment would have paid anything rather than give up his novel, it seemed downright threatening. What have I got myself into, moving down here? he thought. Now it was clear that with this woman beside him he wouldn't read a line.

I must make her realize she's made a mistake, he thought, that I'm not at all the type for a beach courtship; that I'm the sort it's best not to pay too much attention to. "Conversation," he said, aloud. "What kind of conversation?" and he extended his hand towards her. There, now, if I lay a hand on her, she will surely be insulted by such an unsuitable action, maybe she'll give me a slap and go away. But, whether it was his own natural reserve, or was a different, sweeter yearning that in reality he was pursuing, the caress, instead of being brutal and provocatory, was shy, melancholy, almost entreating: he grazed her throat with his fingers, lifted a little necklace she was wearing and let it fall. The woman's reply consisted of a movement, first slow, as if resigned and a bit ironic – she lowered her chin to one side, to trap his hand – then rapid, as if in a calculated, aggressive spring: she bit the back of his hand. "Ow!" Amedeo cried. They moved apart.

"Is this how you make conversation?" the lady said.

There, Amedeo quickly reasoned, my way of making conversation doesn't suit her, so there won't be any conversing, and now I can read; he had already started a new paragraph. But he was trying to deceive himself: he understood clearly that by now they had gone too far, that between him and the tanned lady a tension had been created that could no longer be broken off; he understood also that he was the first to wish not to break it off, since in any case he wouldn't be able to return to the single tension of his reading, all intimate and interior. He could, on the contrary, try to make this exterior tension follow, so to speak, a course parallel to the other, so that he would not be obliged to renounce either the lady or the book.

Since she had sat up, with her back propped against a rock, he sat beside her, put his arm around her shoulders, keeping his book on his knees. He turned towards her and kissed her. They moved apart, then kissed again. Then he lowered his head towards the book and resumed reading.

As long as he could, he wanted to continue reading. His fear was that he wouldn't be able to finish the novel: the beginning of a summer affair could be considered the end of his calm hours of solitude, a completely different rhythm would dominate his days of vacation; and, obviously, when you are completely lost in reading a book, if you have to interrupt it, then take it up again some time later, most of the pleasure is lost: you forget so many details, you never manage to become immersed in it as before.

The sun was gradually setting behind the next promontory, and then the next, and the one after that, leaving remnants of color, against the light. From the little inlets of the cape, all the bathers had gone. Now the two of them were alone. Amedeo had his arm around the woman's shoulders, he was reading, he gave her kisses on the neck and on the ears – which it seemed to him she liked – and every now and then, when she turned, on the mouth; then he resumed reading. Perhaps this time he had found the ideal equilibrium: he could go on like this for a hundred pages or so. But once again it was she who wanted to change the situation. She began to stiffen, almost to reject him, and then said: "It's late. Let's go. I'm going to dress."

This abrupt decision opened quite different prospects. Amedeo was a bit disoriented, but he didn't stop to weigh the pros and cons. He had reached a climax of the book, and her words, "I'm going to dress," dimly heard had, in his mind, immediately been translated into these others: While she dresses, I'll have time to read a few pages without being disturbed.

But she said: "Hold up the towel, please," addressing him as *tu* perhaps for the first time. "I don't want anyone to see me." The precaution was useless because the shore by now was deserted, but Amedeo consented amiably, since he could hold up the towel while remaining seated and continue to read the book on his knees.

Beyond the towel, the lady had undone her halter, paying no attention to whether he was looking at her or not. Amedeo didn't know whether to look at her, pretending to read, or to read, pretending to look at her. He was interested in the one thing and the other, but looking at her seemed too indiscreet while going on reading seemed too indifferent. The lady did not follow the usual method used by bathers who dress outdoors, first putting on clothes and then removing the bathing suit underneath them. No, now that her bosom was bared, she also took off the bottom of the suit. This was when, for the first time, she turned her face towards him: and it was a sad face, with a bitter curl of the mouth, and she shook her head, shook her head and looked at him.

Since it has to happen, it might as well happen immediately! Amedeo thought, diving forward, book in hand, one finger between the pages; but what he read in that gaze – reproach, commiseration, dejection, as if to say: Stupid, all right, we'll do it if it has to be done like this, but you don't understand a thing, any more than the others ... – or rather, what he did *not* read, as he didn't know how to read gazes, but only vaguely sensed, roused in him a moment of such transport towards the woman that, embracing her and falling onto the mattress with her, he only slightly turned his head towards the book to make sure it didn't fall into the sea.

It had fallen, instead, right beside the mattress, open, but a few pages had flipped over; and Amedeo, even in the ecstasy of his embraces, tried to free one hand, to put the book-mark at the right page. Nothing is more irritating when you're eager to resume reading than to have to search through the book, unable to find your place.

Their love-making was a perfect match. It could perhaps have been extended a bit longer: but then hadn't everthing been lightning-fast in their encounter?

Dusk was falling. Below, the rocks opened out, sloping, into a little harbor. Now she had gone down there and was halfway into the water. "Come down; we'll have a last swim ..." Amedeo, biting his lip, was counting how many pages were left till the end.

(1958)

The Adventure of a Near-Sighted Man

Amilcare Carruga was still young, not lacking resources, without exaggerated material or spiritual ambitions: nothing, therefore, prevented him from enjoying life. And yet he came to realize that for a while now this life, for him, had imperceptibly been losing its savor. Trifles: like, for example, looking at women in the street. There had been a time when he would cast his eyes on them, greedily; now perhaps he would start instinctively to look at them, but it would immediately seem to him that they sped past like a wind, stirring no sensation, so then he would lower his eyelids, indifferent. Once new cities had excited him – he traveled often, as he was a businessman – now he felt only irritation, confusion, loss of bearings. Before, in the evening – as he lived alone – he used to go always to the movies: he enjoyed himself, no matter what the picture was; anyone who goes every evening sees, as it were, one huge film, in endless instalments: he knows all the actors, even the character roles, the walk-ons, and this recognition of them every time is amusing in itself. Well: even at the movies, now, all those faces seemed to have become colorless to him, flat, anonymous; he was bored.

He caught on, finally. The fact was that he was near-sighted. The oculist prescribed eyeglasses for him. After that moment his life changed, became a hundred times richer in interest than before.

Just slipping on the glasses was, every time, an emotion for him. He might be, for instance, at a tram stop, and he would be overcome by sadness because everything, people and objects around him, was so generic, banal, worn from being as it was, and him there groping in the midst of a flabby world of nearly decayed forms and colors. He would put on his glasses to read the number of the arriving tram, and all would change; the most ordinary things, even a lamp-post, were etched with countless tiny details, with sharp lines, and the faces, the faces of strangers, each filled up with little marks, dots of beard, pimples, nuances of expression that there had been no hint of before; and he could understand what material clothes were made of, could guess the weave, could spot the fraying at the hem. Looking became an amusement, a spectacle; not looking at this thing or that: looking. And so Amilcare Carruga forgot to note the tram number, missed one car after another, or else climbed onto the wrong one. He saw such a quantity of things that it was as if he no longer saw anything. Little by little, he had to become accustomed, learn all over again from the beginning what was pointless to look at and what was necessary.

The women that he then encountered in the street, who before had been reduced for him to impalpable, blurred shadows, he could now see with the precise interplay of voids and solids that their bodies make as they move inside their dresses, and could judge the freshness of the skin and the warmth contained in their gaze, and it seemed to him he was not only seeing them but already actually possessing them. He might be walking along without his glasses (he didn't wear them all the time so as not to tire his eyes unnecessarily; only if he had to look into the distance) and there, ahead of him on the sidewalk, a bright-colored dress would be outlined. With a now-automatic movement, Amilcare would promptly take his glasses from his pocket and slip them onto his nose. This indiscriminate covetousness of sensations was often punished: maybe the woman proved a hag. Amilcare Carruga became more cautious. And at times, an approaching woman might seem to him, from her colors, her walk, too humble, insignificant, not worth taking into consideration; he wouldn't put on his glasses; but then when they passed each other close, he realized that, on the contrary, there was something about her that attracted him strongly, God knows what, and at that moment he seemed to catch a look of hers, as if of expectation, perhaps a look that already from his first appearance she had trained on him and he hadn't been aware of it; but by now it was too late, she had vanished at the intersection, climbed into the bus, was far away beyond the traffic-light, and he wouldn't be able to recognize her another time. And so, through the necessity of eyeglasses, he was slowly learning how to live.

But the newest world his glasses opened to him was that of the night. The night city, formerly shrouded in shapeless clouds of darkness and of colored glows, now revealed precise divisions, prominences, perspectives; the lights had specific borders, the neon signs once immersed in a vague halo now could be read letter by letter. The beautiful thing about night was, however, that the margin of haziness his lenses dispelled in daylight, here remained: Amilcare Carruga felt impelled to put his glasses on, then realized he was already wearing them; the sense of fullness never equalled the drive of dissatisfaction; darkness was a bottomless humus in which he never tired of digging. In the streets, above the houses spotted with yellow windows, square at last, he raised his eyes towards the starry sky: and he discovered that the stars were not splattered against the ground of the sky like broken eggs, but were very sharp jabs of light that opened infinite distances around themselves.

This new concern with the reality of the external world was connected with his worries about what he himself was, also inspired by the use of eyeglasses. Amilcare Carruga didn't attach much importance to himself; however, as sometimes happens with the most unassuming of people, he was greatly attached to his way of being. Now to pass from the category of men without glasses to that of men with glasses seems nothing, but it is a very big leap. Just imagine: when someone who doesn't know you is trying to describe you, the first thing he says is: "he wears glasses"; so that accessory detail, which two weeks ago was completely unknown to you, becomes your prime attribute, is identified with your very existence. To Amilcare – foolishly, if you like – becoming, all at once, someone who "wears glasses" was a bit irritating. But that wasn't the real trouble: it was that once you begin to suspect that everything concerning you is purely casual, subject to transformation, and that you could be completely different and it wouldn't matter at all, then, following this line of reasoning, you come to think it's all the same whether you exist or don't exist, and from this notion to despair is only a brief step. Therefore Amilcare, having to select a kind of frame, instinctively chose some fine, very understated earpieces, just a pair of thin silver hooks that hold the naked lenses and, with a little bridge, connect them over the nose. And so it went for a while; then he realized he wasn't happy: if he inadvertently caught sight of himself in the mirror with his glasses on he felt a keen dislike for his face, as if it were the typical face of a category of persons alien to him. It was precisely those glasses, so discreet, light, almost feminine that made him look more than ever like "a man who wears glasses", one who had never done anything in his whole life but wear glasses, so that you now no longer even notice he wears them. They were becoming, those glasses, part of his physiognomy, blending with his features, and so they were diminishing every natural contrast between what his face was – an ordinary face, but still a face – and what was an extraneous object, an industrial product.

He didn't love them, and so it wasn't long before they fell and broke. He bought another pair. This time his choice took the opposite direction: he selected a pair of black plastic frames, an inch thick, with hinged corners that stuck out from the cheekbones like a horse's blinkers, side-pieces heavy enough to bend the ear. They were a kind of mask that hid half his face; but behind them he felt himself: there was no doubt that he was one thing and the glasses another, completely separate; it was clear he was wearing glasses only incidentally and, without glasses, he was an entirely different man. Once again – insofar as his nature allowed it – he was happy.

In that period he happened, on a business matter, to go to V. The town of V. was Amilcare Carruga's birthplace, and there he had spent all his youth. He had left it, however, ten years ago, and his trips back to V. had become more and more brief and sporadic, and now several years had gone by since he last set foot there. You know how it is when you move away from a place where you've lived a long time: returning at long intervals you feel disoriented, it seems that those sidewalks, those friends, those conversations in the café, must either be everything or can no longer be anything; either you follow them day by day or else you are no longer able to participate in them, and the thought of reappearing after too long a time inspires a kind of remorse, and you dismiss it. And so, gradually, Amilcare had stopped seeking occasions for going back to V., then if occasions did arise, he let them pass, and in the end he actually avoided them. But in recent times, in this negative attitude towards his native town, there was, beyond the motive just defined, also that sense of general disaffection that had come over him, which he had subsequently identified with the worsening of his near-sightedness. So now, finding himself in a new frame of mind, thanks to the glasses, the first time a chance of going to V. presented itself, he seized it promptly, and went.

V. appeared to him in a totally different light from the last few times he had been there. But not because of its changes: true, the town had changed a great deal, new buildings everywhere, shops and cafés and movie-theaters all different from before, the younger generation all strangers, and the traffic twice what it had been. All this newness, however, only underlined and made more recognizable what was old; in short Amilcare Carruga, for the first time, managed to see the place again with the eyes of his boyhood, as if he had left it the day before. Thanks to his glasses he saw a host of insignificant details, a certain window, for example, a certain railing; or rather he was conscious of seeing them, of distinguishing them from all the rest, whereas in the past he had merely seen them. To say nothing of the faces: a news-vendor, a lawyer, some having aged, others still the same. In V. Amilcare Carruga no longer had any real relatives; and his group of close friends had also dispersed long since; however, he had endless acquaintances, inevitably; the town was small, as it had been in the days when he lived there, and, practically speaking, everybody knew everybody else, at least by sight. Now the population had grown a lot, here too – as everywhere in the well-to-do cities of the North – there had been a certain influx of southerners, the majority of the faces Amilcare encountered belonged to strangers; but for this very reason he enjoyed the satisfaction of recognizing at first glance the old inhabitants, and he recalled episodes, connections, nicknames.

V. was one of those provincial towns where the tradition of an evening stroll along the main street still obtained, and in that nothing had changed from Amilcare's day to the present. As always happens in these cases, one of the sidewalks was crammed by a steady flow of people; the other sidewalk, less so. In their day, Amilcare and his friends, out of a kind of anti-conformism, had always walked on the less popular sidewalk, from there had cast glances and greetings and quips at the girls going by on the other. Now he felt as he had then, indeed even more excited, and he set off along his old sidewalk, looking at all the people who passed. Encountering familiar people this time didn't make him uneasy: it amused him; and he hastened to greet them. With some of them he would have liked also to stop and exchange a few words, but the main street of V. was so made, its sidewalks so narrow, with the crowd of people shoving you forward, and, what's more, the traffic of vehicles now much increased, that you could no longer, as in the past, walk a bit in the middle of the street and cross it whenever you chose. In short, the stroll proceeded either too rushed or too slow, with no freedom of movement. Amilcare had to follow the current or struggle against it, and when he saw a familiar face he barely had time to wave a greeting before it vanished, and he could never be sure whether he had been seen or not.

Thus he ran into Corrado Strazza, his classmate and billiards-companion for many years. Amilcare smiled at him and waved broadly. Corrado Strazza came forward, his gaze on him, but it was as if that gaze went right through him, and Corrado continued on his way. Was it possible he hadn't recognized him? Time had gone by, but Amilcare Carruga knew very well he hadn't changed much; so far he had warded off a paunch as he had baldness, and his features had not been greatly altered. Here came Professor Cavanna. Amilcare gave him a deferential greeting, a little bow. At first the professor started to respond to it, instinctively, then he stopped and looked around, as if seeking someone else. Professor Cavanna! who was famous for his visual memory, because of all his numerous classes he remembered faces and first and last names and even semester grades! Finally Ciccio

Corba, the coach of the football team, returned Amilcare's greeting. But immediately afterwards he blinked and began to whistle, as if realizing he had intercepted by mistake the greeting of a stranger, addressed to God knows what other person.

Amilcare became aware that nobody would recognize him. The eyeglasses that made the rest of the world visible to him, those eyeglasses in their enormous black frames, made him invisible. Who would ever think that behind that sort of mask there was actually Amilcare Carruga, so long absent from V., whom no one was expecting to run into at any moment? He had barely managed to formulate mentally these conclusions when Isa Maria Bietti appeared. She was with a girl friend; they were sauntering and looking in shop windows, Amilcare blocked her way, and was about to cry "Isa Maria!" but his voice was paralyzed in his throat, Isa Maria Bietti pushed him aside with her elbow, said to her friend "The way people behave nowadays ...", and went on.

Not even Isa Maria Bietti had recognized him. He understood all of a sudden that it was only because of Isa Maria Bietti that he had come back, as it was only because of Isa Maria Bietti that he had decided to leave V. and had remained away so many years; everything, everything in his life and everything in the world was only because of Isa Maria Bietti, and now finally he saw her again, their eyes met, and Isa Maria Bietti didn't recognize him. In his great emotion, he hadn't noticed if she had changed, grown fat, aged, if she was attractive as ever, or less or more, he had seen nothing except that she was Isa Maria Bietti and that Isa Maria Bietti hadn't seen him.

He had reached the end of that length of the street fre-
quented in the evening stroll. Here, at the comer of the ice
cream parlor, or a block further on, at the newsstand, the
people turned around and came back along the sidewalk in
the opposite direction. Amilcare Carruga also turned. He
had taken off his glasses. Now the world had become once
more that insipid cloud and he groped, groped with his eyes
widened, and could bring nothing to the surface. Not that
he didn't succeed in recognizing anyone: in the better-lighted
places he was always within a hair's breadth of identifying
a face or two, but a shadow of doubt that perhaps this
wasn't the person he thought always remained, and anyway,
who it was or wasn't mattered little to him after all. Someone nodded, waved; he may actually have been greeting
him, but Amilcare couldn't quite tell who it was. Another
pair, too, as they went by, greeted him; he was about to
reply, but had no idea who they were. One, from the opposite sidewalk, shouted a "Ciao, Carrù!" to him. To judge by
the voice, it might have been a man named Stelvi. To his
satisfaction, Amilcare realized they recognized him, they
remembered him. The satisfaction was relative, because he
couldn't even see them, or else couldn't manage to recognize
them; they were persons who became confused in his memory, one with another, persons who basically were of little
importance to him. "Good evening!" he said every so often,
when he noticed a wave, a movement of the head. There, the
one who had just greeted him must have been Bellintusi or
Carretti, or Strazza. If it was Strazza Amilcare would have
liked perhaps to stop a moment with him and talk. But by
now he had returned that greeting rather hastily, and when
he thought about it, it seemed natural that their relations
should be like this; conventional and hurried greetings.

His looking around, however, clearly had one purpose: to track down Isa Maria Bietti. She was wearing a red coat, so she could be sighted at a distance. For a while Amilcare followed a red coat but when he managed to pass it he saw that it wasn't she, and meanwhile two other red coats had gone past in the opposite direction. That year medium-weight red coats were all the fashion. Earlier, in the same coat, for example, he had seen Gigina, the one from the tobacco shop. Now he began to suspect that it hadn't been Gigina from the tobacco shop but had really been Isa Maria Bietti! But how was it possible to mistake Isa Maria for Gigina? Amilcare retraced his steps, to make sure. He came upon Gigina, this was she, no doubt about it; but if she was now coming in this direction, she couldn't have covered the whole distance; or had she made a shorter circuit? He was completely at sea. If Isa Maria had greeted him and he had responded quite coldly, his whole journey, all his waiting, all those years had been in vain. Amilcare went back and forth along those sidewalks, sometimes putting on his glasses, sometimes taking them off, sometimes greeting everyone and sometimes receiving the greetings of foggy, anonymous ghosts.

After the other extreme of the stroll, the street continued and was soon beyond the city limits. There was a row of trees, a ditch, beyond it a hedge, and the fields. In his day, in the evening, you came out here with your girl on your arm, if you had a girl; or else, if you were alone, you came here to be even more alone, to sit on a bench and listen to the crickets sing. Amilcare Carruga went on in that direction; now the city extended a bit farther, but not much. There was the bench, the ditch, the crickets, as before. Amilcare Carruga sat down. Of all the landscape the night maintained only some great swaths of shadow. Whether he put on or took off his eyeglasses here, it was really all the same. Amilcare Carruga realized that perhaps the thrill of his new glasses had been the last of his life, and now it was over.

(1958)

The Adventure of a Wife

Signora Stefania R. was coming home at six in the morning. It was the first time.

The car hadn't stopped at the door of her building but a bit before that, at the corner. She had been the one to ask Fornero to leave her there, because she didn't want the concierge to see that while her husband was away she came home at dawn in the company of a young man. Fornero, as soon as he had cut off the engine, started to put his arm around her. Stefania R. drew back, as if the nearness of home made everything different. She darted out of the car in sudden haste, bent to signal Fornero to start it again and go away, then began walking, with her quick little steps, her face buried in the collar of her coat. Was she an adulteress?

The door of the building was still locked, however. Stefania R. wasn't expecting this. She didn't have the key. It was because she didn't have the key that she had spent the night out. That was the whole story: there would have been a hundred ways to have it opened, up till a certain hour; or rather: she should have remembered earlier that she didn't have the key; but she hadn't, it was as if she had acted deliberately. She had left the house in the afternoon without the key because she had thought she would be coming back for supper; instead she had let those girl-friends she hadn't seen for ages, and those boys, those friends of theirs, a whole party, drag her first to supper then to drink and dance at one boy's house, then at another's. Obviously at two in the morning it was late to remember that she was without her key. It was all because she had fallen a bit in love with that boy, Fornero. Fallen in love? Fallen *a bit*. Things should be seen as they are: neither more nor less. She had spent the night with him, true: but that expression was too strong, it really wasn't the right way to put it; she had waited in the company of that boy until it was time for the door of her building to be opened. That was all. She thought they opened up at six, and at six she had hastened to go home. Also because the cleaning woman came at seven and Stefania didn't want her to notice she had spent the night out. And today, besides, her husband was coming home.

Now she found the door still locked, and she was alone there in the deserted street, in that early morning light, more transparent than at any other hour of the day, in which everything appeared to be seen through a magnifying glass. She felt a twinge of dismay, and the desire to be in her bed, sleeping there for hours, in the deep sleep of every morning, the desire, too, of her husband's nearness, his protection.

But it was the matter of a moment, perhaps less: perhaps she had only expected to feel that dismay but in reality hadn't felt it. The fact that the concierge hadn't opened up yet was a bore, a great bore, but there was something about that early morning air, about being alone here at this hour that made her blood race not at all unpleasantly. She didn't even feel regret at having sent Fornero away: with him she would have been a bit nervous; alone, on the other hand, she felt a different agitation, a bit like when she was a girl, but quite different.

She really had to admit it: she felt no remorse at all for having spent the night out. Her conscience was easy. But was it easy because by now she had taken the plunge, because she had finally set aside her conjugal duties, or, on the contrary, because she had resisted, because, in spite of everything, she had kept herself faithful? Stefania asked herself this and it was this uncertainty, this unsureness as to how things really stood, along with the coolness of the morning, that made her shudder briefly. In a word: was she to consider herself an adulteress at this point, or not? She paced back and forth briefly, her hands thrust into the pockets of her long coat. Stefania R. had been married for a couple of years, and had never thought of being unfaithful to her husband. To be sure, in her life as a married woman there was a kind of expectation, the awareness that something was still lacking for her. It was like a continuation of her expectations as a girl, as if for her the complete emergence from her minority had not yet occurred, or rather, as if she had to emerge from a new minority, a minority with regard to her husband, and finally become his equal, before the world. Was it adultery she had been awaiting? And was Fornero adultery?

She saw that a couple of blocks farther on, on the opposite sidewalk, the bar had pulled up its shutters. She needed a hot coffee, at once. She started towards it. Fornero was a boy. You couldn't think of using big words, for him. He had driven her around in his little car all night, they had covered the hills, backwards and forwards, the river road, until they had seen dawn breaking. They had run out of gas, at a certain point, they had had to push the car, wake up a sleeping filling-station attendant. It had been a kids' night on the town. Three or four times Fornero's tries had been more dangerous, and once he had even taken her to the door of the Pensione where he lived and had dug his feet in, stubbornly: "Now you're going to stop making a fuss and come upstairs with me." Stefania hadn't gone upstairs. Was it right to behave like that? And afterwards? She didn't want to think about it now, she had spent a sleepless night, she was tired. Or rather: she didn't yet realize she was sleepy because she was in this extraordinary state, but once she got to bed she would go out like a light. She would write on the kitchen slate, telling the maid not to wake her. Maybe her husband would wake her, later, when he arrived. Did she still love her husband? Of course she loved him. And then what? She would ask herself nothing. She was a little bit in love with that Fornero. A little bit. And when were they going to open that damn front door?

The chairs were piled up in the bar, sawdust scattered on the floor. There was only the barman, at the counter. Stefania came in; she didn't feel the least ill-at-ease, being there at that unlikely hour. Who had to know anything? She could have just got up, she could be heading for the station, or arriving at that moment. Anyway, she didn't owe explanations to anybody. She realized she enjoyed this feeling.

"Black, double, very hot," she said to the man. She had acquired a confident, self-assured tone, as if there were a familiarity between her and the man in this bar, where actually she never came.

"Yes, Signora, just another minute for the machine to warm up and it'll be ready," the barman said. And he added: "It takes me longer to warm up than the machine, in the morning." Stefania smiled, huddled into her collar, and said: "Brrr ..."

There was another man in the bar, a customer, off to one side, standing, looking out of the window. He turned at Stefania's shiver and she noticed him only then, and as if the presence of two men suddenly recalled her to self-awareness, she looked carefully at her reflection in the glass behind the bar. No, it wasn't obvious that she had spent the night out; she was only a bit pale. She took her compact from her bag and powdered her nose.

The man had come to the counter. He was wearing a dark overcoat, with a white silk scarf, and a blue suit underneath. "At this hour of the morning," he said, addressing nobody in particular, "people who are awake fall into two categories: the still and the already."

Stefania smiled briefly, without letting her eyes rest on him. She had already seen him clearly in any case: he had a somewhat pathetic, somewhat ordinary face, one of those men who, accepting themselves and the world, have arrived, without being old, at a condition between wisdom and imbecility.

"... and, when you see a pretty woman, after you've wished her a 'good morning!'" And he bowed towards Stefania, taking the cigarette from his mouth.

"Good morning," Stefania said, a bit ironic, but not sharp.

"... you ask yourself: Still? Already? Already? Still? There's the mystery."

"What?" Stefania said, with the air of someone who had caught on but doesn't want to play the game. The man examined her, indiscreetly; but Stefania didn't care at all even if he realized she was "still" awake.

"And you?" she asked, slyly; she had understood that this gentleman was the self-styled night-owl type and not recognizing him as such at first glance would distress him.

"Me? Still! Always still!" Then he thought about it a moment. "Why? Hadn't you realized that?" And he smiled at her, but he wanted only to mock himself, at this point. He stayed there a moment, swallowing, as if his saliva had an unpleasant taste. "Daylight drives me off, makes me return to my lair like a bat..." he said absently, as if playing a part.

"Here's your milk. The Signora's coffee," the barman said.

The man began blowing on the glass, then sipping slowly. "Is it good?" Stefania asked.

"Revolting," he said. Then: "It drives out the poisons, they say. But how can it do anything for me at this point? If a poisonous snake bites me, it'll drop dead."

"As long as you've got your health ..." Stefania said. Perhaps she was joking a bit too much.

And in fact, he said: "The only antidote, I know, if you want me to tell you ..." God knows what he was getting at.

"What do I owe you?" Stefania asked the barman.

"... That woman I've been looking for always ..." the night-owl continued.

Stefania went outside, to see if they had opened the door. She took a few steps on the sidewalk. No, the door was still closed. Meanwhile the man had also come out of the bar, as if he meant to follow her. Stefania retraced her steps, reentered the bar. The man, who hadn't expected this, hesitated for a moment, started to go back too, then, overcome by an access of resignation, he continued, coughing a bit, on his way.

"Do you sell cigarettes?" Stefania asked the barman. She had run out, and wanted to smoke one the moment she was inside her house. The tobacconists were still closed.

The barman pulled out a pack. Stefania took it and paid him.

She went to the doorway of the bar again. A dog almost bumped into her, tugging violently on a leash and pulling after him a hunter, with gun, cartridge-belt, and game-bag.

"Down, Frisette! Down!" the hunter cried. And, into the bar: "Coffee!"

"Handsome!" Stefania said, petting the dog. "Is he a setter?"

"*Épagneul breton*," the hunter said. "Female." He was young, somewhat blunt, but more out of shyness than anything else.

"How old is she?"

"About ten months. Down, Frisette. Behave yourself."

"Well? Where are the partridges?" the barman said.

"Oh, I just go out to exercise the dog," the hunter said.

"You go far?" Stefania asked.

The hunter mentioned the name of a locality not very distant "It's nothing with the car. So I'm back by ten. The job ..."

"It's nice up there," Stefania said. She didn't feel like letting the conversation die, even if they weren't talking about anything much.

"There's a deserted valley, clean, all bushes, heath, and in the morning there's no mist, you can see clearly ... If the dog flushes something ..."

"I wish I could go to work at ten. I'd sleep till nine-forty-five," the barman said.

"Well, I like to sleep, too," the hunter said, "all the same, being up there, while everybody else is still sleeping ... I don't know, I like it... it's a passion with me ..."

Stefania felt that behind his apparent self-justification this young man concealed a sharp pride, a contempt for the sleeping city all around, a determination to feel different.

"Don't take offense, but in my opinion you hunters are all crazy," the barman said. "I mean, this business of getting up in the middle of the night."

"No," Stefania said, "I understand them."

"Hm, who knows?" the hunter said. "It's a passion like any other. " Now he had taken to looking at Stefania and that bit of conviction he had instilled earlier in his talk about hunting now seemed gone, and Stefania's presence seemed to make him suspect that his whole attitude was mistaken, that perhaps happiness was something different from what he was seeking.

"Really, I do understand you, a morning like this ..." Stefania said.

The hunter remained for a moment like someone who wants to talk but doesn't know what to say. "In weather like this, dry, and cool, the dog can walk well," he said. He had finished his coffee, paid for it, the dog was pulling him to go outside, and he remained there still, hesitant. He said, awkwardly: "Why don't you come along too, Signora?"

Stefania smiled. "Oh, if we run into each other again, we'll fix something, eh?"

The hunter said, "Mmm", moved around a bit, to see if he could find another conversational ploy. "Well, I'll be going. Good morning." They waved and he let the dog pull him outside.

A worker had come in. He ordered a shot of grappa. "To the health of everybody who wakes up early," he said, raising his glass. "Beautiful ladies, specially." He was a man not young but jolly-looking.

"Your health," Stefania said, politely.

"First thing in the morning, you feel like you own the world," the worker said.

"And not in the evening?" Stefania asked.

"In the evening you're too sleepy," he said, "and you don't think of anything. If you do, it means trouble ..."

"Me, in the morning I think of every kind of problem, one after the other," the barman said.

"Because before you start working you need a nice ride. You should do like me: I go to the factory on my motorbike, with the cold air on my face ..."

"The air drives out thoughts," Stefania said.

"There, the lady understands me," the worker said. "And if she understands me, she should drink a little grappa with me."

"No, thanks, really, I don't drink."

"In the morning it's just what you need. Two grappas, chief."

"I really never drink; you drink to my health and you'll make me happy."

"You never drink?"

"Well, occasionally, in the evening."

"You see? There's your mistake ..."

"Oh, a person makes plenty of mistakes ..."

"Your health," and the worker drained one glass, then the other. "One and one makes two. You see, I'll explain ..."

Stefania was alone, there in the midst of those men, those different men, and she was talking with them. She was calm, sure of herself, there was nothing that upset her. This was the new event of that morning.

She came out of the bar to see if they had opened the door. The worker also came out, straddled his motor-bike, slipped on his driving gloves. "Aren't you cold?" Stefania asked. The worker slapped himself on the chest; there was a rustle of newspapers. "I'm armored." And then, in dialect, he said: "Goodbye, Signora." Stefania also said goodbye to him in dialect, and he rode off.

Stefania realized that something had happened from which she could not now turn back. This new way of hers of being among men, the night-owl, the hunter, the worker, made her different. This had been her adultery, this being alone among them, like this, their equals. She didn't even remember Fornero any more.

The front door was open. Stefania R. hurried home. The concierge didn't see her.

(1958)

The Adventure of the Married Couple

THE FACTORY-WORKER Arturo Massolari was on the night shift, the one that ends at six. To reach home he had to go a long way, which he covered on his bicycle in fine weather, and on the tram during the rainy, winter months. He got home between six-forty-five and seven; in other words, sometimes before and sometimes after the alarm clock rang to wake Elide, his wife.

Often the two noises – the sound of the clock and his tread as he came in – merged in Elide's mind, reaching her in the depths of her sleep, the compact early-morning sleep that she tried to squeeze out for a few more seconds, her face buried in the pillow. Then she pulled herself from the bed with a yank and was already blindly slipping her arms into her robe, her hair over her eyes. She appeared to him like that, in the kitchen, where Arturo was taking the empty receptacles from the bag that he carried with him to work: the lunch box, the Thermos. He set them in the sink. He had already lighted the stove and started the coffee. As soon as he looked at her, Elide instinctively ran one hand through her hair, forced her eyes wide open, as if every time she were ashamed of that first sight her husband had of her on coming home, always such a mess, her face half-asleep. When two people have slept together it's different, in the morning both are surfacing from the same sleep, and they're on a par.

Sometimes, on the other hand, it was he who came into the bedroom to wake her, with the little cup of coffee, a moment before the alarm rang; then everything was more natural, the grimace on emerging from sleep took on a kind of lazy sweetness, the arms that were lifted to stretch, naked, ended by clasping his neck. They embraced. Arturo was wearing his rainproof wind-cheater; feeling him close, she could understand what the weather was like: whether it was raining or foggy or if it had snowed, according to how damp and cold he was. But she would ask him anyway: "What's the weather like?", and he would start his usual grumbling, half-ironic, reviewing all the troubles he had encountered, beginning at the end: the trip on his bike, the weather he had found on coming out of the factory, different from when he had entered it the previous evening, and the problems on the job, the rumors going around his section, and so on.

At that hour, the house was always scantily heated, but Elide had completely undressed, and was washing in the little bathroom. Afterwards he came in, more calmly, and also undressed and washed, slowly, removing the dust and grease of the shop. And so, as both of them stood at the same basin, half-naked, a bit numbed, shoving each other now and then, taking the soap from each other, the tooth-paste, and continuing to tell each other the things they had to tell, the moment of intimacy came, and at times, maybe when they were helpfully taking turns scrubbing each other's back, a caress slipped in, and they found themselves embracing.

But all of a sudden Elide would cry: "My God! Look at the time!" and she would run to pull on her garter-belt, skirt, all in haste, on her feet, still brushing her hair, and stretching her face to the mirror over the dresser, hairpins held between her lips. Arturo would come in after her; he had a cigarette going, and would look at her, standing, smoking, and every time he seemed a bit embarrassed, having to stay there unable to do anything. Elide was ready, she slipped her coat on in the corridor, they exchanged a kiss, she opened the door, and could already be heard running down the stairs.

Arturo remained alone. He followed the sound of Elide's heels down the steps, and when he couldn't hear her any more he still followed her in his thoughts, that quick little trot through the courtyard, out of the door of the building, the sidewalk, as far as the tram stop. The tram, on the contrary, could be heard clearly: shrieking, stopping, the slam of the step as each passenger boarded. There, she's caught it, he thought, and could see his wife clinging in the midst of the crowd of workers, men and women, on the number eleven that took her to the factory as it did every day. He stubbed out the butt, closed the shutters at the window, darkening the room, and got into bed.

The bed was as Elide had left it on getting up, but on his side, Arturo's, it was almost intact, as if it had just been made. He lay on his own half, properly, but later he stretched a leg over there, where his wife's warmth had remained, then he also stretched out the other leg, and so little by little he moved entirely over to Elide's sice, into that niche of warmth that still retained the form of her body, and he dug his face into her pillow, into her perfume, and he fell asleep.

When Elide came back, in the evening, Arturo had been stirring around the rooms for a while already: he had lighted the stove, put something on to cook. There were certain jobs he did in those hours before supper, like making the bed, sweeping a little, even soaking the dirty laundry. Elide criticized everything, but to tell the truth he didn't then go to greater pains: what he did was only a kind of ritual in order to wait for her, like meeting her halfway while still remaining within the walls of the house, as outside the lights were coming on and she was going past the shops in the midst of the belated bustle of those neighborhoods where many of the women have to do their shopping in the evening.

Finally he heard her footstep on the stairs, quite different from the morning, heavier now, because Elide was climbing up, tired from the day of work and loaded down with the shopping. Arturo went out on the landing, took the shopping bag from her hands, and they went inside, talking. She sank down on a chair in the kitchen, without taking off her coat, while he removed the things from the bag. Then she would say: "Well, let's pull ourselves together", and would stand up, take off her coat, put on her house-coat. They would begin to prepare the food: supper for both of them, plus the lunch he would take to the factory for his one a.m.

break, and the snack to be left ready for when he would wake up the next day.

She would potter a bit, then sit for a bit on the straw chair and tell him what he should do. For him, on the contrary, this was the time when he was rested, he worked with a will, indeed he wanted to do everything, but always a bit absently, his mind already on other things. At those moments, there were occasions when they got on each other's nerves, said nasty things, because she would like him to pay more attention to what he was doing, take it more seriously, or else to be more attached to her, to be closer, comfort her more. But after the first enthusiasm when she came home, his mind was already out of the house, obsessed with the idea that he should hurry because he would soon have to be going.

When the table was set, when everything that had been prepared was placed within reach so they wouldn't have to get up afterwards, then came the moment of yearning that overwhelmed them both, the thought that they had so little time to be together, and they could hardly raise the spoon to their mouth, in their longing just to sit there and hold hands.

But even before the coffee had finished rising in the pot, he was already at his bike, to make sure everything was in order. They hugged. Arturo seemed only then to realize how soft and warm his wife was. But he hoisted the bike to his shoulder and carefully went down the stairs.

Elide washed the dishes, went over the house thoroughly, redoing the things her husband had done, shaking her head. Now he was speeding through the dark streets, among the sparse lamps, perhaps he had already passed the gasometer. Elide went to bed, turned off the light.

From her own half, lying there, she would slide one foot towards her husband's place, looking for his warmth, but each time she realized it was warmer where she slept, a sign that Arturo had slept there too, and she would feel a great tenderness.

(1958)

The Adventure of a Poet

THE LITTLE island had a high rocky shoreline. On it grew the thick, low scrub, the vegetation that survives by the sea. Gulls flew in the sky. It was a small island near the coast, deserted, uncultivated: in half an hour you could circle it in a rowboat, or in a rubber canoe, like the one those two had who were coming forward, the man calmly paddling, the woman stretched out, taking the sun. Approaching, the man listened intently.

"What do you hear?" she asked.

"Silence," he said. "Islands have a silence you can hear."

In fact, every silence consists of the network of minuscule sounds that enfolds it: the silence of the island was distinct from that of the calm sea surrounding it because it was pervaded by a vegetable rustling, the calls of birds or a sudden whirr of wings.

Down below the rock, the water, without a ripple these days, was a sharp, limpid blue, penetrated to its depths by the sun's rays. In the cliff-faces the mouths of grottos opened, and the couple in the rubber boat were going lazily to explore them.

It was a coast in the South, still hardly affected by tourism, and those two were bathers who came from elsewhere. He was one Usnelli, a fairly well-known poet; she, Delia H., a very beautiful woman.

Delia was an admirer of the South, passionate, even fanatical, and lying in the boat she talked with constant ecstasy about everything she was seeing, and perhaps also with a hint of hostility towards Usnelli, who was new to those places and, it seemed to her, did not share her enthusiasm as much as he should have.

"Wait," Usnelli said, "wait."

"Wait for what?" she said. "What could be more beautiful than this?"

He, distrustful (by nature and through his literary education) of emotions and words already the property of others, accustomed more to discovering hidden and spurious beauties than those that were evident and indisputable, was still nervous and tense. Happiness, for Usnelli, was a suspended condition, to be lived, holding your breath. Ever since he began loving Delia, he had seen his cautious, sparing relationship with the world endangered; but he wished to renounce nothing, neither of himself nor of the happiness that opened before him. Now he was on guard, as if every degree of perfection that nature, around him, achieved – a decanting of the blue of the water, a languishing of the coast's green into gray, the flash of a fish's fin at the very spot where the sea's expanse was most smooth – were only heralding another, higher degree, and so on, to the point where the invisible line of the horizon would part like an oyster revealing all of a sudden a different planet or a new word.

They entered a grotto. It began spaciously, like an interior lake of pale green, under a broad vault of rock. Farther on it narrowed to a dark passage. The man with the paddle turned the canoe around to enjoy the various effects of the light. The light from outside, through the jagged aperture, dazzled with colors made more vivid by the contrast. The water, there, sparkled, and the shafts of light ricocheted upwards, in conflict with the soft shadows that spread from the rear. Reflections and glints communicated also to the rock walls and the vault the instability of the water.

"Here you understand the gods," the woman said.

"Hum," Usnelli said. He was nervous. His mind, used to translating sensations into words, was now helpless, unable to formulate a single one.

They went further in. The canoe passed a shoal: a hump of rock at the level of the water; now the canoe floated among rare glints that appeared and disappeared at every stroke of the paddle: the rest was dense shadow; the paddle now and then struck a wall. Delia, looking back, saw the blue orb of the open sky constantly change outline.

"A crab! Huge! Over there!" she cried, sitting up.

"... ab! ... ere!" the echo sounded.

"The echo!" she said, pleased, and started shouting words under those grim vaults: invocations, lines of verse.

"You too! You shout too! Make a wish!" she said to Usnelli.

"Hoooo ..." Usnelli shouted. "Heeey ... Echoooo ..."

Now and then the boat scraped. The darkness was deeper.
"I'm afraid. God knows what animals ..."

"We can still get past."

Usnelli realized that he was heading for the darkness like a fish of the depths, who flees sunlit water.

"I'm afraid, let's go back," she insisted.

To him, too, basically, any taste for the horrid was alien. He paddled backwards. As they returned to where the cavern broadened, the sea became cobalt.

"Are there any octopuses?" Delia asked.

"You'd see them. The water's so clear."

"I'll have a swim then."

She slipped over the side of the canoe, let go, swam in that underground lake, and her body at times seemed white (as if that light stripped it of any color of its own) and sometimes as blue as that screen of water.

Usnelli had stopped rowing; he was still holding his breath. For him, being in love with Delia had always been like this, as in the mirror of this cavern: in a world beyond words. For that matter, in all his poems, he had never written a verse of love: not one.

"Come closer," Delia said. As she swam, she had taken off the scrap of cloth covering her bosom; she threw it into the canoe. "Just a minute." She also undid the other piece of cloth tied at her hips and handed it to Usnelli.

Now she was naked. The whiter skin of her bosom and hips was hardly distinct, because her whole person gave off that pale blue glow, like a medusa. She was swimming on one side, with a lazy movement, her head (the expression firm, almost ironic, a statue's) just out of the water, and at times the curve of a shoulder and the soft line of the extended arm. The other arm, in caressing strokes, covered and revealed the high bosom, taut at its tips. Her legs barely struck the water, supporting the smooth belly, marked by the navel like a faint print on the sand, and the star as of some mollusc. The sun's rays, reflected underwater, grazed her, making a kind of garment for her, or stripping her all over again.

Her swimming turned into a kind of dance-movement; suspended in the water, smiling at him, she held out her arms in a soft rolling of the shoulders and wrists; or with a thrust of the knee she brought to the surface an arched foot, like a little fish.

Usnelli, in the boat, was all eyes. He understood that what life now gave him was something not everyone has the privilege of looking at, open-eyed, as at the most dazzling core of the sun. And in the core of this sun was silence. Nothing that was there at this moment could be translated into anything else, perhaps not even into a memory.

Now Delia was swimming on her back, surfacing towards the sun, at the mouth of the cavern, proceeding with a light movement of her arms towards the open; and beneath her the water was changing its shade of blue, paler and paler, more and more luminous.

"Watch out! Put something on! Some boats are coming, out there!"

Delia was already among the rocks, beneath the sky. She slipped underwater, held out her arm. Usnelli handed her those skimpy bits of garment, she fastened them on, swimming, and climbed back into the canoe.

The approaching boats were fishermen's. Usnelli recognized them as some of that group of poor men who spent the fishing season on that beach, sleeping against the rocks. He went towards them. The man at the oars was the young man, grim with toothache, white sailor's cap pulled over his narrowed eyes, rowing in jerks as if every effort helped him feel the pain less; father of five children; a desperate case. The old man was at the poop; his Mexican-style straw hat crowned with a fringed halo his whole lanky figure, his round eyes once perhaps widened in arrogant pride, now in drunkard's clowning, his mouth open beneath the still-black, drooping mustache; with a knife he was cleaning the mullet they had caught.

"Caught much?" Delia cried.

"What little there is," they answered. "Bad year."

Delia liked to talk with the local inhabitants. Not Usnelli. ("With them," he said, "I don't have an easy conscience." He would shrug, and leave it at that.)

Now the canoe was alongside the boat, where the faded paint was streaked with cracks, curling in short segments, and the oar tied with a length of rope to the rowlock creaked at every turn against the worn wood of the side, and a little rusty anchor with four hooks had got tangled under the narrow plank-seat in one of the wicker basket traps, bearded with reddish seaweed, dried out God knows how long ago, and over the pile of nets dyed with tannin and dotted at the edges by round slices of cork, the gasping fish glinted in their pungent dress of scales, dull-gray or pale blue; the gills still throbbing displayed, below, a red triangle of blood.

Usnelli remained silent, but this anguish of the human world was the contrary of what the beauty of nature had been communicating to him a little earlier: there every word failed, while here there was a turmoil of words that crowded into his mind: words to describe every wart, every hair on the thin, ill-shaven face of the old fishermen, every silver scale of the mullet.

On shore, another boat had been pulled in, overturned, propped up on saw-horses, and below, from the shadow, emerged the soles of the bare feet of the sleeping men, those who had fished during the night; nearby, a woman, all in black clothing, faceless, was setting a pot over a seaweed fire, and a long trail of smoke was coming from it. The shore of that inlet was of gray stones; those patches of faded, printed colors were the smocks of the playing children, the smaller watched over by older, whining sisters, while the older and livelier boys, wearing only shorts made from old, grown-ups' trousers, were running up and down between rocks and water. Farther on a straight stretch of sandy beach began, white and deserted, which at one side disappeared into a sparse cane-brake and untilled fields. A young man in his Sunday clothes, all black, even his hat, with a stick over his shoulder and a bundle hanging from it, was walking by the sea the length of that beach, the nails of his shoes marking the friable crust of sand: certainly a peasant or a shepherd from an inland village who had come down to the coast for some market or other and had taken the seaside path for the soothing breeze. The railway showed its wires, its embankment, its poles, the fence, then vanished into the tunnel and began again farther on, vanished once more. And once more emerged, like stitches in uneven sewing. Above the white and black markers of the highway, squat olive groves began to climb; and higher still the mountains were bare, grazing land or shrubs or only stones. A village set in a cleft among those heights extended upwards, the houses one on top of the other, separated by cobbled stair-streets, concave in the middle so that the trickle of mule refuse could flow down, and on the doorsteps of all those houses there were numerous women, old or aged, and on the parapets, seated in a row, numerous men, old and young, all in white shirts, and in the middle of the streets like stairways, the babies were playing on the ground and an older youth was lying across the path, his cheek against the step, sleeping there because it was a bit cooler than inside the house and less smelly, and everywhere, lighting or circling there were clouds of flies, and on every wall and every festoon of newspaper around the fireplaces there was the infinite spatter of fly excrement, and into Usnelli's mind came words and words, thick, woven one into the other, with no space between the lines, until little by little they could no longer be distinguished, it was a tangle from which even the tiniest white spaces were vanishing and only the black remained, the most total black, impenetrable, desperate as a scream.

(1958)

The Adventure of a Skier

There was a line at the ski lift. The group of boys who had come on the bus had joined it, pulling up side by side, skis parallel, and every time it advanced – it was long and, instead of going straight, as in fact it could have, zigzagged randomly, sometimes upward, sometimes down – they stepped up or slid down sideways, depending on where they were, and immediately propped themselves on their poles again, often resting their weight on the neighbor below, or trying to free the poles from under the skis of the neighbor above: stumbling on their skis, which had gotten twisted, leaning over to adjust the bindings and bringing the whole line to a halt, pulling off windbreakers or sweaters or putting them back on as the sun appeared or disappeared, tucking strands of hair under their woolen headbands or the billowing tails of their checked shirts into their belts, digging in their pockets for handkerchiefs and blowing their red, frozen noses, and for all these operations taking off and putting on the big gloves that sometimes fell in the snow and had to be picked up with the tip of a pole: that flurry of small disjointed gestures coursed through the line and became frenzied at its end, where the skier had to unzip every pocket to find where he'd stuck the ticket money or the badge, and hand it to the lift operator, who punched it, and then he had to put it back in the pocket, and readjust the gloves, and join the two poles together, the tip of one stuck in the basket of the other so they could be held with one hand – all this while climbing up the small slope of the little open space where he had to be ready to position the T-bar under his bottom and let it tug him jerkily upward.

The boy in the green goggles was at the midway point of the line, numb with cold, and next to him was a fat boy who kept pushing. And as they stood there the girl in the sky-blue hood passed. She didn't get in line; she kept going, up, on the path. And she moved uphill on her skis as lightly as if she were walking.

"What's that girl doing? She's going to walk up?" the fat boy who was pushing asked.

"She's got climbing skins," said the boy in the green goggles.

"Well, I'd like to see her up where it gets steep," said the fat boy.

"She's not as smart as she thinks, you can bet on that."

The girl moved easily, her high knees – she had very long legs, in close-fitting pants, snug at the ankles – moving rhythmically, in time with the raising and lowering of the shiny poles. In that frozen white air the sun looked like a precise yellow drawing, with all its rays: on the expanses of snow where there was no shadow, only its glint indicated humps and crevices and the trampled course of the trails. Framed by the hood of the sky-blue windbreaker, the blond girl's face was a shade of pink that on her cheeks turned red against the white plush lining of her hood. She laughed at the sun, squinting slightly. She moved lightly on her climbing skins. The boys in the group from the bus, with their frozen ears, chapped lips, sniffling noses, couldn't take their eyes off her and began shoving each other in the line, until she climbed over a ledge and disappeared,

Gradually, as their turn came, the boys in the group, after many initial stumbles and false starts, began to ascend, two by two, pulled along the almost vertical track. The boy in the green goggles ended up on the same lift as the fat boy who kept pushing. And there, halfway up, they saw her again.

"How did that girl get up here?"

At that point the lift skirted a sort of hollow where a packed-down trail advanced between high dunes of snow and occasional fir trees fringed with embroideries of ice. The sky-blue girl was proceeding effortlessly with that precise stride of hers and that push forward of her gloved hands, gripping the handles of the poles.

"Oooh!" the boys on the lift shouted, holding their legs stiff as they ascended. "She might even beat the rest of us!"

She had that delicate smile on her lips, and the boy in the green goggles was confused, and didn't dare to keep up the banter, because she lowered her eyelids and he felt as if he'd been erased.

As soon as he reached the top, he started down the slope, behind the fat boy, both of them heavy as sacks of potatoes.

But what he was looking for, as he made his way along the trail, was a glimpse of the sky-blue windbreaker, and he hurtled straight down, so that he'd appear bold and at the same time hide his clumsiness on the turns. "Look out! Look out!" he shouted, in vain, because the fat boy too and all the boys in the group were descending at breakneck speed, shouting "Look out! Look out!" and one by one they fell, backward or forward, and he alone was cutting through the air, bent double over his skis, until he saw her. The girl was still going up, off the trail, in the fresh snow. The boy in the green goggles grazed her, passing by like an arrow, rammed the fresh snow, and disappeared into it, face forward.

But at the bottom of the slope, breathless, dusted in snow from head to foot, c'mon, there he was again with all the others in line for the lift, and then up, up again to the top. This time when he met her, she too was going down. How did she go? For them, a champion was someone who sped straight down like a lunatic. "Well, she's no great champion, the blonde," the fat boy said, quickly relieved. The sky-blue girl was coming down in no hurry, making her turns with precision, or, rather, until the last moment they couldn't tell if she would turn or what she would do, and suddenly they'd see her descending in the opposite direction. She was taking her time, one would have said, stopping every so often to study the trail, upright on her long legs: meanwhile, though, the boys from the bus couldn't keep up. Until even the fat boy admitted, "No kidding. She's incredible!"

They wouldn't have been able to explain why, but this was what held them spellbound: all her movements were as simple as possible and perfectly suited to her person; she never exaggerated by a centimeter, never showed a hint of agitation or effort, or determination to do a thing at all costs, but did it naturally; and depending on the state of the trail, she even made a few uncertain moves, like someone walking on tiptoe, which was her way of overcoming the difficulties without revealing whether she was taking them seriously or not – in other words, not with the confident air of one who does things as they should be done but with a trace of reluctance, as if she were trying to imitate an expert but always ended up skiing better. This was the way the sky-blue girl moved on her skis.

Then, one after the other, awkward, heavy, snapping the christies, forcing snowplow turns into a slalom, the boys from the bus plunged down after her, trying to follow her, to pass her, shouting, making fun of each other, but everything they did was a jumbled downhill tumble, with disjointed shoulder movements, arms holding poles out straight, skis that crossed, bindings that broke off boots, and wherever they passed the snow was gouged by crashing bottoms, hips, head-over-heels dives.

After every fall, they raised their heads and immediately looked for her. Passing through the avalanche of boys the sky-blue girl went along lightly; the straight creases of her close-fitting pants scarcely angled as her knees bent rhythmically, and you couldn't tell if her smile was in sympathy with the exploits and mishaps of her downhill companions or was instead a sign that she didn't even see them.

Meanwhile, the sun, instead of getting stronger as midday approached, grew numb, until it disappeared, as if soaked up by blotting paper. The air was full of light colorless crystals flying slantwise. It was sleet: you couldn't see from here to there. The boys skied blindly, shouting and calling to each other, and they were continually going off the trail and, c'mon, falling. Air and snow were now the same color, opaque white, but peering intently into it, so that it almost became less dense, they could make out the sky-blue shadow, suspended in the midst of it, flying this way and that as if on a violin string.

The sleet had scattered the crowd at the lift. The boy in the green goggles found himself, without realizing it, near the hut at the lift station. There, was no sign of his companions. The girl in the sky-blue hood was already there. She was waiting for the T-bar, which was now making its turn. "Quick!" the lift man shouted to him, grabbing the T-bar and holding it so that the girl wouldn't set off alone. With limping herringbones, he managed to position himself next to the girl just in time to depart with her, but he nearly caused her to fall as he grabbed hold of the bar. She kept them both balanced until he was able to right himself, muttering reproaches, to which she responded with a low laugh like the *glu-glu* of a guinea hen, muffled by the windbreaker drawn up over her mouth. Now the sky-blue hood, like the helmet of a suit of armor, left uncovered only her nose, her eyes, a few curls on her forehead, and her cheekbones. So he saw her, in profile, the boy in the green goggles, and didn't know whether to be happy to find himself on the same T-bar or to be ashamed of being there, all covered with snow, the hair pasted to his temples, the shirt puffing out between sweater and belt, and not daring to tuck it in, so as not to lose his balance by moving his arms; and partly he was glancing sideways at her, partly keeping an eye on the position of his skis, so that they wouldn't go off the trail at moments of traction too slow or too taut, and it was always she who kept them balanced, laughing her guinea-hen *glu-glu,* while he didn't know what to say.

The snow had stopped. Now there was a break in the fog, and in the break the sky appeared, blue at last, and the shining sun and, one by one, the clear, frozen mountains, their peaks feathered here and there by soft shreds of the snow cloud. The mouth and chin of the hooded girl reappeared.

"It's nice again," she said. "I said so."

"Yes," said the boy in the green goggles, "nice. Then the snow will be good."

"A little soft."

"Oh, yes."

"But I like it," she said, "and going down in the fog isn't bad."

'As long as you know the trail," he said.

"No, like this," she said, "guessing."

"I've already done it three times," said the boy.

"Good for you. I've done it once, but I went up without the lift."

"I saw you. You'd put on climbing skins."

"Yes. Now that the sun's out I'll go up to the pass."

"To the pass where?"

"Farther up from where the lift goes. Up to the top."

"What's up there?"

"The glacier seems so close it's as if you could touch it. And the white hares."

"The what?"

"The hares. At this altitude mountain hares put on a white coat. Also the partridges."

"Up there?"

"White partridges. Their feathers are all white. While in summer their feathers are pale brown. Where are you from?"

"Italy."

"I'm Swiss."

They had arrived. At the end they pulled away from the lift, he clumsily, she holding the bar with her hand through the whole turn. She took off her skis, stood them upright, took the climbing skins out of the bag she wore at her waist, and fastened them to the bottoms of the skis. He watched, rubbing his cold fingers in the gloves. Then, when she began to climb, he followed.

The ascent from the lift to the summit of the pass was difficult.

The boy in the green goggles worked hard, sometimes her-ringboning, sometimes stepping, sometimes trudging up and sliding back, holding on to his poles like a lame man his crutches. And already she was up where he couldn't see her.

He reached the pass in a sweat, tongue out, half blinded by the glittering radiance all around. There the world of ice began. The blond girl had taken off her sky-blue wind-breaker and tied it around her waist. She too had put on a pair of goggles. "There! Did you see? Did you see?"

"What is it?" he said, dazed. Had a white hare leaped out? A partridge?

"It's not there anymore," she said.

Below, over the valley, cawing blackbirds fluttered as usual at two thousand meters. Midday had turned perfectly clear, and from up there you could see the trails, the open slopes thronged with skiers, children sledding, the lift sta-tion and the line that had immediately re-formed, the hotel, the parked buses, the road that wove in and out of the black forest of fir trees.

The girl had set off on the descent, going back and forth in her tranquil zigzags, and had already reached the point where the trails were more trafficked by skiers, yet her figure, faintly sketched, like an oscillating parenthesis, didn't get lost in the confusion of darting interchangeable profiles: it remained the only one that could be picked out and followed, removed from chance and disorder. The air was so clear that the boy in the green goggles could divine on the snow the dense network of ski tracks, straight and oblique, of abrasions, mounds, holes, pole marks, and it seemed to him that there, in the shapeless jumble of life, was hidden the secret line, the harmony, traceable only to the sky-blue girl, and this was the miracle of her, that at every instant in the chaos of innumerable possible movements she chose the only one that was right and clear and light and necessary, the only gesture that, among an infinity of wasted gestures, counted.

The Adventure of a Motorist

As soon as I leave the city I realize it's dark. I turn on the headlights. I'm driving from A to B, on a three-lane highway whose middle lane is for passing, in both directions. When you drive at night your eyes too in a sense have to disconnect one interior mechanism and turn on another, because you no longer have to struggle to distinguish the specks of distant cars moving toward you or ahead of you amid the dim shadows and colors of the evening landscape but, rather, have to check a kind of blackboard that demands a different reading, more precise but simplified, since the darkness erases all the details of the picture that might distract you, highlighting only the indispensable elements – white stripes on the asphalt, yellow rays of headlights, and red pinpoints of light. It's a process that happens automatically, and if tonight I'm led to reflect on it, that's because now that the external possibilities of distraction are diminished, the internal ones take over, and my thoughts run of their own accord, in a circuit of alternatives and doubts that I can't switch off, so I have to make a particular effort to concentrate on the driving.

I got in the car suddenly, after a fight on the phone with Y. I live in A, Y lives in B. I wasn't expecting to go and see her tonight. But in our daily phone call we said serious words to each other; in the end, driven by resentment, I said to Y that I wanted to break off our relationship; Y answered that it didn't matter to her and that she would immediately telephone Z, my rival. At that point one of us – I don't remember if it was she or I myself – hung up. Not a minute had passed before I realized that the occasion of our quarrel was a small thing in comparison to its consequences. Calling Y back on the phone would be a mistake; the only way to resolve the issue was to hurry to B and have it out with Y face-to-face. So here I am on this highway that I've traveled hundreds of times, at all hours and in all seasons, but which has never felt so long.

To be more precise, it seems to me that I've lost the sense of space and the sense of time: the cones of light projected by the headlights blur the outlines of places into indistinctness; the numbers of the kilometers on the road signs and those which leap into view on the dashboard are data that say nothing to me, that don't respond to the urgency of my questions about what Y is doing at this moment, what she's thinking. Did she really intend to call Z or was it only a threat, flung out in spite? And if she was serious, would she have called him immediately after our phone call, or would she have thought about it for a

moment, let the anger cool before deciding? Like me, Z
lives in A; he's loved Y for years in vain; if she called and
summoned him, he certainly jumped in his car and hurried to B. So he too is racing along this highway; every car
that passes me could be his, and, similarly, every car that
I pass. It's hard to confirm this: the cars that go in the
same direction as me are two red lights when they are
ahead and two yellow eyes when I see them behind me in
the rearview mirror. At the moment of passing I can distinguish at most the make of car and how many people
are inside, but the great majority have just a driver, and
as for the model, I don't think that Z's vehicle is especially recognizable.

As if that weren't enough, it starts raining. The visual
field is reduced to the semicircle of glass swept by the windshield wiper; all the rest is streaked or opaque darkness,
and the only information that arrives from outside is red
and yellow flashes distorted by a swirl of drops. All I can
do about Z is try to pass him and not let him pass me,
whatever car he's in, but I have no way of knowing if he's
there or what it is. All the cars going in the direction of B
feel like enemies: every car that, faster than mine, frantically flashes its turn signal in the mirror, asking me to get
over, provokes a pang of jealousy; and every time the distance that separates me from the taillights of a rival
diminishes, I accelerate triumphantly into the center lane so
that I'll get to Y before him.

All I need is a few minutes' advantage: seeing how
quickly I hurried to her, Y will immediately forget the reasons for the fight; everything between us will go back to
the way it was; Z, upon arriving, will understand that he's
been drawn in only because of a sort of game between us,

and he'll feel like an intruder. In fact, maybe at this moment Y has already regretted everything she said to me and tried to call me back, or she too, like me, thought that the best thing was to come in person, so she got in her car and is speeding along this highway in the opposite direction.

Now I've stopped paying attention to the cars that are going in the same direction as me and look at the ones that are coming toward me and that for me consist only of the double star of headlights that spreads until it sweeps the darkness from my field of vision and abruptly disappears behind me, trailing a kind of underwater luminescence. Y has a very common make of car – like mine, in fact. Each of these luminous apparitions could be her speeding toward me, and at each one something stirs in my blood, as if through an intimacy fated to remain secret: the message of love addressed exclusively to me is mixed up with all the other messages that run along the wire of the highway, and yet I couldn't wish from her a message different from that.

I realize that as I'm speeding toward Y, what I most desire is not to find Y at the end of my drive: I want Y to be speeding toward me, this is the response I need; that is, I need her to know that I am speeding toward her but at the same time I need to know that she is speeding toward me. The only thought that comforts me is the same that most torments me: the thought that if at this moment Y is speeding toward A, each time she sees the lights of a car heading toward B she'll wonder if it's I who am speeding toward her, and she'll hope that it's me but can never be sure. Now, two cars going in opposite directions found themselves side by side for an instant, a flare illuminated the raindrops, and the sound of the engines fused, as in a sharp gust of wind: maybe it was us, or rather, certainly I was I, if that means something, and the other might be her, that is, what I hope is her, the sign in which I want to recognize her, although it's precisely the sign itself that makes her unrecognizable to me. Driving along the highway is the only means that remains to us, to me and to her, to express what we have to say to each other, but as long as we're driving we can neither give nor receive the communication.

Of course, the reason I got in my car was to reach her as soon as possible, but the farther I go, the more clearly I realize that the arrival is not the true end of my journey. Our meeting, with all the inessential details that the scene of a meeting includes, the minute network, of sensations and meanings and memories that would unfold before me – the room with the philodendron, the glass-sliaded lamp, the earrings – and the things I would say, some of them surely wrong or misunderstood, and the things she would say, to some degree certainly jarring or anyway not those which I expect, and the whole progression of unpredictable consequences that every gesture and every word entails: all this would raise a cloud of noise around the things we have to say to each other, or rather that we wish to hear each other say, so that the communication that is already difficult on the telephone would be even more obstructed, suffocated, buried as if under an avalanche of sand. That's why, rather than continue to talk, I felt the need to transform the things to say into a cone of light launched at a hundred and forty kilometers an hour, to transform myself into this cone of light moving along the highway, because certainly a signal like that can be received and understood by her without getting lost in the ambiguous disorder of secondary vibrations, just as, in order to receive and understand the things that she has to tell me, I would like them not to be other (rather, I would like her not to be other) than this cone of light that I see advancing along the highway at a speed (I would say, roughly) of a hundred and ten or a hundred and twenty. What counts is to communicate the indispensable, leaving aside the superfluous, to reduce ourselves to essential communication, to a luminous signal, that moves in a given direction, abolishing the complexity of our persons and situations and facial expressions, leaving them in the shadow box that the headlights carry along and conceal. The Y whom I love is in reality that bundle of luminous rays in motion, and all the rest of her can remain, implicit; and the me whom she can love, the me who has the power to enter that circuit of exaltation which is her emotional life, is the flash of this pass that I, for love of her and not without some risk, am attempting.

And yet with Z (I haven't forgotten Z in the least) I can establish the correct relationship only if he is merely the flash and dazzle that follows me, or the taillights that I follow: because if I begin to take his person into consideration, which is, let's say somewhat pathetic but also undeniably disagreeable, yet also – I have to admit – excusable, with that whole boring story of his unhappy love, and his slightly equivocal behavior ... well, who knows where it would end. Instead, as long as everything continues like this it's fine: Z who tries to overtake me or lets himself be overtaken by me (but I don't know if it's him), Y who accelerates toward me (but I don't know if it's her) remorseful and again in love, I who race toward her jealous and anxious (but I can't let her know, not her or anyone).

Of course, if I were absolutely alone on the highway, if I didn't see other cars driving in both directions, then everything would be much clearer: I would be certain that Z had made no move to supplant me and that Y had made no move to reconcile with me, facts that I could mark on the credit or the debit side in my accounts but that wouldn't leave any room for doubt. And yet if I were permitted to replace my present state of uncertainty with that negative certainty, I would certainly refuse to make the exchange. The ideal condition for excluding doubt would be for only three cars to exist in this entire part of the world: mine, Y's. and Z's. Then no other car could be going in my direction except Z's, and the only car headed in the opposite direction would certainly be Y's. Instead, among the hundreds of cars that darkness and rain reduce to anonymous flashes, only a motionless observer situated in a favorable position could distinguish one car from the other and maybe recognize who is in it. This is the contradiction I find myself in: if I want to receive a message, I would have to give up being a message myself, but the message I'd like to receive from Y – that is, that Y has become a message herself – has value only if I in turn am a message; and yet the message that I have become has meaning only if Y receives it not as an ordinary receiver of messages but as the message that I expect to receive from her.

By now, arriving in B, going to Y's house, finding that she stayed there, with her headache, pondering the reasons for the quarrel, would give me no satisfaction. If then Z too arrived, the result would be an odious and melodramatic scene; and if instead I discovered that Z had refrained from coming or that Y hadn't carried out her threat to call him, I would feel that I had played the role of the fool. On the other hand, if I had stayed in A and Y had come there to apologize, I would find myself in an embarrassing situation: I would see Y with different eyes, as a weak woman who is clinging to me, and something between us would change. The only situation I can accept is this transformation of ourselves into the message of ourselves. And Z? He can't escape our fate either; he too has to be transformed into the message of himself – it would be terrible if I drive to Y, jealous of Z, and Y drives to me, remorseful, in order to escape Z, whereas Z, meanwhile, hasn't even dreamed of leaving the house ...

Halfway along the highway there's a service station. I stop, hurry to the bar, buy a handful of telephone tokens, dial the code for B, then Y's number. No one answers. Joyfully I drop the tokens: obviously Y couldn't stand her impatience, she got in her car and is driving toward A. Now I've returned to the highway, on the other side, and I too am driving toward A. All the cars I pass could be Y, or all the cars that pass me. All the cars in the opposite lane, advancing in the opposite direction, could be the deluded Z. Or: Y too stopped at a gas station, telephoned my house in A, and, not finding me, realized that I was going to B and reversed direction. Now we are driving in opposite directions, moving farther and farther apart, and the car that I pass or that passes me belongs to Z, who also, halfway along the highway, tried to telephone Y ...

Everything is still more uncertain, but I feel I have now reached a state of inner tranquility. As long as we can try our telephone numbers and no one answers, all three of us will continue to flow forward and back along these white lines, without places of departure or arrival that, packed with sensations and meanings, loom over the univocality of our journey: finally liberated from the cumbersome materiality of our persons and voices and states of mind, reduced to luminous signals, the only mode of existence fitting for we who wish to be identical to what we say without the distorting buzz that our presence or that of others transmits to what is said.

Of course, the price to pay is high, but we have to accept it: not to be able to distinguish ourselves from the many signals that pass along this road, each with a meaning of its own that remains hidden and indecipherable, because there is no longer anyone outside of here who is able to receive us and understand us.

SMOG

Translated by Willam Weaver

THAT WAS a time when I didn't give a damn about anything, the period when I came to settle in this city. Settle is the wrong term. I had no desire to be settled in any sense; I wanted everything around me to remain flowing, temporary, because I felt it was the only way to save my inner stability, though what that consisted of, I couldn't have said. So when, after a whole series of recommendations, I was offered the job as managing editor of the magazine *Purification*, I came here to the city and looked for a place to live.

To a young man who has just got off the train, the city – as everyone must know – seems like one big station: no matter how much he walks about, the streets are still squalid, garages, warehouses, cafés with zinc counters, trucks discharging stinking gas in his face, as he constantly shifts his suitcase from hand to hand, as he feels his hands swell and become dirty, his underwear stick to him, his nerves grow taut, and everything he sees is nerve-racking, piecemeal. I found a suitable furnished room in one of those very streets;

beside the door of the building there were two clusters of signs, bits of shoebox hung there on lengths of string, with the information that a room was for rent written in a rough hand, the tax stamps stuck in one corner. As I stopped to shift the suitcase again, I saw the signs and went into the building. At each stairway, on each landing there were a couple of ladies who rented rooms. I rang the bell on the second floor, stairway C.

The room was commonplace, a bit dark, because it opened on a courtyard, through a French window; that was how I was to come in, along a landing with a rusty railing. The room, in other words, was independent of the rest of the apartment, but to reach it I had to unlock a series of gates; the landlady, Signorina Margariti, was deaf and rightly feared thieves. There was no bath; the toilet was off the landing, in a kind of wooden shed; in the room there was a basin with running water, with no hot-water heater. But, after all, what could I expect? The price was right, or rather, it was the only possible price, because I couldn't spend more and I couldn't hope to find anything cheaper; besides, it was only temporary and I wanted to make that quite clear to myself.

"Yes, all right, I'll take it," I said to Signorina Margariti, who thought I had asked if the room was cold; she showed me the stove. With that, I had seen everything and I wanted to leave my luggage there and go out. But first I went to the basin and put my hands under the faucet; ever since I had arrived I had been anxious to wash them, but I only rinsed them hastily because I didn't feel like opening my suitcase to look for my soap.

"Oh, why didn't you tell me? I'll bring a towel right away!" Signorina Margariti said; she ran into the other room and came back with a freshly ironed towel which she placed on the footboard of the bed. I dashed a little water on my face, to freshen up – I felt irritatingly unclean – then I rubbed my face with the towel. That act finally made the landlady realize I meant to take the room. "Ah, you're going to take it! Good. You must want to change, to unpack; make yourself right at home, here's the wardrobe, give me your overcoat!"

I didn't let her slip the overcoat off my back; I wanted to go out at once. My only immediate need, as I tried to tell her, was some shelves; I was expecting a case of books, the little library I had managed to keep together in my haphazard life. It cost me some effort to make the deaf woman understand; finally she led me into the other rooms, her part of the house, to a little étagère, where she kept her work baskets and embroidery patterns; she told me she would clear it and put it in my room. I went out.

Purification was the organ of an Institute, where I was to report, to learn my duties. A new job, an unfamiliar city – had I been younger or had I expected more of life, these would have pleased and stimulated me; but not now, now I could see only the grayness, the poverty that surrounded me, and I could only plunge into it as if I actually liked it, because it confirmed my belief that life could be nothing else. I purposely chose to walk in the most narrow, anonymous, unimportant streets, though I could easily have gone along those with fashionable shopwindows and smart cafés; but I didn't want to miss the careworn expression on the faces of the passers-by, the shabby look of the cheap restaurants, the stagnant little stores, and even certain sounds which belong to narrow streets: the streetcars, the braking of pickup trucks, the sizzling of welders in the little workshops in the courtyards: all because that wear, that exterior clashing kept me from attaching too much importance to the wear, the clash that I carried within myself.

But to reach the Institute, I was obliged at one point to enter an entirely different neighborhood, elegant, shaded, old-fashioned, its side streets almost free of vehicles, and its main avenues so spacious that traffic could flow past without noise or jams. It was autumn; some of the trees were golden. The sidewalk did not flank walls, buildings, but fences with hedges beyond them, flower beds, gravel walks, constructions that lay somewhere between the palazzo and the villa, ornate in their architecture. Now I felt lost in a different way, because I could no longer find, as I had done before, things in which I recognized myself, in which I could read the future. (Not that I believe in signs, but when you're nervous, in a new place, everything you see is a sign.)

So I was a bit disoriented when I entered the Institute offices, different from the way I had imagined them, because they were the salons of an aristocratic palazzo, with mirrors and consoles and marble fireplaces and hangings and carpets (though the actual furniture was the usual kind for a modern office, and the lighting was the latest sort, with neon tubes). In other words, I was embarrassed then at having taken such an ugly, dark room, especially when I was led into the office of the president, Commendatore Cordà, who promptly greeted me with exaggerated expansiveness, treating me as an equal not only in social and business importance – which in itself was a hard position for me to maintain – but also as his equal in knowledge and interest in the problems which concerned the Institute and *Purification*. To tell the truth, I had believed it was all some kind of trick, something to mention with a wink; I had accepted the job just as a last resort, and now I had to act as if I had never thought of anything else in my whole life.

Commendatore Cordà was a man of about fifty, youthful in appearance, with a black mustache, a member of that generation, in other words, who despite everything still look youthful and wear a black mustache, the kind of man with whom I have absolutely nothing in common. Everything about him, his talk, his appearance – he wore an impeccable gray suit and a dazzlingly white shirt – his gestures – he moved one hand with his cigarette between his fingers – suggested efficiency, ease, optimism, broad-mindedness. He showed me the numbers of *Purification* that had appeared so far, put out by himself (who was its editor-in-chief) and the Institute's press officer, Signor Avandero (he introduced me to him; one of those characters who talk as if their words were typewritten). There were only a few, very skimpy issues, and you could see that they weren't the work of professionals. With the little I knew about magazines, I found a way to tell him – making no criticisms, obviously – how I would do it, the typographical changes I would make. I fell in with his tone, practical, confident in results; and I was pleased to see that we understood each other. Pleased, because the more efficient and optimistic I acted, the more I thought of that wretched furnished room, those squalid streets, that sense of rust and slime I felt on my skin, my not caring a damn about anything, and I seemed to be performing a trick, to be transforming, before the very eyes of Commendatore Cordà and Signor Avandero, all their technical-industrial efficiency into a pile of crumbs, and they were unaware of it, and Cordà kept nodding enthusiastically.

"Fine. Yes, absolutely, tomorrow, you and I agree, and meanwhile," Cordà said to me, "just to bring you up to date ..." And he insisted on giving me the Proceedings of their latest convention to read. "Here," he took me over to some shelves where the mimeographed copies of all the speeches were arranged in so many stacks. "You see? Take this one, and this other one. Do you already have this? Here, count them and see if they're all there." And as he spoke, he picked up those papers and at that moment I noticed how they raised a little cloud of dust, and I saw the prints of his fingers outlined on their surface, which he had barely touched. Now the Commendatore, in picking up those papers, tried to give them a little shake, but just a slight one, as if he didn't want to admit they were dusty, and he also blew on them gently. He was careful not to put his fingers on the first page of each speech, but if he just grazed one with the tip of a fingernail, he left a little white streak over what seemed a gray background, since the paper was covered with a very fine veil of dust. Nevertheless, his fingers obviously became soiled, and he tried to clean them by bending the tips to his palm and rubbing them, but he only dirtied his whole hand with dust. Then instinctively he dropped his hands to the sides of his gray flannel trousers, caught himself just in time, raised them again, and so we both stood there, our fingertips in mid-air, handing speeches back and forth, taking them delicately by the margins as if they were nettle leaves, and meanwhile we went on smiling, nodding smugly, and saying: "Oh yes, a very interesting convention! Oh yes, an excellent endeavor!" but I noticed that the Commendatore became more and more nervous and insecure, and he couldn't look into my triumphant eyes, into my triumphant and desperate gaze, desperate because everything confirmed the fact that it was all exactly as I had believed it would be.

It took me some time to fall asleep. The room, which had seemed so quiet, at night filled with sounds that I learned, gradually, to decipher. Sometimes I could hear a voice, distorted by a loud-speaker, giving brief, incomprehensible commands; if I had dozed off, I would wake up, thinking I was in a train, because the timbre and the cadence were those of the station loud-speakers, as during the night they rise to the surface of the traveler's restless sleep. When my ear had become accustomed to them, I managed to grasp the words: "Two ravioli with tomato sauce ..." the voice said. "Grilled steak ... Lamb chop ..." My room was over the kitchen of the "Urbano Rattazzi" beer hall, which served hot meals even after midnight: from the counter the waiters transmitted the orders to the cooks, snapping out the words over an intercom. In the wake of those messages, a confused sound of voices came up to me and, at times, the harmonizing chorus of a party. But it was a good place to eat in, somewhat expensive, with a clientele that was not vulgar: the nights were rare when some drunk cut up and overturned tables laden with glasses. As I lay in bed, the sounds of others' wakefulness reached me, muffled, without gusto or color, as if through a fog; the voice over the loudspeaker – "Side dish of French fries ... where's that ravioli?" – had a nasal, resigned melancholy.

At about half past two the "Urbano Rattazzi" beer hall pulled down its metal blinds; the waiters, turning up the collars of their topcoats over the Tyrolean jackets of their uniform, came out of the kitchen door and crossed the courtyard, chatting. At about three a metallic clanking invaded the courtyard: the kitchen workers were dragging out the heavy, empty beer drums, tipping them on their rims and rolling them along, banging one against the other; then the men began rinsing them out. They took their time, since they were no doubt paid by the hour; and they worked carelessly, whistling and making a great racket with those zinc drums, for a couple of hours. At about six, the beer truck came to bring the full drums and collect the empties; but already in the main room of the "Urbano Rattazzi" the sound of the polishers had begun, the machines that cleaned the floors for the day that was about to start.

In moments of silence, in the heart of the night, next door, in Signorina Margariti's room, an intense talking would suddenly burst forth, mingled with little explosions of laughter, questions and answers, all in the same falsetto female voice; the deaf woman couldn't distinguish the act of thinking from the act of speaking aloud and at all hours of the day or even when she woke up late at night, whenever she became involved in a thought, a memory, a regret, she started talking to herself, distributing the dialogue among various speakers. Luckily her soliloquies, in their intensity, were incomprehensible; and yet they filled one with the uneasiness of sharing personal indiscretions.

During the day, when I went into the kitchen to ask her for some hot water to shave with (she couldn't hear a knock and I had to get within her eyeshot to make her aware of my presence), I would catch her talking to the mirror, smiling and grimacing, or seated, staring into the void, telling herself some story; then she would suddenly collect her wits and say: "Oh, I was talking to the cat," or else, "I'm sorry, I didn't see you; I was saying my prayers" (she was very devout). But most of the time she didn't realize she had been overheard.

To tell the truth she did talk to the cat often. She could make long speeches to him, for hours, and on certain evenings I heard her repeating "Pss ... pss ... kitty ... here, kitty ..." at the window, waiting for him to come back from his roaming along the balconies, roofs, and terraces. He was a scrawny, half-wild cat, with blackish fur that was gray every time he came home, as if he collected all the dust and soot of the neighborhood. He ran away from me if he even glimpsed me in the distance and would hide under the furniture, as if I had beaten him at the very least, though I never paid any attention to him. But when I was out he surely visited my room: the freshly washed white shirt which the landlady set on the marble top of the dresser was always found with the cat's sooty paw prints on its collar and front. I would start shouting curses, which I quickly cut short because the deaf woman couldn't hear me, and so I then went into the other room to lay the disaster before her eyes. She was sorry, she hunted for the cat to punish him; she explained that no doubt when she had gone into my room to take the shirt, the cat had followed her without her noticing him; and she must have shut him up inside and the animal had jumped up on the dresser, to release his anger at being locked in.

I had only three shirts and I was constantly giving them to her to wash because – perhaps it was the still disordered life I led, with the office to be straightened out – after half a day my shirt was already dirty. I was often forced to go to the office with the cat's prints on my collar.

Sometimes I found his prints also on the pillowcase. He had probably remained shut inside after having followed Signorina Margariti when she came to "turndown the bed" in the evening.

It was hardly surprising that the cat was so dirty: you only had to put your hand on the railing of the landing to find your palm striped with black. Every time I came home, as I fumbled with the keys at four padlocks or keyholes, then stuck my fingers into the slats of the shutters to open and close the French window, I got my hands so dirty that when I came into the room I had to hold them in the air, to avoid leaving prints, while I went straight to the basin.

Once my hands were washed and dried I immediately felt better, as if I had regained the use of them, and I began touching and shifting those few objects around me. Signorina Margariti, I must say, kept the room fairly clean; as far as dusting went, she dusted every day; but there were times when, if I put my hand in certain places she couldn't reach (she was very short and had short arms, too), I drew it out all velvety with dust and I had to go back to the basin and wash immediately.

My books constituted my most serious problem: I had arranged them on the étagère, and they were the only things that gave me the impression this room was mine; the office left me plenty of free time and I would gladly have spent some hours in my room, reading. But books collect God knows how much dust: I would choose one from the shelf, but then before opening it, I had to rub it all over with a rag, even along the tops of the pages, and then I had to give it a good banging: a cloud of dust rose from it. Afterward I washed my hands again and finally flung myself down on the bed to read. But as I leafed through the book, it became hopeless, I could feel that film of dust on my fingertips, becoming thicker, softer all the time, and it spoiled my pleasure in reading. I got up, went back to the basin, rinsed my hands once more, but now I felt that my shirt was also dusty, and my suit. I would have resumed reading but once my hands were clean I didn't like to dirty them again. So I decided to go out.

Naturally, all the operations of leaving: the shutters, the railing, the locks, reduced my hands to a worse state than ever, but I had to leave them as they were until I reached the office. At the office, the moment I arrived, I ran to the toilet to wash them; the office towel, however, was black with finger marks; as I began to dry my hands, I was already dirtying them again.

I spent my first working days at the Institute putting my desk in order. In fact, the desk assigned me was covered with correspondence, documents, files, old newspapers; until then it had obviously been a kind of clearinghouse where anything with no proper place of its own was put. My first impulse was to make a clean sweep; but then I saw there was material that could be useful for the magazine, and other things of some interest which I decided to examine at my leisure. In short, I finally removed nothing from the desk and actually added a lot of things, but not in disorder: on the contrary, I tried to keep everything tidy. Naturally, the papers that had been there before were very dusty and infected the new papers with their dirt. And since I set great store by my neatness, I had given orders to the cleaning woman not to touch anything, so each day a little more dust settled on the papers, especially on the writing materials, the stationery, the envelopes, and so on, which soon looked old and soiled and were irksome to touch.

And in the drawers it was the same story. There dusty papers from decades past were stratified, evidence of the desk's long career through various offices, public and private. No matter what I did at that desk, after a few minutes I felt impelled to go wash my hands.

My colleague Signor Avandero, on the contrary, kept his hands – delicate little hands, but with a certain nervous hardness – always clean, well groomed, the nails polished, uniformly clipped.

"Excuse me for asking, but," I ventured to say to him, "don't you find, after you've been here a while, I mean ... have you noticed how one's hands become dirty?"

"No doubt," Avandero answered, with his usual composed manner, "you have touched some object or paper that wasn't perfectly dusted. If you'll allow me to give you a word of advice, it's always a good idea to keep the top of one's desk completely clear."

In fact, Avandero's desk was clear, clean, shining, with only the file he was dealing with at that moment and the ballpoint pen he held in his hand. "It's a habit," he added, "that the President feels is very important." In fact, Commendatore Cordà had said the same thing to me: the executive who keeps his desk completely clear is a man who never lets matters pile up, who starts every problem on the road to its solution. But Cordà was never in the office, and when he was there he stayed a quarter of an hour, had great graphs and statistical charts brought in to him, gave rapid, vague orders to his subordinates, assigned the various duties to one or the other without bothering about the degree of difficulty of each assignment, rapidly dictated a few letters to the stenographer, signed the outgoing correspondence, and was off.

Not Avandero, though. Avandero stayed in the office morning and afternoon, he created an impression of working very hard and of giving the stenographers and the typists a lot to do, but he managed never to keep a sheet of paper on his desk more than ten minutes. I simply couldn't stomach this business; I began to keep an eye on him and I noticed that these papers, though they didn't stay long on his desk, were soon bogged down somewhere else. Once I caught him when, not knowing what to do with some letters he was holding, he had approached my desk (I had stepped out to wash my hands a moment) and was placing them there, hiding them under a file. Afterward he quickly took his handkerchief from his breast pocket, wiped his hands, and went back to his place, where the ballpoint pen lay parallel to an immaculate sheet of paper.

I could have gone in at once and put him in an awkward spot. But I was content with having seen him; it was enough for me to know how things worked.

Since I entered my room from the landing, the rest of Signorina Margariti's apartment remained unexplored territory to me. The Signorina lived alone, renting two rooms on the courtyard, mine and another next to it. I knew nothing of the other tenant except his heavy tread late at night and early in the morning (he was a police sergeant, I learned, and was never to be seen during the day). The rest of the apartment, which must have been rather vast, was all the landlady's.

Sometimes I was obliged to go look for her because she was wanted on the telephone; she couldn't hear it ring, so in the end I went and answered. Holding the receiver to her ear, however, she could hear fairly well; and long phone conversations with the other ladies of the parish sodality were her pastime. "Telephone! Signorina Margariti! You're wanted on the telephone!" I would shout, pointlessly, through the apartment, knocking, even more pointlessly, at the doors. As I made these rounds, I got to know a series of living rooms, parlors, pantries, all cluttered with old-fashioned, pretentious furniture, with floor lamps and bric-à-brac, pictures and statues and calendars; the rooms were all in order, polished, gleaming with wax, with snowy-white lace antimacassars on the armchairs, and without even a speck of dust.

At the end of one of these rooms I would finally discover Signorina Margariti, busy waxing the parquet floor or rubbing the furniture, wearing a faded wrapper and a kerchief around her head. I would point in the direction of the telephone, with violent gestures; the deaf woman would run and grasp the receiver, beginning another of her endless chats, in tones not unlike those of her conversations with the cat.

Going back to my room then, seeing the basin shelf or the lampshade with an inch of dust, I would be seized by a great anger: that woman spent the whole day keeping her rooms as shiny as a mirror and she wouldn't even wave a dustcloth over my place. I went back, determined to make a scene, with gestures and grimaces; and I found her in the kitchen, and this kitchen was kept even worse than my room: the oilcloth on the table all worn and stained, dirty cups on top of the cupboard, the floor tiles cracked and blackened. And I was speechless, because I knew the kitchen was the only place in the whole house where that woman really lived, and the rest, the richly adorned rooms constantly swept and waxed, were a kind of work of art on which she lavished her dreams of beauty; and to cultivate the perfection of those rooms she was self-condemned not to live in them, never to enter them as mistress of the house, but only as cleaning woman, spending the rest of her day amid grease and dust.

Purification came out every two weeks and carried, as a subtitle, "of the Air from Smoke, from Chemical Exhaust, and from the Products of Combustion." The magazine was the official organ of the IPUAIC, "The Institute for the Purification of the Urban Atmosphere in Industrial Centers." The IPUAIC was affiliated with similar associations in other countries, which sent us their bulletins and their pamphlets. Often international conventions were held, especially to discuss the serious problem of smog.

I had never concerned myself with questions of this sort, but I knew that putting out a magazine in a specialized field is not as hard as it seems. You follow the foreign reviews, you have certain articles translated, and with them and a subscription to a clipping agency you can quickly compile a news column; then there are those two or three technical contributors who never fail to send in a little article; also the Institute, no matter how inactive it is, always has some communication or agenda to be printed in bold type; and there is the advertiser who asks you to publish, as an article, the description of his latest patented device. Then when a convention is held, you can devote at least one whole issue to it, from beginning to end, and you will still have papers and reports left over to run in the following issues, whenever you have two or three columns you don't know how to fill.

The editorial as a rule was written by the President. But Commendatore Cordà, always extremely busy (he was Chairman of the Board of a number of industries, and he could only devote his odd free moments to the Institute), began asking me to draft it, incorporating the ideas that he described to me with vigor and clarity. I would then submit my draft to him on his return. He traveled a great deal, our President, because his factories were scattered more or less throughout the country; but of all his activities, the Presidency of the IPUAIC, a purely honorary position, was the one, he told me, which gave him the greatest satisfaction, "because," as he explained, "it's a battle for an ideal."

As far as I was concerned, I had no ideals, nor did I want to have any; I only wanted to write an article he would like, to keep my job, which was no better or worse than another, and to continue my life, no better or worse than any other possible life. I knew Cordà's opinions ("If everyone followed our example, atmospheric purity would already be ...") and his favorite expressions ("We are not utopians, mind you, we are practical men who ..."), and I would write the article just as he wished, word for word. What else could I write? What I thought with my own mind? That would produce a fine article, all right! A fine optimistic vision of an functional, productive world! But I had only to turn my mood inside out (which wasn't hard for me because it was like attacking myself) to summon the impetus necessary for an inspired editorial by our President.

"We are now on the threshold of a solution to the problem of volatile wastes," I wrote, "a solution which will be more quickly achieved" – and I could already see the President's satisfied look – "as the active inspiration given Technology by Private Initiative" – at this point Cordà would raise one hand, to underline my words – "is implemented by intelligent action on the part of the Government, always so prompt ..."

I read this piece to Signor Avandero. Resting his neat little hands on a white sheet of paper in the center of his desk,

Avandero looked at me with his usual, inexpressive politeness.

"Well? Don't you like it?" I asked him.

"Oh, yes, yes indeed," he hastened to say.

"Listen to the ending: 'To answer the catastrophic predictions from some quarters concerning industrial civilization, we once more affirm that there will not be (nor has there ever been) any contradiction between an economy in free, natural expansion and the hygiene necessary to the human organism'" – from time to time I glanced at Avandero, but he didn't raise his eyes from that white sheet of paper – "'between the smoke of our productive factories and the green of our incomparable natural beauty....'Well, what do you say to that?"

Avandero stared at me for a moment with his dull eyes, his lips pursed. "I'll tell you: your article does express very well what might be called the substance of our Institute's final aim, yes, the goal toward which all its efforts are directed ..."

"Hmm ..." I grumbled. I must confess that from a punctilious character like my colleague I expected a less tortuous approval.

I presented the article to Commendatore Cordà on his arrival a couple of days later. He read it with care, in my presence. He finished reading, put the pages in order, and seemed about to reread it from the beginning, but he only said: "Good." He thought for a moment, then repeated: "Good." Another pause, and then: "You're young." He warded off an objection I had no intention of making. "No, that's not a criticism, believe me. You are young, you have faith, you look far ahead. However, if I may say so, the situation is serious, yes, more serious than your article would lead the reader to believe. Let's speak frankly: the danger of air pollution in the big cities is huge, we have the analyses, the situation is grave. And precisely because it is grave, we are here to solve it. If we don't solve it, our cities, too, will be suffocated by smog."

He had risen and was pacing back and forth. "We aren't hiding the difficulties from ourselves. We aren't like the others, especially those who are in a position which should force them to think about this, and who instead don't give a damn. Or worse: try to block our efforts."

He stood squarely in front of me, lowered his voice: "Because you are young, perhaps you believe everybody agrees with us. But they don't. We are only a handful. Attacked from all sides, that's the truth of it. All sides. And yet we won't give up. We speak out. We act. We will solve the problem. This is what I would like to feel more strongly in your article, you understand?"

I understood perfectly. My insistent pretense of holding opinions contrary to my own had carried me away, but now I would be able to give the article just the right emphasis. I was to show it to the President again in three days' time. I rewrote from beginning to end. In the first two thirds of it I drew a grim picture of the cities of Europe devoured by smog, and in the final third I opposed this with the image of an exemplary city, our own, clean, rich in oxygen, where a rational complex of sources of production went hand in hand with ... et cetera.

To concentrate better, I wrote the article at home, lying on my bed. A shaft of sunlight fell obliquely into the deep courtyard, entered through the panes, and I saw it cut across the air of my room with a myriad of impalpable particles. The counterpane must be impregnated with them; in a little while, I felt, I would be covered by a blackish layer, like the slats of the blind, like the railing of the balcony.

When I read the new draft to Signor Avandero, I had the impression he didn't dislike it. "This contrast between the situation in our cities and that in others," he said, "which you no doubt expressed according to our President's instructions, has really come off quite well."

"No, no, the President didn't mention that to me, it was my own idea," I said, a bit annoyed despite myself because my colleague didn't believe me capable of any initiative.

Corda's reaction, on the other hand, took me by surprise. He laid the typescript on the desk and shook his head. "We still don't understand each other," he said at once. He began to give me figures on the city's industrial production, the coal, the fuel oil consumed daily, the traffic of vehicles with combustion engines. Then he went on to meteorological data, and in every case he made a summary comparison with the larger cities of northern Europe. "We are a great, foggy industrial city, you realize; therefore smog exists here, too, we have no less smog than anywhere else. It is impossible to declare, as rival cities here in our own country try to do, that we have less smog than foreign cities. You can write this quite clearly in the article, you *must* write it! We are one of the cities where the problem of air pollution is most serious, but at the same time we are the city where most is being done to counteract the situation! At the same time, you understand?"

I understood, and I also understood that he and I would never understand each other. Those blackened facades of the houses, those dulled panes of glass, those window sills on which you couldn't lean, those human faces almost erased, that haze which now, as autumn advanced, lost its humid, bad-weather stink and became a kind of quality of all objects, as if each person and each thing had less shape every day, less meaning or value. Everything that was, for me, the substance of a general wretchedness, for men like him was surely the sign of wealth, supremacy, power, and also of danger, destruction, and tragedy, a way of feeling filled – suspended there – with a heroic grandeur.

I wrote the article a third time. It was all right, at last. Only the ending ("Thus we are face to face with a terrible problem, affecting the destiny of society. Will we solve it?") caused him to raise an objection.

"Isn't that a bit too uncertain?" he asked. "Won't it discourage our readers?"

The simplest thing was to remove the question mark and shift the pronoun. "We will solve it." Just like that, without any exclamation point: calm self-confidence.

"But doesn't that make it seem too easy? As if it were just a routine matter?"

We agreed to repeat the words. Once with the question mark and once without. "Will we solve it? We will solve it."

But didn't this seem to postpone the solution to a vague future time? We tried putting it in the present tense. "Are we solving it? We are solving it." But this didn't have the right ring.

Writing an article always proceeds in the same way. You begin by changing a comma, and then you have to change a word, then the word order of a sentence, and then it all collapses. We argued for an hour. I suggested using different tenses for the question and the answer: "Will we solve it?

We are solving it." The President was enthusiastic and from that day on his faith in my talents never wavered.

One night the telephone woke me, the special, insistent ring of a long-distance call. I turned on the light: it was almost three o'clock. Even before making up my mind to get out of bed, rush into the hall, and grope for the receiver in the dark, even before that, at the first jolt in my sleep, I already knew it was Claudia.

Her voice now gushed from the receiver and it seemed to come from another planet; with my eyes barely open I had a sensation of sparks, dazzle, which were instead the shifting tones of her unceasing voice, that dramatic excitement she always put into everything she said, and which now arrived even here, at the end of the squalid hall in Signorina Margariti's apartment. I realized I had never doubted Claudia would find me; on the contrary, I had been expecting nothing else for all this time.

She didn't bother to ask what I had been doing in the meanwhile, or how I had ended up there, nor did she explain how she had traced me. She had heaps of things to tell me, extremely detailed things, and yet somehow vague, as her talk always was, things that took place in environments unknown and unknowable to me.

"I need you, quickly, right away. Take the first train. . . ."

"Well, I have a job here . . . The Institute . . ."

"Ah, perhaps you've run into Senator . . . Tell him . . ."
"No, no, I'm just the . . ."

"Darling, you will leave right away, won't you?"

How could I tell her I was speaking from a place full of dust, where the blinds' slats were covered with a gritty black grime, and there were cat's prints on my collar, and this was the only possible world for me, while hers, her world, could exist for me, or seem to exist, only through an optical illusion? She wouldn't even have listened, she was too accustomed to seeing everything from above and the wretched circumstances that formed the texture of my life naturally escaped her. What was her whole relationship with me if not the outcome of this superior distraction of hers, thanks to which she had never managed to realize I was a modest provincial newspaperman without a future, without ambitions? And she went on treating me as if I were part of high society, the world of aristocrats, magnates, and famous artists, where she had always moved and where, in one of those chance encounters that occur at the beach, I had been introduced to her one summer. She didn't want to admit it, because that would mean admitting she had made a mistake; so she went on attributing talents to me, authority, tastes I was far from possessing; but my real, fundamental identity was a mere detail, and in mere details she did not want to be contradicted.

Now her voice was becoming tender, affectionate: this was the moment that – without even confessing it to myself – I had been waiting for, because it was only in moments of amorous abandon that everything separating us disappeared and we discovered we were just two people, and it didn't matter who we were. We had barely embarked on an exchange of amorous words when, behind me, a light came on beyond a glass door, and I could hear a grim cough. It was the door of my fellow tenant, the police sergeant, right there, beside the telephone. I promptly lowered my voice. I resumed the interrupted sentence, but now that I knew I was overheard, a natural reserve made me tone down my loving expressions, until they were reduced to a murmuring of neutral phrases, almost unintelligible. The light in the next room went off, but from the other end of the wire protests began: "What did you say? Speak louder! Is that all you have to tell me?"

"But I'm not alone. ..."

"What? Who's with you?"

"No, listen, you'll wake up the tenants, it's late. ..."

By now she was in a fury, she didn't want explanations, she wanted a reaction from me, a sign of warmth on my side, something that would bum up the distance between us. But my answers had become cautious, whining, soothing. "No, Claudia, you see, I ... don't say that, I swear, I beg you, Claudia, I ..." In the sergeant's room the light came on again. My love talk became a mumble, my lips pressed to the receiver.

In the courtyard the kitchen workers were rolling the empty beer dmms. Signorina Margariti, in the darkness of her room, began chatting, punctuating her words with brief bursts of laughter, as if she had visitors. The fellow tenant uttered a Southern curse. I was barefoot, standing on the tiles of the hall, and from the other end of the wire Claudia's passionate voice held out her hands to me, and I was trying to run toward her with my stammering, but each time we were about to cast a bridge between us, it crumbled to bits a moment later, and the impact of reality crushed and denied all our words of love, one by one.

After that first time, the telephone took to ringing at the oddest hours of the day and night, and Claudia's voice, tawny and speckled, leaped into the narrow hall, with the heedless spring of a leopard who doesn't know he is throwing himself into a trap, and since he doesn't know, he manages, with a second leap, as he came, to find the path out again: and he hasn't realized anything. And I, torn between suffering and love, joy and cruelty, saw her mingling with this scene of ugliness and desolation, with the loud-speaker of the "Urbane Rattazzi", which blurted out: "Noodle soup," with the dirty bowls in Signorina Margariti's sink, and I felt that by now even Claudia's image must be stained by it all. But no, it ran off, along the wire, intact, aware of nothing, and each time I was left alone with the void of her absence.

Sometimes Claudia was gay, carefree, she laughed, said senseless things to tease me, and in the end I shared in her gaiety, but then the courtyard, the dust saddened me all the more because I had been tempted to believe life could be different. At other times, instead, Claudia was gripped by a feverish anxiety and this anxiety then was added to the appearance of the place where I lived, to my work as managing editor of *Purification*, and I couldn't rid myself of it, I lived in the expectation of another, more dramatic call which would waken me in the heart of the night, and when I finally did hear her voice again, surprisingly different, gay or languid, as if she couldn't even remember the torment of the night before, rather than liberated, I felt bewildered, lost.

"What did you say? You're calling from Taormina?"

"Yes, I'm down here with some friends, it's lovely, come right away, catch the next plane!"

Claudia always called from different cities, and each time, whether she was in a state of anxiety or of exuberance, she insisted that I join her at once, to share that mood with her. Each time I started to give her a careful explanation of why it was absolutely impossible for me to travel, but I couldn't continue because Claudia, not listening to me, had already shifted to another subject, usually a harangue against me, or else an unpredictable hymn of praise, for some casual expression of mine which she found abominable or adorable.

When the allotted time of the call was up and the day or night operator said: "Three minutes. Do you wish to continue?" Claudia would shout: "When are you arriving, then?" as if it were all agreed. I would stammer some answer, and we ended by postponing final arrangements to another call she would make to me or I was to make to her. I knew that in the meanwhile Claudia would change all her plans and the urgency of my trip would come up again, surely, but in different circumstances which would then justify further postponements; and yet a kind of remorse lingered in me, because the impossibility of my joining her was not so absolute, I could ask for an advance on my next month's salary and a leave of three or four days with some pretext; these hesitations gnawed at me.

Signorina Margariti heard nothing. If, crossing the hall, she saw me at the telephone, she greeted me with a nod, unaware of the storms raging within me. But not the fellow tenant. From his room he heard everything and he was obliged to apply his policeman's intuition every time the phone's ring made me jump. Luckily, he was hardly ever in the house, and therefore some of my telephone conversations even managed to be selfconfident, nonchalant, and, depending on Claudia's humor, we could create an atmosphere of amorous exchange where every word took on a warmth, an intimacy, an inner meaning. On other occasions, however, she was in the best of moods and I was instead blocked, I answered only in monosyllables, with reticent, evasive phrases: the sergeant was behind his door, a few feet from me; once he opened it a crack, stuck out his dark, mustachioed face, and examined me. He was a little man, I must say, who in other circumstances wouldn't have made the least impression on me; but there, late at night, seeing each other face to face for the first time, in that lodginghouse for poor wretches, I making and receiving amorous long-distance calls of half an hour, he just coming off duty, both of us in our pajamas, we undeniably hated each other.

Often Claudia's conversation included famous names, the people she saw regularly. First of all, I don't know anybody; secondly, I can't bear attracting attention; so if I absolutely had to answer her, I tried not to mention any names, I used paraphrases, and she couldn't understand why and it made her angry. Politics, too, is something I've always steered clear of, precisely because I don't like making myself conspicuous; and now, besides, I was working for a government-sponsored Institute and I had made it a rule to know nothing of either party; and Claudia – God knows what got into her one evening – asked me about certain Members of Parliament. I had to give her some kind of answer, then and there, with the sergeant behind the door. "The first one ... the first name you mentioned, of course ..."

"Who? Who do you mean?"

"That one, yes, the big one, no, smaller ..."

In other words, I loved her. And I was unhappy. But how could she have understood this unhappiness of mine? There are those who condemn themselves to the most gray, mediocre life because they have suffered some grief, some misfortune; but there are also those who do the same thing because their good fortune is greater than they feel they can sustain.

I took my meals in certain fixed-price restaurants, which, in this city, are all run by Tuscan families, all of them related among themselves, and the waitresses are all girls from a town called Altopascio, and they spend their youth here, but with the thought of Altopascio constantly in their minds, and they don't mingle with the rest of the city; in the evening they go out with boys from Altopascio, who work here in the kitchens of the restaurants or perhaps in factories, but still sticking close to the restaurants as if they were outlying districts of their village; and these girls and these boys marry and some go back to Altopascio, others stay here to work in their relatives' or their fellow townsmen's restaurants, saving up until one day they can open a restaurant of their own.

The people who eat in those restaurants are what you would expect: apart from travelers, who change all the time, the regular customers are unmarried white-collar workers, even some spinster typists, and a few students or soldiers. After a while these customers get to know one another and they chat from table to table, and at a certain point they eat at the same table, groups of people who at first didn't know one another and then ended up by falling into the habit of always eating together.

They all joked, too, with the Tuscan waitresses, good-natured jokes, obviously; they asked about the girls' boyfriends, they exchanged witticisms, and when there was nothing else to talk about they started on television, saying who was nice and who wasn't among the faces they had seen in the latest programs.

But not me, I never said anything except my order, which for that matter was always the same: spaghetti with butter, boiled beef, and greens, because I was on a diet; and I never called the girls by name even though by then I too had learned their names, but I preferred to go on saying "Signo-rina" so as not to create an impression of familiarity: I had happened upon that restaurant by chance, I was just a random customer, perhaps I would continue going there every day for God knows how long, but I wanted to feel as if I were passing through, here today and somewhere else tomorrow, otherwise the place would get on my nerves.

Not that they weren't likable. On the contrary: both the staff and the clientele were good, pleasant people, and I enjoyed that cordial atmosphere around me; in fact, if it hadn't existed, I would probably have felt something was lacking, but still I preferred to look on, without taking part in it. I avoided conversing with the other customers, not even greeting them, because, as everyone knows, it's easy enough to strike up an acquaintance, but then you're involved; somebody says: "What's on this evening?" and you end up all together watching television or going to the movies, and after that evening you're caught up in a group of people who mean nothing to you, and you have to tell them your business, and listen to theirs.

I tried to sit down at a table by myself, I would open the morning or evening paper (I bought it on my way to the office and took a glance at the headlines then, but I waited to read it until I was at the restaurant), and then I read through it from beginning to end. The paper was of great use to me when I couldn't find a seat by myself and had to sit down at a table where there was already someone else; I plunged into my reading and nobody said a word to me. But I always tried to find a free table and for this reason I was careful to put off as late as possible the hour of my meals, so I turned up there when most of the customers had already left.

There was the disadvantage of the crumbs. Often I had to sit down at a table where another customer had just got up and left the table covered with crumbs; so I avoided looking down until the waitress came to clear away the dirty dishes and glasses, sweeping up all the remains into the cloth and changing it. At times this task was done hastily and between the top cloth and the bottom one there were bread crumbs, and they distressed me.

The best thing, at lunchtime for example, was to discover the hour when the waitresses, thinking that by then no more customers would be coming, clean up everything properly and prepare the tables for the evening; then the whole family, owners, waitresses, cooks, dishwashers, set one big table and finally sit down to eat, themselves. At that moment I would go in, saying: "Oh, perhaps I'm too late. Can you give me something to eat?"

"Why, of course! Sit down wherever you like! Lisa, serve the gentleman."

I sat down at one of those lovely clean tables, a cook went back into the kitchen, I read the paper, I ate calmly, I listened to the others laughing at their table, joking and telling stories of Altopascio. Between one dish and the next I would have to wait perhaps a quarter of an hour, because the waitresses were sitting there eating and chatting, and I would finally make up my mind to say: "An orange, please, Signorina …." And they would say: "Yes, sir! Anna, you go. Oh, Lisa!" But I liked it that way, I was happy.

I finished eating, finished reading the paper, and went out with the paper rolled up in my hand, I went home, I climbed up to my room, threw the paper on the bed, washed my hands. Signorina Margariti kept watch to see when I came in and when I left, because the moment I was outside she came into my room to take the newspaper. She didn't dare ask me for it, so she took it away in secret and secretly she put it back on the bed before I came home again. She seemed to be ashamed of this, as if of a somehow frivolous curiosity; in fact she read only one thing, the obituaries.

Once when I came in and found her with the paper in her hand, she was deeply embarrassed and felt obliged to explain: "I borrow it every now and then to see who's dead, you know, forgive me, but sometimes, you know, I have acquaintances among the dead. ..."

Thanks to this idea of postponing mealtimes, for example by going to the movies, on certain evenings, I came out of the film late, my head a bit giddy, to find a dense darkness shrouding the neon signs, an autumnal mist, which drained the city of dimensions. I looked at the time, I told myself there probably was nothing left to eat in those little restaurants, or in any case I was off my usual schedule and I wouldn't be able to get back to it again, so I decided to have a quick bite standing at the counter in the "Urbano Rattazzi" beer hall, just below where I lived.

Entering the place from the street was not just a passage from darkness to light: the very consistency of the world changed. Outside, all was shapeless, uncertain, dispersed, and here it was full of solid forms, of volumes with a thickness, a weight, brightly colored surfaces, the red of the ham they were slicing at the counter, the green of the waiters' Tyrolean jackets, the gold of the beer. The place was full of people and I, who in the streets was accustomed to look on passers-by as faceless shadows and to consider myself another faceless shadow among so many, rediscovered here all of a sudden a forest of male and female faces, as brightly colored as fruit, each different from the rest and all unknown. For a moment I hoped still to retain my own ghostly invisibility in their midst, then I realized that I, too, had become like them, a form so precise that even the mirrors reflected it, with the stubble of beard that had grown since morning, and there was no possible refuge; even the smoke which drifted in a thick cloud to the ceiling from all the lighted cigarettes in the place was a thing apart with its outline and its thickness and didn't modify the substance of the other things.

I made my way to the counter, which was always very crowded, turning my back on the room full of laughter and words from each table, and as soon as a stool became free I sat down on it, trying to attract the waiter's attention, so he would set before me the square cardboard coaster, a mug of beer, and the menu. I had trouble making them notice me, here at the "Urbano Rattazzi" over which I kept vigil night after night, whose every hour, every jolt I knew, and the noise in which my voice was lost was the same I heard rise every evening up along the rusty iron railings.

"Gnocchi with butter, please," I said, and finally the waiter behind the counter heard me and went to the microphone to declare: "One gnocchi with butter!" and I thought of how that cadenced shout emerged from the loud-speaker in the kitchen, and I felt as if I were simultaneously here at the counter and up there, lying on my bed in my room, and I tried to break up in my mind and muffle the words that constantly crisscrossed among the groups of jolly people eating and drinking and the clink of glasses and cutlery until I could recognize the noise of all my evenings.

Transparently, through the lines and colors of this part of the world, I was beginning to discern the features of its reverse, of which I felt I was the only inhabitant. But perhaps the true reverse was here, brightly lighted and full of open eyes, whereas the side that counted in every way was the shadowy part, and the "Urbano Rattazzi" beer hall existed only so you could hear that distorted voice in the darkness, "One gnocchi with butter!" and the clank of the metal drums, and so the street's mist might be pierced by the sign's halo, by the square of misted panes against which vague human forms were outlined.

One morning I was wakened by a call from Claudia, but this wasn't long distance; she was in the city, at the station, she had just that moment arrived and was calling me because, in getting out of the sleeping car, she had lost one of the many cases that comprised her luggage.

I got there barely in time to see her coming out of the station, at the head of a procession of porters. Her smile had none of that agitation she had transmitted to me by her phone call a few minutes before. She was very beautiful and elegant; each time I saw her I was amazed to see I had forgotten what she was like. Now she suddenly pronounced herself enthusiastic about this city and she approved my idea of coming to live here. The sky was leaden; Claudia praised the light, the streets' colors.

She took a suite in a grand hotel. For me to go into the lobby, address the desk clerk, have myself announced by phone, follow the bellboy to the elevator, caused endless uneasiness and dismay. I was deeply moved that Claudia, because of certain business matters of hers but in reality perhaps to see me, had come to spend a few days here:

moved and embarrassed, as the abyss between her way of life and mine yawned before me.

And yet, I managed to get along fairly well during that busy morning and even to turn up briefly at the office to draw an advance on my next pay-check, foreseeing the exceptional days that lay ahead of me. There was the problem of where to take her to eat: I had little experience of de luxe restaurants or special regional places. As a start, I had the idea of taking her up to one of the surrounding hills.

I hired a taxi. I realized now that, in that city, where nobody earning above a certain figure was without a car (even my colleague Avandero had one), I had none, and anyway I wouldn't have known how to drive one. It had never mattered to me in the least, but in Claudia's presence I was ashamed. Claudia, on the other hand, found everything quite natural, because – she said – a car in my hands would surely spell disaster; to my great annoyance she loudly made light of my practical ability and based her admiration of me on other talents, though there was no telling what they were.

So we took a taxi; we hit on a rickety car, driven by an old man. I tried to make a joke of how flotsam, wreckage, inevitably comes to life around me, but Claudia wasn't upset by the ugliness of the taxi, as if these things couldn't touch her, and I didn't know whether to be relieved or to feel more than ever abandoned to my fate.

We climbed up to the green backdrop of hills that girdles the city to the east. The day had cleared into a gilded autumnal light, and the colors of the countryside, too, were turning gold. I embraced Claudia, in that taxi; if I let myself give way to the love she felt for me, perhaps that green and gold life would also yield to me, the life that, in blurred images (to embrace her, I had removed my eyeglasses), ran by at either side of the road.

Before going to the little restaurant, I told the elderly driver to take us somewhere to look at the view, up higher. We got out of the car, Claudia, with a huge black hat, spun around, making the folds of her skirt swell out. I darted here and there, pointing out to her the whitish crest of the Alps that emerged from the sky (I mentioned the names of the mountains at random, since I couldn't recognize them) and, on this side, the broken and intermittent outline of the hill with villages and roads and rivers, and down below, the city like a network of tiny scales, opaque or glistening, meticulously aligned. A sense of vastness had seized me; I don't know whether it was Claudia's hat and skirt, or the view. The air, though this was autumn, was fairly clear and unpolluted, but it was streaked by the most diverse kinds of condensation: thick mists at the base of the mountains, wisps of fog over the rivers, chains of clouds, stirred variously by the wind. We were there leaning over the low wall: I, with my arm around her waist, looking at the countless aspects of the landscape, suddenly gripped by a need to analyze, already dissatisfied with myself because I didn't command sufficiently the nomenclature of the places and the natural phenomena; she ready instead to translate sensations into sudden gusts of love, into effusions, remarks that had nothing to do with any of this. At this point I saw the thing. I grabbed Claudia by the wrist, clasping it hard. "Look! Look down there!"

"What is it?"

"Down there! Look! It's moving!"

"But what is it? What do you see?"

How could I tell her? There were other clouds or mists which, according to how the humidity condenses in the cold layers of air, are gray or bluish or whitish or even black, and they weren't so different from this one, except for its uncertain color, I couldn't say whether more brownish or bituminous; but the difference was rather in a shadow of this color which seemed to become more intense first at the edges, then in the center. It was, in short, a shadow of dirt, soiling everything and changing – and in this too it was different from the other clouds – its very consistency, because it was heavy, not clearly dispelled from the earth, from the speckled expanse of the city over which it flowed slowly, gradually erasing it on one side and revealing it on the other, but trailing a wake, like slightly dirty strands, which had no end.

"It's smog!" I shouted at Claudia. "You see that? It's a cloud of smog!"

But she wasn't listening to me, she was attracted by something she had seen flying, a flight of birds; and I stayed there, looking for the first time, from outside, at the cloud that surrounded me every hour, at the cloud I inhabited and that inhabited me, and I knew that, in all the variegated world around me, this was the only thing that mattered to me.

That evening I took Claudia to supper at the "Urbano Rattazzi" beer hall, because except for my cheap restaurants I knew no other place and I was afraid of ending up somewhere too expensive. Entering the "Urbano Rattazzi" with a girl like Claudia was a new experience: the waiters in their Tyrolean jackets all sprang to attention, they gave us a good table, they rolled over the trolleys with the specialties. I tried to act the nonchalant escort but at the same time I felt I had been recognized as the tenant of the furnished room over the courtyard, the customer who had quick meals on a stool at the counter. This state of mind made me clumsy, my conversation was dull, and soon Claudia became angry with me. We fell into an intense quarrel; our voices were drowned by the noise of the beer hall, but we had trained on us not only the eyes of the waiters, prompt to obey Claudia's slightest sign, but also those of the other customers, their curiosity aroused by this beautiful, elegant, imposing woman in the company of such a meek-looking man. And I realized that the words of our argument were followed by everyone, also because Claudia, in her unconcern for the people around her, made no effort to disguise her feelings. I felt they were all waiting only for the moment when Claudia, infuriated, would get up and leave me there alone, making me once more the anonymous man I had always been, the man nobody notices any more than one would notice a spot of damp on the wall.

Instead, as always, the quarrel was followed by a tender, amorous understanding; we had reached the end of the meal and Claudia, knowing I lived nearby, said: "I'll come up to your place."

Now I had taken her to the "Urbano Rattazzi" because it was the only restaurant I knew of that sort, not because it was near my room; in fact, I was on pins and needles at the very thought that she might form some idea of the house where I lived just by glancing at the doorway of the building, and I had relied chiefly on her flightiness.

Instead, she wanted to go up there. Telling her about the room, I exaggerated its squalor, to turn the whole event into something grotesque. But as she went up and crossed the landing, she noticed only the good aspects: the ancient and rather noble architecture of the building, the functional way in which those old apartments were laid out. We went in, and she said: "Why, what are you talking about? The room is wonderful. What more do you want?"

I turned at once to the basin, before helping her off with her coat, because as usual I had soiled my hands. But not she, she moved around, her hands fluttering like feathers among the dusty furnishings.

The room was soon invaded by those alien objects: her hat with its little veil, her fox stole, velvet dress, organdy slip, satin shoes, silk stockings; I tried to hang everything up in the wardrobe, put things in the drawers, because I thought that if they stayed out they would soon be covered with traces of soot.

Now Claudia's white body was lying on the bed, on that bed from which, if I hit it, a cloud of dust would rise, and she reached out with one hand to the shelf next to it and took a book. "Be careful, it's dusty!" But she had already opened it and was leafing through it, then she dropped it to the floor. I was looking at her breasts, still those of a young girl, the pink, pointed tips, and I was seized with torment at the thought that some dust from the book's pages might have fallen on them, and I extended my hand to touch them lightly in a gesture resembling a caress but intended, really, to remove from them the bit of dust I thought had settled there.

Instead, her skin was smooth, cool, undefiled; and as I saw in the lamp's cone of light a little shower of dust specks floating in the air, soon to be deposited also on Claudia, I threw myself upon her in an embrace which was chiefly a way of covering her, of taking all the dust upon myself so that she would be safe from it.

After she had left (a bit disappointed and bored with my company, despite her unshakable determination to cast on others a light that was all her own), I flung myself into my editorial work with redoubled energy, partly because Claudia's visit had made me miss many hours in the office and I was behind with the preparation of the next number, and also because the subject the biweekly *Purification* dealt with no longer seemed so alien to me as it had at the beginning.

The editorial was still unwritten, but this time Commendatore Cordà had left me no instructions. "You handle it. Be careful, however." I began to write one of the usual diatribes, but gradually, as one word led to the next, I found myself describing how I had seen the cloud of smog rubbing over the city, how life went on inside that cloud, and the facades of the old houses, all jutting surfaces and hollows where a black deposit thickened, and the facades of the modern houses, smooth, monochrome, squared off, on which little by little dark, vague shadows grew, as on the office workers' white collars, which stayed clean no more than half a day. And I wrote that, true, there were still people who lived outside the cloud of smog, and perhaps there always would be, people who could pass through the cloud and stop right in its midst and then come out, without the tiniest puff of smoke or bit of soot touching their bodies, disturbing their different pace, their otherworldly beauty, but what mattered was everything that was inside that smog, not what lay outside it: only by immersing oneself in the heart of the cloud, breathing the foggy air of these mornings (winter was already erasing the streets in a formless mist), could one reach the bottom of the truth and perhaps be free of it. My words were all an argument with Claudia; I realized this at once and tore up the article without even having Avandero read it.

Signor Avandero was somebody I hadn't yet fathomed. One Monday morning I came into the office, and what did I find? Avandero with a suntan! Yes, instead of his usual face the color of boiled fish, his skin was something between red and brown, with a few marks of burning on his forehead and his cheeks.

"What's happened to you?" I asked (calling him *tu*, as we had been addressing each other recently).

"I've been skiing. The first snowfall. Perfect, nice and dry. Why don't you come too, next Sunday?"

From that day on, Avandero made me his confidant, sharing with me his passion for skiing. Confidant, I say, because in discussing it with me, he was expressing something more than a passion for a technical skill, a geometrical precision of movements, a functional equipment, a landscape reduced to a pure white page; he, the impeccable and obsequious employee, put into his words a secret protest against his work, a polemical attitude he revealed in little chuckles, as if of superiority, and in little malicious hints: "Ah, yes, that's *purification*, all right! I leave the smog to the rest of you...." Then he promptly corrected himself, saying: "I'm joking, of course. ..." But I had realized that he, apparently so loyal, was another one who didn't believe in the Institute or the ideas of Commendatore Cordà.

One Saturday afternoon I ran into him, Avandero, all decked out for skiing, with a vizored cap like a blackbird's beak, heading for a large bus already assailed by a crowd of men and women skiers. He greeted me, with his smug little manner: "Are you staying in the city?"

"Yes, I am. What's the use of going away? Tomorrow night you'll already be back in the soup again."

He frowned, beneath his blackbird's vizor. "What's the city for, then, except to get out of on Saturday and Sunday?" And he hurried to the bus, because he wanted to suggest a new way of arranging the skis on the top.

For Avandero, as for hundreds and thousands of other people who slaved all week at gray jobs just to be able to run off on Sunday, the city was a lost world, a mill grinding out the means to escape it for those few hours and then return from country excursions, from trout fishing, and then from the sea, and from the mountains in summer, from the snapshots. The story of his life – which, as I saw him regularly, I began to reconstruct year by year – was the story of his means of transportation: first a motorbike, then a scooter, then a proper motorcycle, now his cheap car, and the years of the future were already designated by visions of cars more and more spacious, faster and faster.

The new number of *Purification* should already have gone to press, but Commendatore Cordà hadn't yet seen the proofs. I was expecting him that day at the IPUAIC, but he didn't show up, and it was almost evening when he telephoned for me to come to him at his office at the Wafd, to bring him the proofs there because he couldn't get away. In fact, he would send his car and driver to pick me up.

The Wafd was a factory of which Cordà was managing director. The huge automobile, with me huddled in one corner, my hands and the folder of proofs on my knees, carried me through unfamiliar outskirts, drove along a blind

wall, entered, saluted by watchmen, through a broad gate-
way, and deposited me at the foot of the stairway to the
directors' offices.

Commendatore Cordà was at his desk, surrounded by a
group of executives, examining certain accounts or production plans spread out on enormous sheets of paper, which
spilled over the sides of the desk. "Just one minute, please,"
he said to me, "I'll be right with you."

I looked beyond his shoulder: the wall behind him was
a single pane of glass, a very wide window that domi-
nated the whole expanse of the plant. In the foggy evening
only a few shadows emerged; in the foreground there was
the outline of a chain hoist which carried up huge buckets
of – I believe – iron tailings. You could see the row of
metal receptacles rise in a series of jerks, with a slight
swaying that seemed to alter a bit the outline of the pile
of mineral, and I thought I saw a thick cloud rise from it
into the air and settle on the glass of the Commendatore's
office.

At that moment he gave orders for the lights to be turned
on; suddenly against the outside darkness the glass seemed
covered by a tiny frosting, surely composed of iron particles, glistening like the stardust of a galaxy. The pattern of
shadows outside was broken up; the lines of the smoke-
stacks in the distance became more distinct, each crowned
by a red puff, and over these flames, in contrast, the black,
inky streak was accentuated as it invaded the whole sky
and you could see incandescent specks rise and whirl
within it.

Cordà was now examining with me the *Purification*
proofs and, immediately entering the different field of
enthusiasms, receiving the mental stimulation of his

position as President of the IPUAIC, he discussed the articles in our bulletin with me and with the Wafd executives. And though I had so often, in the offices of the Institute, given free rein to my natural dependent's antagonism, mentally declaring myself on the side of the smog, the smog's secret agent who had infiltrated the enemy's headquarters, I now realized how senseless my game was, because Cordà himself was the smog's master; it was he who blew it out constantly over the city, and the IPUAIC was a creature of the smog, born of the need to give those working to produce the smog some hope of a life that was not all smog, and yet, at the same time, to celebrate its power.

Cordà, pleased with the issue, insisted on taking me home in the car. It was a night of thick fog. The driver proceeded slowly, because beyond the faint headlights you couldn't see a thing. The President, carried away by one of his bursts of general optimism, was outlining the plans of the city of the future, with garden districts, factories surrounded by flower beds and pools of clear water, installations of rockets that would sweep the sky clear of the smoke from the stacks. And he pointed into the void outside, beyond the windows, as if the things he was imagining were already there; I listened to him, perhaps frightened or perhaps in admiration, I couldn't say, discovering how the clever captain of industry coexisted in him with the visionary, and how each needed the other.

At a certain point I thought I recognized my neighborhood. "Stop here, please. This is where I get out," I said to the driver. I thanked Cordà, said good night, and got out of the car. When it had driven off, I realized I had been mistaken.

I was in an unfamiliar district, and I could see nothing of my surroundings.

At the restaurant I went on having my meals alone, sheltered behind my newspaper. And I noticed that there was another customer who behaved as I did. Sometimes, when no other places were free, we ended up at the same table, facing each other with our unfolded papers. We read different ones: mine was the newspaper everybody read, the most important in the city; surely I had no reason to attract attention, to look different from the others, by reading a different paper, or to seem (if I had read the paper of the stranger at my table) a man with strong political ideas. I had always given political opinions and parties a wide berth, but there, at the restaurant table, on certain evenings, when I put the newspaper down, my fellow diner said: "May I?" motioning to it, and offering me his own: "If you'd like to have a look at this one ..."

And so I glanced at his paper, which was, you might say, the reverse of mine, not only because it supported opposing ideas, but because it dealt with things that didn't even exist for the other paper: workers who had been discharged, mechanics whose hands had been caught in their machinery (it also published the photographs of these men), charts with the figures of welfare payments, and so on. But above all, the more my paper tried to be witty in the writing of its articles and to attract the reader with amusing minor events, for example the divorce cases of pretty girls, the more this other paper used expressions that were always the same, repetitious, drab, with headlines that emphasized the negative side of things. Even the printing of the paper was drab, cramped, monotonous. And I found myself thinking: "Why, I like it."

I tried to explain this impression to my casual companion, naturally taking care not to comment on individual news items or opinions (he had already begun by asking me what I thought of a certain report from Asia) and trying at the same time to play down the negative aspect of my view, because he seemed to me the sort of man who doesn't accept criticisms of his position and I had no intention of launching an argument.

Instead, he seemed to be following his own train of thought, where my opinion of his paper must have been superfluous or out of place. "You know," he said, "this paper still isn't the way it should be? It isn't the paper I'd like it to be."

He was a short but well-proportioned young man, dark, with carefully combed curly hair, his face still a boy's, pale, pink-cheeked, with regular, refined features, long black lashes, a reserved, almost haughty manner. He dressed with rather fastidious care. "There's still too much vagueness, a lack of precision," he went on, "especially in what concerns *our* affairs. The paper still resembles the others too much. The kind of paper I mean should be mostly written by its readers. It should try to give scientifically exact information about everything that goes on in the world of production."

"You're a technical expert in some factory, are you?" I asked.

"Skilled worker."

We introduced ourselves. His name was Omar Basaluzzi. When he learned that I worked for the IPUAIC, he became very much interested and asked me for some data to use in a report he was preparing. I suggested some publications to him (things in the public domain, as a matter of fact; I wasn't giving away any office secrets, as I remarked to him, just in case, with a little smile). He took out a notebook and methodically wrote down the information, as if he were compiling a bibliography.

"I'm interested in statistical studies," he said, "a field where our organization is far behind." We put on our over-coats, ready to leave. Basaluzzi had a rather sporty coat, elegantly cut, and a little cap of rainproof canvas. "We're very far behind," he went on, "whereas, the way I look at it, it's a fundamental field. ..."

"Does your work leave you time for these studies?" I asked him.

"I'll tell you," he said (he always answered with some hauteur, in a slightly smug, ex-cathedra manner), "it's all a question of method. I work eight hours a day in the factory, and then there's hardly an evening when I don't have some meeting to go to, even on Sunday. But you have to know how to organize your work. I've formed some study groups, among the young people in our plant. ..."

"Are there many ... like yourself?"

"Very few. Fewer all the time. One by one, they're getting rid of us. One fine day you'll see here" – and he pointed to the newspaper – "my own picture, with the headline: 'Another worker discharged in reprisal.' "

We were walking in the cold of the night; I was huddled in my coat, the collar turned up; Omar Basaluzzi proceeded calmly, talking, his head erect, a little cloud of steam emerging from his finely drawn lips, and every now and then he took his hand from his pocket to underline a point in his talk, and then he stopped, as if he couldn't go ahead until that point had been clearly established.

I was no longer following what he said; I was thinking that a man like Omar Basaluzzi didn't try to evade all the smoky gray around us, but to transform it into a moral value, an inner criterion.

"The smog ..." I said.

"Smog? Yes, I know Cordà wants to play the modern industrialist.... Purify the atmosphere.... Go tell that to his workers! He surely won't be the one to purify it.... . It's a question of social structure.... If we manage to change that, we will also solve the smog problem. We, not they."

He invited me to go with him to a meeting of union representatives from the different plants of the city. I sat at the back of a smoky room. Omar Basaluzzi took a seat at the table on the dais with some other men, all older than he. The room wasn't heated; we kept our hats and coats on.

One by one, the men who were to speak stood up and took their place beside the table; all of them addressed the public in the same way: anonymous, unadorned, with formulas for beginning their speech and for linking the arguments which must have been part of some rule because they all used them. From certain murmurs in the audience I realized a polemical statement had been made, but these were veiled polemics, which always began by approving what had been said before. Many of those who spoke seemed to have it in for Omar Basaluzzi; the young man, seated a bit sideways at the table, had taken a tooled-leather tobacco pouch from his pocket and a stubby English pipe which he filled with slow movements of his small hands. He smoked in cautious puffs, his eyes slightly closed, one elbow on the table, his cheek resting in his hand.

The hall had filled with smoke. One man suggested opening a little, high window for a moment. A cold gust changed the air but soon the fog began coming in from outside, and you could hardly see the opposite end of the room. From my seat I examined that crowd of backs, motionless in the cold, some with upturned collars, and the row of bundled-up forms at the table, with one man on his feet talking, as bulky as a bear, all surrounded, impregnated now by that fog, even their words, their stubbornness.

Claudia came back in February. We went to have lunch in an expensive restaurant on the river, at the end of the park. Beyond the windows we looked at the shore and the trees that, with the color of the air, composed a picture of ancient elegance.

We couldn't understand each other. We argued on the subject of beauty. "People have lost the sense of beauty," Claudia said.

"Beauty has to be constantly invented," I said.

"Beauty is always beauty; it's eternal."

"Beauty is born always from some conflict."

"What about the Greeks?"

"Well, what about them?"

"Beauty is civilization!"

"And so ..."

"Therefore ..."

We could have gone on like this all day and all night.

"This park, this river ..."

("This park, this river," I thought, "can only be marginal, a consolation to us for the rest; ancient beauty is powerless against new ugliness.")

"This eel ..."

In the center of the restaurant there was a glass tank, an aquarium, and some huge eels were swimming inside it.

"Look!"

Some customers were approaching, important people, a family of well-to-do gourmets: mother, father, grown daughter, adolescent son. With them was the *maître d'hôtel*, an enormous, corpulent man in frock coat, stiff white shirt; he was grasping the handle of a little net, the kind children use for catching butterflies. The family, serious, intent, looked at the eels; at a certain point the mother raised her hand and pointed out an eel. The *maître d'hôtel* dipped the net into the aquarium, with a rapid swoop he caught the animal and drew it out of the water. The eel writhed and struggled in the net. The *maître d'hôtel* went off toward the kitchen, holding the net with the gasping eel straight out in front of him like a lance. The family watched him go off, then they sat down at the table, to wait until the eel came back, cooked.

"Cruelty ..."

"Civilization ..."

"Everything is cruel ..."

Instead of having them call a taxi, we left on foot. The lawns, the tree trunks, were swathed in that veil which rose fiom the river, dense, damp, here still a natural phenomenon. Claudia walked protected by her fur coat, its wide collar, her muff, her fur hat. We were the two shadowy lovers who form a part of the picture.

"Beauty ..."

"Your beauty ..."

"What good is it? As far as that goes ..."

I said: "Beauty is eternal."

"Ah, now you're saying what I said before, eh?"

"No, the opposite."

"It's impossible to discuss anything with you," she said.

She moved off as if she wanted to go on by herself, along the path. A layer of fog was flowing just over the earth: the fur-covered silhouette proceeded as if it weren't touching the ground.

I saw Claudia back to her hotel that evening, and we found the lobby full of gentlemen in dinner jackets and ladies in long, low-cut dresses. It was carnival time, and a charity ball was being held in the hotel ballroom.

"How marvelous! Will you take me? I'll just run and put on an evening dress!"

I'm not the sort who goes to balls and I felt ill at ease.

"But we don't have an invitation ... and I'm wearing a brown suit ..."

"I never need an invitation ... and you're my escort."

She ran up to change. I didn't know where to turn. The place was full of girls wearing their first evening dress, powdering their faces before going into the ballroom, exchanging excited whispers. I stood in a corner, trying to imagine I was a shop clerk who had come there to deliver a package.

The elevator door opened. Claudia stepped out, in a sweeping skirt, pearls on a pink bodice, a little diamond-studded mask. I couldn't play the role of clerk any more. I went over to her.

We went in. All eyes were on her. I found a mask to put on, a kind of clown's face with a long nose. We started danc-ing. When Claudia twirled around, the other couples stepped back to watch her; as I'm a very bad dancer, I wanted to stay in the midst of the crowd, so there was a kind of hide-and-seek. Claudia complained that I wasn't the least bit jolly, that I didn't know how to enjoy myself.

At the end of one dance, as we were going back to our table, we passed a group of ladies and gentlemen, standing on the dance floor. "Oh!" There I was, face to face with Commendatore Cordà. He was in full dress, with a little orange paper hat on his head. I had to stop and say hello to him. "Why, it *is* you, then! I thought so, but I wasn't sure," he said, but he was looking at Claudia, and I realized he meant he would never have expected to see me with a woman like her, I looking the same as usual, in the suit I wore to the office.

I had to make the introductions; Cordà kissed Claudia's hand, introduced her to the other older men who were with him, and Claudia, absent as always and superior, paid no attention to the names (as I was saying to myself: "My God! Is that who he is?" because they were all big shots in industry). Then Corda introduced me: "And this is the managing editor of our periodical, you know, *Purification,* the paper I put out. ..." I realized they were all a bit intimidated by Claudia, and they were talking nonsense. So then I felt less timid myself.

I also realized something else was about to happen, namely that Cordà could hardly wait to ask Claudia to dance. I said: "Well then, we'll see you later.... " I waved expansive good-bys and led Claudia back to the dance floor, as she said: "Wait a minute, you don't know how to dance to this, can't you hear the music?"

All I could hear or feel was that, in some way not yet clear even to those men, I had spoiled their evening when I appeared at Claudia's side, and this was the only satisfaction I could derive from the ball. "*Cha cha cha ...*" I sang softly, pretending to dance with steps I didn't know how to make, holding Claudia only lightly by the hand so that she could move on her own.

It was carnival time; why shouldn't I have some fun? The little toy trumpets blared, fluttering their long fringes, handfuls of confetti pattered like crumbling mortar on the backs of the tailcoats and on the bare shoulders of the women, it slipped inside the low-cut gowns and the men's collars; and from chandelier to floor, where it collected in limp piles pushed about by the shuffling of the dancers, streamers unrolled like strips of bare fibers or like wires left hanging among collapsed walls in a general destruction.

"You can accept the ugly world the way it is, because you know you have to destroy it," I said to Omar Basaluzzi. I spoke partly to provoke him, otherwise it was no fun.

"Just a moment," Omar said, setting down the little cup of coffee he had been raising to his lips. "We never say: It has to get worse before it can get better. We want to improve things.... No reformism, and no extremism. We ..."

I was following my train of thought: he, his. Ever since that time in the park with Claudia, I had been looking for a new image of the world which would give a meaning to our grayness, which would compensate for all the beauty that we were losing, or would save it.... "A new face for the world."

The worker unzipped a black leather briefcase and took out an illustrated weekly. "You see?" There was a series of photographs. An Asiatic race, with fur caps and boots, blissfully going to fish in a river. In another photograph there was that same race, going to school; a teacher was pointing out, on a sheet, the letters of an incomprehensible alphabet. Another illustration showed a feast day and they all wore dragon heads, and in the middle, among the dragons, a tractor was advancing with a man's portrait over it. At the end there were two men, still in fur caps, operating a power lathe.

"You see? This is it," he said, "the other face of the world."

I looked at Basaluzzi. "You people don't wear fur caps, you don't fish for sturgeon, you don't play with dragons."

"What of it?"

"So your group doesn't resemble those people in any way, except for this ..." and I pointed to the lathe, "which you already have."

"No, no, it'll be the same here as there, because it's man's conscience that will change, for us as it has for them, we'll be new inside ourselves, even before we are new outside ..." Basaluzzi said, and he went on leafing through the magazine. On another page there were photographs of blast furnaces and of workers with goggles over their eyes and fierce expressions. "Oh, there'll be problems then, too, you mustn't think that overnight ..." he said. "For quite a while it'll be hard: production ... But a big step forward will have been made... . Certain things won't happen, as they do now ..." and he started speaking of the same things he always talked about, the problems that concerned him, day in and day out.

I realized that, for him, whether or not that new dawn ever came mattered less than one might think, because what counted for him was the line of his life, which was not to change.

"There'll always be trouble, of course. ... It won't be an earthly paradise.... . We're not saints, after all. ..."

Would the saints change their lives, if they knew heaven didn't exist?

"They fired me last week," Omar Basaluzzi said.

"And now what?"

"I'm doing union work. Maybe next autumn one of the bosses will retire."

He was on his way to the Wafd, where there had been a violent demonstration that morning. "Want to come with me?

"Eh! That's the one place I mustn't be seen. You understand why."

"I mustn't be seen there either. I'd get the comrades in trouble. We'll watch from a café nearby."

I went with him. Through the windows of a little café we saw the workers coming off their shift walk through the gates, wheeling their bicycles, or crowding toward the streetcars, their faces already prepared for sleep. Some of them, obviously forewarned, came into the café and went at once to Omar; and so a little group was formed, which went off to one side to talk.

I understood nothing of their grievances and I was trying to discover what was different between the faces of the countless men who swarmed through the gates surely thinking of nothing but their family and Sunday, and these others who had stopped with Omar, the stubborn ones, the tough ones. And I could find no mark that distinguished them: the same aged or prematurely old faces, product of the same life: the difference was inside.

And then I studied the faces and the words of the latter group, to see if I could distinguish the ones whose actions were based on the thought "The day will come ..." and those for whom, as for Omar, whether the day really came or not didn't matter. And I saw they couldn't be distinguished, because perhaps they all belonged to the second category, even those few whose impatience or ready speech might make them seem to be in the first category.

And then I didn't know what to look at so I looked at the sky. It was an early spring day and over the houses of the outskirts the sky was luminous, blue, clear; however, if I looked at it carefully, I could see a kind of shadow, a smudge, as if on an old, yellowed snapshot, like the marks you see through a spectroscope. Not even the fine season would cleanse the sky.

Omar Basaluzzi had put on a pair of dark glasses with thick frames and he continued talking in the midst of those men, precise, expert, proud, a bit nasal.

In *Purification* I published a news item I had found in a foreign paper concerning pollution of the air by atomic radiation. It was in small type and Commendatore Cordà didn't notice it in the galleys, but he read it when the paper was printed and he then sent for me.

"My God, I have to keep an eye on every little thing; I ought to have a hundred eyes, not two!" he said. "What came over you? What made you publish that piece? This isn't the sort of thing our Institute should bother with. Not by a long shot! And then, without a word to me! On such a delicate question! Now they'll say we've started printing propaganda!"

I answered with a few words of defense: "Well, sir, since it was a question of air pollution ... I'm sorry, I thought ..."

I had already taken my leave when Cordà called me back. "See here, do you really believe in this danger of radioactivity? I mean, do you really think it's so serious?"

I remembered certain data from a scientific congress, and I repeated the information to him. Cordà listened to me, nodding, but irked.

"Hmph, what awful times we have to live in, my friend!" he blurted out at one point, and he was again the Cordà I knew so well. "It's the risk we have to run. There's no turning back the clock, because big things are at stake, my boy, big things!"

He bowed his head for a few moments. "We, in our field," he went on, "not wanting to overestimate the role we play, of course, still ... we make our contribution, we're equal to the situation."

"That's certain, sir. I'm absolutely convinced of that." We looked at each other, a bit embarrassed, a bit hypocritical. The cloud of smog now seemed to have grown smaller, a tiny little puff, a cirrus, compared to the looming atomic mushroom.

I left Commendatore Cordà after a few more vague, affirmative words, and once again it wasn't clear whether his real battle was fought for or against the cloud.

After that, I avoided any mention of atomic explosions or radioactivity in the headlines, but in each number I tried to slip some information on the subject into the columns devoted to technical news, and even into certain articles; in the midst of the data on the percentages of coal or fuel oil in the urban atmosphere and their physiological consequences, I added analogous data and examples drawn from zones affected by atomic fallout. Neither Cordà nor anyone else mentioned these to me again, but this silence, rather than please me, confirmed my suspicion that absolutely nobody read *Purification*.

I had a file where I kept all the material concerning nuclear radiation, because as I read through the papers with an eye trained to select usable news items and articles, I always found something on that subject and I saved it. A clipping service, too, to which the Institute had subscribed, sent us more and more clippings about atomic bombs, while those about smog grew fewer all the time.

So every day my eye fell upon statistics of terrible diseases, stories about fishermen overtaken in the middle of the ocean by lethal clouds, guinea pigs born with two heads after some experiments with uranium. I raised my eyes to the window. It was late June, but summer hadn't yet begun: the weather was oppressive, the days were smothered in a gloomy haze, during the afternoon hours the city was immersed in a light like the end of the world, and the passers-by seemed shadows photographed on the ground after the body had flown away.

The normal order of the seasons seemed changed, intense cyclones coursed over Europe, the beginning of summer was marked by days heavily charged with electricity, then by weeks of rain, by sudden heat waves and sudden resurgences of March-like cold. The papers denied that these atmospheric disorders could be in any way connected with the effects of the bombs; only a few solitary scientists seemed to sustain this notion (and, for that matter, it was hard to discover if they were trustworthy) and, with them, the anonymous voice of the man in the street, always ready, of course, to give credence to the most disparate ideas.

Even I became irritated when I heard Signorina Margariti talking foolishly about the atomic bomb, warning me to take my umbrella to the office that morning. But to be sure, when I opened the blinds, at the livid sight of the courtyard, which in that false luminosity seemed a network of stripes and spots, I was tempted to draw back, as if a discharge of invisible particles were being released from the sky at that very moment.

This burden of unsaid things transformed them into superstition, influenced the banal talk about the weather, once considered the most harmless subject of conversation. Now people avoided mentioning the weather, or if they had to say it was raining or it had cleared they were filled with a kind of shame, as if some obscure responsibility of ours were being kept quiet. Signor Avandero, who lived through the weekdays in preparation for his Sunday excursion, had assumed a false indifference toward the weather; it seemed totally hypocritical to me, and servile.

I put out a number of *Purification* in which there wasn't one article that didn't speak of radioactivity. Even this time I had no trouble. It wasn't true, however, that nobody read the paper; people read it, all right, but by now they had become inured to such things, and even if you wrote that the end of the human race was at hand nobody paid any attention.

The big weeklies also published reports that should have made you shudder, but people now seemed to believe only in the colored photographs of smiling girls on the cover. One of these weeklies came out with a photograph of Claudia on its cover; she was wearing a bathing suit, and was making a turn on water skis. With four thumbtacks, I pinned it on the wall of my furnished room.

Every morning and every afternoon I continued to go to that neighborhood of quiet avenues where my office was located, and sometimes I recalled the autumn day when I had gone there for the first time, when in everything I saw I had looked for a sign, and nothing had seemed sufficiently gray and squalid to suit the way I felt. Even now my gaze looked only for signs; I had never been able to see anything else. Signs of what? Signs that referred one to the other, into infinity.

At times I happened to encounter a mule-drawn cart: a two-wheeled cart going down an avenue, laden with sacks. Or else I found it waiting outside the door of a building, the mule between the shafts, his head low, and on top of the pile of sacks, a little girl.

Then I realized there wasn't only one of these carts going around that section; there were several of them. I couldn't say just when I began to notice this; you see so many things without paying attention to them; maybe these things you see have an effect on you but you aren't aware of it; and then you begin to connect one thing with the other and suddenly it all takes on meaning. The sight of those carts, without my consciously thinking of them, had a soothing effect on me, because an unusual encounter, as with a rustic cart in the midst of a city that is all automobiles, is enough to remind you that the world is never all one thing.

And so I began to pay attention to them: a little girl with pigtails sat on top of the white mountain of sacks reading a comic book, then a heavy man came from the door of the building with a couple of sacks and put those, too, on the cart, turned the handle of the brake and said "Gee" to the mule, and they went off, the little girl still up there, still reading. And then they stopped at another doorway; the man unloaded some sacks from the cart and carried them inside.

Farther ahead, in the opposite lane of the avenue, there was another cart, with an old man at the reins, and a woman who went up and down the front steps of the buildings with huge bundles on her head.

I began to notice that on the days when I saw the carts I was happier, more confident, and those days were always Mondays: so I learned that Monday is the day when the laundrymen go through the city with their carts, bringing back the clean laundry and taking away the dirty.

Now that I knew about it, the sight of the laundry carts no longer escaped me: all I had to do was see one as I went to work in the morning, and I would say to myself: "Why, of course, it's Monday!" and immediately afterward another would appear, following a different route, with a dog barking after it, and then another going off in the distance so I could see only its load from behind, the sacks with yellow and white stripes.

Coming home from the office I took the streetcar, through other streets, noisier and more crowded, but even there the traffic had to stop at a crossing as the long-spoked wheels of a laundry cart rolled by. I glanced into a side street, and by the sidewalk I saw the mule with bundles of laundry that a man in a straw hat was unloading.

That day I took a much longer route than usual to come home, still encountering the laundrymen. I realized that for the city this was a kind of feast day, because everyone was happy to give away the clothes soiled by the smoke and to wear again the whiteness of fresh linen, even if only for a short while.

The following Monday I decided to follow the laundry carts to see where they went afterward, once they had made their deliveries and picked up their work. I walked for a while at random, because I first followed one cart, then another, until at a certain point I realized that they were all finally going in the same direction, there were certain streets where they all passed eventually, and when they met or lined up one after the other they hailed one another with calm greetings and jokes. And so I went on following them, losing them, over a long stretch, until I was tired, but before leaving them I had learned that there was a village of laundries: the men were all from an outlying town called Barca Bertulla.

One day, in the afternoon, I went there. I crossed a bridge over a river, and was virtually in the country, the highways were flanked still by a row of houses, but immediately behind them all was green. You couldn't see the laundries. Shady pergolas surrounded the wineshops, along the canals interrupted by locks. I went on, casting my gaze beyond each farmyard gate and along each path. Little by little I left the built-up area behind, and now rows of poplars grew along the road, marking the banks of the frequent canals. And there in the background, beyond the poplars, I saw a meadow of white sails: laundry hung out to dry.

I turned into a path. Broad meadows were crisscrossed with lines, at eye level, and on these lines, piece after piece, was hung the laundry of the whole city, the linen still wet and shapeless, every item the same, with wrinkles the cloth made in the sun, and in each meadow this whiteness of long lines of washing was repeated. (Other meadows were bare, but they too were crossed by parallel lines, like vineyards without vines.)

I wandered through the fields white with hanging laundry, and I suddenly wheeled about at a burst of laughter. On the shore of a canal, above one of the locks, there was the ledge of a pool, and over it, high above me, their sleeves rolled up, in dresses of every color, were the red faces of the washerwomen, who laughed and chattered; the young ones' breasts bobbing up and down inside their blouses, and the old, fat women with kerchiefs on their heads; and they moved their round arms back and forth in the suds and they wrung out the twisted sheets with an angular movement of the elbows. In their midst the men in straw hats were unloading baskets in separate piles, or were also working with the square coarse soap, or else beating the wet cloth with wooden paddles.

By now I had seen, and I had nothing to say, no reason to pry. I turned back. At the edge of the highway a little grass was growing and I was careful to walk there, so as not to get my shoes dusty and to keep clear of the passing trucks. Between the fields, the hedgerows, and the poplars, I continued to follow with my eyes the washing pools, the signs on certain low buildings: STEAM LAUNDRY, LAUNDRY CO-OPERATIVE OF BARCA BERTULLA, the fields where the women passed with baskets as if harvesting grapes, and picked the dry linen from the lines, and the countryside in the sun gave forth its greenness amid that white, and the water flowed away swollen with bluish bubbles, It wasn't much, but for me, seeking only images to retain in my eyes, perhaps it was enough.

(1958)

A PLUNGE INTO REAL ESTATE

Translated by D. S. Carne-Ross

1

He raised his eyes from the book (he always read in the train) and rediscovered the landscape piece by piece. The wall, the fig tree, the quarry with its chain of buckets, the reeds, the cliffs – he had seen them all his life but only now, because he was returning did he really become aware of them. Every time he came home to the Riviera, Quinto renewed contact in this fashion. But he had been away so much, come back so often, the thing had been going on for years; what was the fun of it when he already knew the scene by heart? All the same, he still hoped for some chance discovery as he sat there with one eye on the book and the other on the landscape. But now he was simply confirming familiar impressions.

Yet every time there was something that checked the pleasure he took in this exercise and made him look down at the page on his lap, something irritating that he couldn't quite pin down. It was the houses, that was it, all these new houses that were going up, apartment buildings six or eight stories high, their massive white flanks standing out like barriers propping the crumbling slope of the coast and putting out as many windows and balconies as they could toward the sea. The Riviera was gripped by a fever of cement. An apartment building here, the identical window boxes of geraniums on every balcony; there a building that had just gone up, the windows still marked with white, waiting for the Milanese families who wanted a place by the sea; a little farther on, some scaffolding, and below, the cement mixer in action and a sign advertising the local real estate office.

In the little towns on the terraced hillsides the new buildings played piggyback with one another, while in their midst the owners of the old houses added another story and craned their necks to see out. The town where Quinto lived had once been surrounded by shady gardens of eucalyptus trees and magnolias, where retired English colonels and elderly spinsters leaned over the hedges and exchanged Tauchnitz editions and watering cans. Now the bulldozers were churning up the soil with its rotting leaves and its gravel from the garden paths, picks were demolishing the two-story residences, the ax was at the broad-leaved palm trees, which fell with a papery scrunch from the sky so soon to be filled by the desirable, three-room, all-convenience, sunny homes of tomorrow.

When he came home, Quinto had once been able to look out over the roofs of the new town and the poorer quarters down by the sea front and the harbor. In between were the crowded houses of the old part of town, with their moldy, lichenous walls, lying between the hill to the west, where the olive groves clustered thickly above the gardens, and to the east, the green swarm of villas and hotels stretching beneath the bare flank of the carnation fields, glinting with green-houses as far as the Point. But all he could see these days was a geometrical arrangement of parallelepipeds and poly-hedrons ranked one above the other, corners and sides of houses, clustering roofs and windows and blank walls pierced only by the ground-glass bathroom windows, one above the other.

The first thing that always happened was that his mother took him up to the roof terrace. Left to himself, with that idle, vague nostalgia of his which faded almost as soon as it came, he would have gone away again without troubling to go up there. "I'll show you what's new since you were last here," she said, and started pointing out the new buildings. "The Sampieris are adding another floor, that's a new house built by some people from Novara, and the nuns, even the nuns ... You remember the garden with the bamboos that we used to be able to see down there? Just look at all the digging that's going on there now; heaven knows how many floors they're going to have with foundations like that! And the giant Chilean pine in the garden of the villa Van Moen – the finest on the Riviera it used to be – well, the Baudino firm has bought up the whole area and the tree's been chopped down for firewood. What a shame it is; the author-ities ought to have stopped them. Of course, they could hardly have transplanted it; goodness knows how deep the roots went. Now come over to this side, dear. They couldn't take away any more of our view to the west than they've done already, but just look at that roof that's popped up over there. I tell you we have to wait half an hour longer every morning for the sun!"

Quinto would say, "Oh, good Lord, my dear, you don't say!" and things of that sort, mere grunts and chuckles. He couldn't manage anything more. Sometimes he said. "What can one do though?" and sometimes too he felt a positive satisfaction at a particular piece of damage that was quite beyond repair, some residue of a boyish desire to *épater* stirring in him, or perhaps it was the shrugging assumption of wisdom on the part of the man who knows there's no use fighting against History. All the same, Quinto was offended by the spectacle of this landscape, *his* landscape, being overwhelmed by cement before he had ever really possessed it. Basically, though, he was historically minded, anti-nostalgia. He'd seen a bit of the world: hell, what did he care? He was quite prepared to create far more havoc himself, and in the field of his own life. He almost hoped that, as they stood there on the terrace, his mother would minister to these perverse inclinations, and he found himself trying to catch in the resigned denunciations that she accumulated from one visit to the next the note of some feeling more violent than regret for a treasured landscape that was dying. But the reasonable tone of her complaints kept clear of that acrimonious slope that waits for all complaints too long repeated and leads, in its lower reaches, to mania. The disease is revealed by little tricks of speech, the habit of calling the builders "they", for example, as though they were in league to destroy one; it shows in expressions like "Just look what they've done to us now!" of things that damage a great many other people besides oneself. But no, his mother's serene melancholy provided no foothold for that contradictory demon of his, and the longing to stop being merely passive and to take the offensive grew all the sharper in him. The thing stared him in the face. The district, *his* district, that amputated part of himself, had taken on a new life, abnormal and graceless perhaps, but *for that very reason* (such are the contradictions that operate in minds brought up on literature) it was more alive than ever before. And he was excluded. Bound to the place by no more than a thread of nostalgia and by the devaluation of a semi-urban area with no further claim to a view, he was only hurt by what was happening.

These reflections had prompted the remark "If everybody's building, why don't we build too?" He had thrown this out one day in conversation with Ampelio. The Signora had overheard it, and putting her hands to her head, had cried, "Oh, no, my poor garden!" His remark and her response had set in train an already lengthy series of discussions, calculations, inquiries, negotiations. With the result that Quinto was now coming home to try his hand at real estate.

2

But as he thought the matter over by himself in the train, his mother's words came back to him and he felt a sense of discomfort, even remorse. She was lamenting the loss of a part of herself, something she was losing that she knew she would not get back again. It was the bitterness older people feel when every general injury that touches them in some way seems a blow against their own individual life, which has no longer any means of redress; because when any one of life's good things is taken away, it is life itself that is being taken. Quinto recognized in the resentful way he had reacted the cruelty of the *coûte que coûte* school of optimism, the refusal of the young to admit any sort of defeat since they believe that life will give back at least as much as it took away, so that if today it destroys some dear spot, the tone of a particular scene, something charming and beautiful but hardly to be defended, or remembered, on the grounds of its "artistic" value – well, tomorrow it will undoubtedly give you something else in exchange, something that will be destroyed in its turn but that can be enjoyed meanwhile. And yet he felt how mistaken the cruelty of youth is, how wasteful, and how much it bodes the first unseasonable taste of age; and at the same time how necessary it is! He understood it all, God help him! He even understood that basically his mother was perfectly right. Without anything of this sort in mind, she was quite understandably upset. She simply told him, each time he came home, about the way everyone was adding to their houses.

The result was that Quinto hadn't dared tell her what he had in mind. It was this project of his that was now bringing him home. It was all his own idea; he hadn't even discussed it with Ampelio, and indeed only very recently had it come to figure in his mind no longer as a possibility, something that might or might not be done, but as an urgent decision. The only thing that had been agreed – with his mother's resigned consent – was to sell a part of the garden. They had reached the point where they had to sell something.

It was the period when taxation was pressing hard. Two particularly savage taxes had burst at almost the same time, after his father's death. (Signor Anfossi, grumbling and almost too scrupulous, had always looked after these things.) One was the estate surtax, a graceless, vindictive measure passed during the immediate postwar period, which bore particularly hard on the middle class. It had been delayed by the laborious procedures of bureaucracy only to explode now, just when one least expected it. The other was the inheritance tax; it looked reasonable enough from the outside, but once you found yourself face to face with it, you couldn't believe it was true.

Quinto was prey to a variety of emotions. He was worried by the fact that he couldn't raise even a tenth of the money needed to pay the two taxes. And stirring inside him was an ancestral hatred of the tax collector inherited from generations of frugal Ligurian farmers who disapproved of government as such, combined with the irrepressible fury of the decent citizen at being singled out for fiscal massacre – "while the rich, as everyone knows, get away scot free." Added to this was the suspicion that somewhere in those maddening tangles of figures was an obvious trap, clearly visible to everyone except himself. All these sentiments, which the tax collector's pallid communication arouses in even the most innocent breast, were crossed by the feeling that he was an incompetent landowner, unable to make the best use of his property, the kind of person who, in a period when capital was in continual, speculative use, a period of swindling and paper credit, sits back with his hands in his pockets and lets the value of his property decrease. It came to him that this unreasonable malice on the part of the nation against a family without means was the beautifully logical expression of what in official language is known as "the legislator's intent": the intent to strike at un-productive capital. And as for the man without capital, or without the will to exploit it, why, God help him.

Whenever one made inquiries at the tax office or the bank or at one's lawyer's, the answer was always the same: Sell.

Everyone is selling now – they've got to, to pay their taxes. ("Everyone" obviously meant "everyone like you," that is, property owners whose property consisted of a few unproductive olive trees or some houses with fixed rents.) Quinto's thoughts had at once turned to the piece of land known jocularly at home as "the flowerpottery."

The flowerpottery, which had formerly served for raising vegetables, was a small plot of land at the bottom of the garden. On it stood a shed, formerly a chicken coop, now full of flowerpots, tools, potting soil, and insecticide. Quinto regarded it as a marginal addition to the property; he was bound to it by no childhood memories, since everything he remembered about it had gone: the coop where he used to watch the lazy-stepping hens, lettuce seedlings fretted by snails, the tomatoes craning up their slender sticks, the zucchini snaking along under cover of their leaves, which spread out over the ground. In the middle, queening it over the rest of the kitchen garden, there used to be two succulent plum trees, which, after oozing gum and darkening with ants through a prolonged senescence, finally dried up and died. The need for a kitchen garden had gradually lessened, what with the children away at school and then at work, the older generation dropping away one by one, and finally Signor Anfossi, tireless thunderer to the last – and when *he* went, the house really seemed empty. So Signora Anfossi had moved in with her flowers and turned it into a kind of clearinghouse, a nursery, using the ex-hen house for storing flowerpots. The soil had proved to be moist and exposed to the sun, hence particularly suited to certain rare plants, which, having been granted temporary accommodation there, proceeded to make themselves at home. The spot had acquired a mixed air, devoted at once to horticulture, science, and elegance. It was there rather than among the gravel paths and flower beds of the garden proper that Signora Anfossi liked to pass her time.

"We'll sell it," Quinto had said. "It's a good building site."

"Oh, is it?" his mother had replied. "And where, pray, am I going to move my calceolaria? There isn't another place in the garden. And what about the pittosporums, which are *so* high already? Not to mention the espalier of plumbago, which will be ruined." She paused as though an unexpected fear had struck her. "And what happens if once we've sold the land, they decide to *build* there?" As she spoke, there rose up before her eyes the gray cement wall crashing down onto the green spaces of her garden and transforming it into a bleak back yard.

"Of course they'll build there." Quinto felt irritated. "That's why we're going to sell it. Why would anyone want to buy the land if they couldn't build on it?"

But in fact it wasn't easy to find a purchaser. The builders were looking for new sites near the sea, with a view. The district was already overbuilt, and it was scarcely to be expected that people from Milan or Biella who were looking for a neat little apartment would shut themselves up in a hole like that! Moreover, the market was showing signs of saturation and a slight downward curve in the demand for houses was expected. Two or three firms that had gone ahead a bit too fast found themselves neck deep in unpaid debts and went bankrupt. The price originally fixed for the site had to be lowered. Months went by, a year, and still no buyer appeared. The bank was no longer willing to extend further credit required by the unpaid taxes, and threatened to foreclose. Then Caisotti showed up.

3

Caisotti came with the man from the Superga agency. Neither Quinto nor Ampelio were at home, so Signora Anfossi had to show them around the site. "He's quite uncouth," she told Quinto afterward. "He can scarcely speak Italian. But that chatterbox from the agency was there and he talked enough for two."

While Caisotti was busy measuring the borders of the site, the sleeve of his jacket caught on a wild-rose bush. "I don't want you to think I start by taking away what doesn't belong to me," he said, laughing, as she patiently freed his coat from the thorns.

"That would be too bad, wouldn't it?" she said. Then she notcied that there was blood on his face. "Oh, dear, you've scratched yourself."

Caisotti shrugged, and putting his finger in his mouth, rubbed his cheek with spit. There were traces of blood at the corners of his mouth. "Come up to the house and let me put something on it," the Signora said. Gradually the note of severity she had given to the interview, the figure below which she could in no circumstance go ("Anyway I shall have to speak to my sons. I'll let you know definitely one way or the other"), the strict clauses about the maximum height of the building, the number of windows, and so on – all this began to give way before Caisotti's easygoing way of putting things on a conciliatory basis, of making everything a matter of more-or-less, and what's-the-rush?

Meanwhile the fellow from the agency talked ceaselessly. He was a big man in a white suit; he came from Tuscany. "As I was saying, Signora, it's a real pleasure to put through a deal with a friend like Caisotti. Signor Caisotti – believe me, I've known him for years – is a person one can always do business with. He'll meet your terms, you'll see, Signora. You'll find yourself thoroughly satisfied, I promise. ..."

I'd be more satisfied still, she said to herself, returning to her constant preoccupation, if we didn't have to sell. But what else was there to do?

Caisotti was a countryman who had gone into the building business after the war. He always had three or four jobs under way; he would buy some land, put up as large a building as the local regulations permitted, and stuff it with as many tiny apartments as it would hold. He would sell the apartments while the building was still under construction and then, with a tidy profit to show, at once buy some more land and repeat the process. Quinto turned up promptly in response to his mother's letter, in order to see the deal through. Ampelio sent a telegram saying that he was busy with certain experiments which made it impossible for him to come, but urged that they should not go below a certain figure. Caisotti didn't try to go below this figure, and Quinto found him strangely easy to deal with. He commented on this afterward to his mother.

"Yes, but what an untrustworthy face the man has! And those tiny little eyes!"

"Of course he's untrustworthy," Quinto said. "So what? Why should he look honest? An honest face on him – that would really be dishonest!" He broke off, realizing that he was speaking more warmly than he had intended, as though Caisotti's appearance was what principally mattered.

"Well, I wouldn't trust him," she said.

"Of course not," Quinto agreed, "neither would I. And he doesn't trust us. Didn't you notice the way he hesitated at

everything we said and how slow he was in replying?" He
liked this relation of spontaneous, mutual distrust between
Caisotti and themselves and he was sorry that his mother
didn't appreciate it too. This was the proper relation between
people who look after their own interests, between men of
the world.

Quinto was at home when Caisotti paid a second visit to
conclude the negotiations. He came into the room as though
he were in church, his lips curled back. He was wearing a
khaki cap and took his time about removing it. He was a
man of about forty-five, fairly short but solidly built and
broadshouldered. He had on an American-style checked
shirt, which followed the curve of his belly. He spoke slowly,
with that plaintive, questioning whine peculiar to the Ligurian hill country.

"As I said to the Signora, sir, if you'll take a step to meet
me, I'll take one to meet you. You know my offer."

"Your figure's too low," Quinto said, though he had
already decided to accept it.

The man's big, fleshy face seemed made of a stuff too
formless to retain its lineaments or expressions; they at once
tended to subside as though engulfed not so much by the
deep folds at the corners of his eyes and mouth, but by the
sandy, porous texture of his whole face. He was snub-nosed
and there was an unusual distance between his nostrils and
his upper lip, which made him look either stupid or brutal,
depending on whether his mouth was open or shut. His lips
were thick and fleshy in the middle, but they disappeared
altogether at the corners, as though his mouth ended in two
deep slits in either cheek. This gave him rather the look of a
shark, a suggestion heightened by the slightly receding chin
above the broad throat. But the oddest thing was the way

his eyebrows moved. When Quinto said dryly, "Your fig-ure's too low," it seemed as though Caisotti were trying to draw his scanty eyebrows together in the middle of his fore-head, but all he succeeded in doing was to raise the skin above the bridge of his nose by a fraction of an inch. The skin corrugated tentatively until it resembled a navel, and this upward thrust communicated its motion to the brief canine brows, which instead of drooping did their best to stand on end, trembling with the effort to keep stiff. The brows in their turn affected the eyelids, which curled up into a fringe of tiny, quivering folds as though they were trying to make up for the missing brows. Caisotti sat there with his eyes half closed, looking like a whipped dog, and said plain-tively, "All right, then, you tell me what I ought to do. I'll show you the estimates, I'll show you what figure I can hope to get for the sort of building one can put up there, with no view and no sun. I'll show you everything and you can tell me if I'm going to make a profit or if I'm going to be out of pocket. I'll put myself in your hands entirely."

Caisotti's pose of docile victim had already made Quinto feel uneasy. "All the same," he said, in the effort to be con-ciliating, "it's a good central position, you know."

"Yes, central is central," Caisotti agreed, and Quinto was glad that they had found some common ground. He was relieved to see the fold on Caisotti's forehead smoothing out and the eyebrows being hauled down from their unnatural elevation. But Caisotti carried on in the same tone of voice. "Of course, it won't be a particularly fine building," he said, giving what Signora Anfossi called one of his horrid laughs. "You realize I can only have it facing this way." He gestured with his thick, short arms. "It won't be anything very fine, but you say it's central and I agree with you."

The phrase about the building "not being particularly fine" had revived the Signora's anxieties. "We'd want to see your plans first," she said. "After all, we'll have to look at the place every day of our lives."

Quinto's expression during this exchange was a blend of fatalism and arrogance, the expression of a man who knows that the last thing to be hoped of the building was beauty and that, at best, it might achieve a mean anonymity indistinguishable from the anonymous structures all around. This at least would serve to keep it quite separate from the villa.

"But of course," Caisotti said accommodatingly, "of course you'll see the plans. It'll be a four-story house like every other four-story house – that's the maximum height the building code allows. I have to draw up the plans and show them to the engineers in City Hall for approval, and once they're passed, I'll show them to you so that you can tell me what you think." The submissive voice was taking on a threatening edge. "I'll bring everything up here and you can tell me what to do.... I'll even let you see what all this is going to cost me and what profit I can make. You're educated people, you understand these things better than I do. ..."

"It's not a question of being educated," Quinto said, suddenly irritated, as always, by any reminder of his status as an intellectual. "You know perfectly well how much you can offer just as we know what's the least we're prepared to take."

"If you're already thinking of the least you're prepared to take," Caisotti said with a laugh, "what are we talking about?" As he spoke, he shook his head backward and forward, and Quinto noticed the thick, bull-like nape, which seemed to be subjected to a continual strain. The corners of his mouth went up and he was a shark, or bull perhaps, a bull snorting through its nostrils. His grimace might have been meant for a snigger or else an expression of anger. And at the same time he was also a poor wretch who says to himself: What's the use? They're just taking me for a ride, saying one thing and meaning another. I'm bound to fall into the trap.

Quinto felt that after his remark about "the least we're prepared to take," he ought not to say anything more, so he concluded simply, "Anyway, we'll reach some agreement ..." slipping back into the vague formulas in which Caisotti liked to deal.

But Caisotti wasn't satisfied with this either. "Oh, yes, we'll reach an agreement," he said with the sorry little laugh of the man who knows he is being taken advantage of. "You mean you'll tell me what I've got to do, and we'll go on like that, putting things off from one day to the next and if I don't get my work done in the summer, I'd like to know when I can get it done. I can do precious little building once the wet weather comes."

His eyes were blank, his mouth gave nothing away; all his expression was in his cheeks; they alone were unguarded. The left cheek, just above the gravelly expanse where he shaved, still showed the spot where the rosebush had scratched him. It gave a suggestion of fragile innocence to the leathery face, a suggestion intensified by the way his hair was cropped close on his nape, by his plaintive tone of voice and the bewildered way he looked at people. Quinto again found himself wanting to be nice to the man, to protect him, but this image of Caisotti as a little boy did not march with the other image, that of Caisotti as shark, outsize crustacean, crab, which was how he appeared as he sat there with his thick hands spread out loosely on the arms of the chair. Quinto went ahead with the negotiations in this fashion, indulging now the one image, now the other. But one thing was becoming clearer all the time; he positively *liked* the man!

4

"We've found a buyer."

"About time."

Quinto had gone to school with Canal, his attorney. A small man, he sat buried in the big armchair behind the desk, his head sunk into his shoulders. Spasms of fatigue flickered across his expressive face.

"He's a contractor," Quinto said. "I came to ask if you knew anything about him – whether he's honest, solvent, that sort of thing."

For years Quinto and Canal had not managed to sustain a conversation and on the rare occasions when they met in the street, they found nothing to say to each other. Their manner of life, professions, politics were all different, if not antagonistic. But now they had something concrete to discuss. Quinto was delighted.

"What's his name?" Canal asked.

"Caisotti."

"Caisotti?" Canal sat up sharply, bringing his hands down on the table. His air of fatigue was gone. "You've picked a choice specimen."

It was not a promising start. But although he had already decided to stand up for the man, Quinto made an initial concession to his mother's way of thinking. "Of course

you've only got to look at his face to see the sort of fellow
he is. All the same ..."

"It's not his face. It's that every time he makes a deal,
every time he puts up a building, there's trouble. I've taken
action against him in several cases. He's the biggest swindler
in town."

Quinto was delighted to heart that Caisotti was such a
scoundrel. The charm of business, it was just coming to him,
was precisely that it brought one into contact with people of
all sorts. It meant dealing with crooks and knowing that
they were crooks, making sure that they didn't cheat you,
and indeed, if the opportunity occurred, cheating them.
What counted was the "economic moment"; nothing else
mattered. All the same, he felt alarmed at the possibility that
Canal's information might be so unfavorable that he would
have to abandon the project.

"But in an affair like this," he said, "how can he cheat us?
If he pays for the land, it's his, if he doesn't, that's that. Has
he got any money?"

"Everything has gone well for him so far," Canal replied.
"He came down from the hills in patched pants – he could
hardly read or write – and now he's setting up construction
jobs all over the place. He's making a lot of money. City
Hall is eating out of his hand."

The rancor in Canal's voice was familiar to Quinto. He
represented the old middle-class, conservative, honest, eco-
nomical, undemanding, without much go or imagination,
rather inclined to be stingy. For the last half century this
class had witnessed changes that it had been unable to resist
and had seen a new, traditionless class take the field. On
every occasion it had had to give way, affecting an air of
indifference but with teeth clenched. But wasn't Quinto

moved by the same sense of resentment? The difference was that he reacted by going to the other extreme and embracing everything new, everything that did violence to his feelings. At this very moment, as he was coming up against a new race of raw, unscrupulous contractors, he felt something like a scientist's interest in an important new sociological phenomenon, and at the same time a positive aesthetic satisfaction. The squalid cement invasion bore the shapeless, snub-nosed features of the new man, Caisotti.

"How much is he offering?" the lawyer asked.

Quinto described the initial negotiations. He had got to his feet and was standing by the window. Canal's office was in a smart street, but it faced the rear of the building. The roofs and terraces and walls belonged to the windy, sunlit city as it had been in the nineteenth century; but there too the scaffolding was sprouting, the newly painted walls, the flat roofs with the elevator shed on top.

"Given the state of the market, it's a good price," Canal said grudgingly, gnawing at his lower lip. "In cash?"

"Part cash down, part in installments."

"He's made his payments all right so far, I believe. But he's just put up a house; he ought to pay cash."

"That was what I wanted to find out. Now that I know where I am, we can close with him."

"Of course, if it were a question of having him do some work for you or of buying from him, I should have urged you not to go ahead. But in a case like this, I can't see that it matters whether you sell to him or to someone else. ... So long as he pays up. You'll need to take a good look at the contract, though, the maximum height of the building, number of windows, that sort of thing."

Canal went to the door with him. "Are you staying here awhile or are you off again?"

Quinto shrugged. "Who knows? Off again, I expect."

"How are things with you, your work ...?" Canal took care to leave his questions quite general. Quinto was always moving from one job to another, and he was afraid of appearing out of touch.

Quinto's reply was equally vague. "I've got a new thing in hand now, with some friends. It's too early yet to ..."

"How about politics?"

Here again it was difficult to answer. They were on different sides of the fence and since they respected each other's position, they didn't want to get involved in an argument. But this time Quinto was a little more definite. "I've dropped politics nowadays."

"Yes, that's what I heard. Someone ..."

"What's the political situation here?" Quinto asked.

Canal was a Social Democrat and served on the City council. "Oh, you know, the usual sort of thing."

"You're well? Your wife?"

"Yes, thanks, we're all fine. What about you? Still a bachelor, eh. No projects in that line? Ah, well. Look, you get in touch with me again when you've had a word with Bardissone."

5

Quinto emerged from this exchange of pleasantries with his nerves on edge. He had to traverse a stretch of the main street that he normally avoided on account of its crowded confusion. When he came home, he liked to walk in the countrified outskirts of the town or along the sea front, where he could still recapture the pulsations of the past, the marginal deposits which memory had preserved. But today he felt no nostalgia for a passing order. Seen from these sidewalks, the aspect which the city offered was the same as ever, appallingly unchanged, and what new elements there were – faces, young people, stores – didn't count; his adolescence felt disagreeably close. Why in the world had he come back? All he wanted at the moment was to see the thing through quickly and be off. The idea of staying there filled him with disgust.

He noticed a man on a bicycle propped against the curb; his face seemed familiar. A stringy old fellow in a sweater, his sunburned arms resting on the handlebars. He was a carpenter, Quinto now remembered, a Party member who must have been on the committee in the days when he served on it himself.

He was talking to someone. Quinto walked by, supposing that the old man hadn't recognized him, but he didn't look away because he did not want to give the impression that he was cutting him. But the carpenter had seen him, for he said to the other man. "Why, it's Anfossi!" waving to him in a friendly way. Quinto waved back with equal friendliness, but didn't stop. The carpenter, however, put out his hand and said, "Good to see you, Anfossi. So you've come home for a while, eh?"

They shook hands. Quinto had always liked the old man's somewhat owl-like face, with those tortoise-rimmed glasses and the crew-cut white hair; he liked his voice too, with its broad northern vowels, and his strong, soft handshake. All the same, on this occasion he would have been

happy to dislike him; a response to the old man's warm
humanity did not fit in with his present frame of mind,
which was leading him to feel well-disposed toward Caisotti. And anyway he didn't want to stop. He wanted to
stop even less when the carpenter (Quinto was irritated at
not being able to remember his name since he felt that he
could only reply in the right tone of voice if he called him
by his first name) began saying, "We've been following
your career, you know, all those articles in the national
press. The national press!" he repeated for the benefit of
the other man.

Quinto shrugged and tried to explain that he was no
longer writing articles, but the carpenter wouldn't listen.
"No, no, it was fine work! One could see you meant what
you said."

He pointed to the other man, whom Quinto didn't recognize in the least, and said, "You remember him, don't you?"

"Of course," Quinto said. "Good to see you again."

"But it's Comrade Martini, don't you remember?" the old
man insisted, as though Quinto had confessed to not recognizing him. "Comrade Martini of the Santo Stefano
Section."

"You held a meeting at Party Headquarters in Forty-six to
explain the Amnesty to us," Martini said.

"Yes, yes, I remember," said Quinto, though he remembered no such thing.

"Those were the times, though!" said the man called Martini. "Things looked hopeful then, eh, Masera?"

Quinto was much relieved to find that he remembered
the carpenter was called Masera, and as though the end of
his search for the man's name meant the end of his sense
of guilt, he managed at last to look at him in a friendly

way. He now recalled a windy evening when they had bicycled together along a road by the sea, which at the time was partly blocked by potholes. Masera's bike had been as rusty and broken-down as the one he had now. They had been going to a meeting. It was a fine, warm memory.

"Everything looked hopeful then," Masera repeated, but in the manner of someone who takes a pessimistic line in order to be told by a better-informed comrade that "things still look hopeful now, more so than ever. The struggle is on. ..." But Quinto said nothing, so that Masera was forced to add himself, "And they still look hopeful now, eh, Anfossi?"

"Ah," said Quinto, stretching out his arms.

"But it's hard here, I'll say it's hard! Men being fired – ah, the dirty bastards! What are the comrades saying where you are?"

"It's hard there too," Quinto said.

"Times are hard everywhere!" Masera laughed, as though this solidarity in hard times made things a bit better.

"Tell him ..." Martini whispered something to Masera, of which Quinto managed to catch only the word "lecture."

Masera nodded, smiling understandingly and at the same time doubtfully, as though he had had the same idea himself already but dismissed it as hopeless. "Are you still against public speaking?" he asked, turning to Quinto, "or have you finally turned into an orator? Now that you're here, you see, we were thinking that if you could come to Headquarters and give a talk – well, the comrades would certainly appreciate it."

"No, no, I have to leave almost immediately, and anyway I can't make speeches, you know that, Masera."

"Still the same, eh?" said Masera, laughing and slapping him on the back. "Hasn't changed a bit, has he?" he said to Martini, whom Quinto still didn't remember ever having seen before. "Not a bit," Martini agreed. They were honest, friendly people, but Quinto had no desire to feel himself among friends. Quite the contrary, these were the days of every man for himself, pistol at the ready – the kind of relationship you had with businessmen, contractors, wide-eyed men who knew what was what.

He compared Masera with Caisotti: Masera, trusting, expansive, prepared to find everything in line with his dream; Caisotti, wary, reticent, untrustworthy. No doubt about it though, it was Caisotti who was in touch with his time; he was accepting the conditions of the age, shirking nothing, you might say, whereas poor Masera, with all that stuff about being decent, pure in heart, and so forth, was really an escapist. He wasn't living in the real world at all. Quinto shook off the burden of guilt with which Masera's straightforward social conscience threatened him. You were still doing your duty too by taking part in private enterprise and dealing in land and money; it wasn't an epic sort of duty, maybe, in fact it was rather prosaic, rather bourgeois, but hell, he *was* a bourgeois. How on earth had he ever supposed he was anything else?

Quite reassured now about his bourgeois status, Quinto felt the uneasiness he had experienced with the two workingmen give way to a generalized, almost casual good will. It wasn't altogether insincere: now that he was saying goodbye, he really wanted them to think well of him.

6

Nowhere were the reports on Caisotti favorable. As a result, Quinto found himself taking the man's side. He was being victimized, the whole city was out for his blood, all the stuffed shirts were against him, and yet the poor bricklaying peasant, armed only with his shy, uncouth nature, was standing up to them.

The point was that these negative judgments still left Quinto free to go ahead. People disapproved, but they didn't warn him off altogether. He was the sort of person who liked doing things that were moderately controversial but would never court head-on disapproval, and he found himself supplied with approval and disapproval in exactly the proportions that his temperament required.

Moreover, since he still had to fight down a certain personal uneasiness in the first place, he was reassured by the thought that he was in professional contact with his fellow citizens. He felt he had finally returned to the ranks of the traditional middle-class element in the district, united in the defense of its modest interests, which were under attack. And yet, at the same time he realized that every step he was taking was helping the rise of Caisotti and his like, the new shifty, graceless middle-class that matched the graceless, amoral age they were living in. Let's face it, Quinto said to himself; you people have lost every round! And with this his hostility shifted from the small society of his home town, from his mother and Canal – and from Masera the carpenter. His opponents were now his friends in the big cities in northern Italy, where he had lived all these years, years spent discussing the shape of the new society, the role of the workers and of the intelligentsia. Caisotti has won, Quinto told himself.

He couldn't wait to give his friends there a demonstration of his new position. He got on the train and next day he was lunching with Bensi and Cerveteri in the usual modest restaurant in Turin.

They were talking about starting a review to be called *The New Hegel*. The waitress was trying to get their order; it was her third attempt, but they were too deep in conversation to pay any attention.

Bensi looked at the menu and read the list of dishes, but apparently nothing took his fancy.

"Why not call it *The Hegelian Left?*" he said.

"In that case, why not *The Young Marx*? More punch."

"Are you going to order?" The waitress was still at it.

"I propose *The New Rhine Gazette*."

"What about getting hold of the actual heading of the *Neue Rheinische Zeitung* and using the same characters?" Quinto suggested. His remarks were never quite to the point, but they had a casual, professional air about them. He still hadn't found an occasion to reveal his disagreement with the group, though this suggestion was intended to open the way.

"All right, the title is *Encyclopedia* " Bensi said in a different tone of voice, as though up till then they had been joking, and Quinto's proposal was therefore quite irrelevant. "Or maybe that can be the subtitle. The point is to make it clear from the title down that what we are aiming at is a general phenomenology subsuming every kind of conscious activity within a single body of discourse."

This brought Bensi and Cerveteri into conflict, and Quinto was uncertain whose side to take. If everything was to be subsumed within a single body of discourse, should the paper only print what was already included within that body, or should it also print stuff that was still outside? Cerveteri wanted to include the stuff that was still outside. "I'd like a column called 'A Politician Dreams,'" he said. "We'll invite leaders from all political parties and ask them to tell us what they dream. Anyone who refuses has obviously got something to hide."

Bensi was overcome by one of his paroxysms of maniacal laughter. This involved bringing his face down to the level of the tablecloth and covering his eyes with one hand, as though to indicate his pained amusement at the sight of a friend losing himself in a maze from which only he, Bensi, knew the way out. "We go from ideology to dreams," he managed to say, "not from dreams to ideology." And then, as though succumbing to a malign temptation, he added, "All your dreams are pronged on the ideological spike like moths on a pin."

Cerveteri looked baffled. "Moths?" he said. "*Why moths?*"

Bensi was a philosopher, Cerveteri a poet. Poet Cerveteri was a premature gray; his long, spectacled face provided a battleground on which melancholy Semitic features fought a well-matched engagement with more expressive Florentine traits, whether erudite or plebeian it was difficult to determine. The outcome was a face including both aggression and concentration, but which somehow remained deeply inexpressive, like a cyclist, say, or like someone trying to concentrate on one point in the center of an indefinite series of points. "Why did you say moths?" he repeated. "I dreamed of a moth last night. I was sitting here, in this very restaurant, and they brought me a huge moth, on a plate."

And he gestured in the manner of one raising the wing of a huge moth.

"Christ!" said the waitress, who had come to see if they wanted dessert.

Bensi laughed with exaggerated bitterness, the laughter of a man tired of adversaries who give themselves up unarmed. "Dream symbolism is always a deification," he remarked. "That's what Freud failed to understand."

Quinto greatly admired the incessant intellectual activity of both men. (His own mind inclined rather to relapse into a state of sleepy indifference.) And he was impressed by their breadth of cultural reference. Uncertain which part to take in the argument, the terms of which he only vaguely understood, he decided as usual to back the side most opposed to his natural inclinations, namely Bensi's rigidly mechanistic philosophy, and to resist the appeal of Cerveteri's fluid play of sensation. He turned ironically to Bensi and said, sneering at the poet, "Why not go the whole hog and call it *The New Freud*?"

The philosopher was still in the grips of the convulsion of laughter provoked by Cerveteri and he brushed off Quinto's joke like an irrelevant fly. It appealed to the poet, however, who took it up enthusiastically. "That's it," he cried. "Let's call it *Eros and Thanatos*!"

Bensi brought his hands together and rubbed them till they creaked, while his face contracted in a clenched laugh that made him turn purple. "Do you think you're going to checkmate history with those two? The dialectical process pops out between them like a cuckoo from a clock."

Bensi had a round, cherubic face, like the face of those people from the hills who never really grow up. His forehead, under the babyish wave of curly hair, was so convex that it seemed about to explode. It was marked with little bumps and scratches, as though the pressure of thought made it butt into things. Bensi led with his forehead, holding it forward like a millstone, always grinding, grinding, or like a wheel, setting off a complicated system of gears, driven by an inadequately synchronized central force that made it waste itself in countless secondary motions, as for example the incessant quivering of his lips. During the discussion Quinto found himself looking now at Bensi's eyes, now at Cerveteri's. They both squinted, but the philosopher's squint was extroverted; his eye seemed to fly in pursuit of ideas just on the point of vanishing from the field of human vision into some oblique, unrecognizable perspective. The poet's was an inner squint. The pupils of his close-set, restless eyes seemed to strive to register the effect produced by external sensations in some secret, interior zone of consciousness.

"Let's make an anthology of obituary notices," Cerveteri suggested. "We might make it a regular feature. Better still, what about a whole number filled with nothing but obituary notices?" And he ran his finger down the black-barred column of the obituary page in the folded paper he was holding.

Bensi shrugged. "We're just about to house the conscience of mankind in an electronic brain."

Cerveteri's answer was a lengthy quotation in Latin.

"Saint Augustine?"

"Lactantius."

Quinto's attention wandered and he found himself trying to overhear what people were saying at the nearby tables. There was a family to the right, or perhaps they were two different families, country people who had come in to town to meet. A woman was talking about the damage done by rain to the alfalfa fields. She obviously owned land. She was not young, but she was still of marriageable age, and as she spoke the men nodded agreement, their faces blurred with wine and food. They were farming people, perhaps, from different regions, meeting to settle the terms of a marriage. The woman was showing, in the presence of the man's family, that she was a mature, competent person, as though to outdo the other women there by this evidence that she was much more than a mere housewife.

Quinto felt sharply envious of everything that these people represented: the sense of interests at stake, the attachment to things, concrete and in no way ignoble passions, the desire to better oneself in more than a material sense, and in addition there was something placid and earthy and solid about them. There was a time, Quinto reflected, when you could live the life of the mind only if you owned land. But in detaching itself from its economic basis, culture had paid dearly. It depended on privilege in those days, certainly, yet it was still firmly rooted. Nowadays the intellectual belonged neither to the bourgeoisie nor to the proletariat. For that matter, even Masera could do nothing better than ask him to give a lecture.

At another table a waitress was flirting with a couple of men in bow ties who couldn't keep their hands at home. In between the jokes addressed to the girl, Quinto could hear words like "Italian Gas," "General Electric," and stock-market quotations. A pair of stock-market agents, obviously, smooth operators. At any other time he would have disliked them intensely, but in his present mood he found that they embodied his ideals: expediency, cunning, quick functional intelligence. A man who isn't trying to make money doesn't count, Quinto said to himself. Why, even the workers have their trade-union struggles. But we intellectuals make a distinction between the larger historical perspectives and our own interests and in the process we have lost the taste of life. We have destroyed ourselves. We don't mean anything.

Cerveteri had gone back to his dream. "A large moth," he was saying. "It had big wings with minute gray, wavy markings, like a black-and-white Kandinsky – no, a Klee, perhaps. I was trying to lift these wings with my fork and they gave out a fine dust, a kind of gray powdery stuff, then disintegrated between my finger and thumb. I tried to lift the fragments to my mouth, but they turned into ashes and spread over everything, covering the plates, sinking into the wineglasses. ..."

My superiority over these people, Quinto reflected, is that I still have the bourgeois instincts that they have mislaid in the wear and tear of intellectual fashion. I shall stick to these instincts and in so doing save myself, while they'll crumble away. But I've got to start making money. Selling some land to Caisotti isn't enough. I must start building too. I'll use the money I get from him to put up another house next to the one he is building.... . Quinto concentrated on the possibilities of the site that had not yet been exploited, on the ways of putting it to the best use.

Cerveteri's hands fluttered over the tablecloth, which was littered with crumbs, cigarette ashes, stubs crushed on plates or ashtrays, bits of orange peel tortured into strange shapes by Bensi's nails, match sticks shredded away by Cerveteri's fingers, toothpicks dislocated by Quinto's hands and teeth.

I must get into partnership with Caisotti, he said to himself. We'll speculate in real estate together.

7

Quinto had an idea. Adjoining the land they were proposing to sell was a bit of garden with a bed of forget-me-nots in the middle. It was fairly level and about the same size as the flowerpottery. It too offered an excellent site for a small apartment building. But he realized that once Caisotti's building was up, it would lose all value as a site since the law did not allow houses to be constructed right on top of one another. It's clear, Quinto said to himself, that whichever site we sell, we're going to reduce the value of the one immediately beside it. So the only thing to do is to go into partnership with Caisotti and build together. Let him have both sites and put up a single large building there; in return we'll take a certain number of apartments, which will remain our property. I must talk this over with Ampelio at once.

Quinto and his brother did not live in the same town. Their rare meetings took place in their mother's house and it was there that they had now arranged to meet to discuss the sale.

"I've got an idea," Quinto said to Ampelio the moment he arrived. On their way from the station they stopped at the fish market and bought half a pound of limpets. When he got home, Ampelio kissed his mother hurriedly and told her about the limpets that he had bought. He had been away for six months. He was a university instructor in chemistry, and though he earned a wretched salary he hardly ever came home, not even during vacations. He had at one time been more tied to his home town that Quinto, but now he seldom showed his face there. He no longer seemed to take any pleasure in his familiar haunts and in the life he used to lead.

Nobody in fact knew what his tastes were nowadays, except insofar as they were revealed by small, unexpected gestures – like this business of the limpets, for example – and even then it was hard to tell how far they were sincere.

Quinto began telling him about the negotiations with Caisotti. As he explained, Ampelio went into the kitchen and Quinto followed him, talking. Ampelio undid the paper in which the limpets were wrapped and picked up a knife and then a lemon. He stood by the sideboard, opening cupboards and pulling out drawers with quick, confident gestures as though he had left everything in place the day before. He cut a slice of lemon and sprinkled it on the limpets without taking them out of their paper. He made a gesture indicating that Quinto was to help himself; Quinto rejected the offer vigorously – he couldn't stand shellfish – and went on talking.

Ampelio said nothing, giving no sign of either agreement or disapproval. Several times Quinto broke off under the impression that his brother wasn't listening, but Ampelio would say, "And what then?" and Quinto carried on again as though nothing had happened. Ampelio had always been like this, even when he was a boy. The only difference was that in those days, Quinto, being the older brother, would lose his temper, but in time he had got used to it. Ampelio sat there at the polished kitchen table, still in the overcoat and scarf that he had been wearing even though it was late spring. He had a small black beard and was already balding; his eyes were concealed behind the thick lenses of his glasses. Quinto watched him ease the limpets out of their shells with the point of his knife and with his other hand raise the shells fringed with seaweed to his lips. The soft flesh of the limpets vanished between his lips framed by the dark beard, with a sound of breath being sucked in or else blown out, it was hard to tell which. Then he put the empty shells one on top of the other in a little pile.

Quinto had unrolled a map. Still chewing, Ampelio glanced at it out of the corner of his eye. His mouth, surrounded by beard, was like a sea urchin turned upside down, the mouth moving among the black spines. Quinto had explained the present phase of the negotiations and told Ampelio what he had found out about Caisotti. Now, his finger on the map, he said, "I see it like this. If we build in area A, we preclude the possibility of selling area B or of building on it. This means that if we sell area A to Caisotti for its value as a building site, which I call X, we deprive area B of its value of Y. So what it comes to is that if we sell at X, we lose the chance of a possible X + Y. Or putting it the other way, we now own A + B; if we sell A, we are left with only B − Y."

Quinto had been mulling over this little algebraic demonstration for several days, hoping to impress his scientific brother.

Ampelio got up, went to the sink, drank from the faucet, rinsed his mouth, and spat − one after the other. Then he said, "Obviously we've got to use the flowerpottery as capital to invest in any building we erect on the second site. And since the regulations don't permit two buildings to be put up so close to each other, we must think in terms of a single large structure occupying the two plots, to be built by Caisotti, half for himself, half for us."

This was precisely the plan on which Quinto had been racking his brains as though it were the knottiest problem in the world. And here was Ampelio coming out with it as though it followed naturally from the facts of the situation! Quinto didn't know what to say next. Ampelio sat down and started covering the borders of the map with figures, every now and then asking for additional information, which Quinto was never able to provide quite accurately. What was the maximum height allowed by the building code? How many apartments did Caisotti intend to put in? What was the price of cement? Quinto realized that his brother couldn't know any more about building estimates than he did, yet there he was, rapidly jotting down figures with a confidence that Quinto envied deeply.

"Let's reckon eight apartments, plus a couple of shops on the ground floor," Ampelio said, calculating the annual rents and the time it would take to amortize their capital.

"But what about the money we need right away to pay the taxes?"

"We'll apply for a loan and use the prospective building as security."

"Oh, God!" Quinto screeched in desperation. Ampelio, as always, was composure itself. He didn't laugh, no wrinkle creased his massive brow. For him, everything was in the sphere of the possible.

Signora Anfossi came into the kitchen. "Well, boys, have you figured it all out? Is it all right?"

"Yes, yes. We're going to lose though, either way."

"Oh, that Caisotti, with his nasty dishonest face!"

"It isn't Caisotti's doing, poor man. But we're going to be in the red, all the same."

"Then why not drop the whole thing?" the Signora suggested. "That's it, we'll tell him we've changed our minds and that we're not thinking of selling at present. As for the taxes, we'll have to ask the bank again."

"No, no, Mother, look, we were just saying that what we must do is propose something much more complicated to Caisotti."

"More complicated? Heavens!"

"Yes, yes, somehing very complicated. In the long run we'll make a handsome profit."

Quinto bent down to talk to her, gesturing in a nervous, combative way, trying at the same time to convince her and to start an argument. Ampelio stood beside him, tall and serious, his dark beard thrust forward. He looked like a judge whose only task is to pronounce sentence.

"Now, Mother, listen. You know the forget-me-not bed ..."

8

Quinto and Ampelio went out together. They walked rapidly along the familiar streets, talking in a way they hadn't done for ages. It was as though they had never left home, two brothers playing a busy part in the town's economic life, controlling a whole network of interests: brusque, practical people, with both feet on the ground. They were play-acting and they knew it, since they were both very unlike the characters they were assuming at the moment. In the normal way, before the afternoon was over they would have relapsed into sceptical inertia and then gone their separate ways, Ampelio back to his laboratory and Quinto to his intellectual disputes, as though these were the only thing in the world that counted. Yet for the time being their present roles seemed feasible. And how fine it would have been, two brothers against the world together! So many things would have been within their grasp, they could have done so much – what exactly, they would have been hard put to it to say. Here they were, for example, on their way to Caisotti to put the proposition to him, to explore the situation, to ask him – well, to ask him something or other. Hell, why make things difficult? At present they were sizing him up. They would decide later what course of action to take.

Caisotti did not have a telephone. He had an office upstairs: CAISOTTI BUILDING COMPANY. They rang the bell and a girl opened the door. It was a small, low room with a typewriter and some blueprints on the table. No, Caisotti wasn't in; he was always out and about, on the job; he was hardly ever in his office.

"When will he be back?" Shrug. "Where can we find him?" "Try at the Caffè Melina, just over there, but it's a bit too early." "We have to see him at once." Shrug. "I suppose you could leave a message with me."

"Well, thanks anyway, Miss Shrug." Ampelio produced this witticism, greatly to the surprise of Quinto, who had never heard his brother employ such a sarcastic, confidential tone in his family circle. He took a look at the girl. Not bad.

Not more than sixteen or so, she had the look of a country girl, with her pink-and-white complexion, her eyes dark under the well-marked brows, and two soft, black braids of hair falling onto her ample breasts.

"You must be the Anfossi brothers," she offered.

Cunning little bitch, Quinto said to himself, false as hell, with her nose in the air and that butter-wouldn't-melt expression.

Ampelio's joke might have seemed designed to pave the way for an improbable exchange of pleasantries with the girl, but he at once resumed his usual dry manner as though he had gone too far. He asked about the building sites where Caisotti might be found, said good-bye and went down the narrow stairs. But at the bottom he produced one more unlikely witticism. "*Ciao, bella*!" he cried.

On his way down, Quinto turned around and saw that the girl had not yet shut the door. She was looking down through her heavy lashes and smiling in a curious way. He had the impression that behind that country-girl face of hers, Caisotti was staring at them in his enigmatic fashion.

"Not bad, the girl, eh?" he said, wanting to talk about her.

"Mmm," Ampelio said, as though avoiding an indelicate topic.

They went to one of the places she had suggested, where Caisotti's firm was putting up a new house, or rather adding new floors to an existing two-story house. It was in one of the main streets and the addition would fill the gap between two large buildings.

They went in. There were mounds of cement all over the place, but no sign of men at work. The staircase was not in yet, so Quinto and Ampelio had to climb up on some sloping planks. "Hey! Anybody about? Caisotti! Is the boss here?" Their voices re-echoed between the bare walls.

On the third floor two workmen were crouching down, banging away at chisels. They had the air of people doing something they know to be useless. The two brothers at once stopped shouting and asked, almost in a whisper, "Isn't Caisotti here?" "No." "Hasn't he come yet?" "We don't know." "Is the foreman here?" "Next floor up." Quinto and Ampelio went up.

On this floor the walls were in place, but the roof and the floor were lacking. The doors opened onto empty space. A kind of wild gaiety came over the pair of them. *Haie!* they whooped at each other, *haie!* as they climbed along the planks of the scaffolding with arms extended, like tightrope walkers.

There was a noise of scraping shoes. A narrow plank spanned the open floor of a room, resting on the doorsteps at each side. And there, outlined against the doorway, as though in hiding, was Caisotti.

They calmed down, feeling rather silly. "Ah, Caisotti, hello there, we were just looking for you." The man's heavy bulk blocked the frame of the doorway on which the narrow plank lay. He stood there with his hands in his pockets, giving no sign of recognition. Quinto went forward a few steps along the plank, then paused as he felt it bend beneath him. He was waiting for Caisotti to do something, at least put a foot on his end of the plank to keep it steady, but no, he said nothing, did nothing. Suspended there in space, Quinto, simply to break the silence, said, "I want you to meet my brother, Ampelio." Caisotti took one hand out of his pocket and bringing it up to the peak of his cap, struck it with the flat of his hand. Quinto turned around toward his brother, slowly, so as not to start the plank wobbling, and noticed that he was responding to Caisotti's gesture with precisely the same gesture. They both looked serious.

"Don't go there; you'll fall," Caisotti said slowly. Then: "If you'll both go down, I'll be with you."

They went to the Caffè Melina and sat at a noisy table on the sidewalk. Caisotti wanted to buy the drinks. "A Punt e Mes?" Ampelio took Punt e Mes. Quinto, who suffered from stomach trouble, ordered a *rabarbaro*, though secretly convinced that *rabarbaro* was bad for him too. Ampelio offered Caisotti a cigarette. Quinto didn't smoke. The two men were perfectly at ease with each other and Quinto felt rather jealous.

Caisotti was repeating to Ampelio everything he had said to Signora Anfossi and Quinto, interjecting remarks like "As I had the pleasure of saying to your mother," or "You're an engineer, sir; I don't have to explain this to you." Ampelio had his degree in chemistry, but he raised no objection. He listened in silence, the cigarette dangling from his black beard, eyes half shut behind the thick lenses. He asked a question now and then, but casually, as one professional to another, and not, or so it seemed, with anything of Quinto's nagging compulsion to show himself well informed and on his guard.

Indeed, when Quinto raised an objection, Caisotti turned to Ampelio with that plaintive air of his, as though he were asking for protection. "Of course you understand that your brother's point—"

"No, no, Caisotti!" Quinto broke in, to cover himself. Ampelio's only response was a broad gesture, brushing the surface of the table as though to clear away side issues and get back to the heart of the matter.

Caisotti would obviously have liked to go on playing the victim, but his heart was no longer in it. Instead he remarked, still to Ampelio, "You're the elder brother, sir, and you understand—"

"No, look here, I'm the elder brother," Quinto interrupted, feeling slightly embarrassed. Caisotti nonetheless continued to treat Ampelio with markedly greater respect.

"And if you tell me that on your side you want a space between the floors, fine, I'll see you have your space."

"It's you who need the space," Ampelio said, "to avoid dampness in your ground floor."

"I need the space, certainly I need it, but tell me this, please: won't I sell the ground floor just as well without the space, whereas if you should decide one day to build on the site next to me, you'd find the space very handy."

Quinto looked at Ampelio. Slowly he blew a cloud of smoke. He waited until the smoke had drifted away, then said, "And what if we were to build together?"

There was a tiny movement of Caisotti's fingers as he knocked the ash off his cigarette; his eyes were moist, like someone looking into the distance to banish some remote excitement, but at the same time they came to a sharp point and the wrinkles thickened around his lids.

"I'd say we could get along very nicely."

9

Ampelio considered that they ought not to let themselves be influenced by unfavorable reports on Caisotti. "You know how it is here. All you ever hear about people is gossip. Someone new makes his mark and gets ahead, and at once the whole pack is tearing him to bits."

Canal came near to doing just that. "Go into partnership with Caisotti? You two, your mother? With that crooked, loose-living peasant! The way he drags that girl around with him... ."

"We saw the girl," Quinto said, instantly distracted by a facile curiosity. "What about her? Who is she? She looks as though she came from the country." He glanced at Ampelio as though asking his support. I told you what they're like, Ampelio's expression seemed to say.

"She does," Canal said. "He brought her with him from the village where he used to live – he's got a wife and children up there."

"You mean ...?"

"I don't mean anything, I don't know anything about them and I don't want to. There's something dirty about the whole setup."

Quinto described his impression, on first seeing the girl, that there was some resemblance between her and Caisotti, all the more disturbing because it wasn't a physical or external resemblance.

"I wouldn't doubt it," Canal said.

"How do you mean? The idea of him and that girl... she's barely sixteen ... with a man who might be her father. ..."

"Oh, he's got lots of children. He left home because he'd filled the whole valley with his bastards."

"You think she's his illegitimate daughter?" Quinto said, but he felt that the moment had come to react against this gossipy curiosity and show himself in his true colors, a man of the world with no provincial prejudices. "And what if she is, what's the harm? All right, so he's got an illegitimate daughter, and instead of abandoning her he finds her a job and keeps her with him. Is that any reason to stick your knife in him?"

"Oh, I know nothing about it, I assure you."

"And if she were his mistress and not his daughter, what would be the harm in that? He likes girls, they get on well together.... . Why do you people always have to split hairs?"

"It doesn't matter to me what she is. She may be his daughter or his girl friend – or both at the same time, for all I care!"

"How about getting back to the contract?" Ampelio suggested.

It was a bright, cool afternoon, the kind of weather that makes you feel ready for anything. After their meeting with Caisotti, the two brothers had gone at once to see Canal, their lawyer. They had had to wait since Canal was busy with clients, but this in no way diminished their excitement and they had sat in the waiting room putting the finishing touches to their project. They spoke in broken snatches to prevent anyone understanding what they were talking about. From Canal's office came the sounds of a noisy argument in dialect; he had taken over an old-fashioned clientele of country people, small proprietors doggedly pursuing trivial, interminable suits concerning wills or disputed boundaries. For the first time Quinto did not feel guilty at the distance between himself and this ancestral world; he belonged now to another world from which he could look back on the old one with a superior irony. He was one of the new men, who had thrown off the old-fashioned prejudices, who were used to handling money.

Canal, however, had no sooner heard their schemes than he sat up in his chair in alarm. "But you're crazy! You and Caisotti? Why, he'll spit you like a pair of thrushes!"

Quinto smiled. "Steady, now. Let's wait and see who's going to be the thrush, shall we? The deal is entirely in our favor."

"And Caisotti agrees? You don't say!"

Quinto kept on smiling. "Caisotti agrees. We've just seen him about it."

"But you're mad. Go into business with Caisotti! You and your mother!" And so it went on.

"Listen," Quinto said. In explaining the affair to Canal he had adopted an air of indulgent patience, like a grown-up son explaining something to his father, who thinks he is still a child. Resentment at not being taken seriously is never, on such occasions, far below the surface.

Quinto explained that Caisotti was prepared to buy the two sites, paying partly in cash (which would allow them to settle their back taxes) and partly in apartments (which would mean turning an unproductive asset into a profitable source of income, at no cost to themselves). Quinto appeared to be more and more amused by Canal's objections, and even to go out of his way to provoke him. Every new angle that came up made the game more difficult and exciting, and served to put their skill to the test. Quinto had great confidence in Canal and was delighted to give him so complicated a case and to see how skillfully he handled it. Ampelio, on the other hand, was irritated by the way the lawyer kept raising difficulties; it struck him as mere defeatism. It was not that he trusted Caisotti or that he thought their project foolproof, but rather that Canal's scruples went against the brisk, almost aggressive spirit with which he had thrown himself into the affair. He was convinced that it was one of those things that you either handled resolutely, in the way people do who set a dozen such deals going every day and then let them take their own course; or else you got bogged down in ifs and buts, and then the whole thing became an interminable bore. And in that case, God, why start it in the first place?

He was on his feet, smoking, and from the dry, ironical way he spoke he seemed to have grown more pessimistic about the affair than Canal, and he started attacking Quinto. Deprived of his brother's support, Quinto began to hesitate. Of course, if the outlook was really so uncertain, perhaps the best course was to back out and return to their original project – sell the flowerpottery and leave it at that.

But now it was Canal who wanted to go ahead. As he studied the clauses of the proposed contract, he began to enjoy the prospect of anticipating all the ways in which Caisotti might wriggle out of his obligations and to arm himself with more involved clauses, precautions, restraints, guarantees of every description. He was grimacing and rolling his eyes, running a hand through his disorderly hair, speckling the papers on the desk with marginal notes. "I'll draw you up a contract designed especially for Caisotti, one that won't give an inch. He won't have a hope in hell of getting out of it." He giggled as he sat there bent double, imagining a contract as spiky as a porcupine.

Then, with a sceptical shrug, he added, "Insofar as contracts ever really hold, of course."

10

It began during the period of plans, blueprints, estimates. The key man now was Travaglia.

Travaglia was one of the busiest construction engineers in town and he couldn't spare Quinto and Ampelio much time. They conducted their business through brief, harassed sessions while construction plans were unrolled and spread out on the table and Travaglia answered the telephone and cursed his surveyors.

Travaglia did everything by fits and starts, now issuing a spate of orders, now sitting at his desk tracing lines with a ruler, now scrapping everything and making a clean start. But then, every so often, he would raise his clear eyes, smile, stretch his arms down his heavy body, and be perfectly at peace, as though vistas of endless leisure stretched out ahead of him. He was a fat man, but he sat perched on the high swivel stool by the drawing table; he laughed, staring into the distance. "Do either of you two have the faintest idea what a construction contract is?" His manner was protective, contemptuous, artful. His weight and his early baldness gave him an air of maturity, an authoritative appearance which he put to full use. The Anfossi brothers, who lived from hand to mouth and pursued vague ambitions quite out of their reach, represented in Travaglia's eyes a way of life which he had rejected at the start of his career: the life of art, of science, and to some extent of political ideas as well. And he'd been right to reject them, he assured himself as he looked at them: never getting ahead, making no sort of position for themselves. Quinto, a man still without arts or parts; Ampelio, a dishwasher in some university laboratory who might get a chair at the age of sixty. A pair of failures, there was no longer any doubt about it. As he looked at them, he felt more than ever satisfied with himself, and in dealing with them he paraded his own philosophy of life, that of the practical man who puts first things first. But there was something else in his attitude, a note of violence, a sort of aggressive irritation which the Anfossis always aroused in him. "Because, after all, damn it, I like the poor devils! And I'm the only person who understands them."

They were looking at some accounts. Travaglia raised his head and studied the pair of them, then broke into one of his tired, silent laughs. "Tell me," he said, "just tell me one thing: who put you up to this?"

"You don't need to say any more – you've had enough of us for today. We'll be back tomorrow. We'll tackle the question on our own." The Anfossis were on their way to the door.

"Hey!" cried Travaglia, running after them. "You don't think I'd let you go it alone! That fellow Caisotti would swallow you in one mouthful, you poor innocents. You stay where you are. Let's see now, where were we?"

They had to send the surveyor to ask Caisotti about something marked on the plan. His office was not far from Travaglia's. The man returned with the news that he wasn't there. "I asked the girl—"

"Ah, the girl.... ." Travaglia sniggered.

"She said she didn't know."

"That girl doesn't even know where her – But she was there when we saw it. Go back and tell her it's on the table; it was there this morning and it must be there now."

Ampelio had been sitting in his raincoat, his beard sunk on his chest, not saying anything. Suddenly he stood up and said, "I'll go."

Travaglia gave another of his silent laughs, another stare at nothing, as though he had something in mind that he couldn't put into words.

Quinto was confused. After a while, he said, "I don't understand; you wanted Ampelio to go there to ..."

"What?" Travaglia was already thinking about something else. They started checking the figures.

Ampelio was back in twenty minutes. He stood there stiffly without saying anything.

"Well?"

"We'll have to go to the site. There's a mistake in the plan."

In the end they all went. The flowerpottery and the part of the garden with the forget-me-not bed were in a state of confusion; Signora Anfossi had started to transplant her flowers. It was a fine day and under the warm sun flowers

and leaves took on an air of luxuriant gaiety. Quinto had
never realized that so intense and various a life flourished
within that narrow space, and now, at the thought that it
was all to die and be replaced by a structure of bricks and
girders, he was overcome by a sense of sadness, a fondness
even for the weeds and nettles, which was almost repent-
ance. The other two, however, seemed merely to be enjoying
the pleasant weather. Travaglia had been wearing a hat, but
feeling the heat he had taken it off and was carrying it in his
hand; it had marked his forehead with a red, sweaty line.
Before long he began to feel the sun on his bald head and he
put his hat on again, but on the back of his head, which gave
him a gay, Sunday air. Ampelio had finally removed his
unseasonable raincoat and was carrying it, neatly folded,
over one shoulder. They were measuring a section of the site
where the boundary line curved in. Quinto left them to it.
Travaglia, although he was working, was in one of his peri-
ods of contemplative calm. "What are these called?" he
asked Ampelio, pushing aside some plants with his fingers.
Ampelio answered with an air of vigorous authority that
surprised Quinto, who had not realized his brother took any
interest in flowers.

There was a sudden movement among some dahlias in
pots, and who should emerge, peering at them through her
thick lashes, but Caisotti's secretary. She was wearing a
lightweight suit. "Oh, you're here," she said. "I was looking
for Signor Caisotti."

"Certainly we're here," Quinto said, for some reason suddenly furious. "This is still our property; the contract hasn't
yet been signed."

Shrug. "I don't know about that. He said he'd be here,
with a gentleman—" She broke off and covered her mouth

with a letter she was carrying, as though she were embarrassed at having said too much. She stood there stiffly in her
close-fitting jacket.

"That's it, he's not yet bought the site and he's already
selling apartments, even though they're not built yet,"
Quinto said, turning to the other two, denouncing the man
and at the same time forced to admire him.

Travaglia and Ampelio weren't listening. They had turned
toward the girl. The engineer stood with his head inclined
to one side, his eyes half shut, laughing in his tired way.
Ampelio, one finger in the pocket of his jacket, his coat still
draped sideways across his shoulder, his eyes hidden behind
his thick glasses, looked like someone from the nineteenth
century. "Ah, mail," he said, reaching toward the letter that
the girl was holding. She quickly hid it behind her back, as
though they were playing a game. "It's not for you, it's for
Signor Caisotti." "Is it so urgent?" Shrug. "How should I
know?" "Do you or don't you know," Travaglia broke in,
"that Caisotti's measurements are all to his advantage?"
"Oh.... Well, where the land slopes it measures less." "Oh,
so you know that, do you?" Shrug.

Travaglia laughed. "Does Caisotti tell you every morning
what you've got to say or only what you're *not* to say?"

The girl blinked and tossed her hair over her shoulders.
"How do you mean? Caisotti never tells me anything."

"Fine sort of secretary you must be."

The discussion was becoming playful. They were walking
up and down together, the girl between them. She had picked
a flower and was holding it between her lips. Ampelio
brought out a pack of cigarettes, offering them to the girl
first. "No, thank you, I don't smoke," she bleated, the flower
still in her mouth.

"A girl with no vices, eh?" Travaglia said teasingly.

"So what?"

There was a rustling sound from the terrace above and Signora Anfossi looked over the hedge. She was wearing a big straw hat and garden gloves, and carried a large pair of scissors, with which she cut some roses. Travaglia noticed her first; he took off his hat.

"Hello, boys, who is this with you? Oh, Signor Travaglia, it's nice to see you. Have you come to take a look at the site? Do please put your hat on. What do you think about this great project of ours?"

Travaglia replaced his hat carefully. "We'll try to do a good job, Signora, you can count on that."

"And who is the charming young lady? Wait a moment, I think we've met," the Signora went on, sliding her sunglasses down to the tip of her nose. "Yes, it's Lina.'

Quinto, for some reason, said dryly, "No, no, Mother, you don't know her."

"But I do," she insisted. "She came here the other day to get the draft of the contract. Her name's Lina; she's the contractor's secretary – our partner's, I should say."

The girl had drawn back a little when Signora Anfossi appeared, and was looking the other way. Now she stepped toward the hedge. "Yes, it's me, Lina. Nice to see you."

Quinto and Ampelio were both irritated and wanted to put a stop to the proceedings. Ampelio made a start by asking Travaglia about the slope of the ground. "There must be some way of allowing for it, surely?"

But Travaglia continued his conversation with the Signora. "I see you're doing a little gardening," he remarked.

"I'm trying to save what can be saved."

They all went about their business, the Signora to her roses, Travaglia and the two brothers to measure a corner of the site again, while the girl, Lina, stood a little way off, by herself. Travaglia's mind was not on the job; he was bubbling into laughter again.

"You poor jerks!"

"Why?"

"Because of what you're doing to your mother, making her call Caisotti your 'partner.' Your mother's partner."

"You're mad. We've never called him our partner. She was the one who used the word just now, heaven knows why."

"Partner, my ass! Anyway, what has that go to do with it? What's more, this is our affair and we'll finish it ourselves."

"You poor, poor jerks!"

They were going on like this, out of temper with each other, measuring the ground and exchanging sarcastic remarks, when they heard a mumble of voices behind them. They turned around and there was Caisotti, standing beside Lina. He said something to her in an undertone, the slack lines of his face stretched tight with anger, but the girl stood up for herself. He had snatched the letter out of her hand; apparently it enraged him, for he read it several times, spelling it out to himself, syllable by syllable. He put away the letter, stuck his hands in his pockets, and walked on, taking no notice of the rest of them. Apart from the impression of brutality and obstinacy, Quinto was conscious again of something weak and defenseless in this solitary man who made an enemy of everyone. He was striding up and down, his face contorted with anger, his eyes wrinkled. Quinto had never seen him quite so badly dressed. He was wearing a shrunken jacket buttoned over a checked woolen shirt, shapeless yellow pants, and a pair of old shoes spotted with cement. He really looked like a bricklayer now; he needed only the cocked hat made out of newspaper.

With Caisotti, Quinto noticed, the girl dropped her usual air of reserve and looked almost brazen, ready to argue the toss with him. She walked a few steps behind, a little frightened but still aggressive, as though there was a rage against him deep inside her which she'd never let out.

Caisotti continued to walk up and down, looking tense and irritated. Then he turned to the Anfossis and nodded toward them as though they were meeting by chance in the street. "We're here to measure this bit of the site where the ground slopes," Quinto said, then at once regretted that he had spoken, for he caught in his voice a suggestion of apology for their being there at all, although the land still belonged to them. To correct this impression, he turned on Caisotti aggressively. "We're here because your measurements won't do, you see, they're all wrong!"

Caisotti peered forward as though he were looking at Quinto on the horizon. His eyelids were red, his eyes watery, his lips moist like someone in a towering rage, or like a child liable to burst into tears at any moment. "What's this new trouble you're trying to make?" Clearly he could hardly wait to start working off his temper. "You go and do your job and leave me to do mine," he shouted.

"Just a moment, Caisotti." Travaglia stepped forward with the air of someone just then arriving on the scene. "You're a contractor, that's your job, I'm an engineer, that's mine. Right? Well, then ..." And he began explaining the whole thing to him. Caisotti listened to him, but he kept his eyes on the ground and shook his head, as though to say,

Yes, all this is fine, I could get on with you, you know your job, but these two are impossible, you never know what they'll want next, and anyway it's clear they've got it in for me.

"No, no, Caisotti, just listen to me." Travaglia smiled blandly, sleepily, in the manner of someone who understands this sort of situation and knows there's no good getting worked up about it. "But what am I going to do? Just tell me what I'm expected to do!" Caisotti opened his arms wide and his cadences became more plaintive than usual, one long, unending whine, and even Travaglia's vowels grew broader and broader, as though to say, Take it easy, we'll find a way. As they spoke, they both seemed to be trying to lull one another to sleep. Quinto felt excluded from this softly voweled game; he felt expressly singled out as a person who simply didn't count, and not only him but his whole family – as though being property owners and having dictated the terms of the deal, as Quinto was convinced he had done, had no importance whatever. He didn't know whose tone irritated him more, Caisotti's or Travaglia's. This was exactly the occasion when Ampelio should have intervened in that disconcerting way he had; Quinto turned around, but he wasn't there. He was a little way off, at the bottom of the garden where it was greenest. Quinto saw his back, a dark shadow against the sun; Lina was facing him, with that willful little air of hers, twisting a lock of hair around one finger. They were speaking in undertones, and every so often he took a step forward and she stepped back. At a certain point, still with his back to the others, Ampelio said loudly, as though he had been listening to everything the contractor said:

"All right, Caisotti, if that's the way you want it. We're still prepared to drop the whole thing. The contract hasn't been signed yet."

"Drop the whole thing, what do you mean?" cried Caisotti, his voice angry and bitter again, but in the middle of this outburst he changed tactics and forced a laugh. A Caisotti laugh, not pretty to look at, a clenched, gap-toothed kind of laugh. He was looking at the others to see if they agreed that Ampelio had said something absurd. "Drop the deal, you say. Then what are we all doing here?" He laughed again. "We're here to make a deal, right? A friendly deal, that's what we all want, right?"

The Signora looked over the hedge again. "Drop the deal, you say? Oh, dear, my poor plants, pull them up, put them back again, pull them up. ..."

Caisotti was waving his arms now, laughing; he was at his most expansive. "No, no, Signora, we're all friends here; we're going to do things in a friendly way. Don't you worry, we'll do a good job, you'll have nothing to complain about. And while the workmen are here, are there any little improvements you'd like made in the garden?"

"No, no, on no account workmen in the garden."

"Then we'll have no workmen in the garden! We'll have a path here; they can pass in front."

"That wall that'll be facing us – perhaps if it had a few creepers on it..."

"What's that, creepers, eh! Fine, we'll have some lovely plants, just whatever you want. You'll see, we'll get on fine."

As he stood there gesturing clumsily, he knocked down one of the dahlias. "And he didn't even say he was sorry," Signora Anfossi remarked afterward.

11

Oddly, when it came time to sign the contract, Caisotti didn't make a fuss about the points where trouble was expected. He picked on quite trivial points where it was easy to meet his objections. Quinto was positively disappointed. It was a tricky, involved contract, prickly as a thornbush; Canal and the notary had really outdone themselves. Everything was there: the construction contract, the date for final payment of the total sum, as well as date and amounts of the regular installments; the dates when the completed apartments were to be handed over; and the whole thing was tied to a "reversion clause," which meant that if the contractor failed to meet any of his obligations (as specified in the contract), the property reverted to the owners, together with any buildings constructed on it in the meantime, in whatever state they were then in.

"If he signs this," Canal said to Quinto, "you're safe – he won't be able to touch you."

Caisotti had signed, he had let them have their way as though the business of a contract was a mere formality. He came to the notary's by himself, without a lawyer or anyone – "an economy measure," they said, or else, "because every time he hires a lawyer he ends up quarreling with him." The meeting was attended by the three Anfossis, the Signora and her sons, as well as by their lawyer and their notary. As Caisotti came into the office (the atmosphere of the place in itself was presumably calculated to intimidate him) and saw all those educated people writing away, he looked around like a trapped animal who instinctively tries to escape but knows it's no longer any use. Daniel in the lion's den, Quinto said to himself, always ready to see the man in a favorable light. But this image of Caisotti as victim gave him no satisfaction; he needed to see him as some wild, savage beast, a lion, for example, and his own party as a den full of Daniels surrounding the man – relentless, virtuous Daniels goading him like jailers with forked contractual clauses.

Caisotti took a chair near the notary's desk, while the others sat or stood around; he listened attentively as the contract was read, his mouth half open, every now and then silently repeating a phrase to himself. Quinto found himself wondering if the truth of the matter was that the man was simply stupid. But in fact he was concentrating in order not to miss anything, and every so often he would raise one of his big hands and say, "Stop," and the notary would go back and read the passage again, enunciating very deliberately. At times it looked as if Caisotti was on the point of rejecting the whole thing, as if he thought this was all a trap. Quinto half expected him to jump to his feet and say, You're crazy! and slam the door behind him. But no, he waited for the notary to finish, and then nodded to indicate his approval. When he did raise an objection, it was in some part of the contract where no one had expected trouble; he was particularly concerned with the technical details and there was some business about gravel which led to endless argument, all the more so since Ampelio seemed to think it was a matter of principle and refused to budge an inch, even though Canal advised him to let it go.

Quinto was bored, and since everyone was concentrating on the discussion, he went over to the window and looked out at the street, bright in the spring sunlight, and tried to work up some feeling for the place and for the deal, which was going ahead nicely; but he felt as if the whole affair was now really over and that this adventure in real estate was merely a matter of administration, of long, boring discussions. It no longer interested him or excited him and his only hope was that from now on Ampelio would stand by him.

The ground was easy now and everything seemed to be going smoothly; it was at this point that Caisotti succeeded in deferring the date on which one of the payments was due, or rather two of the three payments, and also in lowering the total by two hundred thousánd lire.

They had not yet reached the point of signing the contract when Ampelio looked at his watch and said that he had to go if he was to catch his train.

Quinto had had no idea he intended to leave. "What do you mean? The thing hasn't been signed yet. ..." Suddenly he felt furiously angry with his brother. "Why do you have to go now?"

"I have to go, that's all there is to it. Who's got to be in the laboratory tomorrow, you or me?" Ampelio's voice was insulting.

Quinto felt thoroughly fed up at the idea of having to stay and look after everything himself; he had got it into his head that Ampelio was going to handle the matter, which would leave him free to regard it with a certain detachment. He had hoped that from now on it was going to be like this. They began to argue in a rapid undertone, in front of Caisotti and the notary. "You never said you'd have to go. Leaving me here like this ..." "It's practically finished. Mother has power of attorney; she can sign and then everything is settled." "No, there's still lots to do. We haven't agreed on anything. ..."

"But if Ampelio has got to be at the laboratory tomorrow ...?" Signora Anfossi broke in.

There's more money to be made this way than in all his laboratories put together, Quinto was on the point of saying, as though he were playing the part of an elderly businessman who doesn't want his sons to go to college. But he checked himself, and what he in fact said was, "Yes, but we ought to reach some agreement, so that when one of us is away the other is here."

"If you have to leave too, don't worry," Caisotti said suddenly. "Go ahead. At this stage, if necessary, the Signora and I can settle the rest of what there is to settle."

Quinto remembered something that Canal had said – greatly to their annoyance, at the time – and which Travaglia had repeated in almost the same words: "I tell you what'll happen. You start this wretched business going and that's the last that'll be seen of you. You'll leave your mother to pull the chestnuts out of the fire."

"As a matter of fact," the notary said, "it would be convenient if one of you did stay. There are still some papers to see to."

"I'm staying, of course I'm staying," Quinto said quickly. "I've no intention of going." He was furious because he had really wanted to stay, though admittedly he had had half an idea of going to Milan. Bensi and Cerveteri had called a meeting to set the editorial policy of their new review, and though he didn't really want to go, since he disapproved of their position, he would have quite liked to be there, just by accident as it were. One way and another, he was furious.

Ampelio had left. Everything was dealt with rapidly – the signatures, the promissory notes, and all the rest. As Quinto and Caisotti walked down the stairs, chatting about the time when building would start, Caisotti said, "Everything depends now on getting the green light from City Hall. We'll have to put up the proposal to the technical office, wait till they hold a general meeting, and then if everything goes well—"

"But ... how long will that take?" Quinto suddenly felt alarmed. "I thought everything was settled."

Caisotti snorted. "With those bureaucrats? Not on your life! They can hold us up for months. And if there's something they don't like, oh, that means headaches, I can tell you!"

"But the work?"

"The work doesn't start till we get the green light, that's for sure."

Quinto stopped on the stairs. "Look here, Caisotti, you've just signed a contract committing you to handing over the finished apartments to us by December thirty-first."

"Take it easy!" Caisotti took a step forward. Quinto had not seen this expression before, a look of sullen fury quite different from the occasion when he had lost his temper in their garden. "Take it easy! The contract says I hand over in eight months. And eight months means *eight months after I get the authorization.* Right?"

"The hell it does! Look, Caisotti, the date is on the contract. You're required to let us have the apartments on the last day of December this year."

Yes, and then again, no. December 31st, agreement, contract. ... It appeared that in one place the contract stated that the apartments were to be ready in eight months, and in another, "by December 31st." However, legal opinion was that they needn't worry, since there was no reason to suppose it would take long to get the affair approved.

Moreover, they said, Caisotti is the kind of man who always gets his way. He'd got his hooks into the boys in City Hall.

Quinto and Caisotti said good-bye as they left the notary's office. Quinto was already wondering if he hadn't slipped up somewhere.

12

Work started late. There were a couple of men on the job; they were digging the ground in preparation for the foundations. One was a lean, dark, bad-tempered fellow who wore nothing but a pair of shorts, with a handkerchief tied around his head like a pirate. He was a born idler, always taking time off to smoke or play around with the maids. Every now and then, with a heavy sigh, he would pick up the shovel that he had left sticking in the ground, first spitting on the palms of his hands. The other was a great bull of a man with red, cropped hair; he kept his head down as though he didn't want to see anyone or hear anyone, though in fact he was a good-looking fellow, in spite of his savage, bewildered expression. He laid on with pick or shovel as though he were a bulldozer, and if he replied to the other man's witticisms, it was only in sullen, inarticulate grunts. "A fine worker," commented Caisotti, who paid a visit now and then to see how things were going. This was in answer to Quinto's objection that with only two workmen the job would take a year. "He does the work of three men. Keeps at it for hours on end, without a break. Only wish I'd got a few more of his sort."

The main events of the summer were these: A dispute with
Caisotti about the mounds of earth that were blocking the
road. A two-week break in the work when he had to trans-
fer all his men to another site, where he was badly behind
schedule. And his failure to meet the first payment.

Quinto was enjoying himself. He was always on the move;
seeing Canal to get him to write a warning letter to Caisotti;
seeing the notary about details of the registration of the
contract – there was always something not quite in order;
seeing Travaglia and getting him to the site to check that everything was going according to the terms of the contract – in
fact, the foundations were hardly laid; seeing Caisotti to hurry
him on or complain about something. Quinto's professional
friends were always ready to lend a hand, and though they
didn't take him too seriously they were amused to see him
finally face to face with practical problems. Travaglia did not
spare him a good deal of ironical witticism, the notary provided tactful advice, and Canal, all professional rigor, stuck
his heels in and wouldn't give an inch.

Relations with Caisotti were more difficult, more indirect,
but when Quinto did manage to get hold of him, he felt that
he was enjoying the richest rewards that the project had to
offer. *Moral* rewards, that is, since the question of the material rewards due to follow was shot through with an anxiety,
a shiver of danger, which Quinto recognized – now that he
was experiencing them for himself – as the spice of private
enterprise. He felt morally rewarded when, for example, an
exchange of phrases with Caisotti revealed the mutual
respect between capitalist and contractor – the meaningful
look rewarded him ("we're in this together"), the flicker of
confusion on Caisotti's face, which meant that he had
played his cards well. Their approaches were brusque.

"Look here, Caisotti," Quinto would open aggressively, bearing down on him while he was sitting alone at his usual sidewalk table in front of the Caffé Melina, scowling at a coffee cup or an empty glass (business was obviously going badly), "what's this all about, eh?" Caisotti would reluctantly bring Quinto into his field of vision, then look away again as though he'd rather not have seen him. Quinto, rising a little self-consciously to his theme, would then proceed to justify his complaint. Caisotti would continue to look straight ahead of him, biting his lips as though he were keeping back a violent outburst and just managing to transform it (by means of the jerky movements of his head that followed next) into a general sense of discouragement and distrust. His replies were always wide of the mark, but loaded with an absolute lack of esteem; they were often so insulting as to preclude all further possibility of discussion. The gloves were off now, and the cups and saucers rattled as Caisotti's fists, compact as small footballs, pounded on the table. In these exchanges, Quinto noted with satisfaction, it was Caisotti who seemed anxious to keep his voice down and prevent anyone from overhearing what they were arguing about. Then they would both calm down and act as though the barrier separating them had been removed. They talked about the future, about what they both had to gain from going ahead with the venture. They talked like partners, like equals. The motley, busy crowd that filled the street pressed up against their table. From where they sat, they looked across a gay, vulgar flower bed down to the sea front.

Quinto would go home and find the red-haired workman busy at the foundations – the other man had left ahead of time; he was digging away like a madman.

The appearance and the color of the site were changing. The dark, wet-smelling undersoil was being brought up into the light. The living green of the surface soil was disappearing under shovelfuls of soft earth and big, doughy clods heaped up along the trenches. Tangles of dead roots, snails, and worms showed on the walls of the trenches. Signora Anfossi would stand among the clustering plants and the flowers she was leaving to wither on their stems, the tall bushes and the branches of mimosa, and peer over the hedge to watch the mounds of earth growing day by day more numerous in the waste land which had once been her garden. Then she would turn back to her green.

13

"In the meanwhile, if you find anyone looking for an apartment or a shop, you can send him on to me," Quinto said to the man in the Superga agency, after paying him his commission.

"Send him on to you.... How do you mean?"

"It'll take a few months still, of course," Quinto said. "The apartment building on my land – the one Caisotti is putting up. It'll be ready by December?

"December? Oh, sure." The agent laughed.

"Yes, December – it's in the contract. We've got a reversion clause, you know!" Quinto was by now resigned to the fact that the apartments wouldn't in fact be ready by December, but it annoyed him to hear it put like this, as a matter of course, by this individual who had nothing to do with the affair. "Caisotti has to hand them over by the end of the year."

"Sure, sure, the end of *next* year, eh! No good counting on dates when you're dealing with a guy like Caisotti!"

"Bit late to tell me this now, isn't it? Who recommended Caisotti to me in the first place?"

There was a woman waiting in the office, dark-haired, lean, tanned. "Did you say apartments?" she asked. "In what part of town? How many rooms?" She was about thirty-five, a Milanese or anyway from Lombardy. In her tight-fitting summer dress she looked too thin, even a little wasted, but there was a suggestion of energy, of impulsiveness, in her expression. Quinto looked at her. There was a certain refinement, a harmony of line, in her face and breasts and her bare arms.

"No, no, Signora," the agent said, "they're not ready yet. Anyway, you want to buy an apartment and I gather these are to be rented." He looked at Quinto.

"That's so, yes," Quinto said, and the subject was closed.

"Now, that new house I was telling you about, Signora," the agent went on.

"Good-bye," Quinto said, going out. He was irritated by the way the man at once ruled out the possibility of the woman being interested in one of his apartments. He felt furious, suddenly, at not being able to discuss the matter with her: the number of rooms, the way they were laid out, the conveniences, etc. At his abrupt good-bye, she had looked at him questioningly, a hint of a smile on her face. An interesting woman, not good-looking perhaps, but interesting – very much a woman. What Quinto would have liked was not so much to talk to her about the apartments, but simply to talk to her. And in fact he had not moved far from the agency, as if he was waiting for her to come out. She did appear a moment later, and he went up to her. "Excuse me," he began, "I just wanted to say – about those apartments, if you had thought at all about that part of town, the question of sale or lease is something we could discuss."

"Oh, thank you," she said, "I really don't know yet. As I was saying to the man, I simply wanted to get a general idea of the possibilities. We haven't decided whether to take a place here or in Rapallo. My husband ..."

They walked along together.

"You're from Milan?"

"Well, Mantua really."

"Ah, Mantua. Which part of the beach do you go to?"

"Near the Serenella. Do you know it?"

"Yes, I go there every now and then."

"Well, whenever you're next there, my umbrella is the one nearest the pier."

Quinto went there the next day. There was not much beach and it was packed with people. She was sharing her umbrella with a group of friends, among them a colonel. Quinto had to sit down and join in the conversation, which was a great bore. He was sorry he'd come. She was nothing much to look at in a bathing suit and she didn't interest him the way she'd done the day before. The sea was rather rough and no one wanted to swim, but finally they decided they ought to go in and splashed about in the breakers, making a great deal of noise. There was a rope, half rotten and slimy-green with seaweed, hanging from a row of iron posts. Nelly was nervous and kept close to the rope. As each wave came, Quinto held her by the arm, from behind, to support her. A wave that looked as if it was going to be bigger than the others was just on them, and Quinto managed to get his hands on her breasts. It was in fact quite a small wave. She laughed and did not remove his hands.

They spent the night together. To find a room, Quinto had to spend the whole afternoon searching; it was August and hotels and pensions were all packed. Finally he managed to find a place where they only asked to see the man's papers. The room overlooked a busy street and Quinto, used to his cool house up on the hill, was hot and couldn't get to sleep. It was not a proper double bed and they had to lie close together. They were naked, the sheet was sweaty, and the light of a street lamp shone through the open window. Nelly was sleeping with her back to him and he had to lie on the edge of the bed if he wasn't to be pressed right against her. He thought about waking her up. Being the first time, their love-making hadn't amounted to much, and he felt that perhaps it was up to him to start again. He would only have needed a little encouragement, but she was asleep and he was lazy and it suited him to think that she was the kind of person who didn't mind much one way or the other – not at all the sensual woman he had at first supposed. He looked at the back of her neck; her skin was no longer fresh and her shoulder blades were bony. For years Quinto had gone only with women who slightly repelled him physically. This was a deliberate program: he was afraid of ties, he only wanted casual affairs.

He started thinking about the project, about Caisotti, about the payments.... .

14

There was no cement. That month, apparently, the usual deliveries had not been made and all the building jobs in the district were idle, or so Caisotti said. Travaglia did in fact confirm the story when Quinto went to ask him about it, but then he started to laugh and implied that while cement was not to be had in certain circumstances, in others – well, there was cement. It was a question, in short, of being willing to pay for it. A good many crews had suspended work, but only for a few days; most of them were now busy again. Only Caisotti had no cement; and this was the time to start laying the foundations.

"A put-up job, you say! This is the last straw, with all I've got to put up with – you people coming here to give me hell!" Caisotti turned on Quinto aggressively when he came to inquire what was happening; but then, as usual, he calmed down and started being sorry for himself. "You think this is my idea of a joke?" he whined. "Keeping my men idle, machinery rented for nothing, losing the best time of the year, missing my delivery dates. ... If they won't let me have the cement, what the hell can I do?" Lately the man had become quite impossible to deal with. He had got it into his head that because he hadn't yet been able to meet the first payment, the Anfossis were going around setting people against him.

"Look here, Caisotti, you don't pay us and you try and put the blame on us!"

"Hell, man, I'm having a hard time. Happens to everyone, see. And you go and bring the lawyer into it. He hates me, that guy does; I've known it for ages. And you have to tell the notary all about me, and he blabs it to half the town. Yes, and your mother, she goes around saying that Caisotti doesn't pay his debts. Then what happens? They all start pestering me and I don't get my cement."

"So it's true then.... You don't have the cement because you haven't paid for it!"

Caisotti waved his fist in Quinto's face. "Watch your step, mister," he yelled. "I've had enough! I don't pay for it, eh. ..." They were standing in the most chaotic part of the site, amid piles of earth and planks left here and there. From the tool shed the red-haired workman emerged and stood, towering, behind Caisotti, his back slightly bent, his face expressionless, a cross between an angel and an orangutan.

"Put your hands down, Caisotti, do you mind?" Quinto said. "Starting a fight will settle nothing." Never had the man appeared to him so much an unarmed hero in a hostile world, taking them all on single-handed. He was pleased with himself, too, for having responded to Caisotti's brutal outburst with only a sense of cold superiority; he was aware all the time that he was the one who had the situation under control. And in fact Caisotti quickly put his hands in his pockets, as though ashamed of his outburst, and muttered something under his breath. Then he turned his anger against the big workman, finding some excuse to bawl him out. The man stood there in silence, listening, head down.

Quinto remained master of the occasion. But Caisotti neither paid up nor did he push the work ahead.

Then there was the argument about the pipes. They had been uncovered during the digging and then left lying where they were. According to the terms of the contract, everything recovered from the site belonged to Caisotti. But Signora Anfossi, seeing the pipes apparently thrown away and left to get rusty, leaned over the hedge one day when he was there, and asked him if he meant to do anything with them.

He was in one of his black moods. "What do you expect me to do with your pipes?"

"Well, then," she said, delighted, "if you're not going to do anything with them, they'd be useful to me in the garden. I'll send someone to get them." And so next day she sent the gardener for them and got him to fix up a system of pipes to water a bed of narcissus. This had happened more than a month previously. Then one day she had looked over the hedge (she heard Caisotti moving about on the other side) and she made some comment or other about his failure to meet the first payment or the work being behind schedule. In her quiet, composed way, she never lost an occasion, as she moved about the garden, looking after her flowers, to make some little wounding remark. He had mumbled something, not wanting to be drawn, and they both kept on with what they were doing. That seemed to be the end of it, when suddenly Caisotti started shouting furiously, "It's theft, Signora Anfossi, theft, I say! I'm going to report you to the police! That'll teach you to go about stealing people's pipes! First you sell and then you steal back what you've sold. Fine way for the gentry to behave!"

"You must be mad," Signora Anfossi said, shaking her head.

That was the day Ampelio came home. He had been attending a conference of chemists in Germany. Quinto was upstairs; he heard him talking to their mother, then go out again. She came up to Quinto's room. "Quickly, you must go after Ampelio and stop him. I'm afraid he's going to do something silly. I told him that our nice Signor Caisotti had reached the point of calling me a thief, and Ampelio said,

'Where is he, where is he, I'll bash his head in!' And he went off to look for him."

Quinto ran out into the road after his brother; he was some way ahead, walking fast. "Ampelio, Ampelio," he shouted. "What's the matter with you? Mother's frightened. Where are you going?"

Ampelio kept on walking, not bothering to turn around. "I'm going to bash his head in."

"Look, do we really have to take everything Caisotti says seriously? He's quite irresponsible. ..."

"I'm going to bash his head in."

"That won't help, Ampelio. I nearly poked him myself the other day. The bastard's trying to create difficulties in order to put off the deadline. If you start a quarrel, you'll be doing him a favor."

"But in the meantime I'll have bashed his head in."

This might have been the moment to raise a different type of objection, namely that Caisotti had a pair of shoulders like a brick wall and fists to knock down a calf, while Ampelio was a university teacher who didn't weigh much over a hundred pounds. But neither of them raised this point; it probably didn't even occur to them. Quinto, puffing along behind

Ampelio, developed a different line of argument. Their relations with Caisotti were in a delicate phase, he said; they had to use tact, diplomacy, pay no attention to his tantrums. The great thing was to be flexible.... .

"Flexible!" said Ampelio. "Paid off pretty well so far, your flexibility, hasn't it? There's not one brick on top of another."

It was Quinto's turn to lose his temper. "God! I like that! I've been chasing Caisotti for months and now you suddenly turn up and start taking a strong line! Hail the conquering hero!"

"But I've been at Frankfurt!"

"What the hell's that got to do with it?" But Quinto had paused to think before replying, and now he had lost steam.

They walked on for a little while in silence. It wasn't clear where Ampelio expected to find Caisotti, and Quinto didn't ask him. Then, suddenly, as they were crossing the square, they heard the noise of an engine starting up and there the man was, behind the windshield of a small, three-wheeled truck. The bodywork projected in front like a torpedo; Caisotti was sitting stiffly in the saddle, grasping the shuddering handlebars. He was wearing a cap fastened under his chin and a wind-breaker. Turning to Ampelio as though they had been talking a few hours ago, he said. "They've let me have my cement! I told you you only had to be patient, didn't I? Now I can get the work going again; I'll put on all the men I can. You give me a few days' grace and I'll settle the payment with interest. Right?"

Ampelio was calm and friendly. "Fine. When do you start laying the foundations?"

"Saturday."

"This Saturday? Couldn't start sooner?"

"Saturday will be time enough. The cement will dry over the weekend, then on Monday we'll start work."

"What about the payment? The second one is almost due, you know."

"You'll just have to be patient for a while and I'll settle the two together. That's for sure – I know where I am now. I wouldn't say that if it weren't so."

"We're counting on you, Caisotti."

"We'll beat all the records this time! 'Bye now, and my respects to the Signora." And with a volley of sharp reports, the machine was under way.

Quinto didn't know what to say. "You see?" Ampelio remarked.

"See what? He's played one more trick on us, I see that."

Ampelio shook his head briefly as though excluding this possibility altogether. "No, no, this time he'll keep his word."

"Grow up, won't you! You don't know him. Start laying the foundations on Saturday, hell! You don't realize what state the work's in; go take a look. He's just playing with you. And this business of putting off the payment again, as though it didn't matter! And you stood there calmly and let him get away with everything!"

"What about you? You never opened your mouth all the time."

"I wanted to watch you handle it. But I never expected—" Ampelio shook his head. "You don't understand the situation. He's going through a difficult period right now, but he's got a chance of recovering. If we're always on his back and start taking legal action, we'll start a panic among his creditors and the next thing we know, he'll go bankrupt. Now the question is this: is this in our interest or is it in our interest to back him up? If he goes bankrupt, there'll be the suit about the proceeds, with all the creditors.... . We'll have to hand the project over to another firm, and God knows on what terms. On the other hand, if Caisotti can put his affairs in order, we're all right too."

Quinto wrung his hands. This was his own reading of the situation, reached after much painful thought; he had been trying to explain it to his brother a minute back. And now ... "I thought you wanted to bash his head in," he remarked.

"It wasn't the psychological moment. I realized that at once. And then don't you see, Caisotti has given ground; all that talk of his was intended to make amends, even his final 'My respects to the Signora.' He changed his position in a flash."

They were on the brink of a quarrel. Quinto had only to come out with, "All your doing, eh?" which was on the tip of his tongue; Ampelio had only to give way to the temptation to add, "It only needed a bit of energy," and they would have come to blows. But they kept quiet. After a while, as though there were no other point to raise, Quinto said, "And we should have told him that the first thing to do is buttress the soil on our part of the site, where they've knocked down the wall. They've dumped everything there. The first rain we get, we'll have a landslide on our hands."

"We can leave a note about that in Caisotti's office," Ampelio said. "First things first. That's a secondary matter."

They stopped by his office. Quinto went in alone; Ampelio had gone to buy some cigarettes. The secretary was more evasive than ever. "You can leave the message with me. Oh, all right, put it in writing if you want. If Caisotti comes. ... I haven't seen him for a couple of days." Suddenly she smiled and gestured lavishly. "So! The traveler returns! Got a present for me?"

Ampelio was standing in the doorway. He clicked his heels and bowed low. *"Gnädige Fräulein,"* he murmured.

15

The town's most widely read newspaper was *The Financial Forecast*, a fortnightly published by the Chamber of Commerce. Modest in format, it consisted of only four pages, occupied exclusively with debt failures and defaulters. The names were listed in alphabetical order, with the addresses and the amount of money owing. Sometimes, with an air of reticence or excuse, an explanation was added like "Traveling," "Sickness," "Address Unknown," and often, with something like a gesture of extenuation, "Insufficient funds." A world of small projects and ambitions and failures floated in these columns of faded type: packers and mail florists, ice cream dealers, builders, people with rooms to let.... And the small fry whose financial designs were impossible to make out, people trying to clutch on to the banks of the great money river, people trying to get ahead in spite of their debts, condemned to bear the shame of the paltry sums they owed.

Quinto had now caught the *Forecast* habit too, and every two weeks, when he saw people with the new issue, he hurried to the newsstand to get his copy and studied it in the street like all the others who wanted to check the financial position of the people they had business dealings with, who were looking for the first signs of a crisis or a bankruptcy, or who were simply curious to take a look inside their neighbors' pockets. There was one name Quinto was looking for, *that* name.... And then one day, there it was: Pietro Caisotti. Two loans for 300,000 lire defaulted. Here was the slope that all too many firms had not been able to remount.

The payments, the deadline for the apartments, everything was now problematic. Everything hung by a thread.

It was a ticklish moment. Even Canal, who had made some preliminary soundings himself, recommended calm. In this crisis Caisotti showed his ability; he at once went to see the lawyer, tacitly warning him not to take immediate steps. He explained that his failure to make payment, even though the notice had just appeared in print, was in fact out of date; it referred to the situation of two weeks back, which he had just about got in hand. He was on the point of concluding certain deals, and what's more he was owed money by various people himself and before long he'd be in a position to meet his obligations in full. It was learned through Canal's inquiries that Caisotti was in fact due to collect a certain debt; they succeeded in discovering the date and the amount of the sum. It wasn't a great deal and they would have to hit him quickly if they wanted to collect their debt before anyone else got at him. Caisotti was due to be paid in the morning, and it was arranged that Quinto should make a surprise visit in the early afternoon, promissory note in hand, before he could pretend that he had no money.

Quinto rang and rang again; he was about to go away when the door opened. It was the inevitable Lina, sweating just a little (it was a hot August day); she was now wearing her long black hair in a ponytail. "You're looking for Caisotti? I don't know if he's in." "What do you mean, you don't know?" The office consisted of only two rooms. As Quinto stood there, a door opened down the narrow corridor. It was dark, and in the darkness, wary as a lizard, Caisotti peered out. He looked as if he had been asleep in his clothes; his shirt was sticking out, his belt was undone, his hair was rumpled. He seemed helpless, as though he couldn't see or hear and only wanted to get the gummy taste of sleep out of his mouth. Then he turned about, and going over to the windows, threw open the shutters. The light flooded the room, leaving him blinder than before. It was the familiar office, which, apparently, served as a bedroom as well. The bed, a straw mattress spread on the floor, was behind a screen; there was an iron washbasin. Caisotti went to the basin, and pouring some water from the jug, splashed it over his face, then dried himself. His face still dazed with sleep and his hair wet, he went to the desk and sat down. Quinto took the chair facing him. Lina was no longer there. Outside, the town was lying in the heavy noonday heat shot through with the elusive, tangy smell of burning sand from the beach. Quinto felt as though he'd already said everything he had come to say, even though he'd not opened his mouth. The light had not yet penetrated Caisotti's gluey eyeballs.

He began to talk, slowly, sighing, as though they were in the middle of a conversation. "You know, when things get to a certain point, I give up, I let them do what they want." He carried on in this strain. The light bothered him and he closed the shutters. What a headache it was, he went on, trying to build houses, with everyone putting spokes in your wheel! City Hall wouldn't let you do this, the state hit you for taxes, you have to depend on a dozen people for everything you need. Quinto noticed that Caisotti's complaints were all phrased in such a way as to make it impossible for him to disagree; and it was a special kind of agreement they elicited, being addressed not so much to the business colleague or the creditor, but rather to someone holding the political views which he held himself, or had formerly held.

"And it's the same with the cement," Caisotti continued. "A hell of a situation that is. They've got us by the throat, there's no way out; it's a monopoly. ..." And he began complaining about the big cement companies, quoting instances, restrictions, violations, mentioning places where it would have been easy to get all the cement he wanted if they hadn't been taken over and closed down by the all-powerful cement companies. He showed more skill than Quinto would have expected in identifying the causes of his difficulties and in setting individual facts within a general frame of reference. All the same it was wearisomely familiar, the old, old story about the little man being crushed by the big monopolies that turned up inevitably in every discussion of the Italian economy. Quinto found it particularly irritating since he was not at the moment disposed to consider the situation from this point of view. Not that he didn't agree; Caisotti's case was, in its broad outline, undeniable. But Quinto's role was now that of the owner of real estate and he wanted to look at things the way real estate owners looked at them.

Caisotti described an attempt to start a stone quarry in his village, where he owned a small piece of land; the land was valueless, just a heap of stones, but these stones, according to Caisotti, were perfect for making cement. He'd spent a lot of money on the project, he said, and then the cement companies stepped in and prevented him from going ahead. This reference to "a small piece of land" made Quinto (real estate owner) prick up his ears; this property constituted, in Canal's eyes, a kind of final guarantee, since a foreclosure could be put on it. Now it appeared that it was all stones, the right kind for cement maybe, but useless because the monopoly had succeeded in stopping the project.

"Ah, it's a struggle, it's a struggle," Caisotti said. "Who would have thought, Anfossi, *in those days*, that it was going to be still like this? Remember?"

"Mmm," Quinto murmured. He wasn't sure whether Caisotti's reference was to particular memories or simply to common knowledge.

"We thought that once we'd come down from the hills and chased *them* away, everything would be all right. And now look...."

It appeared that Caisotti had fought with the partisans and indeed in the very outfit to which Quinto had belonged. He had been an inspector in the commissariat, with which Quinto had never had much to do, since the different units of the brigade had been spread out in different parts of the valley and in different valleys. But now it was coming to him that he had once seen the man, wearing a khaki shirt and carrying a Sten gun slung over one shoulder; he had been raising hell about the requisitioning of some beef. Caisotti was much better informed about Quinto and remembered the units to which he had been attached and reminded him of the places where they had bivouacked. Quinto had forgotten the names, but obviously they would be familiar to Caisotti, who came from those parts.

He had gotten up and was standing in a corner of the room. "Do you see this?" High up on the wall, half hidden by a cupboard, was a picture; it was one of those composites with the pictures of all the men of a particular city or formation who died in the war, a white, red, and green ribbon around one corner and underneath, the inscription: "In Memory of the Men of the —th Brigade who Gave their Lives for Freedom." What with the indistinct light and the dirty glass, the picture was hard to make out. Quinto stared at the tiny faces of the fallen, but he didn't seem to remember any of them. He had known so many men who had afterward lost their lives. He was still easily moved by the memory of how even on their last evening he had eaten baked chestnuts with them from the same pot and slept beside them on the straw. He found himself looking for a particular face, a man he had scarcely known who had been killed, stupidly, almost as soon as he arrived. They had been out on patrol together, and it was just chance that one took one side of the road, one the other. He thought for a moment that one of the tiny photographs looked like him, but then he saw another that could just as well have been him. The pictures had been taken ages ago; many of the faces were those of schoolboys, others were men in uniform with their berets and insignia. It was impossible to tell one from the other. Quinto sighed deeply. What was there to say now?

Nothing was settled. Caisotti asked for a deferment on the first payment; he had to finish another building already under way. Once he'd finished it, he could concentrate all his material and all his men on the Anfossi site and complete the work within the stipulated time – which, he reminded Quinto, was to be figured from the date the contract was approved by City Hall, not from the date when it was signed. To make things more difficult for him at this stage, he said, would hurt them as well as him.

Quinto went home in a foul temper. It was not only his failure (once again) to make Caisotti pay up, but also the discovery that he was an old comrade in arms. A fine turn Italian society had taken! Two partisans, one a peasant, the other a student, who had taken up arms together in the belief that they were building a new Italy. And look at them now! Both accepting the world as it was, both chasing money. And they didn't even possess the old bourgeois virtues; they were simply a couple of real estate sharks. It was no accident that they were in partnership and, of course, trying to swindle each other.

However, Quinto reflected, Caisotti had at least retained the habit of looking at his difficulties as part of the social struggle. Whereas in *his* case ...?

16

Shrouded in scaffolding, a chaos of planks, ropes, buckets, sieves, bricks, splotches of sand and lime, the house began to grow in the fall. Already its shadow was falling on the garden; the windows of the villa were shut out from the sky. But it still seemed no more than a temporary structure, a mere obstruction, something that would be pulled down the way it had been put up. That was how Signora Anfossi tried to see it, concentrating her displeasure on transitory symptoms like the objects that fell from the scaffolding onto her flower beds or the piles of planks in the road. She refused to look on it as a *house,* something that would always be there staring her in the face.

Caisotti proposed that in place of the first payment, he should increase the number of rooms to be handed over to the Anfossis. Negotiations were prolonged; during the discussions about the size of the additional rooms, it was discovered that Caisotti had made them all narrower than the contract stipulated so he could squeeze one extra room into each apartment. He was stealing their property, as it were, and proposing to pay them with what he had stolen! Canal spotted the trick in time and a supplement to the contract was drawn up; several clauses of the original contract were revised and the reversion clause was strengthened and extended to cover the delivery of the new apartments. This was fine, but they were still no nearer getting any money out of him, still no nearer the day when the building would be completed.

Ampelio paid a two-day visit during these negotiations. Both he and Quinto were at home, when who should suddenly turn up but Lina. She was bringing some papers: Caisotti wanted her to check some facts before entering the contract on the books at City Hall. Why Caisotti was being so scrupulous was far from clear, since he had never troubled himself about this sort of thing before. Signora Anfossi, as it happened, was out; this was unfortunate since it was always finally up to her to find the papers and accounts which Quinto, as he rushed frantically about, left scattered all over the house. Whenever information was needed, the Signora was the person to see.

Quinto and Ampelio sat down in the study to go over the papers while Lina sat opposite, looking softly at them. "Wait a moment while I look for the account we drew up the other time," Quinto said, and went off next door to ransack his drawers. He turned half a cupboard upside down and hunted through a dozen files, but couldn't find what he was looking for. When he returned, Caisotti's papers were still lying on the desk, but there was no sign of either the girl or Ampelio. She must have left, Quinto supposed. She would be back for the information tomorrow. He called, "Ampelio!" but there was no answer. He hadn't gone out, because his beret was still on the hatrack; he was balding and never went out without it. Perhaps he was upstairs. Quinto went up to the next floor and looked into a number of rooms, calling his name; he even went into the bathroom and from there into his brother's room.

Lina and Ampelio were in bed. The girl at once pressed her face into the pillow; her black hair spread out and around, a pink shoulder emerged from the sheets. Ampelio raised himself up on one elbow; the ribs were clearly visible in his lean, naked body. Mechanically he reached for his glasses on the side table. "Christ," he said. "Do you have to stick your damn nose in everywhere?"

Quinto shut the door and went downstairs, black with rage. He could have killed the man. To start an affair of this sort, here in the house, with somebody in Caisotti's pay – just when their business relations were in such a delicate phase ... To go upstairs at the double with that sanctimonious little tramp ... Ampelio didn't give a hang for the project. He left him all the responsibilities and headaches, and when he did show up, he started criticizing. And there he was upstairs, having himself a good time, leaving his fool of a brother to ransack his drawers. They were probably laughing at him, sending him to look for papers that quite likely had no importance whatever! He didn't put it past that slut. Always "Yes, sir," "No, sir," with him, demure as could be; but when Ampelio showed up, it was *hoop-la!* Or maybe Caisotti had sent her, to fool them. If so, it was clear why he hadn't told her to try her tricks on him; she wouldn't have had a hope in hell there! But even so, loosing her on Ampelio wasn't really very clever. It was a filthy trick though, a filthy trick. And what was he supposed to do? Turn down the sheets for them?

Quinto was on his way out when the doorbell rang. It was
Caisotti. He needed some details, he said; they wanted them
at City Hall.... But was it really so urgent? There was something furtive in his manner that was unlike his usual
wariness; he seemed anxious, unsure of himself. Quinto
took him into the study and showed him the papers that his
secretary had brought; he told him she had been looking for
him. "Oh, she was here, was she? Where is she?" "Why?
Didn't you send her?" "Of course I sent her," Caisotti said,
"but she had some other things to do as well. There was
something I wanted to tell her. Where is she?" Quinto
shrugged. "How do I know? I suppose she's gone back." "In
that case, I'd have met her." Caisotti looked around toward
the other rooms and the staircase, like a baffled animal.

"I suppose she went another way. Where do you imagine
she is?"

It looked in fact as though Caisotti had followed her up to
the villa, and not seeing her reappear, had come after her. He
made one excuse after another to stay; his tone was conciliat-
ing, he made concessions, and even went so far as to propose
some improvements in the building – at no extra cost. And
all the time with that wary, uncertain look, searching Quinto's face as though waiting for him to give himself away. At
times it looked as though the uneasiness that kept him there
was going to harden into some barely controllable violence.
The slack muscles of his pale face grew taut, the blood
showed through his clenched knuckles, the shark mouth
twisted into a nervous, ingratiating grimace that seemed the
prelude to some wild outburst. Quinto was annoyed at being
stuck there with Caisotti and having to shield his brother and
that tart upstairs. His resentment against Ampelio made him
side with Caisotti; and at the same time he was aware that

this was the right moment to force him to make important concessions. He was never going to have the man in his hands again like this, but on the spur of the moment he could remember nothing useful to ask him. Irritated at not being able to show that he was on his side, he could think of no way out except to persuade him to come and take a look at the site to see how the work was getting on.

Caisotti went with him reluctantly, taking care to keep the villa, and especially the garden gate, well in sight. They climbed up the gangplank, onto the second floor, where the cement was still wet. Quinto examined the angles of the walls and the doors. "This wall ought to be thicker, Caisotti," he said, his voice booming through the empty space. "Here, do you see what I mean?"

Caisotti didn't move. He was looking furtively through the bare brick frame of the window, across the dense green of the garden, which Quinto scarcely recognized from that unfamiliar vantage point. "Thicker? Yes, of course, but wait till it's finished, with the mortar, you'll see. ..."

17

Caisotti's stock was starting to go down, among his own following too. Even the red-haired giant – his name was Angerin – burst suddenly into revolt.

Angerin lived on the site in a wooden shack used as a tool shed and night watchman's hut; he slept on the ground, like an animal, never taking off his clothes. First thing in the morning, his face blank and bewildered, he would set off down the hill with that ambling, apelike gait of his to buy a roll of bread, a blood sausage, and a tomato; he would come back chewing, his mouth full. He appeared to live on this, though every now and then he was seen cooking something in a dirty pot balanced on a couple of bricks. Caisotti, apparently, owed him a couple of months' wages. The man was hunger itself and yet, being immensely strong and obedient, he was given all the heaviest work. The other men insisted on being paid regularly; otherwise they would go off and work elsewhere, for jobs were easy to find in the building trade. So Caisotti economized at the expense of Angerin – who was docile and incapable of taking any steps on his own – treating him like a slave. When he first arrived, he had been a frightening, bull-like figure, but he had lost weight, his shoulders curved in and his arms hung listlessly by his side. Lack of food, overwork, and sleeping on the ground were ruining him.

The only person who took any notice of him was Signora Anfossi, and Quinto learned about him from her. She would have him up to the villa and give him sugar and biscuits and old undershirts. She'd offer him advice and ask him about himself, a painful procedure for Angerin, this, since she couldn't understand his inarticulate dialect and made him repeat everything ten times. He was from the mountain hinterland, like Caisotti, who had brought him down to work. "I don't think he's ever had any god except Caisotti," Signora Anfossi said.

"He's probably his illegitimate son," Quinto suggested, laughing.

"Yes, I wondered about that. I asked him if they were related and he seemed confused."

"Him too.... What a man!"

"What do you mean?"

"Oh, gossip, gossip."

On the job, the other men laughed at him and played tricks on him. He exploded quite suddenly. From the villa they heard the sound of blows, the crack of planks thrown down on planks, men shouting. Quinto ran out, down the site. The workmen were in the road, scattering in all directions; one had jumped from the second floor, right on top of the flowers. "Help! Angerin has gone crazy! Help!" The giant was up on the second floor, smashing everything. He sent buckets of mortar crashing against the walls, wrenched the scaffolding apart, toppled over ladders, blindly hurled bricks, cracking the walls and wrecking the fresh cement. The noise re-echoed in the empty building, grew enormous, and this obviously excited him still more. No one could get near him; he was making great flailing strokes with a shovel, which would have killed anyone on the spot. It was his way of working off his resentment against Caisotti – blindly, without caring whom he hit.

"Send for the police!" someone shouted. "No, no, send for Caisotti. He's the only person who can handle him." The foreman had in fact ridden off to look for him. Quinto stood and watched the skeleton of this house, which had risen so slowly and so painfully, being demolished before his eyes, watched the girders buckle under Angerin's blows and the window sills crack. He was already reckoning the time that would be lost in repairing the damage, thinking of all the places that would merely be patched up, all the arguments they would have to go through.... .

Caisotti arrived in his three-wheeler. As soon as the sound of his motor approached, then stopped, the sounds inside the new building stopped too. Caisotti got out, looking pale and drawn, but quite calm. He pushed his way through the men without looking at anyone and went up to the building, then propping a ladder against the wall, he climbed up to the second floor.

Angerin was there waiting for him, shovel raised, tensing himself to strike. Caisotti climbed another step. He spoke quickly, in dialect, not raising his voice. "Angerin, you're sore at me?" The giant stared at him, wide-eyed, and started to tremble. At last he said, "Yes, with you." "You want to kill me?" Angerin hesitated a moment, then: "No." "Drop that shovel!" It didn't sound like an order, more like a question or a statement; or maybe an order to a tame dog. Angerin dropped the shovel. As soon as Caisotti saw that his hands were empty, he came up quickly, and here he made a mistake. Angerin was beginning to be afraid of what he had done, but now his rage flooded back; seizing a trowel, he threw it violently at Caisotti. It hit him on the forehead; it was only a glancing blow but it opened up a long cut, which quickly brimmed with blood. It looked as though Caisotti must be stunned by the pain, but no, he reacted quickly. It was his only chance. The giant would have finished him otherwise. He raised one arm, more as though he wanted to hide the sight of his blood from Angerin than to stop the bleeding, then hurled himself on top of him. They rolled over and it was difficult to see what was happening, then Caisotti was on top and Angerin was no longer trying to hit him but merely to drag him off and then not even that. Caisotti, his knee pressed against the man's chest, started to pommel him, one sledgehammer blow after another thudding dully on his back, his chest, his head, his bones.

"He's killing him!" said one of the workmen standing beside Quinto. "No, he won't kill him," someone else said, "but Angerin won't see a penny of his back pay. It'll all go to repair the damage." The thudding blows continued, then someone cried, "That's enough! He's not defending himself any more." Quinto recognized his mother's voice; she was standing by the hedge, very pale, a shawl wrapped around her.

Caisotti got to his feet and slowly came down the ladder. Angerin's outstretched body began to stir and then he too got up, first on all fours, then onto his feet. But his body was slack and bent and he started to limp about, picking things up and putting them back in their place.

Caisotti walked forward, holding a bloody handkerchief to his face; he pulled his cap over it to keep it in place; his eyes were full of tears. "It was nothing," he said in dialect to the men. "All right, you can go back to work now." "Work with that lunatic? The hell you say! Damn near killed us, he did. We're not going back, we're going for the police." "He won't hurt you; he wasn't after you anyway. He's all right again now. You're not calling anyone. Back to work!" And he got back into his three-wheeler, the bloody handkerchief slipping down over his eyes, and jammed his foot down onto the starter. He pushed for a moment, trembling with the putt-putt of the engine, blinded by the tears that were rolling down his cheeks. Then he was off.

18

Quinto spent most of the winter at Milan, working on the editorial board of the magazine that Bensi and Cerveteri had started. He would come home every now and then and stay a few days. He used to arrive in the evening and on his way to the villa pass by the site. The shadow of the building stood out in the darkness, still wrapped in its trellis of scaffolding, pierced with blank window spaces, roofless. The work was going ahead so slowly that it looked the same from one visit to the next. This, he felt, was as far as it was ever going to get; he couldn't even imagine it finished. So this was where his passion for concrete reality had led him, to this shapeless heap of bricks and beams lying there unused; it had been a mere caprice, something started and then dropped halfway. Only with Bensi and Cerveteri did he feel himself a man of action, and this helped him to overcome his neurotic sense of being less educated and intelligent than they were. There too he was acting in continual opposition to his own instincts, but this was a more manageable kind of opposition. What in the world had ever made him dabble in real estate? He no longer felt the slightest interest in the project and stayed away for months on end, leaving all the headaches to his mother.

As for Ampelio, it was no use relying on him for anything. He was always preparing for some exam or other, the dirty grind, and there was no hope of shifting him an inch from his chosen path. Every three or four months, he came to see his mother for a couple of days, and that was that. During one of these brief visits, it happened that Quinto came home too. They met in the morning. Quinto, who had arrived the night before, was in the bathroom, washing, when Ampelio came in. Quinto went at him at once. "Well, what have you been doing? Have you settled anything? Have you seen to having the property confiscated since the work hasn't been finished on time? And what about the foreclosure?" It was a relief to have someone on whom he could unload his own bad conscience and his resentment at the whole affair, which had seemed so straightforward at first and yet grew more and more involved as time went on.

Ampelio stood by the bathroom door; he was wearing an overcoat. His umbrella hung over one arm. No trace of expression was visible behind his glasses. "There's nothing to be done," he said calmly.

Quinto was in his pajamas. "What do you mean, there's nothing to be done?" he shouted, drying himself hurriedly. "What do you mean? We've got the reversion clause, haven't we?" He went back into his bedroom, shoving Ampelio out of the way. "Caisotti hasn't handed over the apartments. Right. So we take back the site and everything on it. We've got to get moving."

"Well, get moving then," said Ampelio.

When Ampelio took this tone, Quinto always lost his temper completely. He knew what his brother was like, he knew that the angrier he became, the calmer Ampelio's contemptuous irony would be; and yet he lost his temper every time. "So, you've been here five days. You should have been to see Canal and started legal proceedings. And what have you done? Nothing!"

Quinto was sitting on the edge of the bed, getting dressed. Ampelio stood in front of him in his overcoat, his hands on the handle of the umbrella, which was poking into the bedside rug. Ampelio's standing there fully dressed while he was half naked made Quinto feel even more uncomfortable. "You've been here five days," he went on, "and you haven't settled a single thing! Caisotti is selling his apartments before he's finished building them, and we sit here twiddling our thumbs. If we had some tenants who were due to take possession, he'd have to finish the work. Have you tried to find any tenants? Have you been to the agency?"

Ampelio always paused a moment or so before answering, staring at nothing. After a while he said, "You've got the whole thing back to front."

"What do you mean?"

No answer.

"What do you mean?" Quinto shook him by the arm. "What are you talking about? Are you trying to say that I've been doing nothing myself and that I come here and take it out on you, is that what you mean? Is that it?" He continued to shake his arm, but Ampelio had nothing further to add. "All the months I spent here," Quinto went on, "trying to pull the chestnuts out of the fire – your chestnuts too, don't you understand? – sweating my guts out, you didn't take the faintest notice, you didn't even bother to thank me. Can you deny it? Just answer me: can you deny it?"

It was not Ampelio's way to explain himself. He would only have had to say: "You spent three months here on the beach," and Quinto would have been punctured; he wouldn't have known how to go on. But Ampelio would never do what you wanted, not even in a quarrel. All he said was, "O.K., give me my share, we'll divide the apartments between us, I'll sell my part of it just as it is, to Caisotti or to anyone who'll buy it; I'll take what I can get. I don't care so long as I don't have to go on having these squabbles with you. The only thing I regret is leaving Mother in your hands."

"What the hell are you talking about?" Quinto seized him by the wrists. "Don't you know that I've done everything so far, that I've done it for you too?"

Ampelio shook him off. "You're sick, your nerves are shot to hell. You ought to go see a doctor."

"Why do you treat me like this, why do you insult me?" Quinto yelled, and began pounding him with his fists. Ampelio fell on the bed and lay there without even trying to defend himself. He merely held his knees and elbows up so that Quinto's blows, which were passionate rather than powerful, hit only his arms and legs. He was still holding his umbrella, but he made no attempt to use it. His glasses had fallen off and were lying on the bed. He simply waited, hunched up, his beard in the collar of his overcoat, staring at Quinto without resentment or anything else, only the lost look of the myopic and a complete withdrawal.

Quinto stopped suddenly. Ampelio got up and put on his glasses. "Go and see a doctor; you're not normal." And he left the room.

19

At the end of the winter Quinto found a job in Rome, working for a movie company. He left the editorial board of the review after quarreling with Bensi and Cerveteri. The Roman world was lavish and uninhibited; the producer was a man who managed to lay his hands on hundreds of thousands of lire from one day to the next. It was a convivial sort of existence, with ten-thousand-lire notes flying around as though they were small change. In the evenings they all went off to eat together at a restaurant, then on to someone's house to drink. Drinking made Quinto ill; nonetheless, this, finally, was life. He had not yet laid his hands on much actual money, but he was on the way at last.

His mother's letters, full of maddening little details, went into everything exhaustively, and nearly drove him crazy. They had lost a possible tenant because the apartments weren't yet ready; Caisotti had now got the roof on, but the elevator shed on top exceeded the limits permitted by the regulations. Travaglia was supposed to come and note the violation, but he was nowhere to be found. Quinto was now living in another world, where everything was possible, everything could be fixed, everything was done quickly; even so, he was unable to wash his hands of the project, if only because he found that in the movies, the more he earned the more he spent, and it wasn't enough. He was after a French girl who was part of a Franco-Italian co-production team, and he was always on the go. It was a rootless life.

And more and more the thought of that cursed apartment building nagged at him.

As soon as he had a few days off, he went home. I'm going to take the affair in hand and settle everything in quick order, he said to himself. He felt he had adopted the style of the movie world. But one look at that muddy, cluttered site, at that squalid cement structure standing there half finished, and he felt his bustling efficiency draining away. He didn't even know where to start. He listened to his mother listing the principal subjects of dispute (for example, the interminable argument as to whose responsibility the drinking water and electricity connections were), and then to Caisotti, who no longer troubled to conceal his contempt for partners so helpless and distracted.

The man was now selling or leasing apartments, in defiance of the contract, which gave him no rights on the property until he had delivered their part of the building to the Anfossis. He would finish an apartment hurriedly and still be putting in the fixtures and giving it the last coat of paint when the occupants were due to arrive.

"You can finish your apartments when you want, but we have to wait for ours! Is that it, Caisotti?"

"You don't even have any tenants waiting to come in."

Quinto had expected this answer. He had looked for tenants and put the matter in the hands of the agencies, but it was quite clear that nothing was going to be ready in the summer. Someone did come up the hill to have a look, but finding the building still under construction and the whole place covered with mud, went back to the agency to complain that he had been given the wrong address. The only thing ready was a shop on the ground floor, a kind of storeroom, which he hoped to rent to a flower shipper, since the flower market was nearby. He went there early one morning, when business was at its briskest, to explore the possibilities, but the season was already in full swing and no one was going to think of moving at such a time.

One Sunday, the day before he was due to return to Rome, he was passing by the site when he saw someone examining it with interest and then walk inside. Quinto followed him. He was a small, elderly man wearing an overcoat and a hat. He went up the cement steps (still without marble) to the second floor and peered through the black doorways. "Excuse me, is there someone you want to see?" Quinto shouted up the stairwell. The old man passed from one apartment to another, taking care not to trip over the cans lying around. "No, no, I'm just looking."

Quinto went up to the second floor himself and looked everywhere for him; finally he saw him come in from a balcony. "Do you want a place to rent?" Quinto asked. The old man was already on the way to the next floor. "No, no, just looking." Quinto went up to the third floor. "If you want an apartment, the ones to the right are ours. We can discuss terms," he shouted into space, for the man had disappeared again. "We've got three-room and four-room apartments – " Realizing that the visitor was on the floor above, he ran up. "Three-room and four-room apartments," he repeated.

Even if he decided against doing so, the fact remained that the man had come to look for an apartment. Otherwise, why should he be sticking his nose in everywhere as though he wanted to examine every room and every detail of the construction? Everything depended on being able to persuade him now, so that he did business with them and not with Caisotti. "It's a mess just now," Quinto said, "but if you want an apartment, we can have it ready in a matter of days. You can start putting your furniture in ..."

But the old man wasn't even listening. He was checking the washbasins and the sewer lines. Perhaps he was deaf? But no, he had answered promptly enough at the beginning. "If we agree on terms now, you can move your furniture the first of the month," he cried, but the man was gone again – and the stairs joining the fourth and fifth floors weren't yet in place. Quinto had a fright. He was such a nosy old devil. Had he managed to fall down the elevator shaft?

But no, there he was, balancing on the cornice of the flat terrace roof, which as yet had no parapet. He had climbed up there on the planks that the workmen used, and was inspecting the water tanks. He was coming down now, keeping his balance carefully, knees slightly bent, arms thrust forward.

Quinto went to give him a hand. "Look, will you please tell me. If you don't want to buy or rent, why exactly are you so interested in this place?"

The old man, refusing his help, had now reached the landing and was starting to go down the stairs. "It's nothing. I was just taking a look at the building because I have to foreclose."

20

During the spring the film company moved to Cannes for the outside scenes. Quinto went to and fro between Rome and Cannes and sometimes stayed at the French producer's villa at Juan-les-Pins. The journey took him near home, but he didn't stop; he couldn't spare the time, and the transition from the rhythm of moviemaking to that of Caisotti's building firm was too much for him. Financially and intellectually, he was used to living a quiet, modest life and he was finding this new and in every sense of the word extravagant existence a continual strain. The French girl was proving difficult. He was leading a life that seemed to carry every possibility of happiness; and yet he felt miserable.

The situation at home was more and more involved. Someone had bought a garage in Caisotti's part of the building, and then hearing that his ownership was liable to be challenged, had rushed off to Signora Anfossi to ask what the situation was. She advised the man not to buy from Caisotti until he had fulfilled his obligations. There was a fearful squabble when Caisotti heard about this, and he was threatening to sue the Signora for defamation. How could he meet his obligations with the Anfossis slandering him and doing their best to ruin his business? Canal, meanwhile, had drawn up a claim against Caisotti for failure to fulfill the terms of the contract, for damages sustained by his clients due to loss of rents, and for his violation of the clause relating to the height of the building. Unless Caisotti gave satisfaction within a month, he was going to prosecute. But Caisotti now had a lawyer of his own and he too was drawing up a claim: he accused Signora Anfossi of repeated defamation of character, of violation of the contract (failure to drain the cesspool within the agreed time), and even of theft. This referred to the business of the pipes the year before; it continued to crop up whenever there was a quarrel. Caisotti's charges made no sort of sense, but if Canal presented his claim, Caisotti would answer with his. It would at least serve to confuse the issue and drag the thing out. They were at present negotiating in order to try and find some way of reaching an agreement.

In the thick of all this, Quinto was catapulted from Cannes back to Rome. The French producer was withdrawing, the Italian company was neck deep in debts. They shot a few inside scenes at Cinecittà, then the crisis took a turn for the worse and the whole project was suspended. Signora Anfossi wrote to say that she had at last been able to find a tenant for the shop: a certain Signora Hofer, a florist, who exported gladioli to Munich.

In September the Italian producer went bankrupt and the movie was bought by a new company, belonging to a big building-site speculator, which finished it rapidly on a shoestring budget. Quinto was no longer needed, since his job of "production assistant" was considered superfluous. He thought he still had some money due to him, but they were able to show him that according to the terms of his contract they didn't owe him anything. He had already broken off with the French girl at Cannes. He came home without a job and without a penny.

His mother was now mainly involved with Signora Hofer. She didn't pay her rent, she didn't answer letters, and she was nowhere to be found. Apparently she had gone to Germany. She turned up, finally, when Quinto was at home. She was nearly six feet tall, an energetic, handsome woman, a little heavy perhaps, but well built; her suit did not conceal the generous breasts; her legs were a shade masculine, but slender and shapely. She had a hard, plain face, but it showed a kind of pride, the pride of a woman who knows her business. Her blond, curled hair was fastened in back by a quite inappropriate pink ribbon. Quinto was instantly drawn to this heavy German body and he couldn't take his eyes off her, but she addressed herself, impassively, to Signora Anfossi. She had a strong accent, but her Italian was coldly fluent. She told the Signora that she had had to remain in Germany longer than she had anticipated and had therefore not been able to pay the rent. But her affairs were now in order and she would return with the money within the week. And off she went, treading firmly in her mannish shoes. Quinto had not managed to catch her eye.

Toward the end of the week, his mother began saying, "No sign of Signora Hofer." He was stretched out on a chaise longue reading *The Confessions of Felix Krull*. "Signora Hofer, eh? Signora Hofer ... We'll make Signora Hofer pay up all right!" He went on playing, obsessively, with her name and her image until gradually he found himself summing up in her person everything he had missed, everything he had failed to bring off – his real estate plunge, the movies, the French girl. "Signora Hofer," he sniggered to himself. "I'll deal with Signora Hofer."

She was only in her shop first thing in the morning, with a couple of packers; this was when the flowers arrived from the market. She supervised the packing of the gladioli into baskets, which were then taken to the agent who made the trip to the airport at Milan. This done, she pulled down the shutters and left. Quinto got up late and he never saw her. She had, however, left her home address.

When a week had passed, he said to his mother. "Let me have the receipt form, signed, and the revenue stamps. I'm going to call on the Hofer woman and make her pay up."

She was living in an old house on the sea front. She opened the door herself. She was wearing a blouse with short sleeves and her arms were a little softer than Quinto had expected. Her expression was doubtful, as though she didn't recognize him. Quinto at once pulled the receipt out of his pocket and said that since she hadn't been able to find the time to visit them, he had come to her in order to settle their account. She opened the door and let him in. Her room, with its embroidered cushions and dolls, suggested a furnished apartment. On a chest of drawers there were photographs of two men, with some flowers in front of them. One was a German airman, the other was an Italian officer who, thought Quinto (always ready to suppose the worst), looked as though he were wearing the uniform of the Republic of Salò.*

"You really needn't have troubled, Signor Anfossi," she said. "I was coming to see you tomorrow or the day after."

---

*The short-lived "Italian Socialist Republic," proclaimed by Mussolini in September, 1943, after the collapse of the Fascist regime.

Quinto's glance was shuttling between her eyes, still remote and distracted, and the firm, full flesh of her body.

"But why don't we settle the account now? I've brought the receipt. ..." Quinto's voice was trying to sound a little playful, a little suggestive – anything to get away from this dry, business-like relation. But it was no good; these delicate vibrations were wasted on Signora Hofer. "If I say that I am coming to see you tomorrow or the day after, Signor Anfossi, it means that it isn't convenient for me to pay until tomorrow or the day after." A fine nerve the woman had, taking this high tone when she was already a week late. It was not, however, on the field of finance that Quinto was resolved to conquer.

He gave a little laugh and said, firmly, "Signora Hofer, I don't like quarreling with a good-looking woman like you."

Plainly she was not expecting this approach, and there was a momentary glint in her eyes that was on the edge of irony. But Quinto, quick as a sexual maniac, was already reaching out to unbutton her blouse. She started back, indignantly, then stopped. "Signor Anfossi, what in the world do you think you're doing?" But his arms were already around her.

The woman was a tigress; he was no match for her. They lurched violently from one end of the room to another, but he never succeeded in getting her off her feet. He had no idea what he was doing; he wanted his revenge for everything – and this was it. In this state of frenzy, he almost passed out at one point and found himself lying exhausted, surrounded by dolls, on the couch. Signora Hofer was standing looking at him with a faint air of contempt. Not once had she smiled.

Quinto straightened himself, trying hard to keep his mind blank. She showed him to the door. Simply for the sake of something to say, he took the receipt out of his pocket. "Then you'll be coming ..."

She reached out for the receipt, went to the bureau, opened her purse, put the receipt into it, went to the door and opened it. "Good evening, Signor Anfossi."

Quinto left. The days were drawing in. It was dark.

21

The woman whom Caisotti employed as his lawyer didn't seem quite to understand the nature of the dispute. He had to decide everything for himself and she merely tried to give a legal color to what he was saying.

"Come off it," said Canal from behind his desk. "Are you seriously proposing to accuse Signora Anfossi of theft? The judge is going to laugh in your face. You ought to advise your client not to play the fool," he added, turning to the lawyer.

Caisotti was sitting in an armchair, fists clenched, face dark and savage. The lawyer turned over some pages. "Let me see ... Yes, here it is. On the eighteenth day of June, nineteenth fifty-four, four metal drain pipes measuring ..."

Canal did his best. He spoke sensibly, like a practical man, without flights of rhetoric, though there were moments when he had difficulty in controlling himself. He was fed up with all this deception and disgusted by the way the law could be used by scoundrels to protect themselves. But this was how things went and his job was to adjust them as best he could, and repair the damage done by swindlers who think they are smart and by starry-eyed dreamers who think everything should be done for them. They both end up by making the same sort of mess, he reflected. So he just went on trying to persuade the other side that there was really no point in dragging the affair out by introducing legal quibbles: the debt had to be paid, the apartments had to be completed and handed over. As for the exact amount of the sum owed, here there was room for compromise since his clients were aware that they had nothing to gain by ruining Caisotti's business. They therefore proposed a final figure. The alternative was to go to court – and this time they meant it.

It was Canal who had proposed these conciliatory tactics to Quinto. "What are we trying to do?" He said to him the day before the meeting. "You've lost interest in the whole affair, that's perfectly obvious. You're practically never here, you leave all the dirty work to your mother. She has every right to wash her hands of it, but instead she takes the thing seriously. As for Caisotti, it doesn't matter to him what happens; he's got no reputation to lose. He arrived here in patched pants, he lives like a beggar and carries on like a petty crook. It's impossible to corner him. You can't ever tell what he's going to do next. This is his system and he makes it work. He keeps his head above water; he's a person you've got to reckon with."

Canal announced the figure that he and Quinto had agreed on. The woman turned toward Caisotti, who screwed up his lips, then shook his head. "My client feels that this figure does not offer a basis for discussion," she said. Caisotti got up; she too got up, and stubbing out her cigarette, she gathered the papers into a brief case. Then she picked up her handbag, shook hands with Canal and Quinto, and hurried after her client, who walked out with his hands in his pockets.

"Oh, I know!" Canal said to Quinto when they were alone. "He's just a peasant, that's the trouble, and he's an idiot. Heaven knows what he thinks he gains at this stage by refusing to pay and dragging the affair out like this. But that's the way he is." And he stretched out his hand to Quinto to say goodbye.

Quinto would have liked to stay a while and talk about his experiences with the movies, but Canal was busy and he had to go. At last he could talk about something that everyone was interested in – Cinecittà, French actresses, and so on – unlike the days when he could discuss only politics and literature and never knew what to say to his old friends. But now the only subject of discussion was Caisotti.

Caisotti, Caisotti, Caisotti... He couldn't take any more of the man; he was through. Sure, he knew what sort of guy he was, he knew he'd win every round, he had known this before any of them! But how did they all manage to accept Caisotti as something normal? Oh, they criticized him, of course, but only verbally; they weren't concerned to destroy him, to *deny* him. All right, he, Quinto, had been the first to praise Caisotti – against the opposition of all the stuffed shirts in town. But at that time he had appeared in a different light; he had been one of the terms of an antithesis, part of a vital process. But now he was simply one aspect of a gray, uniform reality, of a reality which had either to be denied or accepted. For his part, he was not going to accept it!

The notary, Bardissone, for example, delivered a kind of panegyric of the man when Quinto went to see him. "He'll pay all right, believe me. Don't go by appearances; he's not a bad man. He's altogether self-made, remember, and now he's head of a considerable firm. It's a hard moment for everyone; we all have our ups and downs, you know.... But try and get on with him; he's a decent fellow, believe me."

Travaglia was much occupied with politics. The local elections were due the next year and it was said that he wanted to run for mayor. Quinto met him one day in the street and told him something of what went on behind the scenes at Cinecittà; he did his man-of-the-world act. In front of the Caffè Melina they ran into Caisotti. Since the meeting at the lawyer's, he and Quinto no longer spoke to each other, but Travaglia stopped and shook him by the hand. After a while, he said, "And what about this business with the Anfossis?"

Caisotti started to talk in his self-pitying whine, but he didn't go into details and Quinto made no comment beyond shrugging his shoulders now and then, Travaglia, however, tried to argue with him and convince him, but he put forward the Anfossis' case as though it were patently childish; one had to try to understand it, he implied, but there was no use pretending it made any sort of sense. Caisotti in due course came up with a proposal: he would pay the Anfossis a part of what he owed them, but they would have to let him run the apartments. Obviously *they* weren't going to be able to handle them. He would make it his business to look for tenants and collect the rents, and at the end of the year he would hand over a fixed sum.

This arrangement would leave them wholly at Caisotti's mercy; Quinto saw this clearly, but he also saw that it did provide a way of escaping from all this worry, at least for a year, and moreover it spared him the remorse he would feel at leaving his mother to struggle with the rents. Travaglia too understood that this proposal was not altogether to the Anfossis' disadvantage, and he supported it. Quinto tried to bargain and they ended up in Caisotti's office. There was a new secretary, a redhead, new furniture, and a new fluorescent lamp. Caisotti had them both sit down and offered cigarettes. A woman came in, a countrywoman, obviously, no longer young, with a little boy. "I'd like to introduce my wife," Caisotti said. "She's come to live here too now. She was just about my last link with home."

The understanding was that Quinto would discuss the whole matter with his mother and with Ampelio, who was due to come home for a visit.

He was walking up toward the villa, alone, when he saw the old carpenter, Masera. The man was going down the hill, on his bicycle; he braked when he saw Quinto and said hello.

"So you're home for a while, eh? On business? The building, I suppose. ... It always seems to be in the same state every time I pass by. It must be driving you all crazy. Is it true that Caisotti hasn't paid you yet? Look, I've never liked to ask you, but sometimes I've seen you in the street looking a bit worried, and I've said to myself, I'll just have a word with him now. Then I thought, no, better not... . But we often talk about it, the comrades, you know... . How did you ever go and get yourselves in Caisotti's hands? Didn't you know the kind of guy he is? If I told you some of the dirty tricks he's played on us..."

Quinto's nerves were at the breaking point, and yet at the same time he felt a sense of relief. This plunge in real estate, which he had defended and exalted to himself, as though to protect it from the attacks of Masera and his friends, had now become something he could discuss calmly with them. They were on his side, they were behind him.

"Oh, I know you had to sell quickly, to pay your taxes," Masera went on. "And it was a good idea to go into partnership for your building – leave the work to others, for what that was worth.... But why didn't you come to Party Headquarters to ask us? We could have given you some advice. There are contractors who, even though they're not in the Party, are our friends, or at least they want to keep in with us. Then we've got a cooperative society too; it's a going concern.... Come down and talk things over with us one evening. We're planning a joint action to stop speculation, to stabilize real estate prices, to get the building code respected. It's just not possible to put up with the sort of things that are going on now, all this swindling. ... We can fight back; there's plenty to be done. Look, you'll be needing tenants soon. Well, come and have a word with us. Every now and then we hear of someone; people write to us, from Turin and Milan, people in the Party – with money too, sometimes. If we can give them an idea of the price ..."

Quinto walked home feeling as if he was carrying a corpse on his back. Strangled by Masera's well-meaning chatter, the daring individualism of the free-enterprise building contractor, he rolled romantic eyes wildly in the midday sun.

Ampelio was there. They shut themselves up in the dining room and, covering the table with papers, they went over their accounts from the beginning.

The Signora was in the garden. The scent of honeysuckle was in the air, the nasturtiums were an almost too vivid splash of color. If she didn't raise her eyes to the ranked windows of the apartment buildings all around, the garden was still the garden. She went from bed to bed, pruning the dead stalks, making sure that the gardener had watered everything. A snail climbed up the pointed leaf of an iris. She pulled it off and threw it on the ground. A sudden burst of voices made her look up. There, on the top of the building, they were laying the tar on the terrace. She thought it was nicer when they made houses with tiled roofs and put a flag up to show that the roof was on. "Boys, boys!" she shouted toward the dining room. "They've finished the roof!"

Quinto and Ampelio didn't answer. The shutters were drawn and the room was half dark. They sat with bundles of papers on their knees, calculating once again how long it would be before their capital was amortized. The sun was sinking behind Caisotti's building and the light that filtered through the slats and played over the silver on the sideboard grew weaker and weaker. Now only the upper slats were bright, and slowly the light died, reflected on the polished surfaces of the trays and the teapots... .

(1957)

VINTAGE CLASSICS

Vintage launched in the United Kingdom in 1990, and was originally the paperback home for the Random House Group's literary authors. Now, Vintage is comprised of some of London's oldest and most prestigious literary houses, including Chatto & Windus (1855), Hogarth (1917), Jonathan Cape (1921) and Secker & Warburg (1935), alongside the newer or relaunched hardback and paperback imprints: The Bodley Head, Harvill Secker, Yellow Jersey, Square Peg, Vintage Paperbacks and Vintage Classics.

From Angela Carter, Graham Greene and Aldous Huxley to Toni Morrison, Haruki Murakami and Virginia Woolf, Vintage Classics is renowned for publishing some of the greatest writers and thinkers from around the world and across the ages – all complemented by our beautiful, stylish approach to design. Vintage Classics' authors have won many of the world's most revered literary prizes, including the Nobel, the Man Booker, the Prix Goncourt and the Pulitzer, and through their writing they continue to capture imaginations, inspire new perspectives and incite curiosity.

In 2007 Vintage Classics introduced its distinctive red spine design, and in 2012 Vintage Children's Classics was launched to include the much-loved authors of our childhood. Random House joined forces with the Penguin Group in 2013 to become Penguin Random House, making it the largest trade publisher in the United Kingdom.

@vintagebooks

penguin.co.uk/vintage-classics